DA

'Ahead of him, Khârn saw one of his fellow berzerkers fall, his body riddled with shells, his armour cracked and melted by plasma fire. The berzerker howled with rage and frustration, knowing that he was not going to be in at the kill, that he would give Khorne no more offerings on this or any other day. In frustration, the dying warrior set his chainsword to maximum power and took off his own head with one swift stroke. His blood rose in a red fountain to slake Khorne's thirst.' – *from* **Wrath of Khârn** *by William King*

'The axe's blade slashed again and again, a lightning bolt that struck in a dozen places at once, the energy field lashed against the armour so it split and buckled. The wounds were shallow but they were many, for Aescarion knew she could not fell him with one blow. He had to be ground down, whittled away until he could not resist, with blows his supernatural reflexes could not avoid.'

'*My faith has taken me this far*, Aescarion prayed as she sliced and circled the warrior. *Now my hatred will take me through.*' – *from* **Daemonblood** *by Ben Counter*

IN THE WAR-TORN 41st millennium humanity stands on the shores of damnation. Its only saviour is the immortal God Emperor and the massed armies of the Imperium, in this searing anthology of Warhammer 40,000 stories torn from the pages of *Inferno!* magazine.

DARK
IMPERIUM

Edited by
Marc Gascoigne
& Andy Jones

A BLACK LIBRARY PUBLICATION

First published in Great Britain in 2001 by
Games Workshop Publishing
Willow Road, Lenton,
Nottingham, NG7 2WS, UK

10 9 8 7 6 5 4 3 2 1

Cover illustration by Wayne England

A CIP record for this book
is available from the British Library

ISBN 1 84154 136 2

Set in ITC Giovanni

Printed and bound in Great Britain by
Omnia Books Ltd., Glasgow, UK

See the Black Library on the Internet at
www.blacklibrary.co.uk

Find out more about Games Workshop
and the world of Warhammer 40,000 at
www.games-workshop.com

CONTENTS

APOTHECARY'S HONOUR
Simon Jowett

'APOTHECARY!' The cry crackled over the transceiver in Korpus's battered helmet, then vanished beneath a searing wave of static. Mid-stride, Korpus paused. A wheeze escaped from the joints of his armour, as if the suit he had worn since planetfall on Antillis IV was itself grateful for a moment's respite. The craggy uplands upon which the Avenging Sons had set their base camp were unforgiving of flesh and bone and power-assisted ceramite alike.

Korpus turned one way then the other, searching for the signal. The wind had changed direction and with it the currents of unholy energy which had been unleashed upon the planet, casting a blanket of infuriating static across every transmission. The last communication from the Scout Squad that had accompanied the Avenging Sons' Second Company onto Antillis IV had been swamped by one such obliterating wave. Nothing more had been heard from the squad in almost thirty hours. Every remaining Space Marine silently commended their souls to the Emperor.

Eddies of pale grey ash swirled about Korpus as he continued his sweep. The remains of much of Antillis IV's civilian population, it clogged the joints of every Space Marine's armour and cast a dense pall across his visor. Korpus automatically ran a gloved hand across his eye-plates, clearing away the soft, greasy veil which had collected there. The mud and ash swathed landscape around him jumped into sharper focus. Dispatched to support the beleaguered Imperial Garrison, the Avenging Sons had found themselves immured in a daemon's dream of winter: blizzards of human ash driven by winds that howled with the voices of souls lost to Chaos.

'Apothecary!'

The signal broke through the wail and hiss of static, stronger and more urgent than before. Korpus turned his face away from the steep, broken incline he had been climbing and began to negotiate a downwards path. Automatically, he checked the load in his bolt pistol and activated his power fist. In his heart he would rather have continued upwards, in order to stand beside his commander in the vanguard of the next assault. But he was an Apothecary, and not once in the years since he had first donned the white armour had he ever ignored the call of an injured Space Marine.

It was a matter of pride. It was a matter of honour.

'Avenging Son!' Korpus prayed that his own transmission was able to pierce the blizzard of ash and static.

He stepped over the last of the trail of black-armoured corpses that had led him down this narrow defile. Though of similar design to the armour worn by the Avenging Sons, the garish sigils scrawled across its midnight-black surface declared its wearer's true allegiance: to the Dark Gods of the warp. To Chaos.

He kicked aside an abandoned skull-helm and noticed with grim satisfaction the bloody stump of a truncated neck which lolled into view as it rolled away. Among the scattered corpses and their now-redundant weaponry, Korpus had noted the presence of a boltgun and bolt pistol, both sanctified with the sigil of the Avenging Sons, both discarded. Both empty.

'Apothecary?'

The strained query came from an inky, shadow-cast niche in the gully wall. Korpus restrained his desire to hurry into the darkness, well aware of the tricks that the servants of the warp could play on a man's mind, and edged forward.

The Space Marine lay propped against the rear of the niche, his lower body obscured by what Korpus thought, at first, to be an errant shadow, but quickly realised was another corpse. The Avenging Son's breastplate was scorched by bolter fire and cracked in several places. The blood of his many victims shone blackly in the dim light. One of his arms hung loosely to the side, the elbow bent at an unnatural angle. The other still clutched the handle of the chainsword he had driven between the plates of his opponent's armour.

'It's me, Korpus.' Holstering his bolt pistol and disconnecting his power fist, the Apothecary knelt beside his battle-brother. With practised ease he released the catches of the cracked and dented helmet and lifted it away.

'Pereus!' Korpus had stood beside the veteran sergeant on many worlds. 'You must have killed a battalion of the daemon-spawn.'

'And they me,' Pereus's words came in gasps, his normally rich, deep voice cracking with the effort. He glanced downwards, indicating something. Korpus followed his gaze, then rolled away the body of the sergeant's last kill.

The warp-forged chainsword had been driven through the lower plates of Pereus's armour, deep enough so that only its hilt remained visible, perhaps at the same moment that Pereus had struck his own fatal blow.

'Legs gone. No feeling,' Pereus croaked. 'My service to the Emperor ends here.'

As Pereus spoke, Korpus swiftly removed his own helmet. The ritual he was about to perform did not require that both participants be bare-headed, but Korpus believed it to be more fitting.

'Man is born alone,' Korpus intoned, removing his armoured gloves. The wind struck cold against his exposed, sweat-slick-ened hands.

'And so he dies,' Pereus answered in a halting voice. Reaching forward, Korpus began to release the catches of the sergeant's upper armour.

'You serve the Emperor?' Korpus continued, stripping the plates from Pereus's body, exposing the blood-soaked robe beneath.

'And I die in his service.' Pereus shuddered at the wind's chill kiss.

'You are content?' Korpus asked. In a single swift motion, Korpus sliced through the sodden, sticky robe, using a scalpel he had drawn from an instrument pack bolted to his forearm.

'I am content,' Pereus gave the final answer, his voice barely a whisper. Korpus parted the fabric to lay Pereus bare from waist to throat. 'Work fast, Apothecary,' Pereus whispered. 'There will more of these warp-spawned whoresons come to avenge their brothers.' His face and throat convulsed, as if he was trying to swallow an unpalatable morsel. His head rocked forward and his jaw dropped slackly open. A thick stream of blood ran over his lower lip.

Placing a hand under Pereus's chin, Korpus tilted it back upon the now nerveless neck, exposing the full length of the throat. There: a slight bulge resting atop the sternum. Korpus's first target. Replacing the first scalpel in the instrument pack, he selected a second, whose tapered, hair-thin blade was intended for one purpose only: the excision of a Space Marine's progenoid glands.

'When they come, I pray that I will face them as bravely as you,' Korpus told the unhearing sergeant. He watched as a flake of pale ash settled slowly on the pupil of Pereus's unseeing right eye, then set to work.

'THE PROGENOID GLANDS are the future of our Chapter!' Apothecary Lorus's barking tone echoed around the small room set at the centre of the Apothecarion. The tang of chemical preservatives hung in the air. Seated before him in the cold room, banked with glass phials and porcelain specimen dishes, sat the five candidates chosen to undergo training in the sacred rituals and duties of a Space Marine Medic.

'The Avenging Sons' survival as an arm of the Emperor's will is dependent upon the survival of the glands,' Lorus continued. 'And the survival of the glands will depend upon you.'

Lorus stood behind a gurney which had been wheeled into the room by a servitor, one of the small army of the mechanically enhanced wretches who moved tirelessly through the corridors of the Apothecarion, ferrying wounded Space Marines between wards, preparing beds for new occupants or removing the dead to the Chapel of Martyrs. The gurney's cargo was covered by a grey sheet.

Korpus's eyes kept flickering impatiently between the sallow, sharp-featured face of the instructor and the shape under the sheet. Neither he nor any of his fellow candidates were under any illusion about what lay under there. Their instruction in the other aspects of battlefield medicine was already well under way. Now they were to receive induction into the last and most vital of the Apothecarion's mysteries.

'All men die,' Lorus's tone had taken on a flat, liturgical air, his words echoing the Rite of Extreme Unction that Korpus and his fellows had already committed to memory and upon which they were expected to meditate each night before retiring. 'But, in death, an Avenging Son carries within him the means of ensuring that the Emperor's crusade against the tide of Chaos continues.

'Each gland is grown from the seed provided by the gland that came before it and that gland from a similar seed, in an unbroken chain which lies within every Space Marine of the Adeptus Astartes, until the point of death. At the end of a Space Marine's life, it is the duty of an Apothecary to remove the glands and see that they return here to provide seed for the future.

'Without it, there can be no more of us. Without it, the Emperor's crusade ends. Without it, Chaos has free rein.'

Lorus drew back the sheet, revealing the naked corpse of an Avenging Son, whose journey to the Chapel of Martyrs had been delayed for the sake of this demonstration. Korpus's gaze lingered for a moment on the dead man's face as he wondered what battles he had seen in the life of righteous conflict that had led him here. By the time the young apprentice medic looked back at his instructor, the old man had drawn a scalpel, longer and much thinner than those Korpus had seen thus far, from a stiff leather pouch strapped to his forearm. Lorus cast his eyes across the five who sat before him.

'Now you will learn what it truly means to be an Apothecary.'

THE LONG-DEAD instructor's words always echoed in Korpus's memory while performing an Excision. The ghost of the preservatives' tang pricked the back of his throat as he carved the tiny, delicate vesicles from the base of the throat and deep within the chest. Had the wind that howled along the gully not increased while he worked on Pereus, the scent memory would have been augmented by the more powerful odour of the fresh fluid in the phials he unlatched from the storage bays set beneath his armour's thigh-plates. Each of the pair of glands was deposited in a phial, their tops sealed and then replaced in their sheaths.

Korpus secured the catches on the plates of double-thickness ceramite, intended to shield the precious cargo from damage that would doubtless blow the rest of Korpus to the winds of space. Replacing the scalpel in the instrument pack and donning his gloves, he prepared to leave. But there was one last ritual to perform.

'You are a martyr to the Emperor's will,' he intoned over Pereus's eviscerated remains.

The dead man would have met the Apothecary's gaze, had not a dense layer of ash settled across his face, covering it completely.

'You shall be remembered. You shall be avenged.'

'APOTHECARY!' Commander Selleus's voice rang in Korpus's ears during a sudden lull in the static.

'Apothecary Korpus reporting, praise His name,' he replied. Having worked his way out of the defile, Korpus was retracing his steps up the long, rocky incline, heading once more towards the base camp. The number of loaded phials he had been carrying, excised from the bodies of Avenging Sons who had fallen in the battle to hold the perimeter, had prompted his initial decision to return, to place the glands in more permanent storage to be returned via Thunderhawk to the Avenging Son's chapter ship. Pereus's glands had filled the last of the bays and made his return all the more imperative.

'The order to regroup went out an hour past,' Selleus said. 'Where are you?'

'Incoming, my lord.' Korpus lifted his visored gaze. There, visible through the ash-storm, sat the fortified chateau from which Selleus spoke. In his mind's eye, he saw the remaining Avenging Sons, gathered around their commander, preparing themselves for the assault that would inevitably follow the regrouping. Longing to join them, to feel the holy fire of battle leap within him, he increased his pace over the uneven ground.

'Pereus fell. Excision was required,' he continued. 'Your order did not reach me. This damnable static…'

As if summoned by his words, a fresh wave of storm-generated interference engulfed much of Selleus's reply.

'...new incursion...'

Korpus slammed an armoured fist against the side of his helmet. As if mocking his frustration, the static rose in volume. The import of the commander's words was not lost on Korpus: yet more Chaos Marines had landed on Antillis IV.

'Cognis dead...'

The glands which resided within the Company Librarian were of especial value. Implanted in the correct candidate, they would provide the Chapter with a replacement for the veteran psyker, whose reading of the Emperor's Tarot and subtle awareness of the aetheric shifts that heralded the arrival of daemonic forces had turned the tide of battle against greater numbers than had thus far been encountered on Antillis IV. However, the idea of a psychic shock wave powerful enough to end Cognis's long and loyal service almost beggared the imagination. The odds against the Avenging Sons had, it seemed, become much worse.

The hiss and crackle faded and Korpus grabbed the opportunity to reply. 'I am almost with you, sir. I will perform the excision on Cognis and be ready to stand with you...'

'NO!' Selleus cut vehemently across his Apothecary's transmission. He spoke quickly, obviously mindful of possible interference. 'Your orders are to quit the planet, taking all excised glands with you. If that proves to be impossible, you are to destroy them all, including your own. Do you understand?'

For a heartbeat, Korpus struggled to digest the message. Quit the planet? That was not the way of the Avenging Sons. Fight, yes. Die, if necessary. But run?

'Apothecary, respond,' came Selleus's voice. 'Did you receive my last transmission?' A faint crackle had begun to edge his words.

'Transmission received, commander.' Korpus forced his reply from between numb lips. 'But not understood. I can store the glands on my return to base. Surely we can fight on?' Korpus glanced up at the chateau, still maddeningly far above him.

'Negative.' A susurrating hiss washed over Selleus's words, growing steadily in volume. 'Cognis's last message was clear... Outer wall breached... compound overrun... Imperative... all viable glands... out of enemy hands... Imperative!... We embrace... Mercy's Kiss.'

Mercy's Kiss: the name given to the small pistol which hung at Korpus's belt – and the belt of every Apothecary. With it, Korpus would ease the pain of the fatally wounded, thus buying his patient an easier demise and himself more time to perform an Excision. The message in Selleus's use of the name was clear.

The commander's voice erupted into a series of howling whoops and squeals – interference caused by the close proximity of a large concentration of warp energy. The picture in Korpus's mind's eye changed from one of his company preparing to take the war to the enemy, to one of a beleaguered outpost fighting a last-ditch battle against the warp hordes.

'Message received and understood!' Korpus shouted his reply in the hope that it might reach his commander. 'You shall be remem–'

Before he could complete the litany, the distant chateau dissolved in a series of explosions. Gouts of rock and ash flew into the air. A multiple concussion swept down the hillside, pushing a roiling cloud of ash before it. Korpus dropped to the ground, curled so as to present his back to the avalanche and protect the phials loaded in his thigh-packs.

For what seemed like an eternity, the falling debris beat a relentless tattoo against Korpus's ceramite carapace. As he lay there, his commander's last words rang in his ears – and with it, the questions he longed to ask: how had the situation become so dire that his entire company would choose suicide over continued resistance? Why was it so important for the glands in his care to be taken off-world or destroyed?

Eventually the rock fall subsided and Korpus climbed to his feet, ash falling from his shoulders like snow. Looking up at the smoking remains of the chateau, reduced to a ragged collection of charred fragments by the detonation of the company's entire store of munitions, he completed the ritual. Never before had he said the words with such fury and such determination: 'You shall be avenged!'

GUIDED BY THE advice of Tiresias, the Company Astropath, Selleus had ordered the Avenging Sons' Thunderhawk gunships to make landfall at the edge of the greatest concentration of warp energy. Never one to waste time picking a way through the opposition's perimeter, he preferred to strike at the enemy's heart. The reports received from Antillis IV's Imperial garrison upon their company ship's shift out of warp made it clear that any such tactical niceties were already redundant. The planet's Imperial Governor had waited too long before sending a request for help – whether this was due to misplaced confidence or sheer incompetence no longer mattered. The Avenging Sons would have to drive straight for the centre of the enemy's forces, or all was lost.

But all, it seemed, was lost. Korpus's mind nagged at the fact as he made his way towards the drop zone: a garrison airfield still several hours distant. Defended by a unit of Imperial Guardsmen, the Thunderhawks offered his only chance of obeying his commander's final order.

Turning his back on the rocky outcrop which now bore only the smouldering remains of his brothers, Korpus forged across a landscape littered with evidence of Antillis IV's damnation: shattered hulks of Chimera troop carriers, their tracks blown from under them while attempting a strategic withdrawal. A Leman Russ tank, presumably the troops carriers' escort, had been tossed aside like a discarded toy, its armour plating shredded, its crew reduced to bloody daubs. Korpus picked his way between the hulks, wary in case the Chaos-inspired troops that had inflicted such damage had posted a rearguard.

'Apothecary!' The faint plea drifted across the field of static that filled his transceiver's earplug and was gone so quickly that Korpus couldn't be sure it had come from beyond the confines of his own skull. Perhaps it was just a memory of cries he had heard on many battlefields on many worlds. He shivered, then picked up his pace, heading for a stand of flash-blasted trees, the ash-blizzard howling at his back.

Just inside the tree line, Korpus found more wreckage: a battery of Basilisks, reduced to so much scrap, their crews torn to pieces. As he surveyed the organic detritus that lay, draped across the remains of the artillery pieces, the cry came again.

'Apothecary!'

'An echo, nothing more,' he told himself, though he could not suppress the shiver that ran through him. The call of a wounded Space Marine, broadcast hours ago, bouncing back to the planet's surface from the warp-clogged troposphere. The rest of his company had answered the order to regroup and died beside their commander. Korpus was the last of them.

'And you have your orders,' he reminded himself, his voice sounding dead and flat inside his helmet. He should have been with them to meet that last assault. Selleus's last transmission made no sense. The righteous determination with which he had promised his commander vengeance had faded, leaving only questions and confusion.

'Confusion is the seed-bed of Chaos,' Korpus intoned, remembering an aphorism from the Avenging Sons' Chapter Book as he marched on through the trees. Their branches had been stripped and blackened in the wake of the Chaos army's progress. Massive boles had been overturned; wind-blown ash now gathered among their roots.

'Uproot it, in the Emperor's name,' he continued. *If only it were that simple.*

HOURS PASSED, every one of them eating up the distance between Korpus and the airfield. Rugged, mountainous countryside gave way to flat plains and occasional patches of woodland. By nightfall, the Apothecary could see the gap-toothed outline of a city on the horizon, backlit by a dull reddish glow, which could mean only one thing: the forces of Chaos had reached the city. The firelight would be the result of the massive pyres built from the corpses of the city's inhabitants, gouting oily smoke and adding to the ash storms which continued to swirl about him as he marched.

The Thunderhawks' drop zone was located on the outskirts of the city. Had the Imperial troops left to guard the attack ships been able to hold off their attackers, then Korpus would be able to fulfil his commander's orders. If not…

'We may yet meet in the Book of Martyrs, Pereus,' Korpus muttered grimly as he strode on, step after tireless, servo-assisted step.

The night passed in a barely-remembered monotony of motion. Implanted in the early stages of a Space Marine's genetic conditioning, the Catalepsian Node allowed such a warrior to reduce all non-essential mental processes to a minimum, mimicking the effects of sleep, yet retain full awareness of his surroundings and objectives.

Korpus returned to full wakefulness as the first rays of the Antillis system's bloated sun rose between the buildings that now towered above him. He had reached the outskirts of the city and now marched along its cracked and buckled highways, still heading towards the airstrip. The ruins of what had once been an industrial area flanked the highway with shattered factories and storage yards.

As he marched, Korpus recited the Morning Prayer of the Avenging Sons: 'If this day be my last, I shall spend it in the service of your will, Emperor, Saviour, Last Hope of Mankind.' Light years away, aboard the vast, cathedral-like chapter ship that was the home of the Avenging Sons, the morning bell would be tolling. Every Avenging Son not on assignment would be gathered in the Great Chapel, reciting the same prayer as if with one voice. 'For I am an instrument of your will, a scourge of your enemies. I am an…'

The voice that burst from his transceiver stopped Korpus in his tracks, the remainder of the Morning Prayer unspoken. The voice was high and clear, uttering a battle cry he never expected to hear again.

'Avenging Sons!'

'AVENGING SONS!' Scout Vaelus swung his bolter left and right, pumping bolt after bolt into the Traitor Marines which advanced towards him between the high towers of containerised foodstuffs that would now never leave this storage yard for other star systems.

'Avenging Sons!' Scout Salvus, to Vaelus's right, took up the war cry, as did Scout Marus, to his left. Their bolters spat explosive death into the faces of the servants of the warp, vaporising heads, severing limbs – but it was not enough.

Their black-armoured opponents seemed not to feel the pain of their injuries. Shrieking with daemonic laughter and crying, 'Khorne! Khorne!' even as another bolt detonated against their armour, they pressed forward. And there were so many of them, jostling with one another to be the first to taste the flesh of a fledgling Space Marine. So many…

Something slammed against Vaelus's back. Scout Tallis, flanked by Scouts Orris and Flavus, forced back by the Khorne-inspired berserkers that advanced towards them, equally as heedless of the cannonade of bolter fire that was being pumped into their midst, now stood back-to-back with their battle-brothers.

'For the Emperor!' Vaelus cried. They might fall here today, but their enemy would know in whose name they died.

'For the Emperor!' came the unexpected reply, moments before Vaelus heard the muffled crack of a bolt pistol being discharged against an armoured body from closer than the two arms-lengths which separated the Scouts and their attackers. The concussive report sounded again and again, counterpointed by the high-pitched crackling whine of a power fist at full charge. High-voltage detonations punctuated the whine as it connected with armour. The copper tang of boiling blood reached Vaelus as he caught his first glimpse of the figure that was cutting a swathe through the berserkers, fighting with an almost equally mindless fury: a figure whose armour bore the insignia of the Avenging Sons. A figure in white.

'FOR THE EMPEROR!' Korpus's blood sang as he parried the downward sweep of a chainsword with his power fist. The whirring blade shattered against the glove's energy field. Korpus slammed his bolt pistol against the black, sigil-etched breastplate of his attacker and pulled the trigger twice. Still laughing, the berserker fell back, his chest a smoking ruin. Stepping past him, Korpus placed the open palm of his power fist against the back of another skull-helmed traitor. The Chaos Marine, still too mindlessly intent on reaching the Scouts to react to the new threat, stiffened as his armour's servos went into spasm.

'Vengeance!' Korpus breathed, and he closed his fist.

MINDS LOST TO the berserker fury of the Blood God, the Chaos Marines reacted with fatal slowness to the whirlwind of death that had appeared in their midst. Pressed close in their desire to reach the Scouts, they found turning to meet the white-armoured killer difficult: ablative plates snagged and took valuable seconds to disengage, seconds that allowed Korpus to step close, press the muzzle of his bolt pistol against the grinning, fanged skull of a face plate and pull the trigger.

Seeing this, Vaelus closed the gap between himself and the nearest Chaos Marine – and was almost decapitated by his intended target's chainsword. Dropping to one knee to avoid the chattering blade, the Scout pressed his bolter against the nearest of the Chaos Marine's knee joints and fired. Rising as the crippled berserker fell, Vaelus fired again, three times, vaporising the traitor's head.

'Forward, Avenging Sons!' Vaelus cried. 'The day can still be ours!' He turned, searching for a new target, and found himself visor-to-visor with the Scouts' white-armoured saviour. Without a word, the Apothecary stepped past him, heading for the line of Chaos Marines which had closed upon the three Scouts at Vaelus's back and now threatened to overwhelm them.

Before turning to follow Korpus, Vaelus glanced along the narrow passageway between the containers. Moments before, there had been a seething mass of black armour and grinning skulls. Now a tangled carpet of shattered, smoking corpses lay before him.

'Emperor be praised. He has delivered us!' Vaelus breathed, then hurried to join the battle that still raged.

'ALL OF THEM?' Salvus's voice betrayed the mixture of disbelief, confusion and fear felt by all of the Scouts as they listened to Korpus's account of the last hours of the Second Company.

'The entire Second Company, yes,' Korpus, helmetless, replied as he worked on the stump of Marus's right arm, using a long-needled syringe to inject unguents into the raw pink flesh. The Scout's genetically-altered blood had already clotted, sealing the wound, but necrotising infections were still a risk to one who had yet to complete the full course of enhancements that would elevate him to Space Marine status.

'Time is a factor here,' Korpus said, after binding Marus's arm and re-securing his helmet. 'This world is lost. My orders are to save the glands in my keeping. There will be other traitorous abominations such as these who will try to stop me. I may require an escort.'

'We stand ready,' Vaelus declared. At his words, the Scouts snapped to attention. Korpus surveyed them and nodded approvingly. Of the five survivors who stood before him, only Marus had suffered serious injury.

'Then we move,' he said. 'Bring his weapons.' He gestured to the body which lay against one wall of the container-canyon – Flavus, his torso all but bisected by a berserker's chain-axe – then stabbed a finger first at Salvus, then Tallis, both busily donning their helmets while Orris clipped Flavus's bolt pistol and chainsword to his equipment belt. 'You take point. You guard the rear.'

As Korpus expected, decisive orders served to ease the Scouts' disquiet. Since the death of their sergeant, incinerated by a Chaos Marine's melta while leading them in a probing mission beyond the Avenging Sons' former perimeter, the Scouts had been playing a deadly game of cat-and-mouse with the enemy, zig-zagging across the battlefield in the hope of re-locating the Second Company. Bearings lost, communications frustrated by the blizzard of ash and static, they had sought shelter in this vast container yard, believing that they had shaken off their pursuers, only to find themselves trapped by a pincer attack.

'The Emperor sent you,' Vaelus had told Korpus. 'We were daemon-fodder, but for your arrival.'

'The Emperor watches over us all,' Korpus had replied automatically. His blood was still singing in his ears, the urge to rend and kill without thought, without emotion had yet to subside – and, in truth, he wished that it never would. The killing rage – the 'Vengeful Heart' as it had been dubbed, centuries ago – was the state aspired to by every Avenging Son. A unit of Avenging Sons in such a condition were all but unstoppable on the battlefield; their only desire was to move forward through whatever enemy stood before them, their only desire to kill.

Which is what made Selleus's last act so incomprehensible. As an Apothecary, Korpus understood that he should temper his own Vengeful Heart in order to perform his duties. It was an honour and he accepted it as the Emperor's will. But for Selleus to deliberately extinguish the hearts of his entire company...

Such doubts had crept back as the killing rage subsided. To quiet them once again, Korpus turned his mind to his new role as leader of the Scout Squad. But deep within the cage of his soul, his Vengeful Heart beat strong, demanding to be heard.

'THERE'S MOVEMENT,' Vaelus reported as he peered through the ocularius. He adjusted the focusing dials. Lenses spun within the brass casing, allowing him a greater depth of field. 'Possibly human.'

'Doubtful,' Korpus said. He and the Scout crouched behind a pile of discarded aero-engines at the edge of the airfield. Warehouses and hangars curved away to either side, many of them punctured by heavy cannon and las-fire. The field itself was pock-marked with craters, dotted with the remains of commercial and military aircraft. When their drop-ships had landed, both the aircraft and the buildings had been intact.

'The Thunderhawks?' he asked. Vaelus adjusted the dials again.

'Not good,' the Scout reported. 'Two are complete wrecks. The other three have all taken a pounding. There's no way to tell if any can fly.'

'We only need one,' Korpus replied, all too aware of the irony of his words, but determined to remain focused on the mission.

The sudden cough of bolter fire from the rear drew their attention from the attack ships. Vaelus stowed the ocularius and followed Korpus, who was already running towards the nearest hangar.

They arrived to find the other Scouts standing over the bodies of three Imperial Guardsman, members of the unit assigned to guard the Thunderhawks. Their bodies bore the marks of impacts both old and new, but also the buboes and other malformations that spoke of only one thing.

'Necromancy,' Korpus stated flatly. 'This world is now securely in Chaos's grasp. Time is short. Soon even the living will be unable to resist its influence.'

As if to underline his words, one of the corpses began to twitch. Impossibly, it raised itself on one shattered arm, opened its exploded eyes…

Tallis's chainsword sliced through the ex-guardsman's head, rupturing it like an overripe fruit. Its brains, turned black and fluid by the same necromantic power which had re-animated its hours-dead corpse, splashed across the ground. A rank sewer-stench filled the air.

'Any sentient being in the vicinity will know we're here by now,' said Korpus. 'Make for the nearest Thunderhawk. Stay tight and stay alert.'

Korpus led the Scouts from the cover of the hangar, jogging swiftly across the open ground between it and the attack craft. The closer they got the worse the situation looked. Even the three Thunderhawks which remained upright on their landing skids looked ready for the reclamation plants of the Adeptus Mechanicus.

Bolter fire sounded from his left. He turned. Orris had dispatched another re-animated guardsmen.

'Head shots are not enough,' he reminded the Scout. 'Dismemberment is the only way to ensure they don't come after you again.'

'Understood,' Orris replied and set about the corpse with his chainsword. More gunfire erupted from the far side of the group of Thunderhawks. Tallis and Marus had encountered more of the foul things.

'Who here has received flight training?' Korpus demanded. 'I need someone to check the instrumentation.'

'Salvus!' Vaelus called. The Scout had stayed close to the Apothecary, adopting the role of aide-de-camp. Salvus ran back between two of the Thunderhawks, ducking to avoid the blackened and twisted remains of a sensor array.

'We need to know which of these can fly, if any,' Korpus told him. 'They may look like wrecks, but I've known them to take off in a worse state than this.' As Salvus ran up the ramp into the belly of the nearest craft, Korpus offered up a silent prayer that his words would prove to be more than a mere panacea.

The bark of Imperial-issue munitions echoed from the interior of the Thunderhawk. Both Korpus and Vaelus turned, stepped onto the drop-ramp, then dodged the selection of body parts that flew from the hatch, accompanied by a chainsword's chattering.

'Best check the others,' Salvus called out from the belly of the ship. Before Korpus could issue an order, Vaelus was already halfway up the ramp of the neighbouring craft.

Good soldiers, Korpus thought. For the first time, he dared believe that they might escape this doomed world and reach the chapter ship, where the Scouts would undergo implantation of the gene seed from the glands that he carried in his armour. Perhaps they might form the basis for a new Second Company. If so, they would bring honour to the memory of the corpses they would leave on Antillis IV.

'Pressurising,' Salvus's voice crackled over Korpus's transceiver. He and Orris had spent the last hour jury-rigging the seal around the main hatch, using parts from interior hatches, making frequent reference to the Adeptus Mechanicus Prayer Book he had found in a locker on the flight deck.

Korpus stood outside the hatch, listening to the hiss and pop as the seal closed. After checking over each of the three

Thunderhawks, Salvus had declared the first one to be the most spaceworthy. While he and Orris worked, the others continued to prowl the airfield, using bolter and chainsword to dispatch the necromantically resurrected.

On the flight deck, Salvus watched the icons on the control board. Several relating to non-essential systems were dead; others – including the weapons board – glowed red, indicating failure, but they too should not prevent spaceflight. Salvus narrowed his eyes, concentrating on the set of icons that related to the craft's internal environment. They showed green – for the moment.

Long moments passed. Through the gunship's view-screens, Korpus scanned the edge of the airfield. It was a miracle that they had been allowed so much time, that the Chaos Marines and the daemons that commanded them had not scented their presence here and closed in to finish them off.

'The Machine God is with us!' Salvus's relief-filled words jerked Korpus from his thoughts. Another hiss and pop, and the main hatch swung open. The smiling Scout stood in the doorway. 'With your permission, Apothecary, I could transfer the weapons system from Hawk Four...'

'No time,' Korpus interjected. 'Begin pre-flight rituals. We've been sitting around like targets on a shooting range for too long as it is.'

'Understood.' Salvus disappeared back into the craft.

Korpus strode up the ramp, following Salvus inside. While the Scout made for the raised flight deck, Korpus stooped to open a locker set into the wall beside the Navigator's chart table, which bore the seal of the Apothecarion. Removing his helmet and gloves, Korpus released the catches on the locker door and felt the gentle kiss of air as its vacuum seal was breached. The door swung open, revealing the racks of empty phial-holders within. Minutes later, all were full.

'Soon, my brothers. Be patient.' In his mind, Korpus addressed the Avenging Sons Scouts who, like those with him here on Antillis IV, were awaiting implantation of the gene-seed. The glands he had harvested – and which now floated before him, their preservative-filled phials nestling securely in the locker's racks – would help ensure that the Emperor's crusade would continue.

Korpus closed the locker door, secured its vacuum seal, then refastened the long ceramite thigh-plates over his suit's now empty storage bays. As he had placed each phial into the locker, he had felt a weight lift from his shoulders. Though he had performed this act on countless other worlds, never had the special duty of an Apothecary weighed so heavily upon him, nor had he felt such relief at its completion.

'Apothecary!' Vaelus stood at the Thunderhawk's main hatch. Korpus hurried the length of the craft's interior, re-attaching his gloves, automatically checking the load in his bolt pistol's magazine and the charge in his power fist.

'Report,' he demanded of the Scout, though the sound of bolter fire and a discordant, guttural chanting provided all the answer he needed.

'Brother, the enemy has found us!'

BEHIND THEM, the Thunderhawk's engine ratcheted upwards in pitch. At Korpus's order, Salvus had rushed through the last verses of the pre-flight incantation. The engines didn't sound too healthy – what should have been a smooth rise in tone and volume was interrupted by coughs and judders that had more in common with a chronic chest infection – but the Scout remained confident that the craft would fly.

Korpus and Vaelus had paced away from the Thunderhawk, sheltering from the ash-storm kicked up by its back– and down-drafts under the fuselage of Hawk Four. Korpus held the Scout's ocularius to his eyes, scanning the perimeter of the airfield, while Vaelus continued his report. 'We made contact with their point men during a sweep of the southern perimeter. We hit them hard and fast – I don't think they had time to send out a warning. The others hung back. We still have a few frag mines. They were to lay the mines beyond the perimeter and then retreat. They should have been back by now.'

'Here they come,' Korpus said. 'And they are not alone.'

Through the lenses of the instrument, Korpus watched as the three Scouts raced through the ragged remains of the airfield's southern gate. Bolter fire chewed up the ash-covered ground all around them. A black-armoured horde was at their back, howling, scenting blood and one more victory in the name of their foul masters. From the unevenness of Tallis's stride, Korpus judged that he must have taken a serious hit to one leg. Shifting focus, he tried to assess the exact size of the threat they were facing, when his gaze fell upon a sight that could mean only disaster.

'Emperor's mercy!' he breathed as the vast, obscene bulk of a Dreadnought filled his view, towering over the troops around it, lurching as it stomped through the ash and mud. Its black armour was covered in twisted sigils proclaiming its daemonic allegiance, blasphemous verses in praise of the Dark Gods, and what looked like dolls hanging from chains attached to its carapace.

Despite his revulsion, Korpus adjusted the focusing dials again… Not dolls. Human corpses, some still wearing the tattered remains of Imperial Guard uniforms; faces bloated, limbs torn away, guts slit open and their contents hung like grotesque garlands around their necks. Final proof, if proof were needed, that Antillis IV had fallen.

'They need covering fire!' Korpus barked as he tore the ocularius from his eyes. His mind raced. Even if the jury-rigged Thunderhawk was air-worthy, it would need time to achieve sufficient altitude to be out of range of the Chaos army's guns. He tried not to think of the range of the Dreadnought's cannon. It could swat the fleeing craft from the sky long after it had outdistanced the Chaos Marines' bolters.

'Hawk Four's weapons system is still operational,' he told Vaelus. 'Get to work.' With a nod, the Scout ran for the main hatch. Korpus donned and secured his helmet. By the time he spoke into his transceiver, he had come to a decision: 'Scout Salvus, immediate dust-off. Do you understand? Go. Now!'

'Apothecary, please repeat!' came the uncomprehending reply. 'Leave now? What about the others? Yourself? I cannot–'

'My job is done. The future of the Second Company is in your hands. We'll keep them busy until you're out of range. Tell our brothers that we took the Emperor's holy vengeance into the mouth of Hell. For are we not Avenging Sons?'

'Avenging Sons!' Salvus answered, his voice firm once again. 'Your name shall live forever in the Chapel of Martyrs, Apothecary Korpus!'

The engine's pitch changed again, rising to a scream as the control surfaces swung into the correct alignment. The landing skids groaned as the gunship's bulk began to shift.

'Avenging Sons!' Vaelus's voice echoed in the Apothecary's ears as the Scout fired a first volley from Hawk Four's las-cannon into the approaching black horde. As he ran to meet the other Scouts, Korpus saw their impact: dark-armoured bodyparts flew in all directions like confetti, leaving holes in the oncoming line, which were quickly filled by more of their treacherous brethren. Vaelus fired again, punching more holes in the onrushing tide of Chaos. Behind him, the engines of Salvus's Thunderhawk had taken on the unmistakable tone of an airborne craft. His precious cargo was on its way home.

'Avenging Sons!' Korpus cried, his blood singing as he raced to battle. His last duty performed, he was an Apothecary no longer. Now he was just a warrior. A warrior with a Vengeful Heart.

KORPUS HIT THE Chaos line like a weapon wielded by the Emperor himself. Black-armoured abominations flew left and right, skull-helms shattered by close-quarters bolter fire and blows from his power fist at full discharge. To either side of him, Tallis, Orris and one-armed Marus carved sections from their enemy with their chainswords, blew away limbs and punctured breastplates with their bolters.

Marus was the first to fall. His bolter empty, he reached across his body to unhook his chainsword. In the few seconds it took for him to grasp the hilt of his weapon, a Khorne-chanting Chaos Marine tore his head from his shoulders with a chattering, sigil-etched chain-axe. Tallis returned the favour, severing the Chaos Marine's axe-arm with a well-placed sword-strike to its elbow, followed by a bolter volley in the face, but there was nothing to be done for Marus and no time to mourn. Tallis and Orris surged on, keeping pace with Korpus, cutting a gory swathe through the servants of the Outer Dark. The black tide closed behind them, still making for the Thunderhawks, some already wasting bolts in an attempt to bring down the accelerating Thunderhawk, already several hundred feet above them.

Korpus and the others ignored them. Vaelus, still at the weapons board of Hawk Four, scythed them down with the lascannon. Korpus had issued fresh orders as he ran, leading the Scouts into battle. They knew their target: the Dreadnought.

It already loomed above them, marching with implacable, earth-shaking strides to meet them. In one steel-clawed arm it held a mace the size of a man; its other upper limb had been replaced by a double-linked las-cannon which was aimed far above the heads of the Marines. Korpus didn't need to turn to see its target. The half-dead, totally insane Chaos Marine encased within its inches-thick hide was drawing a bead on the fleeing Thunderhawk gunship.

Kicking aside the last, headless victim of his bolter, Korpus holstered the weapon and made an adjustment to his power fist. Already buzzing with energy, the glove began to emit a continuous high-pitched squeal. The plates of Korpus's battle suit rang with sympathetic vibrations. His teeth began to chatter insanely as the energy from the overloading glove hummed through his bones. His head felt as if it might explode within his helmet.

A single Chaos Marine stood between Korpus and the Dreadnought. Rapid fire from its bolter sprayed diagonally across the Apothecary's armour, knocking him back several steps, but the ceramite plates held. Korpus stepped up to his assailant and punched him squarely in the chest.

But for the lingering smell of ozone and the fragments of fused flesh and armour that lay scattered at Korpus's feet, the Chaos Marine might never have existed. For a heartbeat, the power fist was silent. Korpus feared that its power cell was already empty, that his plan would be undone by his unwise, pre-emptive strike. Then the glove resumed its ear-splitting squeal. Korpus smiled, then sprinted for the Dreadnought's nearest leg.

A VOLLEY OF LAS-FIRE arced up from the Dreadnought's cannon. Flashing across the intervening space, it missed the nose of the still-rising Thunderhawk by what felt like inches. The craft's superstructure groaned and creaked as it was buffeted by the shock-waves of super-heated air. As he jockeyed the flight controls, Salvus muttered a short prayer to the Machine God.

'Whatever you plan to do to that cursed thing, Apothecary,' Salvus added, sparing a thought for the comrades he was leaving behind, 'do it now!'

THE DREADNOUGHT paused in its march to adjust its aim. Korpus knew that it would not miss a second time. Shucking his power fist, whose squeal had passed beyond the range of human hearing, he jammed it between the web of struts and power conduits that ran behind the unholy war machine's knee joint. Blue fire played across the surface of the glove. Tendrils of the barely-tamed lightning began to arc across the surface of the Dreadnought's lower extremities.

For a moment, Korpus stared, entranced by the sight. Orris's cry of pain as his armour was breached by bolter fire from a dozen attackers jerked him back to the deadly present. Spinning on his heel, Korpus made to rejoin the fray.

Orris lay where he had been defending the Apothecary's back, his chest a smoking ruin. One more son of the Emperor to be avenged. Tallis was nowhere to be seen; had he also fallen? Korpus noticed also that Hawk Four's las-cannon had fallen silent. Was he the last Avenging Son alive on Antillis IV? If so the hordes of Chaos would remember his name.

'Avenging Son!' he bellowed, launching himself at the nearest of the surrounding Chaos-spawn, chainsword raised, bolter spitting death.

He never reached his target. The power fist detonated, vaporising the lower half of the Dreadnought. The corrupt war machine tumbled backwards, las-cannon firing a wild, ineffectual volley into the sky. The shock wave from the blast slapped Korpus in the back, scattering him and the Chaos Marines around him like so many model soldiers, swept off a table at the end of a game. Ears ringing, Korpus momentarily lost consciousness.

Blinking back to awareness, Korpus found himself on his back, staring up at the sky. Above him arched a single vapour trail – the Thunderhawk, powering through the stratosphere, safe from attack.

His killing rage, his Vengeful Heart, had subsided. He felt a strange sense of peace, one borne of exhaustion and the knowledge that he had done his duty. He tried to move, to get to his feet, but his legs wouldn't respond. Something had been broken by the power fist's detonation. Was he dying? He thought briefly of Sergeant Pereus.

'Man is born alone,' he whispered. A grey mist edged his vision. He knew he should complete the Rite of Extreme Unction, but felt too tired to continue. The grey mist enveloped him.

'Apothecary!' It was the voice he had heard earlier, while marching alone across Antillis IV. He had thought it to be an echo, an old transmission bounced off the upper atmosphere. Now, undisguised by static, it sounded close to his ear. It was not the voice of any of the Second Company. It had a soft, unpleasant tone.

He tried to turn his head, open his eyes, see to whom the voice belonged. But his head wouldn't turn and his eyes wouldn't open.

The grey mist turned to black.

'APOTHECARY?'

Surprised that he was able to do so, Korpus opened his eyes. Rather than the sky above Antillis IV, or the ruins of the airfield, he found himself staring at the walls of what might have been a laboratory in the Avenging Sons' Apothecarion – might have been, were it not for the nightmarish collection of specimens that hung upon the walls and sat in clear jars of preserving fluid. The malformed limbs, misshapen heads and torsos bore no relation to humanity, but to the breeding grounds of the warp. In the shadows cast by the dull reddish light which illuminated the room, Korpus thought he saw movement. Narrowing his eyes, he saw that he was right. A collection of what resembled nothing so much as clawed, fanged foetuses thrashed against the glass of one large vessel.

'Apothecary!' The tone of the voice at his ear shifted from enquiry to satisfaction. Korpus tried to turn his head, move any of his limbs, but found that he could not. He was all but naked, stripped of his armour and robe, secured by metallic straps to a table of some kind, tilted at an angle close to the vertical. 'Of course,' the voice purred. 'You would like to see your saviour.'

A figure stepped into Korpus's field of view. Covered from throat to floor in a robe made from a slick, vulcanised fabric, he held in one hand a pair of gloves of the same material. The hand which held the gloves appeared normal, but the other was twisted, possessed of too many knuckle joints.

Noticing the direction of Korpus's gaze, the figure held up the hand – his left – and flexed the fingers before Korpus's eyes. The digits moved with an unnatural, insectile grace, each of the extra joints allowing the fingers a range of movement that Korpus, dedicated to the preservation of the human form, found appalling.

'One of my first refinements,' the vile figure said, proudly. 'I find it allows for a more subtle surgical approach.'

For the first time, Korpus focused on the stranger's face. With the bald pate, the sallow skin and sunken cheeks, Korpus might have been looking at his old instructor, Apothecary Lorus. But the skin was stretched too tightly over this man's skull, as if it had been removed, the fat scraped away from under the skin and then reapplied too closely. The black eyes shone out from under heavy brows. A warped intelligence, perhaps genius, danced in those eyes.

'It has been some time since I sought to preserve a human life,' the stranger continued. 'I am pleased that I have not forgotten how.'

Korpus tried to speak, but his throat was clogged as if from an unnaturally long sleep. He coughed, tried again, his voice cracking. 'Who…?'

'Of course!' the stranger laughed. 'How impolite of me! It has also been some time since I received a guest schooled in simple social manners.

'I am Fabrikus. Apothecary Fabrikus.'

The words froze Korpus's heart. Fabrikus's name was a dark legend in the Apothecarion of every Space Marine Chapter. A brilliant man, he served with the First Company of the World Eaters, gaining distinction as a warrior and as a surgeon, before following Primarch Angron into the service of the Ruinous Powers. In the centuries since the Great Heresy, his name had become a byword for perverse experimentation. Some said he was even behind many of the mutations undergone by Chaos Marines: the fusion of flesh to armour of the World Eaters, the hellish combination of near-dead warrior and implacable war machine that was a Chaos Dreadnought.

'I see you have heard of me,' Fabrikus smiled at the look of horror on Korpus's face. 'And I imagine you are wondering what my interest might be in a fallen Space Marine on a fallen world. The answer is simple: the gene-seed.'

Korpus's mind spun back in time, to his last communication with Commander Selleus. He heard again his words, obscured by the waves of static: 'New incursion… Cognis dead…'

'Your Librarian was a truly powerful psyker,' Fabrikus purred, as if reading his mind. 'Fortunately my… allies… were more than his equal. It seemed, however, that before his death he gleaned enough of our purpose in joining the assault on the planet you knew as Antillis IV to warn his commander. Their suicide destroyed all of our advance party. Had it not been for our interception of your leader's last transmission, we would have believed our cause was lost.'

'All viable glands... out of enemy hands...' Selleus's words rang in Korpus's memory.

'You see, my masters require more troops, more than can be provided by the harvest of the seed from those already serving their holy purpose. I have spent centuries experimenting with the other races available to me, but the seed refuses to take, or else it produces mutations that are... unhelpful,' Fabrikus's words carried a hint of frustration. As if hearing them, the fanged things thrashed against the confining glass walls of their preservative-filled prison.

'Though I would never say this to my masters, I believe the warp causes problems with the seed from our own warriors, affects their potency. I have, therefore, decided to return to take up my earlier role and harvest glands from a more pure source, unaffected by the energies of my masters' home.' To hear Fabrikus speak, he and Korpus might have been fellow professionals, discussing the results of a failed experiment and the new measures that might be taken to ensure future success.

'I believe that the seed from those who continue to stubbornly serve the False Emperor might provide me with the material I need to create new types of warrior, loyal to the Dark Lords of the warp, unstoppable in battle.'

'You... you knew I had the glands,' Korpus whispered.

Fabrikus nodded. 'We tracked you across half the world,' he said, smiling. 'And we found you!'

Now it was Korpus's turn to smile. 'But I have them no longer! By the time I blew your Dreadnought to oblivion, they were already off-world! You have failed, Fabrikus! Failed!'

'By the time I found you, all the glands you carried so heroically were indeed off-world,' Fabrikus conceded, apparently unaffected by Korpus's mocking words. 'All of the glands – bar two.'

The import of his words crashed in on Korpus. Nestling at the base of his throat and deep within his naked chest, were the glands he had carried since the day of their implantation, the day that he truly became a Space Marine, a day of such pride, such honour.

'No!' he gasped, wide-eyed with horror. He had been so intent on vengeance, of dying as an Avenging Son should.

Believing his duty as an Apothecary was complete, he had delivered the future of his breed, perhaps of the entire human race, into the hands of this monster, this twisted reflection of all he held dear.

'Oh, yes,' Fabrikus purred. Before Korpus's horrified gaze, the skin around his left eye began to bulge, the eye itself change shape, elongating in an impossible manner, as if supplementary lenses were pushing forward from within the confines of his skull, improving his focus for the surgery to come.

He reached towards an instrument gurney set beside the table upon which Korpus now struggled vainly. The multi-jointed fingers of his left hand selected a scalpel. Longer and thinner than the others, it was designed for only one purpose: excision.

'I prefer to operate without analgesia,' he said, stepping up to the table. 'I think the absence of pain always dulls the experience, don't you?'

Apothecary Fabrikus set to work. His subject's screaming served only to excite the thrashing abominations within their tank into a frenzy, snapping and clawing at their fellows. Korpus cried out, not for himself, but for his honour, lost in the heat of battle. Lost forever.

DAEMONBLOOD
Ben Counter

THE SPACE MARINE and the Battle Sister gazed across at the sight before them. It was an ocean of corruption. It was a continent of evil.

The morass undulated gently, lit by the phosphorescence of vast colonies of bacteria and fungi. It spread so far through the subterranean darkness that it formed the horizon, and far away island-sized buboes spurted like volcanoes. Rivers of ichor oozed across the slabs of fat and tattered, stretched skin, bursting with the sheer immensity of the creature it contained. Here and there huge spires of splintered bone jutted up from the vile sea, picked clean of flesh by the layer of flies that hung as thick and vast as a city's smog and obscured the cavern's ceiling. This sea of flesh was dead, yet alive. It was the diseased green-black of decay, and yet it pulsed with the life of the pestilences which had made this rank, boiling ocean of filth their home.

Sister Aescarion of the Ebon Chalice tore her eyes away from the sight, bile and vomit rising in her throat. What she saw was a manifestation of everything she had been taught to fear, and then to hate, throughout all of her life. Yet there was little room for fear here, or even hatred. It was a blank revulsion that overwhelmed her.

She was lying on her side, still wearing the fluted angel-wing jump pack, for she had landed badly on the thin promontory of rock which arced over the sea. Instinctively she checked her auto-senses. The respirator in her power armour was working hard to filter out the toxins in the air, and warning runes flashed all over her retinal display.

Hurriedly she tried to remember where she was, and the image of the heretic city flitted back into her mind. Far above them, on the planet's surface, the city of Saafir raged as the heretics and their daemonic allies fought her brothers and sisters. And here was surely the heart of Saafir's evil, encapsulated in an unimaginable sea of writhing corruption.

Beside her stood Sergeant Castus, the deep blue armour of the Ultramarines glinting strangely in the half-light. He had removed his helmet, and held his bolter by his side. His centuries-old armour sported several fresh dents and bullet scars, a testament to the ferocious battle which he and the Sister had fought to get here. Like all Space Marines he was tall, and his dark hair was cropped close. His face was as strong and forbidding as a cliff of rock, his eyes fixed grimly on the sight before him.

Aescarion grasped her simulacrum, rolling the ivory beads in the black gauntlet of her power armour. In spite of its comforting presence she knew the sea was alive, and that it could tell they were there. She knew that it would not make do with merely killing them.

'Brother Marine,' she called to Sergeant Castus, her voice small and quiet when usually it was strong and inspiring. 'Close your mind to it. Look away!' Castus did not seem to notice her.

I have my faith, she told herself. *I am alive where no human should have a right to survive. The Emperor is with me always. I have my faith. But I fear for the Space Marine. Why do I fear so?*

A ripple of movement shivered through the air. Aescarion reached out and grasped the haft of her power axe where it had landed next to her. Its head, like a giant chiselled shoulder blade, thrummed angrily with the power field around it. She could not hope to hurt the creature in front of her, but she was not ready to die on her knees, and death in battle with such a thing would be a glorious end in itself.

But am I really going to die here? asked that voice of faith deep inside her. *A spirit true to the Imperium never dies. And the*

Marine? He would have great strength of mind, as he had been trained – but strong enough?

A mile or so across the corpse-ocean, a chasm many leagues long sluiced apart, revealing layers of fat and necrotic muscle beneath, bloated and useless organs. Further away, two orbs the size of cathedrals rose up from the mire with a great, vile sound like a hundred bodies being pulled from a swamp. They shed their filthy membranes to reveal a gleaming black surface. Castus took a few steps away from the rock's edge, but he did not take his eyes off the monstrosity.

It was a face. A mouth and two eyes. When it spoke, it was with a voice felt rather than heard, deep and slow, and Aescarion could feel the waves of malice that swept across the promontory along with the thing's noisome breath.

'What curiously small creatures you are to present such a thorn in my side.' The words roared and rumbled through the air, thick with dark amusement. 'What little bundles of ignorant flesh. I am Parmenides, called the Vile, chosen Prince of Nurgle. I am the virus which the Plague God sends to infect your mortal worlds. I am the festering in your wounded empire. Do creatures as insignificant as yourselves have names too, I wonder?'

'Sergeant Castus of the Ultramarines, Second Company,' the Marine replied in a defiant voice, as if he were trying to impress the daemon prince.

The horrific gaze turned to Aescarion, questioning.

'I would not give you my name, though it cost my soul,' the Battle Sister snarled, and she gripped her axe tighter.

'Such a shame,' Parmenides replied. 'But the girl I can understand. Her mind is most infertile. What has she ever questioned? They teach her and she believes.' The corners of the chasm turned upwards. The thing was smiling. 'But you, my man. You are different, are you not? You can travel across the stars – but you do not know what lies between them. I could show you, my boy. I could show you why your omnipotent Emperor chooses to let his Imperium of toy soldiers be eroded by Chaos.'

Parmenides's immense face rose up in a vast static tidal wave that surrounded them like an amphitheatre of flesh. Now he gazed down on them from above, drowning them in his blank gaze. Sister Aescarion took an involuntary step back, then held firm. Sergeant Castus continued merely to gaze upon the corrupt being, his eyes steely, jaw set in righteous defiance.

'Now ask yourself, who is in the ascendancy? Every year more and more worlds are lost to you. No matter how you lie to yourself that the warp is held at bay, you know deep in that untaught part of yourself that humanity will fall. The girl cannot see the inevitable. But you can. And do you really want to be dragged down by the Imperium as it sinks? You will die knowing your efforts were futile. You will die knowing that you know *nothing!*'

Castus shook his head slightly, but whether he was refuting the monster or agreeing with it Aescarion could not tell.

'I can give you flesh that will not wither, only change and become home to a civilisation of pestilence. Do not follow the Imperium when it falls. With my help you can crush it beneath your heel, and become an Imperium yourself, my boy! I can show you what secrets this dark little universe contains. I can show you what it really means to exist in a world your Imperium is blind to.'

Castus's face was set but uncertainty flickered in his eyes like lightning. Aescarion could sense the insidious psychic worming that would even now be burrowing for his soul, but the Ultramarine was fighting it, trusting in the Emperor, refusing to bow before Parmenides's strength.

Castus tried to hold his hands up to his face and block out the sights and sounds that were trying to change him, but he was pinned by great chains of psychic energy, to the rock where he stood, utterly immobile, held wide open and totally vulnerable to the mental ambush. He tried to remember the years of training and conditioning in the temple of his fortress-monastery. He felt himself getting more and more desperate as he tried to recall all those words of steel that had been spoken to him by the Chaplains ever since he had first set foot in the chapter's aedificium. But they were all slipping away, as his mind was dissolved by Parmenides's will.

'Nnnoo... nnnnn...' the Space Marine grimaced as he tried to form the words of defiance spinning in his mind.

It was a new type of fear he felt now. He had known what it was like to feel the air shredded by bolter shells and laser fire, to anticipate, every second, the hot bloom of pain. And he had become used to it over the years, until it was not a real fear, but an understanding of the constant danger that accompanied a sacred duty to defend the Imperium.

This was so different. Here, his body was not at stake. His mind was the prize, his spirit, his very soul. A Space Marine should never feel fear. But Castus felt it now, a fear of change to the part of him that had always remained the same, a part of him that was as sacred to him, in its own way, as the Imperium itself.

'Domina, salve nos...' he hissed through his teeth, grimacing, a thin trickle of blood running from one nostril.

With a mental shrug, Parmenides cast a dark psychic mantle around Castus's soul – a vast, terrifying emptiness, crushing, draining his spirit.

Castus knew that if he had ever been strong enough to earn the armour of a Marine, he would have to be stronger now. 'Imperator, in perpetuum, in omnipotens, in umbrae...'

Aescarion tried to drag herself towards him but the very air was drenched with power and she, too, could barely move – she felt as if she were entombed in rock. Her ears buzzed with a low, savage laughter, and the abhorrent image before her was shot through with red flecks as her head pounded. 'Never break!' she yelled at the top of her voice, unsure if Castus could hear her. 'Never break!'

From between Parmenides's eyes a shimmering psychic lance leapt out and transfixed Castus, laying him open, white arcs of energy leaping off his armour to the rock, lighting him up like beacon in the a darkness. Every fiendish trick the prince could muster was poured into Castus's disintegrating soul.

The crushing power smashed Castus to his knees with an involuntary scream of panic. Deep in his mind he scrabbled madly, grasping for the memories that were stripped from him and were incinerated by the force of Parmenides's malice. Endless hours of battle blistered and died. The liturgies of the Ultramarines were blasted from his memory. And below even that, a past, a childhood, all were flayed away and burned. The threads of personality that had held him together melted in the psychic fire until all that was left were the most base instincts. The flame left him seared clean of all that had made him a Space Marine of the Emperor. Castus was reduced to an animal with no morals, no duty, no memory of the almighty Imperium that had borne him.

And no faith.

A tide of cold horror rose in Aescarion's heart. Castus was limp, swaying where he knelt, his skin pale, blood running from his nose and ears. All his mental defences had been peeled away and the shrill scream that she could hear in her soul was the sound of Parmenides's foul mind savaging the Marine's spirit like a predator tearing apart its prey. Castus had been strong – but this foul Chaos filth had been stronger.

'Do you join me? Do you belong, fleshy little ignorant man?' the daemon prince's voice rose amidst a screeching psychic crescendo. 'Answer! Answer! Do you embrace knowledge, and the plague, and the true path of humanity? Do you transcend your sad little species? Will you watch them fall beneath you, while you walk the stars?

'Do you join me?'

In a heartbeat the mental chains shattered, and Aescarion could move again. But she knew that this was the worst sign, because it meant that Castus had succumbed.

'Yes!' Castus yelled in a monstrous, throaty voice that was not his, throwing his arms wide apart as if offering himself to sacrifice. 'Oh yes!'

Parmenides laughed, and great walls of flesh pounded against the walls of the promontory, sending debris crashing around them. Aescarion was not going to die here. She was not going to join the Emperor, not just yet. The moment Castus gave himself to Chaos, he had given her something to avenge.

She swung her power axe above her head and rushed at Castus, smashing the blade down amidst its howling blue power field. Castus blocked it with his forearm and his hand was severed in a waterfall of sparks. He looked back at her, not with the eyes of a man, but with the same black, filmy, liquid eyes of the Daemon prince, and smiled at her with Parmenides's malevolent grin. His skin was scarred and pockmarked by the heat generated by the daemon prince's invasion, his teeth were cracked and shattered. His body had been wracked and broken enough – but that was nothing compared to the mutilation of his soul.

He did not bother to draw his combat knife or raise his gun. He simply drove the heel of his remaining hand into Aescarion's breastbone and sent her sprawling across the rock with a strength not even a Space Marine should have.

The Sororitas clung to the rock and saw the waves of filth rising towards her. She drew her stiletto combat knife from its sheath, but instead of rushing at her new nemesis and dying a good death, she drove it into the casing of her own jump pack. In two strokes the fuel inhibitor was sliced out, clear fuel spurting onto the stone.

'Damnation tuum,' she growled through clenched teeth. A heartbeat passed and her jump pack erupted into life. She rocketed into the air on a plume of flame as all the fuel was ignited at once. Her ears were filled with the roar of superheated air. The savage heat slammed against her and knocked her half-unconscious. The pack fused solid. The armour on her back began to melt and her hair caught fire.

As she soared upwards and prayed that she should be immolated before falling back into the cavern, far below her the enfolding waves of Parmenides's corrupt flesh covered Castus. In the darkness below Saafir, a new champion of Chaos was born.

As THEY WITHDREW from the burning ruins of the city of Saafir, the Imperial forces found Sister Aescarion, broken and shattered. Her fellow Sororitas had taken her from the rubble and transported her to the Order Hospitaller in the Ecclesiarchal Palace on Terra. In the dark majesty of that most ancient of worlds, the priests and apothecaries grafted new skin on to her back and furnished her with a new suit of black power armour and white dalmatic from her Order's vaults. They gave her back her hair, so her red-brown ponytail hung between her shoulder blades as if it had never been seared away. But she still had her scars, tiny scorches around her hairline, like hundreds of toothmarks.

When she gained consciousness in one of the wards of the Order of the Cleansing Water, they told her a story she already knew. They told her how the Ultramarines and the Sisters of the Ebon Chalice had been selected to support the Imperial Guard in assaulting and recovering the heretic city of Saafir. About how the cultists they found there were cut down in hails of bolter fire until suddenly a tide of foulness had bubbled up from below the streets, carrying daemons of the Plague God with it: grinning, one-eyed abominations carrying swords of venomous black metal, tank-sized beasts that killed with a touch of their bestial tentacles, and millions of tiny, pestilent abominations, which giggled insanities as they swarmed into armoured vehicles and even between the joints of power armour. Aescarion was familiar with the way the Marines and Sisters had been forced back, selling every inch of ground for a few drops of daemons' blood, but finally forced to abandon the city to its fate as the forces of Nurgle grew overwhelming in number and ferocity.

Aescarion answered with a tale of her own, telling how her Seraphim squad had been cut down in mid-air by the poisoned blades of the Plaguebearers and vast thunderheads of fat, purple flies. How she and Castus had found themselves alone in the carnage, facing an assault that oozed straight up from hell. And finally, how the streets had given way beneath them and delivered them into the underground chamber containing the vilest creature imaginable.

She told them of Castus's fall from the Emperor's light, and they hung their heads in shame.

AT ONCE THE Ultramarine armour had been fused to his muscular frame. The blue surface and white chapter symbol blistered off and the plasteel plates transformed into a living metal which thickened and split, drawing itself into biological curves which oozed dark fluid at the joints. Sometimes he could catch scenes reflected in the dull surface – a darkness descending from the skies, the tear that splits reality in two, Nurgle himself emerging laughing from the shattered remains of the galaxy.

The Plaguebearers that attended to him brought him a morningstar. The haft was cut from the leg bone of some monstrous beast, and the head had been hacked from a stone so black it drank hungrily at the light, and a dark halo played about it constantly. To hold it, he had a new hand made of overlapping plates of dark purple crystal, which flexed and gripped with a cold, alien strength.

On his other arm was a shield as tall as he was, bound in layers of human skin. The varying shades had been wrought into the triple-orbed symbol of Nurgle, and it was drenched in such sorcerous elixirs that it could turn the blows of gods.

The helm they placed on his head had a single eye-slit through which he seemed to see better than with any autosenses. This was just as well because his implants had soon fled him, wriggling out of his new flesh like metallic maggots.

The Plaguebearers looked upon him with approval in their single glowing eyes, their ever-grinning mouths stretching wider. Castus held his new arms high above him and screamed a never-ending scream, so that even Nurgle on his throne of decay would hear him in the warp and perhaps smile a little at the dedication of his new servant.

THE CULTISTS HAD no time to react as the circle of angels dropped around them from the ceiling of the space hulk's dormant engine room, stitching vermilion threads through their bodies with twin bolt pistols. The cultists were naked to the waist, their bodies and faces daubed with crude symbols in woad of strange colours, their skin white and tarnished by the touch of decay, their eyes black and empty. But armour would have helped them little here, as the concentrated fire cut them down before they could hope to fight back.

The graceful black Sororitas armour flashed in the light of Sister Johannes's hand flamer as it spat a gout of blue-hot flame into the centre of the circle, carving a charred canyon through the torso of one and setting two others alight. The cultists howled, spinning like madmen as the blazing chemical adhering to their skin tore its way into their muscles and organs, until their unholy life was burned from them. They slumped to the ground, skeletons of smouldering ash.

Aescarion's axe-head sliced down into one cultist's shoulder, severing the left side of his body to leave him staggering, almost comically lopsided as his organs spilled out onto the floor. Canoness Tasmander had wanted to present Aescarion with an ancient power sword, in recognition of her famous strength of faith beneath Saafir. But she had refused it: it was too elegant a weapon with which to despatch heretics – they should be slaughtered like animals and pounded into the very earth. That had been a long time ago now – now she was in command of a new Seraphim squad who had become her sisters – but the axe remained beside her just the same. And it was that axe which descended upon the hulk's ill-prepared defenders, lopping off limbs and splitting carcasses like a butcher's cleaver.

A spattering of lasgun fire broke against the walls; one impacted on Aescarion's greave. 'By sections!' she yelled and the Seraphim broke their killing circle, their jumps pack hauling them into the air from where they swooped down onto the remaining cultists. The last heretics died so quickly they didn't even have time to scream.

The hulk seemed to have been built by giants. In itself it was the size of a hive city, and everything inside it was immense. In the engine room, ornate turbines as big as city blocks loomed above, too high for their crenellated tops to be visible, and immense pistons bridged the shadows. Everywhere had been daubed with the primitive slogans and symbols of the Plague God, and a reek of death and despair hung in the fetid air. This was a dark, terrible place. But for Aescarion, that was good – because it meant she must be close.

The majority of the hulk had been deserted, and they had spent days picking off the few lifeforms on the scanner. This squad was now as familiar to her, after years of missions, as the Sisters she had lost on Saafir, and they were good, even for the chosen Seraphim.

She was good, too, she knew, for she had learned a great deal of warfare since Saafir. There was a new purpose to her, beyond the service of the Ecclesiarchy. It had driven her to pursue Castus across the stars for almost longer than she could recall, and now her nerves were on fire, because she had found him.

'How far now, Ismene?' she asked.

'Not far, my sister,' Ismene said, the ancient scanning device's pale green glow lighting her face. It showed that she was no longer a young maiden, fresh from the Schola Progenium – they had been hunting darkness for a long time now together. Strong, but not young.

'Then follow.' Aescarion strode through the darkness towards the corridor leading towards the ship's control centres.

Sister Johannes looked up from examining the smoking corpses she had created. While Aescarion's scars were unobtrusive, Johannes's formed a web of chewed-up skin spread across her face. They were a relic of a past mission to a hive city and an altercation with a chainsword, and made her look like a savage. 'Forgive me, Sister Superior, but how can you be sure it is him?'

'I do not know him well,' Aescarion replied, fixing her Seraphim with a cool gaze, 'but I know him well enough. Follow.'

The rest of the squad checked their ammunition and marched into the corridor. The walls were streaked with foulness, blood and viscera. Scraps of skin clung to the edges of the

metal. The passage grew narrower and narrower, until finally
they came to a bulkhead that blocked their way. The symbol of
Nurgle was smeared on it, in blood both human and otherwise.

'Grenades,' Aescarion commanded, and hacked the door off
its hinges.

The Sisters threw their krak grenades into the space beyond.
Aescarion's auto-senses snapped her pupils shut in front of the
sudden light.

She was not afraid. She just wanted to see if he really was
here, at last.

The flare died down and the captain's suite was revealed in
tatters, its elaborate hangings and fine furnishings first defiled
by the presence of corruption, then scoured clean by the
armour-piercing shrapnel. The intricate murals on the ceiling
could just be made out under the filth and scorching, and at
the far end a huge, ornate window looked out into space, a
black velvet tapestry studded with a billion points of light.

The quartet of blasts had not killed him. Aescarion had not
expected them to.

He stood in the flickering wreckage, a standing stone of a
warrior, his bright armour twisted beyond recognition and corroded gunmetal grey. One hand was composed of dark
amethyst cut into a thousand facets, catching the starlight in
sinister forms. The eye-slit of his helmet pulsed with a sickly
yellow glow, and his hands bore a full bodyshield and a monstrous ball and chain. He swung the morningstar slowly above
his head, thrumming in the air and leaving an eldritch trail of
reeking black fire behind it.

Aescarion felt a cold shadow of the horror she had felt many
years ago. But that was not all. There was some pride, sinner
that she was, that she had managed to track him down even
though he had been sowing decay across the galaxy since he
had first been turned. And most of all she felt that most wonderful thing: the blank hate of the Sisters of Battle, the refusal
to accept that such an enemy could exist, the absolute certainty
that to kill him would be right. Aescarion unholstered her bolt
pistol and levelled it at Castus's face.

'Damnatio tuum,' she cried, and the Sisters fired in unison.

Castus took most of the shots on his shield, the rest going
wide or ricocheting from his armour. Two penetrated and

raised sprays of blood, but he stood firm. The champion of
Nurgle swung his morningstar once and drove it downwards,
shattering the face of the nearest Seraphim in a shower of
bone. The next he drove to the ground with his shield.
Instinctively she flipped her jump pack switch and hurtled
away from him, hitting the far wall and tearing like a fly
against glass.

Aescarion yelled with rage and dropped the pistol, taking her
axe in both hands and rushing at her nemesis. Castus turned to
catch her on his great shield, flipping her over with her own
momentum. She hit the ground hard and felt something break.

A cataract of flame caught the champion off balance.
Johannes's mutilated face was twisted into a grimace – she
made ready to sell her life dearly, drawing the hulking warrior
away from her Sister Superior. Castus covered his face from the
heat and swung the morningstar into her midriff, flinging her
across the room, still trailing flames. A staccato burst of pistol
fire from Ismene lasted only as long as it took Castus to behead
her with a swipe of his shield.

Aescarion, bruised and broken but still alive, struggled to her
feet. Castus had changed, too – he was faster and stronger than
any Marine. But she had her faith, which was something Castus
could not claim. She had her faith – and that had been enough
once before.

The two circled slowly through the debris. Aescarion's auto-
senses told her that the armour was pumping painkillers
through her battered frame at an alarming rate. The pain was
stemmed but she could clearly feel that the whole left side of
her body had been badly damaged.

She looked to where Castus's eyes should be, to see if there
was any semblance of humanity left there. Past the menacing
glow, she thought she could just make out the shadows of a
face, a pair of eyes that had once belonged to a human being.

This might be my only chance, she thought. *This may be the last
time I will ever be able to ask him.*

It was a question that she had meditated upon for many
years, something she simply could not understand. It was
something that would keep her awake at night, and now that
she had the opportunity, she had to ask.

'Why did you turn?' she asked calmly. 'Why did you surren-
der and desert your Emperor?'

In what was left of Castus's mind something flickered and a memory sparked. He had seen the woman before, long ago, rising on a column of flame. This was something Parmenides had not told him about. Could it be that he had not always been a servant of blessed Nurgle? Was there something else, a life that also happened to be his?

But that spark of recognition was drowned out in an instant. There was nothing else. Nothing else but an eternity of beautiful decay, for that was the inevitable path of everything that lived: to rot, to collapse, to die.

'Why?' Castus's voice was thick and dark. 'Why not? He is no Emperor of mine. His Imperium is dying beneath him.'

Aescarion tried to hold his gaze, but it was gone, taken over by something inhuman. She slowly swung the comforting weight of the power axe, ready to strike, knowing that he would not hesitate to kill her as quickly as he had done her Sisters. 'It is dying because of weak souls like yours. You defile the spirit of humanity. Eventually you will not even care if you see defeat or victory – all that will matter will be the blood which is shed around you. Your damnation will make a shell of you in the end.'

There was a sound that might have been laughter from inside Castus's helmet. He held the morningstar high, ready to bring it down in a brutal arc.

'My beloved master Parmenides was right,' he sneered, recalling words that he was sure he had never heard before. 'You have no imagination.'

'Really?' Aescarion took a teleport homer from her belt and flicked it to *Transmit*. 'I would beg to disagree.'

A score of punctures opened up in space-time as the teleport beams locked onto the signal and sent their cargo. Three squads of Battle Sisters materialised with a thunderclap.

In the time it took them to pull the triggers of their bolters, Castus had realised that the woman had used his savouring of the victory to her advantage. Raising both arms above his head and yelling a vile Chaotic curse, he drove the shield and the morningstar into the floor with such force that it shattered and he fell, through the maze of decks and into the darkness below.

The Battle Sisters poured volley after volley into the hole, but as the tongues of fire leapt from the boltgun muzzles a great column of flies twisted upwards from the lower decks. So vast in number were they that the swarm of tiny bodies absorbed every bullet. The insects fell dead to the floor in drifts, many ablaze, but by the time those still living had dissipated, there was no sign of the abomination which had summoned them.

Johannes, still alive, hauled herself over to the edge of the hole and peered down. She spat a gobbet of blood-flecked phlegm into the darkness. 'This isn't getting any prettier.'

Aescarion kneeled behind her, exhausted. 'His master has pulled his puppet strings and dragged him back through the warp to Saafir.' She turned to the Sister Superior of the first squad. 'Search the ship. Kill everything.'

As the Sororitas rushed to do her bidding, Aescarion pondered. She had lost him now. But she had found him once and she could find him again. A link between them had been forged. And if Castus had a weakness, that link would be it.

ON TERRA, THEY SAID, the very air tasted different, it had the tang of age and of honour. It was heavy with the smell of power. And they were right.

The Ecclesiarchal palace dominated a continent, as if the ground itself had sprouted a great gothic mountain range, fluted and pinnacled, shot through with uncountable temples and monasteries, all the myriad departments of the Adeptus Ministorum.

Deep within this vast creation were the quarters of the Ebon Chalice, the Convent Sanctorum. And within this, the chambers of Canoness Tasmander. Aescarion was not young but Tasmander was definitely old, a white-haired bull of a woman with a heavy face and deep, imposing voice. Her campaigning days were over now, and she administered to the practical and spiritual needs of her younger Sororitas. Once she had been a warrior of rare skill and ferocity, so strong and brutal in the pursuit of her duty that she gained respect even from the squabbling bureaucrats of the Administratum and the immensely proud Space Marines.

She sat in her quarters, at a desk carved from black marble. The room was of similar black stone, an elaborate mosaic of the Order's symbol covering the floor, and all around hung ancient standards and litanies held in power fields to prevent their ageing. In many ways, the canoness herself was a holy relic, old and revered – and still powerful.

Canoness Tasmander had seen many faces come and go on Earth. She had learned to recognise how they changed. Aescarion's had changed more than most.

Stood in the centre of the room, stripped of her armour and dressed only in her simple Sororitas robes, Aescarion lost half of her bulk. She was slender but wiry, with a strange pent-up energy that marked her out as a fine leader. She had been called before the canoness few times before, and then it had been only for praise. But this was different, she knew it.

'Sister Aescarion,' the canoness began, 'you know that I value you as a stalwart of this order. There is not one in the Ministorum who would not have cause to praise your faith. Let that not be doubted – you are one of the foundations upon which the Ebon Chalice is built.'

'Thank you, my canoness.' Aescarion knew that Tasmander would not approve of her pursuit of Castus. She had undertaken it as a personal task, an act of vengeance, while at all times, the Canoness had stipulated, the Order must act as one. But surely, Aescarion told herself, the destruction of such foes as Castus was the reason the Orders Militant existed?

The canoness leaned forward, her voice turning cold. 'There are paths down which our faith may take us which are false. I have seen it many times and it is one of the saddest aspects of my post, may He forgive me. For a servant of the Emperor to pursue harmful goals through nothing worse than devotion is a tragedy.

'I have long approved of your determination and purity of hatred towards the Darkness which threatens us all. But if you look within yourself, you will find that it is personal wrath that drives you to actively hunt Castus, not the good of the Imperium or my orders. A Sister's duties are to the Emperor and the Imperial cult, to the Adepta Sororitas – but not to her own lust for revenge. Your rage takes you away from this order and you are too valuable an asset for us to lose.

'You will no longer be party to any military operation that may bring you into a confrontation with Castus. Are my orders clear?'

Aescarion turned her eyes to the floor. She knew that she had not done anything wrong. Her faith was strong. She could not do anything to harm her blessed Order, she knew that. But now she was barred from acting upon that faith.

Which is the greater? she thought. *The orders of my canoness, which have been the word of law since I was not much more than a child? Or my faith, which has driven my soul through this savage universe and never once failed me?*

'I understand and obey. But if I may presume, this is a matter which affects me greatly. Castus's turning by Parmenides was the greatest act of abomination I have ever witnessed.'

Tasmander nodded. 'And you could not let that go unavenged. I am not attributing any wrongdoing to you, Aescarion. But the Ebon Chalice is an Order Militant. I can accept absolutely nothing other than total obedience. This order is a legion of Sisters acting as one. I cannot let you fracture that allegiance. Now will you heed the word of the Ministorum and cease this dangerous pursuit?'

Aescarion raised her head and looked the formidable canoness in the eye. The war inside her was over. The decision was made.

'Of course,' she lied.

The next time he stopped to think about what he had become, Castus did not recognise a human being. He had died, and not noticed. Where once his blood flowed there was stagnant, brackish sludge. Where once organs had throbbed with life, there were desiccated twists of petrified flesh. He was not truly alive, but knitted together and animated by the millions of diseases which Nurgle's unholy touch had introduced.

The shield's covering of skin had developed senses – when it fended off blows, he felt pain. The morningstar had become a part of him, the crystalline fist fused around the haft of bone. The helmet had slowly melted and reformed until it and his skull were one. Through its slit he saw only mottled shades of green and purple, the more diseased the brighter. He was something he no longer recognised.

But what did that matter? He had transcended mere humanity. He was the greatest of men. He would see the Imperium fall and live to triumph in its ruins. He should accept these petty changes and rejoice. Shouldn't he?

The warrior gazed down from the promontory. The cavern had not changed after all these decades. Above, the city of Saafir was a mass of festering rot, seeping through the ground, making the whole planet unclean. In the night sky, the nearest and brightest points of light were planets which had fallen to his daemonic hordes. But down below it all, the cavern was the same, with its long, narrow isthmus of stone on which Castus now stood.

And Parmenides, of course. The daemon prince was still there. Castus had long given up wondering if Parmenides was really a majestic demi-god who would deliver all he had promised, or a malevolent beast who was laughing at him. He had grown to realise that there were more important things. To serve Parmenides was to serve the greater powers which linked this world to the next with chains of their will. Castus told himself this every second of waking.

But behind his thoughts, wasn't there something else? Wasn't he a little more than the champion of the Plague God? Hadn't there been a Castus before, a different man but the same? There was only one thing he could say for certain. He had not always been like this.

Below him, the immense waves of decaying flesh rolled and split, and Parmenides's vast face appeared once more, with its malignant grin and dead black eyes.

'My boy,' the daemon prince said, 'You have done much for me. Led my armies. Carved out an empire. Nurgle is much pleased. But now your talents must be turned to another task.'

Castus kneeled on the rock, laying his shield in front of him, ready to receive his holy orders.

'I must confess,' Parmenides continued, 'I cannot see how these little fleshy creatures can be such a nuisance. But now they prepare to strike back at us. A ship is coming, my boy. It is heading for this very planet, such is their insolence, so it is you, my treasured champion, who will demonstrate to them the insanity of their actions. Lead my fleet and be sure to show them the true way of all flesh before you break them. They must not breach Nurgle's sacred boundaries.'

Castus bowed his head. A cancerous shock rippled through the air. The warfleet's ancient teleporters took hold of the warrior's altered frame and hefted him up into orbit to make ready for the foe's arrival.

THE HALL IN THE centre of the Convent Sanctorum had been sealed for many days. Although a questioning nature was not encouraged in the Adepta Sororitas, Battle Sister Aescarion could not help but wonder what political machinations could be going on in there, carried out by men who arrived in secret, dressed in shadows. When she was summoned there, she realised the truth almost at once. It had been a long time since the canoness had sought to separate her loyalty from her faith. While Aescarion had done everything she had been told, on all her campaigns skirting the furthest reaches of the Imperium, throughout the savagery of her many battles, she never forgot her thirst for the blood of Castus.

The hall had been a chapel thousands of years ago, rebuilt and absorbed as the Ecclesiarchal palace spread itself across the continent. The grey stonework had been carved with stern gothic fluting, the ceiling was high and vaulted and the air was cold. In the middle of the hall was a large table around which were sat the delegates, perhaps a score of them. All but one of them were mere presences. The lights set high in the chapel's ceiling hid their hooded faces.

In the centre of them all sat the only visible being, the inquisitor. He was still dressed in his ceremonial Terminator armour, elaborately inlaid with precious stones, with the massive scarlet Inquisitorial seal on the ring of the power-glove. He had an intense face, drawn and lined, not with age, but with the terrors his calling had forced him to endure, and it looked incongruous amongst the great shifting plasteel plates that gave him the bulk of a walking tank. He indicated Aescarion's designated seat with a wave of the power-glove. It was at the head of the table, and her invisible judges sat in an intimidating crescent before her.

'Sister Aescarion... I am aware of the differences the Ministorum has had with the Inquisition in the past,' the Inquisitor began. His voice echoed grandly around the old stone. 'But I am sure you have seen enough in your service to realise that, while we may go about things differently, we both have similar goals at heart.'

Aescarion had always been suspicious of the Inquisition. With their obsession with secrecy, they seemed to her not far removed from the heretics they monitored. She had herself refused any part in dealing with them in the past. But now, she knew, there might be a chance to realise the wish that she had harboured for most of her career in the Ebon Chalice.

The inquisitor raised his unarmoured hand and a servitor somewhere in the back of the room caused a stellar map to be projected into the air above the centre of the table. A network of fine lines and icons appeared, marking out the western edge of the Segmentum Pacificus. One planet was highlighted.

'The activities of Chaotic forces have always been our primary concern,' the Inquisitor continued. 'The planet indicated is Saafir, which we have been monitoring very carefully for over twenty years. Now, we understand that there is an official position held by your canoness regarding Castus and yourself. Is that correct?'

'That is so.' Aescarion felt a ripple of excitement in her blood. It had been a long time since anyone had dared to even mention that name around her.

The inquisitor nodded gravely. 'A point has been reached where it is no longer feasible, we believe, for this to stand.' He gestured again and several planets lit up around the marked one. 'These are the planets which Parmenides and his foul hordes have secured so far. They are mostly barren worlds in which we have little interest. However, Saafir itself is of considerable material value, with incalculably important mineral resources.'

'I know,' Aescarion replied. 'I was in the force sent to recover it in the first place.'

The inquisitor allowed himself a smile. 'Quite. For these reasons we have been content merely to contain this threat.' A dozen more planets lit up on the map. 'These worlds are under attack now. If Parmenides secures them they will give him a considerable sphere of influence. His empire is, in effect, a Chaotic centre of operations within Imperium-controlled space. This is a state of affairs that cannot be tolerated.'

Aescarion glanced from the inquisitor's face to the shadowy figures on either side. She could feel they were studying her intently, trying to gauge her reaction. What could have brought them here, officials of the Imperium so important their identities had to be kept from her? Then she knew.

'The Exterminatum,' Aescarion breathed.

The inquisitor raised his eyebrows. 'You are perceptive, sister.'

'With respect, inquisitor, though you will know I am not disinterested in the fate of Parmenides, I fail to see why I have been called here. I have pressing duties elsewhere on Terra.' She knew full well why they needed her. But she wanted, she needed to hear them say it.

'Sister Aescarion, Parmenides's area of influence has recently become off-limits to all Imperial craft. Any warfleet we send will be intercepted.' His voice dropped – he was saying this with reluctance, Aescarion realised, because he was so unused to telling such important information to a member of the Ecclesiarchy. 'We know that the forces sent to attack any Exterminatus mission will be lead by Castus. Now, in truth, all of our intelligence concerning Castus and most of that concerning Parmenides has come to us indirectly from you. Records from his days in the Ultramarines are next to useless – only you know his mind now.'

Aescarion looked at the inquisitor slyly, 'You need me?'

The inquisitor looked at one of his companions, and the silhouette nodded to him. 'Yes, sister,' he replied. 'We need you.'

'Because only I know how Castus might think.'

'That is not the only reason you are here.' The inquisitor shifted uneasily in his seat, the servos of his armour whirring. This was not something he wanted to say. 'One of the forces which governs this galaxy, and the Imperium within it, is Fate. It is a strange force which cannot be manipulated, only accepted and worked around.

'Part of the reason the Imperium has endured is because we take Fate into account.' Above the table, the map winked off, leaving only the inquisitor lit. 'Lesser leaders ignore it, which is why they all eventually fall. In this matter, it is Fate that connects you to Castus. You are a thread running through his life. Without you, he is completely in the thrall of Chaos. But so long as you are alive, there is a link between him and the Imperium that he cannot escape.

'You were there at the start of this. Fate may well decide that you should be there at the end. This situation may require you to die alongside Castus. I am led to understand that you will accept this.'

Aescarion could feel shadow-hidden eyes examining her. In her mind, she could still see that foul stain of Chaos spreading across the map.

'I could serve my Emperor in no greater fashion,' she said quietly, 'than by scouring Saafir utterly of the filth which infests it.'

* * *

ONCE AGAIN, Castus had changed. Standing there on the bridge of the Chaos vessel, *Defixio*, Aescarion could see the armour around his barrel chest breathing as he did. Where it had been scored it bled a green, brackish ichor. There were no longer eyes behind the helmet, just a single slash of malevolence. He moved, not like a man clad in armour, but like something wholly biological, primeval and strange.

Castus, for his part, knew that he should recognise her. He had seen her before, more than once, but he could not name her. The face had been younger, certainly, with fewer lines; the eyes brighter, the hair a deeper colour. He recalled dimly that age did these things to humans. But it was definitely the same person, the same black-armoured woman, the same symbol of the flaming chalice embroidered on her white robes. But her name… what was her name? Where had he seen her?

Aescarion had seen this moment a million times in her imagination. All around her lay the shattered wreckage of the *Defixio's* bridge. The ancient computation banks were torn apart, spilling brass rods and gears onto the floor. The floor and walls were scarred with gunfire. The bodies of the ship's crew lay all around, alongside the mangled corpses of Castus's daemons. Great swathes of daemons' blood spattered across the walls and pooled around the bases of the control consoles, still smoking and bubbling. None had given any quarter, and all had died for their devotion, either to the god of the Plague or to the purity of the Imperium.

Through the great observation port which served for a ceiling, the stars outside marked the fringes of Parmenides's corrupt domain. The warfleet had barely entered the disputed space when the metal fangs of something alive had burrowed into the *Defixio's* hull and disgorged a horde of Nurgle's finest. One by one the ships protecting the Defixio had fallen to the same fate, their huge empty hulks drifting lazily through space like bodies in the water. Only the defenders aboard the *Defixio* had been able to stem the tide, and then only at the expense of their own lives. The two forces had ground each other down in the corridors and engine rooms of the ship, until only two stood.

Aescarion, whose axe blade still smouldered from the blood of a dozen daemons. And Castus, whose morningstar was heavy with gore and whose shield was blistered and slashed.

So, as Fate and the Emperor's divine will had decreed, they faced each other once again.

Wearily they began to circle once more, weighing their weapons in their hands. Aescarion knew her chances were slight. She was Castus's match in skill but not strength, and she had none of his toughness. She had faced him twice before, and each time her broken body had needed the attentions of the Orders Hospitaller to heal. And Castus would be a greater warrior than he had ever been. He was wholly Chaotic in form, and lacked the weaknesses of humanity.

But, of course, he had not fought this duel out in full, in every waking second of his life, as Aescarion had done. She had mapped out the tides of the struggle, every move, every outcome. She had seen how he fought. She knew even before she had moved how he would react. Aescarion brought her axe down towards him. Castus thrust his shield in front of him but she knew he would. She drove the blade into the top edge of the shield and split it clean in two. Blood fountained from the torn panels, the warrior letting out a bestial roar of pain. His morningstar swept in a wide black path but the Seraphim ducked it, slicing upwards into his armoured torso.

The axe's blade slashed again and again, a lightning bolt that struck in a dozen places at once, the energy field lashing against the armour so it split and buckled. The wounds were shallow but they were many, for Aescarion knew she could not fell him with one blow. He had to be ground down, whittled away until he could not resist, with blows his supernatural reflexes could not avoid.

My faith has taken me this far, Aescarion prayed as she sliced and circled the warrior. *Now my hatred will take me through*.

Castus was forced back under her onslaught. For the first time he felt panic welling up through long-dead avenues of his mind. He fell to his knees, the blows battering his head now. The blade of bone lashed into his body, the flesh exposed, the armour falling away in chunks. He fell onto his back, his altered blood spurting all around, his blackened, dead flesh drying and contracting as it was exposed to the air. He waited for the final blow that would break him.

This was a feeling he had felt before, so many years before. This helplessness, being laid open before an enemy. This was what it had been like when his mind was flayed away. His faith blasted from him. His soul laid bare for Parmenides to corrupt. The heart-rending memories of that day bubbled up into his mind from the dark corner of his soul where they had festered, just as he had festered for all of these years. He had not always been as he was now. He had been changed. This woman! She had been there when it happened – and now she had come back.

Aescarion looked down at Castus. He was at her mercy at last. Now came the part that could so easily become undone. The speech she had rehearsed all these years.

'It makes no difference if I kill you now,' she spat. 'You are bound to the Plague God. If you die, your soul will join a billion others in damnation. If I let you live, you might wait a thousand years more, and by then you will have no mind left to care what happens to my species. Parmenides offered you knowledge. Now you have it, from me. You have seen both sides of reality – you have served both the Imperium and Chaos. But there is one thing you don't know, one fragment of experience you have not claimed. You do not know how it would feel to become righteous again.'

Castus looked up at her. He knew that he would not live for long, not with his stagnant blood running so freely onto the floor. He stared up at her lined face, and the strands of grey in the hair that he had once seen burning above him.

'You are old,' he whispered through his time-ravaged throat. 'I did not realise it had been so long.'

Aescarion switched off her axe's energy field. The air fell still. 'You have all the knowledge you ever will. You are stronger than any man alive, than any Space Marine I have ever known of. But is it enough? It cannot get any better, Castus. It will only get worse. It might take thousands of years, but it will get so much worse.'

Castus felt his life draining away. He knew well, by now, the ways of death. He had minutes, not years. The words of this woman would not leave his mind. He had thrown everything he had believed in away to be one with the blessed Plague God. Surely he could not return?

Aescarion was virtually unarmed now, but she knew Castus was harmless. Even if he wasn't dying, his thoughts were keeping him docile. There was a war going on in his mind of a kind she knew so well. 'You may think that you cannot be forgiven, that you can never be a part of humanity again. But there is more than one path to redemption.'

More than one path. There is always another way. Castus had walked two paths in his life. He had abandoned one. Could he do it again, with the time he had left?

'Look what the years have done to us both,' Aescarion continued. 'They turned you into an animal. They forced my faith away from the commands of my Order. But all that time has let me come to see that whatever happens here, you will never have the chance to change the galaxy again.

'You have an imagination. Use it. Change your path once more before you draw your last breath.'

THE SICKENING FLASH brought him back into the cavern, returning him to the very place where his new life had begun, so long ago. The Chaos champion struggled, but struggled in victory. His steps were laboured as he dragged his bleeding bulk along the promontory once more to his position above the roiling face of the daemon prince.

'Castus, my boy!' Parmenides had been waiting for his servant's return. 'I see it has been a taxing task I set you. But are you victorious?'

Castus nodded slowly, his last reservoir of energy draining dry.

'The Exterminatus? Is it averted?'

'Better... better than that,' Castus croaked. 'It is... unnecessary.'

The face reared up in its slow tidal wave, a mile-wide frown furrowing the cascade of reeking flesh. 'Meaning what, my servant?'

Castus pulled himself up to his full height. With the force of sheer will he unclenched his altered hands. The fingers reluctantly peeled away, the crystal splitting, the morningstar falling from his grip and spiralling down into the corrupt sea.

He spread those fingers and, with what little strength he had left, plunged them into his breastplate. The metal split along the lines which Aescarion's axe had scored, laying open the diseased torso which had been enclosed since he first set foot on Saafir.

The dead organs had been hollowed out and the rotting loops of viscera were gone. Now in his distended ribcage there hung a slim metal cylinder, harmless in appearance – until the daemon prince's psychic sight perceived the gothic letters inscribed upon it:

IN EXTERMINATUS EXTREMIS.
DOMINA, SALVE NOS.

Sergeant Castus of the Ultramarines looked Parmenides the Vile in the eye, and tasted joyfully the fear he saw there.

'Damnatio tuum,' he whispered, and the white light of purity blasted him clean for all eternity.

NIGHTMARE
Gav Thorpe

JOSHUA WAS DREAMING. He knew he was dreaming, because he could distinctly remember laying down to sleep, wrapped in a thin, ragged blanket, out in the desert that he now called home. Inside his dream he found himself standing in a dank grotto of trees, the light dim and the air tinged with the thick, musty smell of rotting vegetation. The trees' leaves hung limp and almost lifeless, pale and sickly on thin, twisted branches. Overhead the watery light of an unfamiliar moon broke through fitfully as a desultory breeze sighed through the foliage around him.

Looking around, Joshua could see that the grotto was surrounded by steep-sided cliffs, broken only by a single cave entrance. It was carved in the shape of a giant mouth, jagged stalactites hanging down just inside the opening like a row of fangs. The dark pits of a pair of hollows just like skull eyes glared at the young man from above the cave entrance.

Greetings, young friend.

The Voice was inside Joshua's head, felt rather than heard. He knew the Voice well, for it had spoken to him many times over the last few years. At first the young man had been afraid of the Voice, but over time he had felt less and less threatened, despite

the strange things it sometimes said. This was the first time that
the Voice had been in one of his dreams, though, and it was
stronger, somehow louder than normal.

'What is happening?' Joshua asked, his words also thought
rather than spoken aloud.

*You are dreaming, that is all. There is nothing here that can hurt
you. There is no need to be afraid,* the Voice replied.

'How are you here too? You have never spoken to me while I
slept before. Why have you never spoken to me in my dreams
until now?' Joshua was not afraid. The Voice was soothing,
calming him.

*You would not let me into your dreams before. You did not trust me
until tonight. Now you know that I am your friend, I can speak to
you anywhere. It was you who let me into your dream, Joshua.*

'Where is this place? Is it real, or is it a dream-land?' Joshua
asked, though he was unsure why, for he knew that he was
dreaming. There was no place on the whole of arid Sha'ul
where plants could grow in such abundance, except perhaps
the gardens of Imperial Commander Ree.

*It is not a real place, I helped you create it. We are going to have
an adventure together. Do you remember when you were just a child,
you used to have adventures in your mind. You would slay the
Emperor's foes, those daemons and monsters, with a bright sword.*

'I remember my daydreams, yes. But that was when I was little. I am fifteen now, too old to have childish adventures,'
Joshua argued.

*You are never too old to have adventures, Joshua. In this land you
are a hero. People will welcome you, adore you even. Not like in the
world of the waking, where you are shunned, where you were driven
from your village by your own friends and family. Here, no one will
hate and despise you for what you are.*

The Voice was very persuasive. It knew everything about Joshua;
his childhood, his thoughts, his emotions. In the lonely times
since Joshua had fled from the mob who had once been his
friends and relations, it had been his companion, soothing his
troubled thoughts with its presence. The Voice always knew the
exact right things to say to make him forget the loneliness. It had
taught him so many things about the gifts he had been given, the
gifts the ignorant peasants of his village had called witchery.

The Voice had explained everything. It had taught Joshua
how others were jealous of his talents and how, out of jealousy,

they became angry. It had shown him the way to practice his skills, so that he could control them, rather than letting them take him over. Sometimes it had asked him to do things, unpleasant things, but Joshua had always refused, and the Voice had never been angry, never shouted or complained. It had been like a father to Joshua, ever since his real father had reported him to the Preacher and Joshua had been forced to flee or be burnt at the stake.

Come, Joshua, in this world where you are a hero. Your adventure awaits you.

As JOSHUA STEPPED towards the sinister cave mouth, two strange figures appeared, as if out of nowhere, and barred his path. The creatures were hunched and deformed. Pale, lidless eyes glowered at him from sunken sockets. One opened its mouth to speak, revealing a circle of razor-sharp teeth lining its mouth, but all that issued forth was an incomprehensible burbling and hissing.

'They will not let me pass,' Joshua told the Voice without speaking.

Then you will have to make them, Joshua.

'How can I fight them? I have no weapons, no armour,' Joshua replied. His heart felt heavy with a sense of inevitability, as if he knew what the Voice would say next.

Here in the dream you can create weapons. Your mind is your weapon, use it!

Joshua stared at his hands, picturing them holding a long-bladed sword. As if at his command, a hefty metal falchion appeared in his grasp, its semi-transparent blade shimmering with an unearthly blue light.

See! the Voice crowed. *Here in this world you have real power, Joshua. Here you are the master. Now – strike them down!*

Joshua hesitated for a moment. The daemons were backing off from the holy fire of his sword, panicked gurgling sounds spewing from their lips.

They are foul, Joshua thought to himself. I am the master here. Taking a deep breath, he stepped forward decisively. One of the daemons lunged for him and he reacted without thought. The blade screamed as it swung through the air. Without pausing in its sweep, the sword sliced through the outstretched arm of the attacking daemon, which howled in pain.

Another stroke cleaved the daemon from shoulder to groin. The other creature turned to run, hobbling away on its twisted legs, but Joshua was faster, striding effortlessly after the fleeing beast. A single backhanded stroke separated the daemon's neck from its head, and Joshua watched with distaste as its dark blood spread across the ground, soaking into the dead leaves, making them hiss with wisps of acrid vapour.

Good, good, the Voice congratulated Joshua. *You have vanquished your foes. Now, enter the cave, pursue your quest.*

Casting one last look back at the fetid woodland, Joshua stepped beneath the tooth-like stalactites and plunged into the darkness of the cave.

INSIDE, THE CAVE had turned into a twisting, downward-sloping tunnel, with smaller paths branching off in all different directions. As he progressed through this maze, the Voice was unerringly guiding Joshua as he sped through the depths. Joshua didn't feel like he was walking, the sensation was more like floating, moving speedily through the network of passages. As he reached another fork in the tunnels, more daemons ran into view, each as twisted and ghastly as the first he had encountered. They held wands and staffs that began firing bolts of white lightning at Joshua. As they exploded against the walls all around him, the young man ducked back into a side passage. Joshua used his mind to weave a shield around himself. Glorious power flowed through his limbs, creating a shifting miasma of miniature stars which whirled around his body. Stepping out into the main tunnel once more, Joshua advanced towards the daemons. Their energy bolts flared harmlessly off Joshua's mental shield, but more and more were arriving.

Eradicate them. They must not stop you!

Joshua held up his hands and concentrated. Each fist burst into eye-searing purple flames and he hurled the balls of magical fire at his foes. The sorcerous flames exploded around the tunnel, engulfing a handful of daemons, burning them in an instant and scattering their ashes through the air. Joshua hurled more fireballs, incinerating the daemons as they charged towards him, the storm of their lightning blasts dissipating harmlessly around him. Joshua was filled with elation – he was unstoppable. More and more daemons fell to his attack. Soon the daemons were dead and none rushed forward to replace them. The air was heavy with the stench of charred flesh. Seeing the scattered lumps of burnt carcass, Joshua was suddenly struck by a deep sorrow. He stopped dead.

'They stood no chance, did they?' he asked the Voice.

Of course not. Spare them no pity! Inferior creatures exist only to serve. If they fight against that purpose, they are utterly worthless. Destroying them was a mercy, for they had wandered from the path of service. They are nothing.

Joshua found the Voice's words disturbing. It had not been the first time the Voice had spoken of destroying inferior beings. Often it was callous and heartless, it seemed to him.

The Voice seemed to have sensed his thoughts.

Did not your own people try to destroy you? Did they pause to listen to your pleas for mercy? Did they try to understand you, to comprehend your innocence? No, they did not. They wanted to kill you for what you represent to them, driven by their misguided fear and loathing. It was they who forced you into the wilderness, condemned you to a life of loneliness and misery. Were it not for me, you would have died out there, young, weak and vulnerable as you were. But I protected you, nurtured you. They are below your consideration, they deserved to die!

'But these were daemons, not people, weren't they?' Joshua demanded, worried by the Voice's tirade.

Of course, of course. This is all a dream, Joshua. None of this is real.

Joshua paused for a moment, considering the Voice's words. It had spoken hurriedly, as if trying to cover up a mistake, angry with itself for letting something slip. There was a glimmer of a thought forming at the back of the young man's mind. But before Joshua could work things out, the Voice was telling him to move on, insistent and urgent. Joshua gave up trying to figure out the Voice's purpose and let himself be guided further into the winding labyrinth of caves.

IT WAS NOT long before Joshua was forced to stop once more. Ahead of him, the narrow, sloping passage was barred by a great iron portcullis. He sidled up to it and looked miserably at its bars, each as thick as his arm.

'You've led me the wrong way!' Joshua complained unhappily to the Voice.

I have not! You must trust me. This is no real obstacle. Merely break the bars and continue.

'But how can I bend these?' Joshua demanded. 'Even the strongest man could not move this portcullis, and I am weak and feeble.'

You hear me, but you do not listen, Joshua! Others have said you are weak, but you know that you are strong. You are stronger than any full grown man. Listen to me, not the doubts placed in your head by fools who do not understand you. Who would you believe? Peasants who grub in the dust and dirt all day, or me, who has already shown you so much, brought you so much?

I guess you're right, Joshua thought, though he was still unsure. He grabbed two of the bars in his hands and strained with all of his meagre muscles. They did not move an inch. Panting, with sweat dripping down his cheeks, Joshua stood back.

'I told you! I'm not strong enough,' he complained.

Stop whining, Joshua, you sound like one of those pathetic preachers who sermonise about the follies of the universe without ever having left their shrines! Bend the bars with your mind, not your body. There you are strong, there you have power.

Joshua took several deep breaths and stepped up to the portcullis once more. Closing his eyes, he grasped the bars again. The metal felt hard and cold in his hands, but he began to pull at them, this time imagining them to be as flimsy as reeds. When he opened his eyes the bars of the portcullis were rent from the frame, leaving a twisted gap wide enough for him to slip through.

As he stepped through the hole, Joshua felt the tunnel constricting around him, suddenly becoming very narrow.

'It is too small,' he told the Voice.

Why is everything an obstacle to you, Joshua? You complain endlessly.

'I'm sorry,' Joshua apologised. Almost contritely, he focused his mind, making his body supple and lithe, almost boneless. With this achieved, he found he could pass through the narrow crevasse with ease.

Well done. You see, nothing is impossible to one such as you.

Joshua grinned to himself, basking in the Voice's delighted praise, and continued to move through the winding fissure.

* * *

FOR WHAT STARTED to seem like an eternity, Joshua eased himself through the small tunnel, around turns and corners, always heading gently downwards. Suddenly, though, the tunnel stopped and Joshua felt himself fall for a moment. He landed with a thick splash and, as his eyes grew accustomed to the dull light, he saw he was standing knee-deep in filthy swamp water, at the bottom of a deep pit. The smell was truly nauseating and Joshua felt bile rise in his throat as he gagged at the stench.

Joshua waded a couple of steps through the murk, looking around him. To his right, a massive, formless thing rose from the mud, filthy water cascading off its slimy hide. Tiny eyes peered at him across the shadows, and its true shape was hidden by gigantic folds of blubbery flesh. It reached towards him with a spindly tentacle, uttering a high-pitched mewling noise. Disgusted, Joshua slapped the tentacle away.

'I don't like this adventure any more,' Joshua told the Voice, feeling sickened and tired.

This is the object of your quest, Joshua. Kill it and you can return home.

'Why do you always ask me to destroy something?' Joshua demanded. 'You've always nagged me to go back to the village to kill them, always told me that I have to destroy others if I want to survive. Why?'

It is just the way things should be. For us to rise to the power which is rightfully ours, we must dispose of those who would oppose us. People will always willingly follow a master, but you must first remove their existing master before they will follow you.

'But I don't want to be anybody's master.' Joshua hung his head sullenly. Beside him, the marsh-thing was huddled against the wall, murmuring with a low, gurgling noise.

Then kill this creature and we will go home. I will never communicate with you again. You can be all alone in the wastelands – friendless, homeless, a vagrant who will never be welcome. Is that what you wish?

'I could get used to the loneliness,' Joshua argued, staring down at the marshy ground as gas escaped in a flurry of bubbles beside him.

You could get used to the loneliness? How often did you weep, that first year in the wilderness? How often did you stand atop the high cliff at Korou and think of leaping off? How often have you longed to return to your family, dreamt that they will welcome you back with

smiles on their faces and open arms? This will not happen, Joshua.
You will always be alone if you do not let me help you. Never again
to know friendship. Never will you meet a pretty girl and wander in
the marketplace buying gifts for each other. Never will you meet the
woman of your dreams and marry her, to the jubilation of those
around you. You are loathed, hated, cast out. You are a vagrant, a
menace, a mutant. You are in league with daemons! You have
betrayed the Emperor! You will ultimately destroy those who you once
loved and who once loved you!

'That's not true! It's not!' Joshua screamed aloud, his voice
echoing off the damp pit walls.

It is what they thought of you, loathsome wretch that you are. You
were a weakling, a failure. They had no choice but to want to kill
you! Now you have no choice but to kill them!

With a howl, Joshua turned on the bloated fiend of the pit,
his hands reaching through the folds of flesh to grab its throat.
'They never understood!' he screamed. 'It wasn't my fault! I
never did anything wrong! I never chose to be like this! They
should have listened to me! I tried to tell them! I tried! Damn
them all to hell! I never did anything wrong! I would never
hurt anyone!' Joshua's screaming became primal and incoher-
ent, a high-pitched wailing which carried a lifetime of
suppressed anger and bitterness. The desperation that only an
abandoned child could know reverberated around the chamber in a rending banshee screech that seemed to last forever.

As he howled, Joshua's hands closed tighter and tighter on the
monster's throat, slowly choking the life from it. Its feeble limbs
thrashed wildly in the mud, throwing up sprays of foul liquid.
Joshua felt all of his anger and hate pouring into his arms,
imbuing his grip with a vice-like strength. With a final effort he
snapped the creature's neck, its tentacles falling limply into the
murky water, a foul dribble of slime trickling from its fat lips.

Suddenly Joshua released his grip and he stood back, horrified, watching the foul corpse slip silently back into the filth.

'I'm going now,' he told the Voice with his mind, panting, his
whole body trembling with emotion. 'I don't like your adventures. I don't like what you say to me, what you've made me do.
I never want to hear you again. I will learn to cope with my life,
without your venomous whispers in my ear. I never again want
to feel as ashamed as I do know. Return me home and then
leave me.'

As you wish, Joshua. You have already done all that I need of you. Simply think of yourself back in the woods and you will leave this place. You will not hear my voice again. But I will be near, of that you can be certain.

JOSHUA WOKE UP WITH a start, his eyes snapping open. For a moment he did not know where he was. All around him grew lush plants, and he found he was resting against the thick trunk of a tree, whose branches spread high into the air above him. Looking around, he saw a high wall encircling the area, broken only by an ornate gate, wrought in the shape of a grinning mask.

With a shock, Joshua realised that these must be the gardens of Imperial Commander Ree's palace. To be caught here would mean imprisonment for him, despite his young age. He stood quickly, putting the tree between himself and the gate.

But how had he come to be here? He had been dreaming, but he couldn't remember of what; the dream had slipped away like morning mist. And why had the guards not found him sleeping and oblivious to everything, right here in their midst?

Trying to calm himself, Joshua relaxed his mind, letting it flow from the restricting confines of his body, just as the Voice had taught him to do. He found a group of guards not far away, could feel their agitated thoughts. Gently, he slipped his mind next to theirs, one by one, touching them only briefly so that they would not know he was there.

Lasguns had no effect on them...

Just burnt them, Emperor's mercy. Bodies everywhere...

A rat would've had problems getting down all the way to the Imperial Commander's bedchambers...

Sentries on the gate cut down...

Strangled and his neck broken. What kind of person would do this...

Nobody could have removed that ventilation duct without heavy machinery...

No sign of them since, either of them. Just disappeared without trace...

Somebody had killed the Imperial Commander? Joshua was desperately confused. It would go ill for him if they found him here after the Imperial Commander had been murdered. They might think he had something to do with it.

As he looked around desperately for a way to escape, Joshua had a sudden flash of recollection. The dank woods from his dream were a twisted version of the gardens that now surrounded him. Had it really been him? Was this where it had started?

He closed his eyes and hung his head in his hands. The Preachers had always warned that the daemons of the warp could possess a person, drive him to do things like this. Joshua's mind reeled.

They had said that... that the ancient, formless denizens of the Empyrean were formed from the sins of the impure and craved after the material universe like a starving man hungers for bread. They could not normally enter the realm of the living, but instead guided unwitting mortals, and sometimes willing servants, to help them break through the boundaries separating the spaces between the stars.

They sought to dominate other creatures, to make them subservient to their immortal and alien whims and needs. It was why they sought out witches and warlocks, because they were the best tools for such monstrosities. It was why the Inquisition and Ecclesiarchy was always hunting down those of magical prowess.

But the Voice had always told Joshua this wasn't true! It was a lie propagated by the Imperial authorities because they feared the power of the blessed ones. Joshua's thoughts were lurching, but through the muddled haze of his mind he caught a strange smell, the metallic reek of blood.

Opening his eyes, he looked about him, but could not see anything. Then he looked at his hands for the first time. Both were stained red, smeared with dried blood.

The Voice, his only friend when all else had deserted him so cruelly, had lied to him, had lied from the very first moment. It had used him, manipulated him. And now it had made him do the most terrible thing ever, and then deserted him, just as his own family had deserted him before. Joshua's howl of fear and desperation echoed off the stone walls.

And in the warp, something laughed.

THE LIVES OF FERAG LION-WOLF
Barrington J. Bayley

FERAG LION-WOLF, champion of Tzeentch, ruler of five worlds, rose from the slab of sparkling white alabaster on which he slept and prepared to receive his honoured visitor. Young maidens bathed him, anointing his body with pleasant-smelling oils so that he gave off an enchanting aroma. The same slave-girls dressed him in garments of shimmering heliotrope silk, decorated all over with the sinuous symbols of the greatest of the gods, and accoutred him with his weapons.

When they had finished, an officer wearing the uniform designed for the palace staff by Ferag himself entered and bowed, waiting for permission to speak.

'The chariot of Lord Quillilil has been sighted entering our planetary system, my great and gracious lord,' the officer announced, once Ferag had impatiently signalled him to continue. 'It will arrive within the hour.'

'And is everything ready?'

'All has been made ready, my great and gracious lord.'

'Good...' Ferag purred.

He dismissed the officer and then turned to examine himself in a full-length mirror. He could not help but be pleased with what he saw. Ferag Lion-Wolf had always been a striking figure, even before he found favour with the Changer of the Ways, to give the great god Tzeentch just one of his many titles. Rugged, strong and handsome, Ferag had earned the admiration of all on his home world, as well as on the many worlds where he had fought and adventured before becoming a champion of Chaos.

But now! Ferag was almost beside himself as he beheld the magnificent transformation wrought on him by the Great Conspirator's marks of favour. In place of his left arm was a powerful, flexing tentacle with twice the reach. His right foot was a scrabbling claw, particularly exciting to behold as it so much resembled the claw of a Chi'khami'tzann Tsunoi or Feathered Lord, the rank of daemon closest to Tzeentch him-self! An extra pair of eyes was set in his forehead, above the others but closer together, giving his face a curiously watchful appearance, like the face of a lurking spider. Those eyes could look into someone's mind and see if plots were being laid there. They could also kill with a single baleful glance. His mouth was also changed. It could pucker into a long tube, half the length of his arm, with which to suck pure magical energy from the souls of others. Tzeentch had given him power and change! And this was not the end of the rewards he was to receive...

Ferag made a magical sign, causing a shimmering oval sur-face to appear in the air, looking like a vertical pool of water or maybe quicksilver. With his forefinger he traced runes in the Dark Tongue, which could only be spoken in the warp. The runes spelled out his Chaos name, so recently bestowed upon him by his greater daemon patron.

With another gesture he dissolved the writing screen.

And now to welcome Quillilil!

Ferag strode from the lofty-ceilinged chamber and on to the spacious balcony overlooking the extensive palace, looking around him and, as always, taking immense satisfaction in his accomplishments. He was ruler of an entire planetary system within the Imperium of Chaos, called by outsiders the Eye of Terror. Five of the system's eight planets were inhabited. Several billion beings all lived in dread, in obedience, in utmost respect and adoration, of Ferag Lion-Wolf.

Ferag had designed his palace to resemble what he imagined the heavenly palaces of Tzeentch and his Feathered Lords to be like. Tier upon tier of terraces rose to the cloud layer, sparkling and glowing in iridescent colours. Towers and minarets and convoluted galleries twisted and twined like snakes. But none of it, of course, was restricted by gravity. The towers and galleries jutted out at crazy angles, as if they had been constructed in space or – as was the impression Ferag had striven to create – the vast unknowable reaches of the warp.

His aides and guards gathered around him. It was time for Quillilil's chariot to arrive. A magnifier had been set up on the balcony. Through it, events in the upper atmosphere became visible as though they were only a short distance away. So they were able to watch as the chariot from the neighbouring planetary system, an elaborate, burnished affair decorated with gold and silver curlicues, appeared in the lemon-yellow sky and swooped through the upper air. Diving for the cloud layer, it descended towards the palace.

Ferag and his aides carefully watched the surrounding countryside, dotted with towns and villages whose privilege it was to share a landscape with their mighty ruler. Yes, there it was! The plot was afoot! Shark-like craft were hurtling over the horizon, three altogether, coming from different directions. In addition, from hidden places nearer at hand, a dozen wild-looking figures mounted on flying discs were soaring upwards, long hair flying behind them, waving weapons.

There was magic at work, or those discs would not have been able to fly here. They were K'echi'tsonae, steeds of Tzeentch, and their proper medium was the warp. Peering closely at the magnifier, Ferag could see the rows of teeth around their rims.

Both shark-craft and riders were converging on the interstellar chariot. Ferag had a consummate sense of timing. He raised a hand, staying his aides who were ready to release a barrage and destroy the raiders. Instead, he allowed the raiders to get closer to their prey.

'Let me deal with this,' Ferag murmured in his melodious baritone voice.

When it seemed there could be no help for the descending foreign vessel on its state visit, he pointed with all five fingers of his right hand. The air became charged with power. It crackled. All present felt the waves of prickling sensations over their entire bodies. And from the fingers of master magician Ferag Lion-Wolf there issued streams of raw magic, crossing the intervening

miles instantaneously, sizzling, swaying, touching all three
shark-craft and all dozen disc raiders.

For a brief moment the great stream of energy flickered
around them, and then, in that same moment, they shivered
and were gone.

Ferag Lion-Wolf smiled knowingly. Lord Quillilil's chariot
settled itself onto a marbled landing bay further down the terrace. Ferag and his party had already made their way there
when the ornate door of the chariot swung open. Flamboyantly
clad guards emerged and took up station on either side, glancing nervously around them.

Lord-Commander Quillilil stepped down from the threshold. Unlike Ferag, he had never been a Space Marine, and so
was much shorter in stature than the hulking Lion-Wolf. He
wore a cloak of brilliant blue. His hands were small, with a
shrivelled, talon-like look. In place of a mouth, he had a compact, curved beak, turquoise in colour. A straw-coloured plume
sprouted from the top of his otherwise bald pate. His eyes were
round and unblinking, and seemed unable to stare in any
direction but straight ahead, so that he looked about him continually with sudden nervous movements.

'My Lord-Commander Quillilil!' Ferag greeted breezily,
spreading arm and tentacle in welcome.

'My Lord-Commander Ferag!'

Quillilil's voice was high and chirping. He allowed Ferag to
embrace him briefly, then stepped back to gaze at the palace
around him. He was clearly impressed.

'I am happy to have been able to protect you, my lord
Quillilil,' Ferag said. 'It appears some of your enemies have
gathered here.'

Twittering laughter rose from Quillilil's throat. His eyes glittered. 'Yes! Subversives from my own planet who fled here
some time ago. I knew my visit would flush them out! Why do
you think I came here? You should be flattered, my lord Ferag,
at the trust I have placed in you. My chariot is unarmed!'

'I, too, have used the occasion to my benefit,' Ferag told him.
'Your renegades could not have acted without help from some
of my own subjects. They are now paying the penalty for their
disloyalty.' He glanced at the surrounding countryside, taking
pleasure in knowing of the death and torture being inflicted
there.

'I have prepared a banquet for tonight,' he continued to tell his guest. 'You are particularly partial to human flesh, I believe?'

Quillilil clacked his beak rapidly, in eager affirmation.

'Skinned specimens have been marinading in spices for the past week. Tonight they will be roasted for your delectation. Tomorrow we will discuss a treaty between us. For the present, though, allow me to show you round my palace. But first–'

Ferag raised arm and tentacle and swept them through the air, making magical passes. There came an immense rumbling sound. The huge edifice all around them was coming apart. Towers, terraces, galleries, halls, all separated and began gyrating in the air, performing a gigantic dance. The landing bay on which they stood itself took part in the display, whirling lazily through a cloud and back again.

Then, with meticulous precision, everything came together again. Stone block met stone block in silent harmony, mortared together as before. In seconds the palace had reassembled itself.

Quillilil trilled in feigned pleasure. 'Most impressive, my lord Ferag! And if you will allow me in return…'

He too made an elaborate sign with his hand. Further along the terrace, a jutting arcade detached itself, floated a short distance away into the ether and then began spinning at speed.

Quillilil made delicate pulling motions with his fingers. The minaret ceased spinning and returned to its place with a deep grinding of stone upon stone. There was a gentle murmur of approval from the assembled aides and retainers.

It was common for Tzeentchian magicians to show off to one another on first meeting. But for all his chirpiness, the visitor could not hide the fact that he had been bettered by his host.

Surreptitiously, Ferag cast his guest a passing glance with his upper pair of eyes, not wanting Quillilil to see the dark flash that would show he was looking into his mind. It was as he had expected. Quillilil was not happy at being ruler of a mere one-planet system. He envied Ferag his domains. The visit was but the first step in an elaborate, convoluted plan to take his place, stretching far into the future. Quillilil's brain was a maze of plot and counter-plot, intricate to the point of madness.

Which was as it should be in a champion of Tzeentch, the Great Conspirator and Master of Fortune. Quillilil would not, however, see his plans come to fruition. Ferag had laid a strategy to add his guest's planet to his own dominion. As for Quillilil himself, he would be disposed of as easily as one of the feeble humans he was about to feast upon.

Ushering his visitor from the landing bay, Ferag began conducting him through the great vaulted halls of the palace, pointing out feature after feature. But his mind was not on the task of being a tour guide. The promise made to him by his greater daemon patron recently – given to him at the same time as his Chaos name – had left Ferag in a state of pure exultation. It was not long, therefore, before he began talking instead of himself.

'Know, my friend, that I have lived a most eventful life, even for one of our kind,' he said seriously to Quillilil as they strode. 'Have you wondered at my name? Its meaning can tell you much about me. I was born on a primitive planet in the Imperium, outside of our Chaos realm. Life there was dangerous. What few human beings there were knew only how to make tools and weapons of stone, and they had it hard. Among my people one did not receive a permanent name at birth. One had to earn it as one grew to manhood. Now the lion-wolf is the most fierce animal on that planet. Standing twice the height of a human, with jaws that can crush a horse, able to outpace the fastest runner – it would take twenty armed warriors to defeat it! When I was eight years old, one of these beasts killed my father...'

THE REMINISCENCE took his mind back. He was a naked boy, standing on the dusty scrubland of the world of his birth. In the sky was the looming globe of its smouldering red sun.

And barely ten paces away, the lifeless body of his father was being tossed back and forth in the jaws of a lion-wolf! When the beast had come loping across the landscape towards them, they had both run for the protection of a rocky tor. But when he heard his father's stout timber spear clattering to the ground behind him, he had turned to witness the dreadful sight.

The boy hesitated. While the beast devoured its prey he could, perhaps, gain the summit of the tor and the fearsome animal might forget him.

But it had killed his father!

A screaming rage gripped him. He ran back and laid his hands on the spear. It was almost too heavy for him to lift, but he raised its fire-hardened point and yelled at the fearsome lion-wolf for all he was worth.

'You killed my father!'

The creature dropped the torn, mauled body and turned its massive face towards him, sniffing the air. He could smell its shaggy coat as it came towards him to investigate. He made jabbing motions with the spear, yelling and retreating. He was at the bottom of the tor now.

The lion-wolf gathered itself together and leaped!

The boy stood his ground, determined to gain revenge for the death of his father. He jammed the butt of the spear in a crevice in the rock and aimed the spearpoint at the gaping jaws of the lion-wolf as it sprang.

The lion-wolf had intended to bite off his head with one snap of its great teeth. Instead, the spear rammed itself down the beast's throat and bore the full impact of that huge body's momentum. Sprawled on the scrubland, the lion-wolf struggled to extract the offending shaft, coughing up great gouts of blood. The boy gave it no chance to do so. On he came, pushing with all his might – pushing the spear down and down, until he came within reach of those deadly claws! But by then it was too late for the animal. The spear had entered its heart.

Even so, the end was long coming. The lion-wolf did not die easily. It writhed and thrashed as its lifeblood poured from its mouth, watched by the fascinated, exultant, grieving eight-year-old...

'So THEN THE tribe gave me my permanent name,' Lord-Commander Ferag said to his guest. 'In my native tongue "Ferag" means "killer", so I was known as "Killer of the Lion-Wolf". I have retained the first word out of respect for my original people.

'No other warrior had ever borne such a name, for no one else had killed a lion-wolf single-handed, and probably has not even now.'

'A stirring tale!' Lord Quillilil chirruped. 'When did you become inducted into the Adeptus Astartes?'

'No more than forty days later, a squad of Purple Stars Space Marines landed near our village. They were told of my courage with the lion-wolf. They tested me in every way, then took me back with them to their monastery.

'I served the Purple Stars for the next twenty years, learning all their ways, going on their campaigns as a scout, as a messenger and in countless other roles. At the end of that time I was judged fit to be transformed into a Space Marine. I was given the extra organs, the progenoid glands, the sacred gene-seed. For two hundred years I served with the Purple Stars, and saw more action than I could hope to relate, eventually rising to the rank of company commander. I particularly distinguished myself in a raid on a tyranid hive ship...'

ONCE AGAIN Ferag Lion-Wolf found his mind regressing to the far past. A squad of Purple Stars Space Marines was cutting a way through the shell of a vast, snail-like form, its motive power crippled by laser fire so that it had become separated from the hive fleet. None of them knew what to expect on the inside, and what they did find was nothing they could have expected.

They were in a round tunnel which pulsed and throbbed like a living organ, branching at irregular intervals. A huge thumping sound was all around them, like the beating of a gigantic heart. The light was dim, blood-red, and seemed to seep from out of the very walls themselves.

Then, scrabbling down the tunnels which were scarcely large enough to contain them, came the tyranid warriors, huge bossed beasts, six-limbed, worse than the worst nightmare, each head a mass of razor-sharp teeth, each front pair of limbs whirling twin swords that could cut straight through a Space Marine's armour!

With horror Ferag saw his bolter shots bounce off the tyranids' armour while his men were butchered around him. There was no chance of retreating to the assault craft.

Then his mind flashed to the time he had fought the lion-wolf as a boy, and he took heart at the memory. He drew his chain sword in his left gauntlet. Sparks flew as he parried the tyranid boneswords, as he later came to know them. This enabled him to get close in – and the muzzle of his bolter went straight between the tyranid's massed teeth!

The monster jumped then slumped as the bolt exploded inside its body. Ferag let out a roar of laughter. He barked into his communicator.

'That's the way to do it, men! That's the way to do it!'

THE HEROIC DEED faded as Ferag brought his mind back to the present. 'The tactics I developed on that day became standard for fighting the foul tyranids at close quarters,' he finished.

He paused for a moment. 'Most warriors would be satisfied with such a life, I dare say, but I was not. The Imperium began to seem too confined for me – I wanted something grander, something to give scope for my abilities! In secret I began to study the ways of magic. I knew, of course, that there had once been a great heretical war, when fully half the original Space Marine legions took refuge in our Imperium of Chaos. I became attracted to the study of Tzeentch. And eventually I did the unthinkable. I deserted my Chapter, and made my way here to devote myself to his service.' He grinned.

'And now I am his champion! Commander of five worlds! It has been a glorious time! I could not begin to regale you with my adventures, or say how long I have lived. In the Eye of Terror a day is a thousand years, a thousand years is but a day, and time means nothing, until death comes.'

'Your fame spreads far and wide, my dear lord commander,' his guest cooed.

'And so it should!' Ferag made a face. 'Do you know, my lord Quillilil, with what contempt I was treated at first? I am a Space Marine of the Second Founding, raised after the Horus war. The Chaos Legionaries are all of the First Founding. They thought themselves harder, and me as soft and weak. Well, they soon learned their mistake.'

Ferag's hand slashed through the air. 'I have killed thirty-five Traitor Marines in hand-to-hand combat! Twenty of them followers of Khorne, the berserker Blood God! And a dozen of those World Eaters, the most feared of all! There is no greater warrior than Ferag Lion-Wolf!'

His voice dropped and became more conciliatory. 'Forgive my boasting, my lord, but I only speak the truth.'

Quillilil twittered flattering laughter. 'It is no boasting at all, my fellow champion. Why, you are too modest. You almost deprecate yourself. Everyone knows of your great victory on the bowl planet.'

'Yessss.' Ferag grinned. It was one of his most beloved memories, perhaps his greatest exploit since coming to the Eye of Terror.

A great army had been assembled, an unholy alliance between the forces of Khorne, the Blood God, and Nurgle, the Great Lord of Disease and Decay, also Tzeentch's most implacable enemy! The battle had been fought in a planet shaped like nothing so much as a shallow bowl, governed by its own special physical laws. It was, in fact, possible to fall off the rim of this bowl and into some inescapable hell.

Ferag had commanded a much smaller Tzeentch force. At first sight the twin hordes looked invincible. The Khorne core of Chaos Space Marines had drenched themselves in blood before the battle even began, butchering their own massed soldiery and driving them towards the enemy. As for the Nurgle horde… a vast, filthy Chaos daemon, a great unclean one, had been at its head, and he had come up with a special tactic. The millions-strong army had been rotted with amoeba plague. Its soldiery were no longer separate individuals, but combined into one sticky, putrid mass which came rolling on, engulfing everything in its path.

Against all this, Ferag had only the special strengths of Tzeentch: strategy and sorcery! It had been a battle of titanic proportions. The bowl world had glowed and seethed with magical forces for months. But in the end it was Ferag's tactical genius that had won the day. The vile hordes of Khorne and Nurgle had been driven over the planet's rim to go toppling into an eternal hell-world.

Ferag had gathered together what survived of the planet's original inhabitants and had given them a generations-long task – to erect in the middle of the bowl a monument to Tzeentch that towered above the rim itself.

It was no wonder, when he looked back over his life, that the Changer of the Ways appreciated his services. Further, was about to reward him with the greatest possible fulfilment. His greater daemon patron, appearing before him in person, had informed him that he was to receive the ultimate gift.

He was to become a daemon prince. He would be immortal, no longer subject to death, able to live forever in the heavens of the warp!

But there was still his guest. Almost reluctantly, Ferag Lion-Wolf returned his attention to the tour of inspection.

'Step this way, my lord Quillilil. There is a most delightful aerial esplanade through here.'

They walked under an ornate archway, through which shone the lemon-coloured sky. Ferag Lion-Wolf heard a grating sound overhead. Looking up, he saw that a block of stone had dislodged itself from the masonry and had begun to fall.

In that instant it occurred to him that perhaps this was the section of the palace upon which Quillilil had demonstrated his magic. But whether this was so or not, Ferag had no time to act. The stone block struck his head with great force, knocking him unconscious.

HE RECOVERED his senses in what seemed like a split second. He was standing on dusty scrubland, naked except for a rag made of woven grass tied loosely around his waist. A vast, murky red sun hovered near the horizon, producing a lurid sunset.

A circle of a dozen men stood around him. They were all looking at him with a sort of avid expectancy.

He looked back, searching one face after another, utterly bewildered.

Until the change came, sweeping through his mind in an unstoppable rush.

The memory of another life flooded into his mind. The life he had really lived. Not the life of the surgically adapted, battle-hardened ex-Space Marine he had thought himself to be, or of the glory-drenched champion of Tzeentch who for uncounted centuries had faithfully served his master.

He was not a warrior at all. He had never left his native planet. His name was not even Killer-of-the-Lion-Wolf. He never could have earned such a name, not even as a man, let alone as a boy! He was known as Ulf Dirt-Creeper, and he was acknowledged by all to be puny physically and a coward morally.

But he did belong to a Tzeentch coven. He had an aptitude for lying, cheating, and low cunning, for which the worshippers of the Change God found uses. Now, however he had been found wanting. It was a small matter, really – he had been sent to murder a man in his sleep, an enemy of the coven, also his sister's husband, and he had been unable to find the courage. Now he stood condemned.

Condemned to end his life as Chaos spawn.

But because he had been of service in the past, Tzeentch had rendered him a final gift. In the last instants before he descended into mindlessness, he had been allowed to stand at the end of a completely different life, one of glory and power. Of course, he could not be allowed to retain the delusion to the end. That would be un-Tzeentchian. The cruel truth had to be revealed.

The coven leader was intoning a formula redolent of untold power in a high-pitched voice. Ulf Dirt-Creeper felt a horrid crawling sensation within him. He whimpered and flailed miserably. Despite himself, his body bent double. His hands touched the earth and became flat, flappy feet. He felt his face swelling into a round, ridiculous travesty of anything thought of as human. His mouth elongated into a long, narrow tube, not for drawing magical force out of his adversaries, but for sucking up the worms and grubs which were to be his only food from now on.

The awful mutation continued, playing out before the disgusted yet fascinated gazes of his fellow cult members. Then Ulf Dirt-Creeper recalled having heard, so long ago now, another name for Tzeentch: the Great Betrayer. Sometimes, instead of the promised spiritual reward, would come the greatest betrayal of all. Not daemon prince but...

A burning question seized his petrified mind in the scant moments before it descended into gibbering insanity. Who was he, really? Ulf Dirt-Creeper or Ferag Lion-Wolf?

Which one is true?

Which one is true?

SMALL COGS
Neil Rutledge

COLONEL SOTH believed in order, in preparation and attention to detail. But as he stood by the shining, silver doors of the Water Temple he felt far from prepared for the coming battle. True, his face was always somewhat drawn, his sparse flesh stretched tightly over his bones, his body all sinew and muscle; no more room for padding on his frame than there was for luxury in his austere life. And his dark eyes flickered restlessly around the rocky bowl in which the temple stood but this, too, was quite normal.

The colonel, rigid and controlled, did not readily display his emotions and only those who knew him well could have detected the slightest signs of anxiety. The sporadic running of his wiry fingers through his tight, greying curls. The thin lips compressed even more tightly and the occasional barely audible sniff as he straightened his dress uniform.

His dress uniform! That indeed was one of his irritations. Perhaps it was fortunate that his unit of the Ulbaran VIIIth was on ceremonial guard duty for the Water Temple festival when the infernal eldar raided. At least they were able to deploy quickly to secure the area. But to be going to war in their dress uniforms, the splendid attire of a bygone era; clumping old-fashioned

boots, the traditional white fibre-cloth itching at the neck and
cuffs and the gleaming, lovingly polished pectorals, it was ridiculous! No helmets, no webbing. Praise be to the Emperor that
they always paraded armed and with a full complement of heavy
weapons! But a slight clenching of his long fingers was another
clue to the colonel's worry as he reflected that ammunition was
not plentiful. He trusted that Headquarters would get some reinforcements to them soon – and in the meantime they would
manage with what they had.

The enemy worried him too, the mysterious eldar! What
were they doing here on the agri-world of Luxoris Beta?
Colonel Soth was an experienced and well-trained officer but
other than the ork pirates his men had defeated to liberate this
planet two years previously, he had never faced aliens before.
Nor had any of the men. They had manuals, training materials
and holo-exercises, but these were not reality. Even the supposedly simplistic orks had constantly produced harrowing
surprises in action. What would the inhumanly sophisticated
eldar do?

Routine, practice and experience produced confident warriors. This had long been one of Colonel Soth's basic maxims.
But they had had no experience against this foe. Lack of practice and experience meant uncertainty – and uncertainty meant
fear.

Soth remembered the nervous eyes of the young lasgunner
catching his, and the boy's anxious question. 'Do they really
skin their captives alive, sir?'

With an outward calm which did not entirely reflect his inner
feelings, the colonel had reassured the guardsman. Such bar-
barity he had explained, was not practised by these eldar and
besides, if the guardsmen followed orders and shot straight, no
alien would capture them anyway. Colonel Soth was almost
confident in his advice. From what he had gleaned, these were
not the so-called dark eldar, the notorious piratical renegades,
but then what was the difference anyway? They were all aliens,
all humanity's enemies.

He mentally castigated himself for such futile speculation
and was about to return to his command post when a soft foot-
fall behind him made him stop and turn. It was the priest from
the temple, Jarendar. He was a tall man and, in his full ceremonial costume, he made a striking figure. Even in the shade

of the temple portico, his long white kilt gleamed and the elaborate gold pectoral, set with rubies to form the symbols of the Ecclesiarchy, glinted brightly, catching the light reflected from the huge doors. As Soth looked into the priest's face he was struck by a similar effect. The man had a strong jaw and jutting nose and though his gaze was even, there was a sense of masked strength and confidence.

A strength more than spiritual, the colonel thought, as he noted how the heavy gold and red leather head-dress spread down across powerful shoulders more like those of a labourer or warrior than a priest.

'The Emperor's light shine upon you,' the priest greeted him formally. The worship of the Divine Emperor here on Luxoris had acquired its own unique trappings in the eighteen hundred years since it had first been settled, but its people were devoted servants nevertheless.

'And also on you,' Soth replied.

'Are your defences prepared, colonel? Is there more my servant or I can do to assist you?' The priest's voice was calm, Soth noted with approval. He had courage even on the verge of an alien attack.

'We are as ready as we can be.' The colonel gestured towards his gleaming parade boots with his gilded ceremonial baton. 'But we are not exactly conventionally attired for action.' There was another slight sniff.

'Who can fully understand the will of the Emperor?' Jarendar asked. 'Had it not been for the festival you would not have been here to deploy to protect us. As you said yourself, if the cursed eldar realise the irrigation controls are here and they can flood the levels to impede our reinforcements, they will certainly attempt to capture the temple.'

'It is not an orderly way to conduct a defence.' Soth spoke almost to himself. 'We are not properly attired or equipped.'

'Properly attired?' The priest smoothed his kilt. 'These garments go back to the dark days of our slavery to the orks, before the Emperor gathered us once more to his bosom, praise him always. Yet even in those terrible times some were able to resist.'

'And,' he added, pointing at the rubies on his pectoral, 'these garments are marked now with the symbols of the Emperor's constancy. Even when we struggled alone we were not forgotten.

Why is this temple here, Colonel Soth? It is to thank the Emperor for his blessing, in giving us the means to control the irregular rains of this harsh land so that we may offer him this land's bounty. In the short term we may see difficulties. In the long term, the Emperor cares for his children.'

Soth was irritated – and was even more annoyed that he could not control his irritation in the presence of this calm priest. 'But how,' he asked sharply, 'can a commander exercise proper control without even adequate comm-links?' He tapped the low-powered wrist communicator he was wearing to emphasis his point.

The priest pointed to where his servant, a young novice, stood by one of the pillars of the portico. 'Rigeth, my servant, he understands. He knows he is only a novice, a servant, a minute component in the Emperor's divine plan. We priests in charge of temples, or colonels in charge of regiments, are inclined to forget that we are merely servants too; only one tiny piece in the Emperor's great whole. Would you allow your men to question–'

A sudden, shrieking whine and burst of laser fire from the great ridge above them cut off the priest's homily. 'The eldar!' Soth spat. 'It's begun! Get to safety. I must reach my command post!' Leaving the priest, he began sprinting up the slope to where he had set up his headquarters on the rocky edge.

The section of the ridge surrounding the depression in which the temple sat was not the steepest. To gain some cover, Soth kept off the road but the surrounding terrain was rough. He needed to concentrate on his footing and as he raced on, he dared only to glance around himself from time to time, sporadically catching sight of the blurs of red screaming along the edge of the crest, their progress marked by staccato spurts of rock dust. The ghastly screech of projectiles ricocheting off the boulders was audible even over the shriek of their engines. These, he assumed, were the eldar's notorious jetbikes, a first wave of attack to soften up his defences and keep his men's heads down.

He paused just before the lip of the great ridge, crouching against a boulder. The tumbled rocks of the ridge offered good cover and he could see the bright stab of lasgun fire as his troops offered up some form of defence. Praying that the eldar weren't trying some form of jamming against which his own dress-issue communicator would be useless, he barked into his wrist unit, 'Soth to Captain Hoddish.'

'Hoddish receiving, sir.' The captain's voice was crisp even over the vox-link.

'Pass the order to cease lasgun fire against the jetbikes. We haven't the ammunition to waste.'

The colonel continued up the slope, his teeth clenched. He could hear Hoddish using the command vox-link. 'Hoddish to all units: no lasgun fire on jetbikes. Don't waste power against those lightning spirits. Save it for the infantry.'

The jetbikes continued their attack passes and Soth had to hurl himself behind a boulder as one craft hurtled straight for him, its projectiles singing an unearthly war-cry as they fragmented the rocks all around him. He caught a split-second glimpse of the alien's helmet as its craft howled overhead. This was certainly a far cry from fighting orks. Even the very sounds of battle were different.

Now, as he approached the top of the ridge, the enemy fire was more intense – but the eldar were not having things all their own way. As one larger jet craft tore across the wide depression there was a flash and a spurt of smoke as a missile was launched by the fire-team posted on the ornate roof of the ancient temple. The eldar craft jerked sharply and dived for the far rim of the rocky bowl but Soth watched the flare of the missile as it blasted towards the enemy, guiding true to catch the vehicle and detonate with a thunderous explosion just short of the crest. The blazing wreckage seemed to fall in mesmerising slow motion and it was only with some effort that Soth managed to tear his eyes away and dash for the summit.

AMIDST A SERIES of blasts from some unseen enemy heavy weapon down the far side of the great slope, the colonel dived into his hastily improvised command post. There, amidst the slightly better shelter of the hurriedly piled rocks and scraped depressions (no text book trench could be dug in this terrain!), Colonel Soth rapidly appraised himself of the developing attack. He led sound troops and they held a strong defensive perimeter, commanding both the temple depression and its surrounding approaches. If it hadn't been for their lack of proper equipment and the unknown nature of their enemy he would have been as confident as any Imperial Guard officer should dare to be.

Crouched under the shadow of a huge sandy-coloured boulder, he hastily conferred with Hoddish and his other staff, while the command comm-link operator – a small, leathery skinned veteran of many anti-pirate operations with the Ulbaran VIIIth – coolly passed them updates from other sections as best as their limited equipment allowed.

'I do not think they are fully pressing us yet, sir,' Hoddish was saying when a deathly howl, followed by a rattling storm of shrapnel and rock fragments made all the men suddenly crouch even lower. Hoddish grinned as the noise subsided, patting a long tear in the still smartly-creased sleeve of his dress jacket. His round face had always struck Soth as peculiarly boyish, with his thin moustache only serving to further the impression of a youth trying to pass as a man. He had a cool head though and continued, unperturbed.

'The main attack has yet to develop. This is just to soften us up. There do not seem to be many enemy and they do not appear to have much armour or heavy weaponry. The best information we can gain from central command is that the whole assault is some form of raid rather than an invasion. I suggest our opponents are a force dispatched to attempt to flood the levels to stop our armour from getting into action. I expect they will press all our perimeter from the air but concentrate on the ground, attempting a breakthrough at just one point.'

'Here, perhaps?' Soth mused out loud. 'We have the widest view but it is the easiest section of the ridge to break through.'

'Yes, sir,' the captain agreed.

As if on cue, there was a shout from a nearby trooper: 'Enemy advancing, sir!'

Soth crawled forward cautiously. The slopes of the ridge raked back on both sides of the spur on which he had located his command post but the guardsman who had called the warning gestured down the left slope. He was another younger man and he looked pale, his knuckles showing white where they gripped his meltagun. His cap was jammed down ridiculously tight on his head, perhaps to try to shield his ears from the ghastly racket of the jetbikes.

'Sir…' He looked nervously at the colonel.

'Yes, guardsman?'

'They're not really spirits, are they sir?'

Soth was mystified. 'Explain yourself.'

'The flying eldar, sir. They're not… spirits, are they?'

Suddenly the words of Hoddish's warning not to waste ammunition against the flying craft came back to Soth. He looked the young guardsman in the eye. 'No, they are not spirits. Captain Hoddish spoke only figuratively. Did you not see the one downed by the missile? And, guardsman…'

'Yes, sir.'

'Straighten your cap!'

'Yes, sir!' The young man showed a slight smile as he carried out the colonel's order.

Soth scrutinised the scene down the slope. He didn't even have viewers but Hoddish passed him a lasgun with a targeter and he was able to search for the enemy more effectively. The slope was a mass of tumbled rock dotted with thorny scrub. It made good concealment for them but also offered the enemy ample cover for a cautious advance. Soth forced himself to concentrate carefully amidst the growing barrage along their section of ridge. They were coming all right! Overhead the jet-bike sweeps seemed to intensify yet further. The colonel doubted if they were causing many casualties but they were keeping the guardsmen from grouping to counter the mounting attack.

'Pass the order to hold fire until range band amber,' he instructed Hoddish without taking his eye from the targeter. 'Heavy weapons to target armour or support troops only!'

He could pick out occasional movements but no clear targets. Suddenly, further along the ridge some form of dreadnought or similar fighting machine appeared from behind a tangle of thorns. There was the crackling whoosh of a lascannon shot from their left and beyond that the staccato tattoo of a heavy bolter, but with frightening speed the machine strode across some open ground and with a grace more organic than mechanised vaulted into a gully and out of sight.

The colonel could hear the young guardsman swearing nervously beside him. In truth Soth could remember scant details of such machines but said clearly, loud enough for the melta-gunner to hear, 'An eldar dreadnought. Fast but poorly armoured. They always suffer at shorter ranges.'

There were increasing signs of movement downslope and the eldar infantry were starting to open fire. The air was full of the

whine of their strange projectiles and sharp cracks as they ricocheted off the rock. As they came closer the storm intensified
and the guardsmen began to reply. Soth nodded approval to
himself at the disciplined nature of his men's firing. The eldar
advance slowed but now under cover of the fire of their sup-
porting infantry and the continuing, howling passes of the
jetbikes, a new threat showed. In several places turrets were rising above scrub patches and rocky outcrops and a torrent of
heavier fire was poured on the guards. A deadly duel began
between the well-placed and concealed cannons of the guards
and the bobbing and weaving grav-tanks of the eldar – and all
the time the alien infantry pressed gradually closer.

The guardsmen were taking casualties but the constant drill
and practice that Colonel Soth had always insisted on, was paying off. One grav-tank exploded, setting ablaze the patch of
scrub in which it had been inadequately concealed. The smoke
drifted across their front and under this cover the strange
dreadnought machine ventured out of the gully – only to be
caught in a torrent of heavy bolter fire that buckled one of its
legs, tumbling it back into the gulch.

The enemy continued to advance, however, and suddenly the
storm of doom broke loose. The jetbikes broke off but the
remainder of the aliens charged, firing their bizarre weapons as
they came. The guardsmen poured down a fusillade of fire but
still the tide surged up the slope. One more grav-tank exploded
away to the left but, almost directly in front of them, another
whined forwards, weapons blazing as it outstripped its escort-
ing infantry.

'In the Emperor's name: where is that lascannon?' Hoddish
was shouting. The tank was getting closer, heading for a dip in
the crest, the red-armoured alien troops storming after it.

Soth grabbed the meltagun off the young guardsman beside
him. 'Cover me!' he cried as he sprinted across the slope. He
could hear shouts behind him and lasgun bolts echoing off the
rocks but it was the sudden zing of eldar projectiles around
him that he was most conscious of as he ran, desperate to cut
across the advance of the grav-tank and get close enough for a
shot. He was closing the range when something snatched at his
leg and he fell, tumbling wildly down the slope. With a painful
tearing he was brought up, caught fast in a thorn bush, staring
at the red wall of the passing grav-tank. Too shocked even to

aim properly, he raised the meltagun and fired. There was the distinctive hiss and then a crashing as the blast tore into the plates at the rear of the alien vehicle, which whined on by.

Soth could see an eldar approaching and struggled to free himself from the thorn bush to bring the meltagun to bear. The alien figure was raising its long, strangely-fashioned weapon, its tall, almost insectoid helmet a blank mask of menace. But before it could fire there was a flash on its chest as it was hit and it dropped.

There was a fusillade of fire from behind Soth as the guardsmen counter-attacked. The colonel found his arm grabbed by the young guardsman whose weapon he had snatched. The youth was shouting and waving his laspistol as, with his other hand, he helped Soth out of the bush. 'You got it, sir! You got the tank.'

But he had no time to say more before two of the red aliens charged them. Soth dropped back to his knees as a shot knocked the meltagun from his hands. His young companion managed to drop one eldar with his pistol and the other was dispatched by the bayonet of a huge sergeant with a bald and scarred head almost as inhuman as the aliens' helmets.

The firing and tumult of battle continued but it faded slightly and moved downhill. The enemy were being driven back. Soth, eagerly assisted by the young guardsman, took cover behind a jagged boulder and examined his leg where he had been hit. There was a good deal of blood on his now less-than-pristine dress trousers but he had been fortunate and the wound was only a long gash across his calf. Lacking his webbing and full kit he had to improvise a dressing with cloth torn from his shirt. Even so, he managed to staunch the bleeding and prepared himself for action once more. The hiss and whine of the eldar infantry's weapons was less noticeable now but the air was once more filled with the awful howl of the jetbikes as they shrieked back to the attack.

'Back to the command post,' Soth ordered the men. 'And keep your heads down.'

It was a short stretch to cover but it was a tense dash as they raced back to the improvised headquarters. Captain Hoddish knew his commander too well to waste time on congratulating him on the destruction of the grav-tank. He merely grinned his boyish grin and, after a simple, 'Good to see you back, sir,'

quickly updated the colonel on the situation. They had taken
some casualties, ammunition was holding, for the present, but
the eldar had probably only paused in their assault. If they
were to impede the Imperial advance and gain any benefit from
flooding the levels, their enemy would have to move fast.

THE SUN WAS beginning to sink and throw long, jagged shadows
amongst the rocks and thorns. The low light brought an astonishing warmth to the reds, sand yellows and ochres of the
broken terrain. It was a harsh land but under this light it
achieved a mellow beauty that struck even the practical Soth.

But there was no time for pondering on such beauty now.
The rich, blue sky of evening was suddenly full of the streaking
red of the jetbikes once more and the colonel again had some
anxious moments as he made his way to inspect their positions
prior to the expected second alien attack. Of particular concern
to him was the lascannon emplacement that had been silent.
He had feared the crew were dead but finally, after crawling and
sliding through jagged rocks and grasping thorns he finally
reached their position and found the men alive.

Coated in sweat and dust, a stocky corporal was feverishly
stripping the weapon mounting down. His fellow crewman,
forearms and tunic front stained with oil, was examining the
components closely.

'Praise the Throne, I have it!' he shouted, his proud face a
picture of relief. Sighing and wiping the sweat from his forehead, he only succeeded in smearing his face with oil;
wide-eyed with delight, he presented more the aspect of an
ancient barbarian than a smart guardsman. Both men looked
up to notice Soth at the same time and simultaneously they
moved to stand and salute him.

'At ease!' Soth ordered curtly, waving them to stay put. 'What
have you got, trooper?'

'Grit, sir!' the oil-smeared gunner replied. 'It was jamming
the traverse cog.'

'How did grit get in the traverse gears?' The colonel's voice
was sharp and full of meaning.

'I don't know, sir. It must have been as we emplaced.' The
gunner's voice had acquired a slightly nervous edge. Soth was a
strict officer and the lascannon's failure to track the grav-tank
had jeopardised both their own position and their colonel's life.

There was a short pause before Soth asked, 'Carelessness, gunner?'

'Yes, sir!' It was the corporal who spoke now. He was still on his knees but he had stiffened to a sort of attention. Eyes rigidly front, his strong jaw thrust out but caked in grime and his dark curls blonde with dust, he made a bizarre picture. He continued quickly, 'I must have rushed too much while emplacing the gun, sir.'

The colonel gave one of his soft sniffs of irritation. This whole action was so disorderly! 'These are difficult conditions, corporal, but that makes attention to detail even more important. It is often the smallest cogs that are the most important. Neatness, care, dedication, these are all as necessary to a guardsman of the Emperor as being able to shoot straight!'

The slight flicker of a smile cracked the flat face of the other gunner. Soth swung on him at once. 'Yes, soldier?'

The man instantly stiffened too. 'Sorry, sir! I was just thinking that we are not too neat just now, sir.'

Soth clenched his fingers. 'No, soldier – but we can still maintain our weapons, even if our uniforms suffer. Get this cannon re-assembled and let me see your training pay off!'

'Yes, sir!' both men chorused and Soth continued his rounds with caution.

As THE COLONEL was heading carefully back to the command post the jetbike passes seemed to ease once more and a rising thunder of las-fire from over the ridge heralded a further eldar attack. Soth had climbed higher to just beyond the ridge top in an attempt to find a path where he could make faster progress. Now with the aerial attack switched to other sections of the ridge, he risked less cover and managed to jog and scramble along just below the crest. It was still tough going and the sting from his flesh wound made him wince as he scrabbled up out of a gully. Still, there was a smoother section ahead and he was prepared to chance a dash across it.

As he stood on the gully edge, he unconsciously moved to straighten his uniform, re-adjusting the bronze pectoral on his chest. It was a misplaced gesture of habit – but it saved the colonel's life. As he moved the bronze plate, something slammed into it with a sharp shock and hiss. It was more a reflex action than the impact that hurled Soth back over the lip of the gully.

A sniper! His brain whirled as he instinctively switched his position, sliding and slipping as carefully as he could, following the gully downhill again. How had an alien sniper penetrated their position?

As Soth pulled himself up to where an overhanging thorn bush offered some chance of concealment for a cautious reconnaissance, he glanced at the small, melted hole in the pectoral. He had no doubt that embedded in that hole was a deadly, toxic dart. When the attack had first started he had considered discarding the pectoral but his own sense of neatness and propriety had stopped him. After all, it was part of the regulation dress uniform. The Emperor be praised for his own fastidiousness!

All this spun through Soth's mind as, with the utmost caution, his laspistol ready in his hand, he pulled himself up behind the thorn bush. His view was restricted but he gained a reasonable grasp of the sweep of slope in front of him. The most likely place of concealment for the alien was another patch of stunted thorn slightly up slope from where he watched. The ground was relatively open, as he had noted previously. It would be hard for his adversary to move without being spotted, but then what of those cameleoline cloaks he recalled from long-past training? As he pondered, straining his eyes for any clue to the alien's whereabouts, a brief movement caught his eye, a quick reddish flick behind a rock. Soth's vision, long used to the arid terrain and hardened wildlife of his homeland, at once discounted it as one of the large chaser lizards that lairled amongst these tumbled boulders.

Just a lizard... but what had startled it?

He carefully scoured the area around where he had seen the creature move. Each rock and tuft of dried vegetation was scrutinised. Every shadow evaluated.

Got it! Only Soth's long training and habitual discipline prevented a hiss of amazement from escaping his compressed lips. As it was, his grip tightened involuntarily on his laspistol. It seemed a rock had moved! Now that he had spotted the alien it was easier to track its wary progress. Its camouflage was truly incredible, making it almost impossible to spot as, crouching almost double, it crept across the rocks.

'Are they really spirits, sir?' The young guardsman's words came back to him. It would be easy to believe it!

To be moving thus across the open, the alien probably thought him dead but it obviously retained some caution. It was too far away for Soth to risk a shot with his pistol. He would somehow have to get closer. One pistol-armed guard colonel in ragged dress uniform against a near-invisible, needle rifle toting and possibly armoured alien? He didn't give much for his chances!

His best hope was to drop back into the gully, crawl higher up the slope and pray he could spot the eldar by peering from behind the larger boulders there. All the time he hadn't taken his eyes off the ghostly progress of the alien but now he was going to have to. He judged the sniper's line of progress as best he could and inched back into the gully. He felt the prickle of sweat on his palm where it gripped the laspistol and his heart thumped in his ribs as he moved, carefully judging each step, back up the small gorge.

It seemed agonisingly slow progress but eventually he was in place to risk a glimpse from behind the boulders. Setting his cap to one side and holding his breath he peered round. No dart pierced him but, look as he might, he could see no sign of the alien. A knot began to form in his stomach when there was a sudden crackle and voice beside him.

'Hoddish to Colonel Soth!' his communicator crackled.

There was a sudden confusion of the rocks almost directly ahead of him, as if his vision had blurred for a second. Reflexively Soth fired.

'Hoddish to Colonel Soth. Are you all right, sir? Hoddish to Colonel Soth.'

The colonel, somewhat shaken, raised his wrist communicator. 'Soth receiving. I'm fine, captain.'

'We are holding the enemy, sir, but ammunition is depleting.'

'I'll be with you shortly, captain. Take extreme care to be alert for infiltrating snipers and ensure the men are warned also. I've just bagged an alien scout. Soth out.'

The colonel had heard rather than seen the eldar fall but by looking carefully he could now make out the body, only partially covered by the concealing cloak. The needle rifle had fallen separately and he could see its oddly graceful stock protruding from some dried weeds. The alien appeared dead but Soth took no chances and, keeping his pistol trained on the body, he advanced carefully.

Soth stood over the body of the dead scout, staring down at the strangely flowing features of the alien's respirator mask. These eldar devils made him shudder. The neat hole in the creature's forehead, burned by his laspistol shot, seemed a more natural eye than the opalescent crystalline lenses beneath it. The lowering sun cast strong shadows amongst the harsh tumbled rocks and, even dead and prone at his feet, the cameleoline cloak broke up the eldar's outline in a most disconcerting fashion. The colonel concentrated on the more clearly defined respirator mask but the sun's rays, lacing over the yellow heights, made the iridescent lenses flicker with eerie life and he turned away.

Soth knew he should get back to the battle, the fury of which he heard just down-slope beyond the boulders. It had been a close run thing though and he was content to snatch a moment's rest. He was still breathing heavily, but more importantly something was nagging him, jabbing the back of his mind with anxiety and the pit of his stomach with persistent adrenaline.

How had the scout infiltrated their perimeter?

In an unconscious gesture of order, he straightened the life-saving pectoral on his chest and started as if a revelation had come directly from the metal itself. The grav-tank! Who had cleared it? A ghastly dread washed over him as he sprinted across the steep slope of the bowl towards the still gently smoking wreck. Dust and small stones skittered from under his boots as he gingerly negotiated the steep flow of the scree across which the enemy tank had ploughed before landing against a rock spire.

The Falcon was clearly a wreck. It had spun around to face up the slope and the front end was burnt out. The rear seemed less damaged however and it was to here that Soth carefully made his way, the sharp edges of the rocks scratching his hands, the stink from the burnt vehicle scouring his nostrils.

The door of the internal compartment hung slightly ajar. Prudence dictated proper clearance procedure but the colonel was on his own and besides, he reckoned it was too late now for prudence. He confidently expected to find something more awful, in its own way, than an armed and lurking eldar. Steadying himself against the rock spire, laspistol at the ready, he kicked the hanging door aside.

Cursing, he lost his balance as the door seemed to bounce from his foot. What hellish stuff did these aliens build their vehicles from? It certainly wasn't the weighty metal of their own Chimeras! But no attack from within caught him off guard. Instead he stared at the charred and twisted bodies of more eldar scouts. Most still sat strapped to their seats in death. One, torn free by the mad careering of the doomed vehicle, was flung mangled, against his comrades. But this time Soth's eyes were not held by the blank stare of the alien respirator masks, they were riveted to the empty seats. He desperately counted and re-counted.

Five empty seats. One scout torn free. One killed by him... There were three of the devils alive out there. And he knew where they would be heading!

COLONEL SOTH gazed down at the distant Water Temple, thinking furiously. Three camouflaged alien snipers! The temple, covered by the guards' ridge top heavy weapons, was defended by only an anti-aircraft section. From his own experience with the alien heretic, Soth didn't doubt that the three remaining eldar could easily evade or dispatch the unwitting guardsmen. He must act fast!

Quickly he radioed Hoddish. 'How pressed are you, captain?'

'It's quite tough, sir.' The statement was given in Hoddish's usual cheerful manner but Soth knew that this mild phrase meant that the guards were under heavy attack. 'Ammunition is getting low but we're holding out.'

'Hoddish, I am sure our perimeter has been breached by three alien scouts and they will attempt to infiltrate the Water Temple. Use the command link to alert the missile teams there. Warn them that the enemy are extremely difficult to locate due to their camouflage cloaks, and that their weapons are silent. Spare me just three men, experienced guardsmen, and I'll attempt to contain the situation. Get them to bring me an extra lasgun. I'm just over the ridge from you, holed up by the wrecked grav-tank.'

'Yes sir! I'll dispatch them at once.'

Soth racked his brains to try to think of how best to combat the alien scouts. As he pondered, he threw away his officer's cap and stripped some of the more prominent braid from the

grimy tatters that had so recently been his best uniform. There
was no point in providing the alien devils with an even more
obvious target than he already was. Appearing like this and carrying a standard lasgun he hoped he would not stand out from
the other men. Soth was no coward but he wanted to deal with
the alien scum personally.

As he straightened up from checking the makeshift dressing
on his leg, he caught sight of the men Hoddish had sent to
assist him. They skittered and slid briskly down the loose scree,
before jogging up and saluting.

'Sergeant Tarses reporting for duty sir!'

It was the bald and scarred NCO who had led the counter-
charge that had saved Soth that afternoon. This afternoon! It
seemed an age away! Soth was pleased with Hoddish's choice.
The sergeant was a tough customer and a veteran of several
operations against the orks. He was an expert in close combat
and fairly bulged out of the white cloth of his uniform – which
he had somehow managed to preserve in a far neater state than
his comrades. Tarses had a reputation for ferocity that went
beyond the wild looks given to him by his heavy brows, missing right ear and the pale scar that twisted across his cheek and
chin. But, as he handed Soth a lasgun, his face was as calm as
if on parade.

'Also, Corporal Nibbeth and Guardsman Sokkoth, sir.
Guardsman Sokkoth specifically volunteered to assist you, sir.'

Both the other men saluted. Nibbeth was another veteran, a
short man but of the same wiry build as Soth himself. He had
a calm sureness in his stance and movement, even on the loose
scree, and the colonel noted with interest the sniper's badge on
the torn sleeve of his tunic. Sokkoth was the young meltagun-
ner who had rescued Soth from the bush. He was
inexperienced but he had certainly acquitted himself well on
that occasion. There was an earnestness in his thin face and
bright eyes as he saluted. Soth had seen such devotion before
in many young recruits. He hoped the lad was not to pay heavily for his keenness.

They moved off as rapidly as they could over the difficult terrain, Soth issuing orders for the advance on the temple as they
went. There was a plan but a sketchy one, the kind of plan Soth
hated and had often chided junior officers for on exercise. Too
much was being left to chance! But they had been caught on

parade by this ghostly enemy and their options were severely limited. Not even Tarses had any form of comm-link and Soth judged it prudent that they should operate as one group to maintain contact.

Hoddish had alerted the missile teams and there was little else they could do other than proceed with caution and hope for the best. As they cleared the slopes and moved out onto the flat base of the depression, Soth attempted to use his wrist communicator to raise the guards stationed at the temple but without success. The sun had dipped behind the ridge and he strained to see the temple clearly in the fading light. The missile team should have been contactable with even the short range unit by now and the colonel feared the worst. Several times as he was descending, he had thought he had heard the crack of a lasgun shot from the direction of their goal, once even a faint cry, but against the background noise of battle from over the ridge top it was impossible to be sure. Soth knew his fears of infiltration to be well-grounded but how much was his proper concern turning to feverish imagination? His mind's eyes locked in memory with the eerie stare of the dead sniper he had so luckily managed to defeat and a brief shiver, owing nothing to the evening chill, ran down his spine. Grimly he pushed the memory aside and signalled to the other men to increase their separation as they hastened on.

THE GROUND was flat at the bottom of the depression and, although still rocky and scattered with clumps of brush, offered little cover compared to the ridge walls. The colonel felt his heart beat faster as they reached the broad, paved ceremonial road which led to the temple. Sweat slicked his hands and his eyes scanned each boulder and bush as he prepared to dash across the road. Never had he felt so appallingly vulnerable. Was it even worthwhile attempting to find cover from these fiendish, invisible death dealers? He looked over to where Sokkoth was ready to cover his dash over the road, nodded and ran. The slap of his boots on the paving stones rung in his ears even over the noise of battle echoing from the ridge tops and it was with clear relief that he finally dropped into the broad drainage conduit at the far edge of the road.

At once, he sprinted further on and took up position to cover Nibbeth, who was to follow him, and Sokkoth and Tarses, who were to advance up the other ditch. The others were across in seconds. Nibbeth sprinted over the road and sprang into the trench with the speed and ease of a desert gazelle and Soth made a mental note to commend Hoddish on his choice of men.

The conduits, paved to carry and channel the surging flows of water that accompanied the irregular rains, offered the best chance of a covered approach to the temple. Now dry, their reddish stones warm in the afterglow that just reached them from the over rim of the bowl, they would provide at least the illusion of concealment while, closer to the temple, the towering sandstone statues, erected to the glory of the Emperor and the great amongst His children, would offer further cover.

Soth wiped his hands on the torn remnants of his tunic and cautiously jogged forward up the conduit. Suddenly he froze as there was a dull detonation from somewhere ahead. There was still a constant backdrop of noise from the fighting beyond the ridge behind them but this explosion had been to the front.

The colonel thought of the massive temple doors. A demolition charge? He knew clearly now they could expect no help from the missile team at the temple. What were these aliens? How could three of them wipe out an entire anti-aircraft squad with such ease and so silently? But then Soth had met one of these devils face-to-face and he knew only too well.

He attempted to hasten forward but he felt strangely weak. This was not war as he knew it, calmly facing the hulking brutality of the orks, meeting their primitive power and ferocity with nerve and disciplined firepower. Now it was he and his guardsmen who seemed the primitives. The memory of the dead eldar's remarkable camouflage haunted Soth as he moved on, his eyes sweeping the rocks on either side. How could he hope to spot the enemy? Only luck had saved him before. There was a knot in his stomach quite different from the normal adrenaline he felt before combat. Soth was a veteran. A cool head, discipline and training had always carried him through but now, just as the sweat ran under the high collar of his ceremonial tunic, the first tingling of fear chafed under his normal tempered resolve. There was a sound ahead. All at once he leapt sideways, swinging up his lasgun. But it had only been the slight rustling of dead stems in the first stirrings of a light evening breeze. The colonel forced himself to breathe deeply, calm as he turned to signal the all-clear to Nibbeth who followed on behind.

THEY SOON reached the lines of colossal statues which flanked the roadway on its final approach to the temple. Soth had always found the giant figures, sculpted stiff in the style of the ancient, desert-dwelling ancestors of the Luxorisians, the first colonists, to be foreboding. Now, looking up at the august images of priests, commanders and dignitaries, he felt not that these pillars of the Empire were watching over him, but rather that they held a vague menace, frowning disapproval on his unkempt appearance and fast beating heart.

He paused under the enormous stylised feet of the statue of the Adeptus Astartes commander who had been the first person to set foot on this planet in the name of the Emperor. The evening breeze blew more steadily and as it ruffled through Soth's tight curls, drying his sweat, he felt chilled. What would that ancient commander have done here? He would have hardly had to have come skulking up a drain! Soth had a sudden mental image of the Space Marine trying to manoeuvre his bulky power armour up the conduit and, oddly, it cheered him. He suddenly grinned to himself. After all, wasn't the kind of covert approach, lightly equipped, that he was performing exactly how his ancestors would have raided from the cold deserts back on his own homeworld? This land was his to protect now and he would deal with these alien devils yet! Tradition should be, must be, upheld.

He waved his men to continue and soon they were at the point where the conduit swung to go around the temple. He still felt vulnerable, still felt tense but the relief he had felt under the statue had not dissipated entirely. They had a plan, if only a rough one. This was the rear of the temple, the side opposite the building's only entrance. There were probably only three enemy scouts facing them. There was a chance they might all be able to dash to the relative shelter of the surrounding portico and make an attempt on the temple doors. Each of them had his duty and his part to play and, to Soth, duty and a clear role were sacred.

He was exceptionally careful as he moved into his covering position, crawling warily up the steep side of the conduit in the shadow of another giant statue. He felt calmer, though, and was thankful that his hands were no longer damp with nervous sweat. He checked to his right and saw Nibbeth silently inching himself into position alongside him. In front of them, across the flagged rear court, the massive octagonal columns of the temple portico rose out of the deep gloom at their base. Predictably perhaps, he could see no sign of the enemy but he tensed as he spotted the brutal evidence of their actions. Slumped on the broad steps of the raised portico, leaning back against one of the great, sandstone pillars was one of the missile team. In other circumstances, he might almost have been taken as asleep but Soth knew better. The aliens had reached the temple. But where were they?

The colonel found that his hands had tensed once more as he waited for Trooper Sokkoth to make his prearranged dash for the portico. The young soldier had volunteered to make the first advance and Soth had seen no reason to refuse him. Sokkoth himself had said, his eyes bright with ardour, that he was the least experienced and most expendable if the aliens had to be drawn into revealing themselves. He was correct, of course and the colonel wondered if this had been in Hoddish's mind as well when he let the recruit come in the first place. But there was no time for such melancholy thoughts.

A soft scrape of stone made Soth turn, to see Sokkoth vault out of the ditch on the other side of the road and sprint for the columns. The lad was fast and had almost reached the steps when he seemed to stumble and next second was face down, a small puff of dust rising with the soft thud of his fall, the clatter of his lasgun a brief underlining of his fate. Sokkoth himself made no sound. Of the alien sniper there had been not a trace.

Some of Soth's previous feeling of powerlessness returned as he scanned the shadows between the pillars. No sign! He scrutinised each section of the rim of the gently pitched, stone flagged roof. No sign! Their next, prearranged tactic in the event of the rear being guarded was to wait five minutes and make a concerted rush from three different directions. The colonel glanced to his right to check that Nibbeth was moving off, further down the conduit, prior to the charge but the wiry little man was standing pressed against the wall at the bottom of the ditch. He was signalling frantically for Soth to join him. In spite of his curiosity, Soth forced himself to descend with the greatest of care and crept along in the shadow of the wall, taking pains not to make any sound, until he was alongside the guardsman. Nibbeth's soft whisper was quick but clear: 'The alien's not on the roof. It's by the end column on the far side.'

'Where? Can you see him?'

'No.'

'But... how can you know?'

'It's where I would be.'

Nibbeth's tone was very matter-of-fact and he slightly shrugged his shoulders as he said it, as if to emphasise his own sniper's badge. He continued, 'The roof's not high enough for a decent view and to get any kind of shot it would have had to skyline itself. With that ghost suit it can just stand against a corner column and watch both ways. It's on the far side because Sokkoth was almost across before it had a clear shot and dropped him.' The guardsman glanced briefly at the timepiece on his wrist, before looking his commanding officer straight in the eye. 'When the time to charge comes, sir, let Tarses go alone. It's a terrible risk for the sergeant but if we watch that end pillar, we'll have the best chance we'll get of nailing the devil.'

Soth thought back to when Sokkoth had saved his skin earlier that day. The young guard had been aided by the determined charge led by the big NCO, who would even now be working himself into a position to charge the other side of the portico. One of the colonel's saviours was already dead. Was the other to perish too? And to die charging alone, without his expected support? All this flashed through the commander's mind but in the end all he said, glancing at his own watch, was, 'Very well. Into place, quickly!'

As fast as caution allowed, he took up his position again, wondering with every cautious movement of his lasgun if a silent death was about to follow. He carefully sighted on the end column and, seemingly immediately, he heard Tarses' stentorian shout as he charged from the conduit. A shadow bulged from the pillar and there was the crack of a lasgun from beside him even as he fired himself. He took two more shots at the column but Nibbeth was out of the ditch and charging the portico. After a moment Soth leapt forward too and the two men reached the columns together. As they dashed into the shadows they saw Tarses pulling his bayonet from the fallen eldar. He looked up, his long scar pale against his dark skin and the gloom. He had no questions, no reproach or surprise, his quiet 'Sir?' merely a request for orders.

Soth lost no time. 'Nibbeth, far side. Tarses with me, this side.'

Nibbeth's compact form vanished silently into the dimness of the further reaches of the portico while Soth crept along the temple wall and the sergeant dashed in short sprints between the outside columns. Two filthy alien scouts dead; two left to deal with. There would probably be one at the temple front. Could they somehow spot that alien too? The colonel moved quickly but kept close to the wall. Shaded by the portico it had captured none of the day's heat and felt chill where he brushed against it. It gave some sense of safety even if, as Soth grimly reflected, it was a purely illusory security.

As they approached the temple forecourt they moved far more cautiously. Soth crept around the corner column as Tarses moved to drop down the steps and crawl around the front of the building. It was quiet except for the barest rustle as the wind tumbled some dead thorn leaves across the flagstones.

Tarses died so quickly that his commander barely noticed. The colonel heard a slight hiss and then a series of thumps as the big sergeant's body tumbled down the steps. Heart in his mouth, Soth pressed his back to the pillar and stood, immobile.

Where was the devil? He dare not move and, tensed against the cold stone, he stared across at the shining doors of the temple. One had been blasted with some kind of alien demolition charge, a surprisingly neat hole blown clean through. The other remained intact, still glowing in all its glory, reflecting what little light there was left. Soth was surprised at how effective a mirror it made and, suddenly hopeful, he scanned it for any sign of the alien.

But he could see nothing other than the leaves, scraping in fits and starts over the stone as the wind caught them. They blew fitfully, barely moving, occasionally lodging against a column base or… Why had those leaves stopped, when others, close by, were still moving? There was no stone to stop them!

The colonel's heart skipped a beat. It must be the eldar scum! He stared at the reflection, desperately trying to make out even a hint of the shadowy outline he had been able to see up on the slopes when he had tackled the first scout. The reflection was too poor but he had a reasonable idea of where his enemy crouched. And, with a shock colder than the stone at his back Soth realised that in turn the eldar now knew exactly where he was! Even now his enemy was probably studying his reflection, waiting for him to move.

The commander had never felt so hopeless but the solid knot of anxiety in the pit of his stomach was hardening further to become a clenched mass of frustrated rage. He would have to try his luck. Perhaps his attempt would distract the alien enough for the wily Nibbeth to nail it. He stared at the reflection and prepared himself to move. Not normally religious, Soth surprised himself by mentally intoning a prayer to the Emperor that came back to him from his childhood – and then he lunged. Swinging around the column he let loose a volley of lasgun shots, their cracks echoing wildly off the stone and the vicious, red stabs tearing the gloom. There were further thuds and the clatter of falling arms.

Astonished, Soth realised he was still alive and that, from the outline he could now see sprawled on the flags, his enemy was dead. He fired a further shot into where he could see the fallen alien's head was and, as the echoes died, he cried out to Nibbeth. But there was no answer.

Where was the final scout? Deep within the temple or, alerted by the noise, hurrying to stalk them? Where for that matter was Nibbeth? There was another of the colonel's soft hisses of irritation as he strode forward. The irritation vanished in an instant as he stepped clear of a pillar and saw Nibbeth's body. The soldier lay face down, his lasgun under him. It was he, not Soth, who had distracted the alien at the crucial moment. Abruptly, the colonel turned on his heel and plunged through the blasted temple entrance.

IMMEDIATELY inside the great doorway, Soth leapt to one side and took cover behind one of the double row of pillars which mirrored those of the exterior. His eyes took a moment to adjust as the interior was brighter than the evening shade of the portico. It was not glaringly lit but soft lights, carefully hidden amongst the carved reliefs of the high walls, gave out a gentle glow. The long hall that comprised the bulk of the temple was flagged with the same worn sandstone as outside and seemed completely empty.

Cautiously Soth surveyed the chamber. It was a plain room, without furnishings, only the pillars breaking the view to the end. Even the carvings were subdued, seeming as natural as the grain in the stone itself. All seemed clear and he began to jog to the end where he knew an ante-chamber gave access to a staircase which led to the control room for the irrigation system, as well as to the passages and cells of the priest's quarters. He felt a curious confidence. He had always liked the building, not from any particular spiritual motivation but for its lack of ostentation and the manner in which it blended the Imperial discipline so dear to him, with the shadowy past of the desert peoples of this world. If he was to face such a lethal foe as these aliens, here was a suitable battleground.

That he was to face the third eldar was clear as he approached the ante-chamber. Its door had been forced and from somewhere down the stairs he could hear the sounds of a struggle. He quickened his pace, while still trying to move as quietly as possible.

The steps down were worn and steep but the lighting was now brighter and Soth took them two at a time. On the small landing, one doorway, its ancient wooden door closed, led to the priest's apartments. Another entrance, its modern steel door blasted through, led into the control chamber. Lasgun at the ready, the colonel charged through. His quick brain, tuned to action, took in the scene in an instant.

The priest, Jarendar, had obviously surprised the alien as it tried to manipulate the irrigation controls. The two were now locked in a desperate struggle. The slight form of the eldar was backed against the bank of instruments while the massive priest, his back towards Soth and blocking any chance of a shot, was attempting to crush his squirming adversary. The priest was a powerful man but, for all that, he was no fighter and just as Soth entered, the foul alien heretic managed to break his hold, draw its laspistol and fire. The priest died with a grunt, the shot blasting through his chest. His body shielded the alien and Soth caught only a glimpse of a raised pistol and ghastly, gem-like lenses before there was another spurt of lasfire and the world went black.

Soth was unsure how long he had been unconscious. It couldn't have been more than a few moments as, when he came painfully back to his senses, the alien was still working at the irrigation controls. His chest seemed a mass of searing agony as, with blurred eyes, he watched the eldar working. It was tall yet slight, and even its small movements, as it passed some glowing, crystal device over the control panel, seemed to have an inhuman grace about them. The other-worldly effect was heightened by its cameleoline cloak which even in the stark and brightly lit control room, still broke up its slender form to a remarkable degree.

Soth's thoughts were as fuzzy as his vision. He thought he saw Nibbeth's body lying next to the dead priest. Had they died, Sokkoth and Tarses, too, only for he, himself to fail? He must try to reach his lasgun. It was just beside him, its stock temptingly near. Could he retrieve it without alerting his enemy? The harrowing vision of the face of the first alien he had killed, the extra blank eye of the pistol wound staring from its forehead, seemed to superimpose itself on the back of the head of the scout working in front of him. It appeared to watch him, daring him to move. He screwed shut his eyes and tried to concentrate, driving the visions from his brain.

Wracked with pain, the colonel tensed himself and tried to move. The only result was even more agony somewhere under his ribs and an uncontrollable gasp that hissed from his lips. The alien turned, the strange crystal device still glowing, its strangely sensuous laspistol drawn in a movement of fluid grace. Soth stared helplessly up into the opalescent lenses of the blank mask as the creature walked lightly over, covering him with its weapon. It paused and almost in one movement, a quick flick from one of its gracile boots sent Soth's lasgun sliding well out of reach, and it was back working at the controls.

Soth trembled with agony and frustration but could do nothing. His head felt as if it was swimming from his body on a haze of pain and his vision seemed to be deteriorating further. He was sure he saw the ghost of Sokkoth creeping towards the alien from behind. He wanted to shout at the dead youth. To tell him it was all futile; that the lad had been correct, the aliens were spirits and they could not be thwarted.

His lips quivered but no sound came. Sokkoth's wraith was almost upon the eldar now and was raising his lasgun to club the scout. The colonel stared at the apparition, his hazy world hovering between dream and reality. Why was this ghost carrying a non-regulation weapon? He would have to discipline it!

But somewhere on a deeper, more rational level of his brain, Soth recognised that it was not Sokkoth's ghost but the young temple novice Jarendar had talked about earlier, the minor component in the Emperor's plan. The weapon was not a las-gun but a candlestick. The candlestick came crashing down just as darkness descended once more on the colonel.

THIS TIME his period of unconsciousness must have lasted longer for when Soth came to again he was floating up the temple stairs. His head swam. Was his spirit being carried off to the Emperor? A face looked down at him, pallid in the bright lights. Soth recognised the insignia around the face's collar. They were the badges of a guard medic.

The colonel's eyes flickered and his lips moved soundlessly as he tried to speak. The medic, concern clear in his dark eyes, addressed him firmly: 'Don't try to talk, sir. You're badly wounded but we'll patch you up. The enemy have been driven back. The reinforcements are here as well and Captain Hoddish is organising the clean-up operations.'

Soth weakly shook his head. The pain was terrible but he felt he must speak. His lips shook but this time a weak, croaking voice was audible, 'Warn him!'

'Warn who, sir?' the medic frowned, plainly not understanding.

'Warn Hoddish. Tell him… tell him to look out for the minor components. Tell him it's the small cogs that count.'

The medic looked forward to where his companion was lifting the front of the stretcher. 'I think the colonel's delirious,' he said.

ANGELS
Robert Earl

IT WAS ALMOST forty summers ago, but I still remember. Sometimes, though, the remembering is hard. In the warmth of a high summer's sun or in the smog of the inn, surrounded by familiar faces, it seems that it was only a dream or an old man's tale grown tall with the telling.

But when the wolves came last winter it was as clear as the summer's sky over the fields. And when Mary lay screaming in her first labour, the memory was the only thing that kept the fear from freezing me.

When it happened, Pasternach was smaller than it is now, much smaller. There was nothing north of the stream but the shadow of the mill, for all of the cottages, and even the workshops, were tucked safely behind the stockade. They huddled around the green, their backs to the world, but between their sturdy gables we could see the battle of distant treetops against the wind.

The stockade itself was higher back then. It had to be, for we had worse to worry about in those days than the prices come harvest time. The Emperor, may the gods protect him, had yet to start clearing the forest hereabouts. And the forest was near.

From time to time, lying in our beds, we would hear cries
floating through the darkness of the night, savage cries that
were neither human or animal. When they became too much
to ignore the council and the rest of the men would meet on
the green.

There, amidst the comforting smells of smoke and stew and
dung, they would drink and argue for a day or so. Then they
would decide to do what they always decided to do – which
was to send out a patrol. But always by daylight and never with
very much enthusiasm. Sometimes the patrols would return in
triumph carrying with them rabbits or even deer, but mostly
they just returned hurriedly.

They were fools to avoid finding the enemy before he found
us, but one cannot blame them, not really. Which of us would-
n't rather pull the blankets up over our heads and hope for the
best?

One autumn the shadow of the forest grew longer. Rumours
pulsed along the narrow tracks and open rivers of the land,
rumours of northern sorcery and a hideous new progeny of the
terrible art.

One of the scrawny, haunted-looking rangers who occasionally drifted through on the road to the city stopped for long
enough in the village to frighten us all. He told a tale of lights
in the sky, great fiery displays to rival the borealis, of villages
found mysteriously deserted and gutted by fire, of horribly
cloven two-footed tracks in the cooling ash.

After he had left, everybody told everyone else that he had
been mad or a liar, and what else could you expect from a
ranger? But even I noticed that after this the men of the patrols
stayed nearer to home and kept their eyes more firmly shut.
They even stopped bringing back game. Then, after Mullens was
taken, the patrols from Pasternach stopped all together.

MULLENS WAS a scarred old bull of a man. He had arrived at the
village two years before, still dressed in his patched halberdier's
uniform, and I think that my brother and I were only slightly
more overawed by him than our parents were.

Even Alderman Fauser was at a loss for words when the old
soldier took his hand in a painful, white knuckled grip and
allowed the two massive war dogs that comprised the whole of
his luggage to sniff his new neighbour's breeches.

In spite of his strange manners and southland accent, Mullens soon became popular in Pasternach. His hounds brought down many a wild boar which he would arrange to be roasted for the whole village in return for his fill of ale. When these feasts were finished apart from bones to gnaw and the dying embers of the fire, he would fill our imaginations with blood-curdling tales of death and glory from his time in the Emperor's great army.

Even more welcome was the fact that he was willing to hire any man who needed the coin. A couple of miles to the west of the village lay a derelict way station with a few neglected fields which Mullens had bought for his retirement. Because he always asked for the villagers' advice, as well as paying their sons to help him, the whole village took some pride in the way that Mullens rebuilt the crumbling stone walls of the gatehouse and cleared the land that it stood over.

It was some small measure of the affection in which he had become held, then, that when the old soldier didn't turn up at the village for two whole weeks a patrol went almost willingly to see if anything was amiss with him.

Though I was but young then, I will never forget the grim silence with which they returned to their families that afternoon and the sense of outrage that clung to them like the smell of the smoke. And the sight and sound of Gustav the blacksmith, iron-faced and iron-handed, suddenly choking and rushing into his hut. I tried to convince myself that the agony of sobbing we could all hear from within was the smith's wife. The thought of this, the hardest of men breaking down, was too unnerving.

None of the men who went to check on Mullens's farm, then burned it to the ground, ever did tell of what they had found there. Today, all being safely buried in the hallowed ground next to the village shrine, they never will. But over the years I have managed to piece together fragments of whispered conversations or the drunken rambling of men quickly hushed by their fellows. Not much, I grant you, but enough to give some idea of the bloody nightmare those men encountered.

I know that, amongst other things, they found Mullens at the farm – or at least what was left of him. He had been eaten right down to the bone, but even as he fell he had not abandoned his weapon. Skeletal fingers locked desperately around the heft of a bloodied spear. Even now, the image fills me with a kind of horrified wonder.

His dogs were found lying on either side of their master. Their ruined and convulsed bodies bore witness to the desperate resistance they had put up. They had died as they had lived, full of courage and loyalty. Few men can hope for such an epitaph and my eyes sting even now at the memory of those fine animals.

Of the attackers who had committed this foul atrocity, there was scant sign. A few bones, a few fly-encrusted brown stains on the stone of the walls and the splintered wood of the door. It seems that their flesh had tasted as sweet to their companions as any other.

To witness such scenes at first hand must have been like stepping into a waking nightmare – and though it sounds almost perverse to say it, I thank the gods for it. The horror of Mullens's farm was enough to shock the whole village into wakefulness at last. It was no longer possible to ignore the danger, and all of our lives were changed and reordered overnight.

There was a meeting on the green the next morning. Nobody drank. The only argument was when Frau Henning, our young farrier's mother, tried to prevent his volunteering to ride to the nearest Empire town for help and men-at-arms. But Gulmar's father overruled her tears and protestations with a fervour that was close to rage. He was proud of his son's courage, I think, and didn't want to deny him the chance to prove it. That pride began to turn into a cancerous mixture of bitterness and regret a few short weeks later. Fuelled by grain alcohol and a nagging wife, it eventually killed him.

Of course we weren't to know that as we watched father and son bid each other farewell in the clear light of that bright morning. They were alive and together for the last time on this world and perhaps sensing it they shook hands as equals, maybe even friends, for the first time. Gulmar Henning never made it back but at least he didn't die a child.

As the hoofbeats of the farrier's borrowed horse faded into the distance, we all stood in a long, solemn silence, broken only by the accusing sobs of the boy's distraught and inconsolable mother. Then the discussion began and incredibly, insanely it seemed at the time, it was decided to do the unthinkable.

We abandoned the harvest.

THAT YEAR'S AUTUMN wheat was left to ripen then wither outside the palisade, a feast only for the teeming birds and vermin. While our golden lifeblood rotted back into the dark earth, the whole village worked at a fever pitch. The great mill wheel was lifted off its pole and wrestled through the gates, leaving a naked patch on the overgrown stone of the wall. Karsten the miller himself supervised this piece of necessary vandalism with shrill cries and fluttering hands. As he capered around he reminded me, despite his fleshy jowls and shiny head, of a hen that has lost its chicks. Even at that age, though, I had the sense to keep the thought to myself, as I did the private grievance that my brother and I would no longer be able to use the great wooden wheel as our private staircase over the wall into the village.

Most of the work was done in the forest, as more trees were felled to strengthen the stockade. By then I was confined to the village with the rest of the children, but even there I could hear the harsh cracks of axes biting into green wood and the occa-sional shocking crash of a falling tree. Throughout the next few weeks the sound of the men nibbling away at the edge of the forest became a constant rhythm that we all lived to.

Meanwhile Gulmar Henning's mother had taken to haunting the parapets in a painfully desperate vigil. She stood silently above the frenetic activity of the village, gaunt and crow-like in a windswept black cloak. She finally broke her silence after three days with a piercing shriek that sent us all rushing to the wall. My eyes followed the line of her trembling arm as it pointed to the east, and I saw it.

There was nothing much, just an orange glow on the hori-zon. Through the jagged arms of the black forest, the distant flames even looked a little comforting. The fire came from the direction of Groenveldt, thirty miles away, and I wondered aloud, quite innocently and without malice, if they were hav-ing a bonfire.

I turned to ask my father, but his tight-lipped expression of angry relief silenced me. I left the chill of the parapet and retreated to my bed, confused and afraid. The next day we began to work even harder.

I didn't have much time to reflect on the strange new turn
our lives had taken, which was perhaps just as well. My days
were spent with cleaning and splitting feathers for the growing
bundles of arrows or spinning the sharpening stone at just the
right pace to avoid Gustav the smith's wrath. My only break
from all this was the occasional errand or, much to my disgust,
doing the women's work and drawing the village's water.

Even though the work was hard, I do remember enjoying it,
for the novelty made all of this excitement and panic a great
game for a child as young as I was, albeit a slightly uneasy one.
I couldn't understand why everyone was so gloomy and foul-
tempered. Even Stanislav the brewer, usually the jolliest and
certainly the reddest-faced man in the village, snarled at me
when I knocked over a pile of hoops he was finding for the
smith.

Then came the night, just as winter was starting to tighten its
icy grip on Pasternach and all the land around it, when I did
understand.

I WAS SHOCKED from my sleep in the steely grey hour before
dawn by the awful sound of a man screaming, screaming and
never ceasing. I clambered out of the cot I shared with my
brother, still too groggy with sleep to be truly alarmed, when
my father burst through the door half dressed and crazy-eyed.

Even in the gloom I could see his knuckles were white from
the grip he had on his scythe, as sharp and gleaming now as it
had ever been. He shouted at my brother and me to get under
the bed, but the undercurrent of terror in his voice froze me
where I stood. I'd never heard the like before.

As my father charged outside I saw the other villagers dashing
to the north wall in the torchlight. Alderman Fauser was already
high on the stockade with half a dozen other men, hacking
down into the darkness beyond. I was almost as surprised to
hear the alderman spitting out such obscene oaths as I was to
see the blood that ran from his pitchfork as he pulled it from
one of the shadows. My father had his foot on the lower rung of
the ladder when he stopped, turned, and bellowed a warning.

Over the south wall, with a hideous snarling and squealing,
poured a wave of dark, misshapen forms. They clambered over
the eaves of the cottages and squeezed through the gaps between
the walls like a boiling mass of gargoyles brought to life by the

night's pale moon. When they reached the torchlit sanctuary of the village green I felt myself shrink at the sight of them.

The things were an obscene combination of man and beast, horribly melted and twisted together. But their deformities, far from weakening them, seemed to give them an abnormal strength. Their clothes were ragged strips, shredded and filthy, but the claws lashing at the end of their arms were sharp and bright enough to freeze me, my cry stopped in my gaping mouth.

The miller, who stood equally open-mouthed and incredulous in their path, was the first victim of this hellish tide. Without breaking their pace these twisted daemons tore him to pieces with a mercifully brief rending and shrieking. Even as they continued their charge I saw, with a rising gorge, shreds stripped from the man's separated limbs being crammed into their fanged, bestial mouths.

With a dreadful roar my father and the rest of the villagers turned to meet this vile onslaught. In the middle of the green, steel met claw in a nightmare of blood and savagery. The men of Pasternach fought with the burning madness of fear that night, but even so they were no match for the savage breeding and sheer weight of numbers of the enemy.

Gradually, remorselessly, the villagers were pushed back to the north wall by the ravenous horde before them. Every man who went down was fallen upon in a hideous feeding frenzy that merely seemed to fuel the enemies' bloodlust rather than sate it.

Then, in one terrible moment, two terrible things happened at once. The alderman, our appointed leader, was torn from his perch atop the wall by a second, slashing swarm of the monsters. And, infinitely worse, my father collapsed under a crushing blow. His opponent, a writhing bundle of fang, claw and muscle, roared in delighted triumph and lunged forward to feed.

There was no bravery in what I did, for without fear to overcome there can be no real courage. It's true that I had to plunge through the wave of horror which engulfed me to seize a rock and run yelling defiance at the beast-thing. There was no fear, though, only a sort of divine rage at the abomination before me.

Turning to face me, the beast let out a dreadful baying laugh. It towered above me, so close that I could smell the reek of it and see with crystal clarity a single drop of saliva roll down one curved yellow fang. Still, in the face of its laughter and in the face of its power I raised my feeble weapon and leapt towards its claws.

My blow never landed, nor did it need to. For in that dread moment, knowing my weakness and knowing my faith, the gods heard my raging prayers and struck for me! With a piercing whine and a blinding flash of light brighter than any storm, the corrupt beast in front of me burst apart in a spray of blood. The struggle around me stuttered into silence as man and monster alike looked in wonder at the astonishing, blinding death of my enemy.

Then the angels appeared.

THERE WERE FOUR of them, one on each wall of the village stockade, and they were both beautiful and terrible. They were clad as great armoured knights, and they moved as if they had the power of giants contained within them. Their huge, shining armour was of a strange and wondrous design, the sweeps and curves of it coloured in hues of blue and green. In their hands they held bizarre weapons: swords bearing teeth; ornate, carved metal wands; incomprehensible bundles of steel pipes which gleamed dully with a strange menace.

One of their number wore hugely distorted gauntlets, vast hands made of some worked metal which sparked and crackled with bound lightening. He lifted the flaring blue gloves above his armoured head and closed the steel fingers into a fist. It was the signal to begin.

In total silence, and in perfect harmony, three of the armoured figures plunged into the squalling mass of daemons below. The killing began as soon as their vast iron-shod feet hit the ground.

Fanged swords squealed and screamed like cats on a fire as they bit down into flesh and bone. They spat great gouts of blood and flesh high into the black vault of the night, and the shrieks of their victims added to the din.

I felt a curiously warm drizzle begin to fall and casually licked a droplet from my lips. It had the salty, coppery taste of fresh blood. Suddenly I was bent double, wracked and spasming, seized by a fit of vomiting.

Through my tears I saw the terrible blue fire of the steel fists. The being that wielded them strode amongst the shadows of his enemies with a hypnotic grace, a terrible dance of death. As he twisted and swung, the massive burning hands snatched at heads, limbs, torsos. Muscle and bone split asunder at his divine touch into hideous steaming wounds. The stink of burning carrion started to drift through the village.

At first the corrupt pack of abominations teeming within the stockade had reeled under the wrath of our saviours. They died like animals in a slaughter-house, shocked and bewildered, until an enraged roar cut through their stupor. The chilling cry was returned from another beast-thing, and then another, until it echoed back and forth from a score of deformed throats. It rose to a savage crescendo and once more the daemons flung themselves into the attack with a terrifying ferocity.

But as the fiends hurled themselves towards the blood-spattered angels, a staccato shriek from above suffocated their war cry. Hands clutched desperately over my ears, I looked up and saw the fourth of our saviours, still standing atop the wooden stockade, thrown into sharp and flickering relief by guttering flames. The bundle of steel pipes he held whirled and flared as they spat burning lances of fire into the charging forms of the enemy.

The living were lifted, torn into bloody ruins, and hurled to the ground. The dead were shredded further, their remains beaten deeply down into the wet soil. Jaws snapped open in rictus howls of agony, inaudible over the awesome noise of their execution.

Still the daemons fought. Despite the lines of holy, magical fire that sliced through them like a new scythe through ripe corn, despite the fresh meat afforded by the rising piles of the dead, despite everything they fought back against the angels. Their blood lust drove them to total annihilation. Claws and fangs cracked and splintered on celestial armour. Divine weapons ate eagerly through verminous hides into the twisted bones beneath. Tainted blood splashed, stinking and steaming, into the cold night air. It was a massacre.

At the last, some semblance of realisation must have come to the last few survivors from the warband, and the last of the monsters tried to flee. I watched the panic, the sheer terror, in their rolling yellow eyes with grim satisfaction, barely able to understand what I had witnessed. They rushed past the angel with the blazing steel fists, leaving two of their number slashed and dying at his feet, and leapt for the stockade.

There was to be no escape from the divine wrath of our saviours. Burning spears chased them, found them, and ripped them apart in arcs of blood and fire. The sizzling gore splattered across the splintered timber of the stockade in glistening sweeps and curves. I stared into the grisly patterns, my mind a shocked blank, and suddenly I imagined I could see the bloodied face of Gulmar, the young farrier, staring back out at me.

I began to shake and gag with the dry heaves. My ears still shrilled and rang painfully from the noise of their deafening weapons. For a time I could do nothing but crouch and heave and cry. It was a long while before I realised that the battle was over.

The angels stood amongst great banks of corpses, silent and still in the gloom like terrible statues. Even then, covered in gore and stinking of burnt flesh, they were beautiful. For one long moment we stood together, angel and boy, in the midst of the carnage. Then, as silently as they had appeared, they faded from our sight and were gone.

I like to think I was the only one who saw the star rise from the forest that night. It was no more than a silent, distant flash of light and I would have missed it too if I hadn't looked up from the well at precisely the right moment. As I carried the water back to bathe my father's wounds I marvelled at the glimpse I had been afforded of their celestial chariot. And even now I still smile to myself when some travelling sage or other tries to tell us what the stars are.

IT WAS ALMOST forty summers ago, but still I remember. When the wolves came last winter the memory gave me the courage to find and destroy them in their own lair and when Mary lay screaming in her first labour the memory gave me the strength to break the taboos and deliver my son.

Now, as the voices of my people fade away and all I can hear is the ticking of the deathwatch in my ears, I remember the events of that singular night and I am not afraid. For I know that in the darkness that I soon must face, the gods will send their angels to watch over me again.

And this time they will not fade.

HELLBREAK
Ben Counter

'YOU WILL NEVER know, scum,' the mechanically translated voice hissed in Commissar von Klas's ear, 'just how lucky you are!'

An unseen hand thrust him up the last few stairs, out of the darkness and into the searing glare of the arena. He stumbled in the sudden light and slipped, hitting the coarse sand face-first, scouring a layer of skin off his cheek. From all around him there rose a cackling cheer. He looked up and a terror shot through him that his training couldn't banish.

An area the size of a landing field spread out before him, its sandy floor streaked with crescents of maroon that could only be the bloody traces of those who had come before him. Around the edge of the arena was a ring of spikes as tall as a man, with a head impaled on each tip. There were heads of men and orks, the long slender faces of eldar, the twisted alien features of a hundred different species.

Beyond them, the amphitheatre rose, huge and dark, forged of black iron into forms which seemed to have been pulled, fully formed, from a madman's imagination. Wicked spikes and curving galleries formed the mouths of leering faces; immense claws of iron held up the private boxes of the elite. The whole edifice rose to join the myriad black pinna-

cles and spires of Commorragh which speared upwards, a
mockery of beauty, to puncture a sky the colour of a wound
gone bad.

But that was not the worst of it. As von Klas hauled himself
to his feet, feeling his muscles complaining with the sudden
release from the steel bonds which had held them for so
long, he felt their eyes upon him, and he heard their laughter. The audience of eldar renegades, many hundreds of
thousands strong, sat in great serried ranks, their pale alien
faces shining like lanterns against the purples and blacks of
their clothing. Silver blades gleamed everywhere, and he
could hear them talking to one another in low voices – perhaps wagering on whether he would live or die, or just
mocking a man who didn't know he was dead yet. In the
prime position, right at the edge of the arena, sat a great dignitary, with a face that even from this distance von Klas could
tell was as long and cruel as any he had ever seen. His purple
robe only half-concealed ceremonial armour with great cres-
cent-shaped shoulder guards. The dignitary was surrounded
by a bodyguard who stood stone-still and carried spears
tipped with bright silver blades, and any number of hangers-
on and courtiers lounged nearby.

Von Klas had barely time to take all this in when the dignitary raised one slender hand to the crowd, who screamed their
approval with a deafening rising screech. Von Klas looked
around him to see what had just been signalled – but he was
alone in the vast arena. The doorway through which he had
been pitched had sunk back into the sand behind him.

Something flickered in the corner of his eye. In the time it
took him to turn and face it, it had got much closer. As a storm
of thoughts and fears rushed through his commissar's mind,
his old, trained instincts took over and he tensed his aching
muscles for the fight.

THE HUMAN HAD maybe a second and a half to see the wych as
she backflipped and cartwheeled her way across the sand
towards it. She wore armour only to display her body, which
was lithe and supple to an extent which no human could
match. Her long red-black hair flowed out in a stormy trail
behind her as she moved, along with the glistening metallic net
that she held in one hand. In the other, twirling like a rotor

blade, was a halberd, as long as she was tall and tipped with a broad, wickedly curved blade.

In his luxuriously fitted box at the front of the audience, the eldar who had signalled, Archon Kypselon, leaned across to Yae, who reclined next to him, her long, slim body draped over the seat, showing off her snake-like muscles. The leader of the Cult of Rage, Kypselon's most valuable ally, Yae looked every bit as formidable as her reputation, her dark hair braided with lengths of silver chain and her glassy, emerald eyes enough to intimidate any lesser eldar into submission.

'I hear this is one of the finest of your wyches,' he said off-handedly. 'Rather wasted on a single creature.'

'Perhaps, my archon,' she replied. 'But I hear it is one of their ruling class. It might provide some sport. They can breed them remarkably tough.'

Out in the arena, the human turned, holding its body low and hands high preparing for the wych's first strike. Through the blur of violent motion it would just be able to make out her face, twisted with exertion and hate, her eyes burning with the sacred narcotics which coursed joyfully through her veins. The delicately pointed eldar ears and large eyes would do nothing to offset the base savagery.

'I hope she is as fine as they say,' Kypselon continued. 'The Kabal of the Broken Spine needs fine warriors. There are others who would take away the authority that I have earned.'

'You know the Cult of Rage are with you,' Yae smiled. 'Power and wisdom such as yours is enough to secure our loyalty.'

Kypselon smirked indulgently. He had been around long enough to know such words were nothing more than a cipher on Commorragh – he had seen enough eldar die by treachery, his included, to know that. But Yae's wyches were truly vital to him. Uergax and the Kabal of the Blade's Edge were threatening to shatter the delicate savagery of his territory. But those were matters for his court. He tried to concentrate on the entertainment at hand; it had, after all, been put on specifically for him. Such honour was really born of fear, of course, but on Commorragh fear and honour were much the same thing.

The wych let out a piercing shriek of pleasure and rage as she whipped the halberd back over her shoulder, leaping high into the air and preparing to bring the blade down on the human in a shining arc.

Yae gave a sudden, sharp gasp of excitement, like a child, sitting up with a glint of rapture in her eyes. Kypselon smiled – an old eldar like him could still appreciate the simple pleasures. A dead human was a pleasure indeed.

The man drove one foot into the arena's sand and thrust itself sideways, away from the shimmering blur of the wych's limbs, just as her blade scythed down in a silver-white blur past its face. Anyone else would have lost their balance and pitched into the bloodsoaked sand, but the wych somersaulted elegantly, landing on her feet and turning on a heel to face her quarry. But the human was ready too, and quicker than most men could, it drove the palm of one hand into the wych's face, snapping her head back, splitting her nose open in a vermilion spray.

There was a dark, displeased hiss from the galleries. Kypselon heard low obscenities muttered around him. Yae stood up, her eyes still shining with glee – for a true wych loves combat whoever wins. But the rest of the audience were not so happy.

The wych in the arena rolled onto her front in a heartbeat, ready to rise and face the upstart human, but it stamped a booted foot into the small of her back, pinning her to the ground.

'Kill it!' yelled an incensed spectator. 'Kill the animal!'

A hundred other voices joined in, rising to a roar – that became a cheer as the wych caught one of the man's legs with her own and tipped it sprawling on its back. She sprang up for the kill, her net forgotten, ready to swipe off its head with her halberd.

The audience noticed before she did: she was no longer holding the weapon. Her opponent was. Before she had time to respond, it drove the blade towards her. She held up the net in front of her neck and face, knowing its metallic strands would parry the blow and keep her head on her shoulders.

But the human was not aiming for her neck, for it did not care for the elegant decapitation that was the most graceful of murders. Instead, the blade went right through her stomach and out between the wych's shoulders. As her lifeblood gouted upwards, she looked unutterably surprised, still coming to realise that her weapon had been stolen.

The man drew out the blade and pulled itself to its feet. The wych slumped to the ground, amidst a growing crimson stain upon the sand.

The yells from the audience became a wordless howl of rage that rang violently around the amphitheatre. Yae was still on her feet, breathing in sharp, shallow gasps, her eyes wide.

Kypselon rose to stand at her side.

'Never fear,' he whispered to her under the din, 'This is as grave an insult to me as it is to you. I shall have the human given to the haemonculi. Then I shall deliver the skin to you once I am sure it can take no more pain.'

Yae did not answer. Her eyes burned and a snarl grew on her face. With a silent gesture, Kypselon ordered his black-armoured bodyguards to fetch the man and remove the body of the wych.

Seeing the dark eldar approaching, the man dropped the wych's halberd, perhaps expecting a quick despatch as a reward for its victory. The crowd continue to howl its derision as one of the warriors knocked it unconscious with the butt of his spear, and the body was dragged away to a fate that it could never have imagined.

It was always the same with aliens, Kypselon reflected. They are simply too stupid to realise when they would be better off dead.

THE ROOM WAS mercilessly lit by a bright glowing ceiling. Two of the alien warriors stood guard at the back wall. The floor was of bare metal, sloping towards a drain in the centre through which his bodily fluids were supposed to drain away. The walls were hung with skins, complete human pelts, presumably the finest of those taken by the torturer over the years. Tattoos had been favoured, and von Klas could recognise the regimental insignia and devotional versus inscribed on the skins: Catachan, Stratix, Jurn, even his own Hydraphur. The words of the Ecclesiarchy in intricate script. Primitive tribal scars. Even a green-brown ork hide with kill tallies gouged into the chest.

He looked down at himself. He was not bound. Presumably they thought the fear alone would keep him here. They were probably right.

'I won't die,' von Klas said aloud, every word like a hammer blow to his aching head. 'I'm a difficult man to kill.'

The warriors said nothing. The door between them opened with a hiss, and the torturer shuffled in. Von Klas had heard rumours about the torture artists of the renegade eldar, but it was only now that he started to believe them.

The eldar looked at von Klas with eyes which had long since sunken out of sight, the sockets now just deep, ravaged tunnels. His skin was a dead blue-grey, stretched and striated by age and untold torment, the lips drawn back like a corpse's, the nose crushed and misshapen, the scalp hairless and paper-thin so white bone showed through.

The robes that covered his shuffling frame were fashioned from skins too, and he had picked out the best designs for them: rare metallic tattoos, the elaborate medical scars of an Astartes veteran. From a belt of gnarled hide, perhaps from an ogryn, hung a multitude of implements, scalpels and syringes, strange arcane devices for lifting the skin or teasing out nerve endings like splinters from a finger. There was something else, too, an articulated silver gauntlet with a medical blade tipping each digit, so sharp their edges caught the acidic light and scraped incandescent curves in the air.

Behind him was a slave, a young human female, dressed in rags with long, lank, once-blonde hair, who scampered along behind the torturer like a fearful pet. She bore few obvious scars, the torturer needing her alive and lucid, since she acted as his interpreter.

The torturer hissed some words in his own language, a tongue as dry as snakeskin slithering between the exposed teeth.

'Verredaek, haemonculus to Lord Archon Kypselon of the Broken Spine Kabal,' began the translator in hesitant Imperial Gothic, 'wishes his... his subject to know that he does not rely on mindless devices to perform his art. Some haemonculi employ cowardly machines which produce mediocre results in the art. Verredaek will only use the ancient talents passed on by the torturers of the Broken Spine. He is proud of this.'

Von Klas stood up, still aching. He was tall, as tall as the guards and far taller than the shrivelled haemonculus. 'I am not going to die here. I am going to kill every single one of you myself.' He kept his voice level, as if he was instructing his own men. 'I might not see it, and I might not even be there. But I will kill you.'

The terrified girl stammered his words back in the eldar language. Through her, Verredaek replied, 'It is good that you do not give up. The bodies and souls of creatures who do not believe themselves to be on the edge of death have long... fascinated me. The first cut will be sweet indeed.'

Without any discernible motion, a blade as long as an index finger, so sharp it disappeared when turned edge-on, appeared in Verredaek's hand. The torturer stepped forward, the skins of his robes hissing as they rubbed together. 'You will know fear, but know also that it is not in vain you die. The art of pain continues through souls such as yours, their agony distilled and passed on, and one day you shall become part of a much greater work.'

Von Klas looked from the knife to Verredaek's sightless eye-sockets, and saw his mistake. This was how he managed to torture his victims without strapping them down or tying them up. Those desperately empty caverns, the ridges of desiccated skin picked out by the harsh light, seemed to bolt him to the ground and drain his limbs of strength.

His superiors had decided that von Klas was officer material, but he had never been a greatly distinguished officer, never led charges that shattered armies, never held the line against awesome odds. He had the medals they give commissars as a matter of course, and nothing more. He might have been in effective command of twenty thousand men, but in the Imperium that made him one amongst a million.

But he had survived the battle in the arena. He had proved to be something special to his captors, so much so that he had been given to Verredaek as a punishment. And now he would be something again. He would survive this, too. He didn't care if it was unknown. He would still do it.

For a second, Verredaek's hypnotic aura was broken as von Klas made his vow to survive. He closed his eyes, and his body was his own again. He would not get a second chance.

With all his strength, he punched, low and hard. His hand hit spongy flesh and drove deeper. The haemonculus gasped in astonishment. The commissar grabbed Verredaek so he would not fall, and spun both of them around, just as the eldar guards began to shoot. One shot sprayed Verredaek across the back, his skin splitting and bursting like a rotten fruit under the assault of a hundred splinters of crystal. The second caught von Klas on the shoulder, a glancing blow but one that drove a dozen splinters deep into the muscle.

The translator screamed and scampered across to the far side of the room, wrapping her arms around her head so she couldn't see.

Von Klas drove Verredaek's body forward into one guard, smashing the eldar into the back wall, knocking him senseless. The second eldar hesitated. It was enough. Von Klas scrabbled at Verredaek's belt until he felt the cold steel of his gauntlet. He thrust his hand into it, feeling the woven metal mesh close around his hand. With one motion he snapped it off the tendon that bound it to the belt and thrust it deep into the second guard's chest. The eldar let out a muffled cry, then slumped lifelessly to the floor.

Von Klas stood up once more, Verredaek's limp body sliding off his shoulders and down the wall. The first eldar lay motionless against the back wall where he had been rammed. He might have been dead, but behind the lifeless jade of the alien's helmet's eyes von Klas couldn't be sure. The second was certainly dead, though, his blood running down into the drain at the room's centre.

Verredaek shifted slightly and suddenly there was an alien gun pointing at von Klas, slender and strange, held in a gnarled blue-grey hand. Without thinking, von Klas slashed the torturer's gauntlet downwards as the eldar turned his head to aim. The blades swiped cleanly through his face, slicing the withered skin to ribbons. The haemonculus slumped to the floor at last.

He had been difficult to kill. But then so am I, thought Commissar von Klas.

He considered taking one of the guard's rifles, but he would have needed two hands to fire it and he wanted to keep hold of the razor-gauntlet. And the splinters that had hit him, though they were sending occasional flashes of pain through his muscles, had still left him alive. Not very efficient, he thought coldly. The torturer's gun might prove more useful. He prised it from Verredaek's dead hands. It was oddly light, and very strange to look at, with a barrel so slender only a needle, surely, could be fired out.

He turned to the translator slave still cowering in the corner behind one of the hanging skins.

'You coming?' he asked. 'We can escape from here if we hurry.'

The translator didn't seem to understand him, as if she wasn't used to having Imperial spoken directly to her and wasn't sure how to respond. She shook her head and redoubled her efforts to hide from him. Von Klas decided to leave her.

The door through which Verredaek had entered opened with a simple touch of his hand on a panel set into the wall. Beyond it, the corridors were made of the same polished metal, but bent and buckled into strange shapes, as if the whole place had been picked up and twisted by a giant. Von Klas jogged down the corridor, mind buzzing, trying to work out if the place had a pattern to it, one part of his brain keeping watch for signs of more guards.

He came to a row of cells, four of them, the doors again opening easily with a press of their inset panels. Behind the first was a human, an Imperial guardsman, still dressed in his grime-grey uniform, his head shaved and his face aged beyond his years.

The man blinked in the sudden light, for the cells were pitch black inside, and looked up at what must have been von Klas's silhouette. 'You're one of us,' he said, surprised into stupidity.

'Come on. We're getting out,' von Klas replied.

The guardsman smiled sadly and shook his head. 'They'll be here any moment. We won't stand a chance.'

'That's an order, soldier. I'm a commissar and I've got scores to settle. If I say we're leaving then we're out of here already. Now move!'

The guardsman shrugged and shuffled unsteadily out of the cell – prisoners weren't manacled, Verredaek must have thought he was above that. Von Klas hurried to open the other three cells.

'Sir! Trouble!' yelled the guardsman. A sketchy reflection of the approaching eldar warriors shimmered on the metal wall and splinters began shattering against the walls.

As three other guardsmen emerged, stumbling and confused, von Klas levelled Verredaek's pistol to defend them. He fired at the first hint of purple and silver that came round the corner, tiny darts leaving a glittering trail as they raced for their target.

There was a strangled cry and the first renegade eldar pitched forward, clutching at the shattered mask of his helmet. As his cries became garbled howls, the warrior convulsed, his body splitting and twisting as it was ripped apart. Hot blood and shards of bone spattered and ricocheted across the walls. The guardsmen – two in sand-coloured uniforms, Tallarn maybe; the last in the remains of a dark red uniform that could have been Adeptus Mechanicus – ducked back into the cells for cover. Von

Klas might not have understood the eldar tongue but he knew fear when he heard it, and that was what he heard now, as the remaining eldar guards howled in fright or pain and fell back.

'Move!' von Klas said quickly. 'They're scared of us now!'

The first man he had released darted forwards and grabbed two rifles from where the guards had dropped them, throwing one to one of the Tallarn. After a moment to scrutinise the controls, they started pumping fire back down the corridor, before hurrying after the others.

Von Klas and his men – they were surely his men now, his unit – hurried away from the cells, von Klas leading, the two armed men jogging backwards with their rifles ready to offer covering fire. All the while von Klas could hear voices, the guards calling for help, trying to organise a pursuit, or perhaps just cursing the guardsmen in their vile alien tongue.

The labyrinth of prison corridors rolled out in front of them in ever more tormented designs. As they stumbled along, von Klas was beginning to believe that surviving might be impossible after all, even for a commissar. But no more guards came. It was not the guards that were supposed to stop prisoners escaping – it was the torment and brutality that were meant to break their will. Von Klas and his men passed the threshold of scarred iron, and emerged, breathless, bloody and exhausted, hearts racing, into the open air, the bowels of Verredaek's torture machine behind them.

But von Klas knew with an officer's instinct that they were not safe. Because they had only freed themselves in order to enter the dark eldar world-city of Commorragh.

VERREDAEK LOOKED OLDER, thought Kypselon, older even than the shattered, wizened specimen that first came into the archon's employ. But, of course, it could just be the vile old creature's shredded face. It had been a long time since Kypselon had seen Verredaek – not since the haemonculus had first retreated into his underground complex to pursue the art of torturer at his command, in fact.

Verredaek shuffled pathetically across the floor of Kypselon's throne room, across the milky marble shot though with amethyst veins. He looked small and feeble under the gaze of the three hundred or so eldar warriors who stood around the room's edge, weapons held ready, constantly at attention.

'Fallen One's teeth, what happened to him?' slurred Exuma, Kypselon's dracon, who was lounging in a seat held aloft by anti-grav motors so he didn't have to walk anywhere. A quietly gurgling medical array pumped a steady steam of narcotics into Exuma's blood.

'He failed,' Kypselon replied with feeling. When he rose from his black iron throne, the wide window behind him cast the shadow of his shoulder guards across Verredaek in two great crescents. The torturer seemed to shrink, and though his eyes were hidden, Kypselon could detect fear in the dark sockets.

'Verredaek, you will recall that when you first entered my services, I had my servants take a little of your blood.' Kypselon's deep voice echoed faintly off the high, vaulted ceiling and purple-draped marble walls.

'Yethhh, archon,' Verredaek replied, his speech impeded by his newly-forked tongue.

'I still have what I took. The reason I keep it, and that of all my followers, is to make real the notion that I own you. You are mine, you are a part of my territory, just like the streets and palaces. Just like my temple. The price of belonging to the Broken Spine is total subservience to me. Yet you failed to carry out my commands.'

Verredaek tried to speak, but he too had been alive longer than most on Commorragh, and he knew that words would not save him here.

'I ordered you to bring the human here, skinless and broken, so I could watch him die. This you failed to do. The reasons are irrelevant. You failed. By definition, being a possession of mine, you must be discarded.'

Kypselon shot a glance at the front row of warriors and four of them strode forwards, grabbing Verredaek and holding him fast.

The haemonculus didn't struggle as Yae flipped her lithe body from the shadows into the centre of the room. Her eyes and smile flashed, as she drew twin hydraknives. They turned to lightning bolts in her hands as she danced – and killed.

As Yae twirled and slashed a thousand cuts into Verredaek's body, Kypselon turned to his dracon. 'What is the situation with the Blade's Edge?'

Exuma looked back with glazed eyes. 'Little has changed, my archon. Uergax has the mandrakes, and the incubi favour him as well. Some remain loyal to us, but what Uergax lacks in territory he makes up with most admirable diplomacy.' The dracon paused to gasp with pleasure as another bolt of drugs shot through his veins.

Kypselon shook his head. 'It is not good. Uergax may soon crush us as I would wish to crush him. The Blade's Edge covets our corner of Commorragh and if incompetence like this persists he will get it. Yae!'

The wych span to a halt and let her lacerated handiwork collapse to the floor. 'Archon?'

'The human we wished to see dead is more resourceful than we thought. It is now loose on Commorragh. Find it.'

Yae smiled with genuine relish. 'It is a great honour to perform a task that would give me such pleasure in the name of one so great.'

'No time for blandishments, Yae. Uergax is bleeding us dry and I do not need this creature running loose to complicate matters. I fully expect you to succeed.'

'Yes, lord.'

'And be wary. This one has a colder heart than most. You may go.'

Yae flitted away, as only a wych could, to fulfil his commands. Kypselon turned to the great window behind him. It was a view of Commorragh, a riot of dark madness and broken spires, bridges that crossed to nothing, mutilated cathedrals to insanity and evil, a planet-wide city at once unfinished and ancient, swarming beneath a glorious swirling thunderstorm sky. And in the centre, obscene, bleached and pale, was Kypselon's temple. A temple to him, because living so long and rising to such power on Commorragh was such an impossible task it might as well be that of a god. A thousand pillars made of thigh bones held up a roof tiled with skulls. Whole skeletons acted out scenes of violation and murder on friezes and pediments.

'Every eldar, human, ork, every enemy I have ever killed stands there, Exuma. Every one. My temple is a testament to the fact that I will not give up, not ever. I have carved a path for myself through the very bodies of my foes.'

Exuma allowed himself to drift back into lucidity long enough to reply: 'Archon, none can say that you have failed in anything you have attempted.'

'That is the past. I have risen to power and I will not relinquish it to a boy like Uergax. I am not ashamed of fear, Exuma, even though young upstarts like Uergax and yourself are. And I feel fear now. But I will use that fear, and my temple will grow.'

Outside, the cancerous rain of Commorragh began to fall.

'IN THE CITY, you need those who want your money or your honour. On the plains, in the desert, you need brothers.' Rahimzadeh of Tallarn was a wiry, intense man, not long a soldier but already well versed in the hot fear and desperation of war. 'Though there are only two of us left, we are brothers still.'

Ibn, the second Tallarn, looked up from the ornate eldar splinter rifle he was examining. 'You would not understand. On your Hydraphur, a million men live within sight of one another. No room for true brothers.'

Von Klas winced as Scleros, the lexmechanic, pulled another shard from the commissar's raw shoulder. It felt like the razor-sharp crystals were doing as much damage coming out as they did going in. 'Brothers or not, we still have a chain of command. I am a commissar and you are now my men.'

'Why?' Ibn asked with a sneer. 'What good can orders and rank do here?' He waved an arm to indicate their surroundings – a shattered shell of a building, the carcass of some vast cathedral of soaring flutes and arches, now gutted and decrepit. It was deserted, which was why they had stopped here, but they all knew that there were malevolent eyes everywhere on Commorragh and they could soon be found wherever they hid.

'We can get out of here,' the commissar replied. 'There's a spaceport nearby, close to the temple.'

'Temple? This place has no gods,' Rahimzadeh said. 'Even the Emperor's light is faint upon us here.'

'It is consecrated to the foul leader of this part of the planet. The scum raised a temple to himself. The spaceport's nearby but it's garrisoned. We'd have to occupy the temple, draw in the garrison troops and make a break for the spaceport.'

'Death would claim us all before we reached it,' said Ibn.

'Not all of us. Not if there were enough. Would you rather let them recapture you? They wouldn't let you run away twice. If we try to escape we'll either make it or die trying. Whatever happens then, it's better than skulking here until one of them finds us.'

Rahimzadeh thought for a second. 'What you say is true. I think you are a good man. But we need others.'

'We'll need a whole damn army,' Ibn said.

Von Klas turned around. 'Scleros?'

The commissar had been right – the tattered dark rust-red uniform was that of the Adeptus Mechanicus. Scleros was a lexmechanic, his brain adapted to allow him to absorb a huge amount of information, produce calculations and battlefield reports. His augmentation was belied by the intricate web of silver tracery surrounding his artificial right eye. 'You said there is a chain of command. As commanding officer, the decision is yours.'

'Fine. And you?'

The fourth guardsman had said little. His head was shaven and he wore the grey uniform that could be from one of a thousand regiments. 'Sure. Whatever. As long as I get a shot at some of those freaks.'

Von Klas studied the Imperial guardsman: his hollow eyes, his scowl, the nose that had been broken two or three times. 'What's your name, soldier?'

'Kep. Necromundan Seventh.'

Ibn let out a short, barking laugh. 'Lucky Sevens? The sands do not lie so much. You are penal legions, my friend. The tattoo at the top of your arm, they can read it. You have the scar on your wrist where the machine makes your blood mad.'

Kep shrugged and held up his hand. Von Klas could see the scar where a frenzon dispenser had once been implanted. 'Guilty. I am from the First Penal Legion.'

'The First?' Rahimzadeh said with a hint of awe in his voice. 'The Big One?'

'What's your crime?' asked von Klas, his words straining as Scleros removed the last of the eldar shrapnel.

'Heresy. Third class. Standard practice – if eldar pirates show up you feed them the penal legion. They get their slaves, the Imperium ditches a few more scum, everyone's happy.'

The bruise-coloured clouds above had coagulated. Large, filthy grey raindrops started to fall, grey with the pollutants. Kep and the Tallarn ran, hunched, into a corner of the old cathedral, where some of the roof remained and there was cover.

Von Klas looked round at Scleros, the remaining soldier. The lexmechanic, as he expected, had no expression. 'You had the surgery?'

The thick rain sent strange trails across the circuitry on Scleros's face. 'Emotional repression protocol, sir. It allows me to deal with information of an ideologically sensitive nature.'

'Thought so. Scleros, you realise that we're never going to get off this planet, don't you?'

'I was unable to understand how we could escape through a spaceport. We would not be able to use a spacecraft, even if we were able to understand eldar technology. We would be shot down. We can not escape this place.'

'I trust you not to tell the men. This mission's objective does not allow for our survival.'

Scleros held out a hand and let a little of the rain collect in his palm. It swam with grey trails of impurity. 'We should get out of the rain. This could infect us.'

The two headed for shelter, while all around them, the soul of Commorragh seethed for their blood.

SYBARITE LAEVEQ gazed down from the gantry at the immense metallic beast, powered by the exertions of the many hundreds of deliciously emaciated human slaves that were chained to its pneumatic limbs. Great clouds of acrid smoke and steam from the huge cauldron of molten metal obscured their faces, and Laeveq felt as if he were striding in the clouds, a god looking down upon the wretches who both feared him and needed him to survive.

The eldar guard watched as another of them fell, limbs flopping loose as the clanking, screeching steel mill machinery carried on without it, head snapping back and forth as the machinery threw it about blindly. Soon Laeveq's eldar would go onto the factory floor and take away the battered corpse and replaced it with another faceless barbarian.

'Sybarite Laeveq,' a hasty voice came through his communicator. 'A problem has presented itself.'

'Elaborate, Xaron.'

'It's Kytellias. She didn't call in on her patrol so we went to find her. Her throat had been slit, ear to ear. Very pretty. Very clean.'

Laeveq cursed his fortune. 'Fugitives. Bring every armed eldar to me, on the gantry above the main hall. We will sweep this entire factory and disembowel them on top of the machinery so all these brute animals will see the cost of denial.'

'It may not be that simple, sybarite. Lady Yae has sent word of dangerous escaped arena slaves.'

'Then we will take much reward for bringing them in. Send everyone here. Is that understood?'

There was no answer. A dim static crackled where the warrior's voice should have been.

'I said, "Is that understood?" Xaron?'

Nothing. Laeveq looked around him at the web of gantries spanning the great space of the main factory hall. Through the billowing sheets of steam, he could see nothing. He felt suddenly alone.

When Laeveq caught sight of the human figure running towards his position along the gantry, he was sure he could take him. It was a tall and strong man, to be sure, with hair cut close and a muscled torso riven with many old scars. It had found a scissorhand and a stinger pistol from somewhere, too, but it would not be skilled with them.

Laeveq whipped out his own splinter pistol and took pleasure in the aiming, fancying he could take the animal in the lower abdomen, and watch it squeal in bestial pain before taking its head.

Before he could pull the trigger, however, the human leapt into the air, swiping the glittering blades of the scissorhand through one of the chains that suspended the gantries from the high ceiling. It landed again, almost falling onto its face. Laeveq smiled, knowing that he could not miss such a fallen target.

The room soared upwards around him as the gantry fell vertical, the chain holding it sliced through. The last things Laeveq saw were the pale, frightened upturned faces of the slaves swirling towards him through the smoke, and the violent red heat of the cauldron, before the liquid fire enveloped him.

VON KLAS arrived at Kep's side. The guardsman was just watching as the molten metal finally covered the top of the eldar's head.

'Your heresy might be third-class,' the commissar said, 'but you're a first-rate murderer.'

'It's what kept me alive.' Kep looked over the gantry rail, and the factory floor below. Hundreds of frightened eyes gazed back. 'So what now?'

Von Klas got to his feet. 'We start our little war. Get Rahimzadeh and Ibn and start unchaining those slaves. And send Scleros up here, we'll need his logistics. We've got an army now.'

THE MOST INTOLERABLE thing of all, thought Kypselon, was that he could see it from his own throne room. The beautiful cold temple of bone, the icon of perfection which would place the seal of immortality on his long and brutal life, now stained by the presence of two thousand barbaric aliens.

'How long have they occupied it?' he asked, his voice quiet and low, as it always was when Kypselon was at his most wrathful, and thus his most dangerous.

Exuma's eyes unclouded slightly. 'Since the turning of the second sun,' he replied. 'Attacked the temple and slaughtered the garrison. Some of them will be armed by now, they had quite an armoury there. It's your human all right. It must have recruited the slaves when it took over Laeveq's factory a few hours ago. Remember Laeveq? Bright boy.'

Kypselon waved a hand brusquely and the great window dimmed into shadow. He turned, his dark purple robes sweeping out behind him, and strode into the centre of the throne room. The eyes of his elite warriors followed his every move. He raised his arms as he spoke, his voice deep and resonant with hate.

'To your strike craft, my children!' he howled. 'This is an insult to you as it is to me. There will be no animals defiling my temple. There will be no barbarian aliens defying our natural dominion! Take up arms and we shall revel in the blood of slaves!'

The warriors held up their weapons and screamed. Their keening war cry drifted through the palace and out into Commorragh, echoing across the nightmarish spires, through the evil air.

FROM WITHIN, the temple was a vast hollowed carcass, bleached white, monstrous vertebrae spanning the ceiling, an altar of skulls the size of a command bunker towering above them all. The slaves crouched behind the barricades they had made from the shattered architectural debris of Commorragh, fragments of broken arches, bouquets of iron spikes. Those that were armed had their rifles and pistols pointed at the horizon – those that were not found themselves jagged shards of metal or heavy bars to fight with at closer quarters.

Rahimzadeh and Kep were in the front line, the slaves formed up around them. It occurred to von Klas that the wasted, broken slaves were the first command the guardsmen had ever had. Near the altar, Ibn was organising those slaves who seemed the strongest, the ones who had been given the few heavy weapons they had found.

'How many do we have?' Commissar von Klas asked of Scleros.

'Eighteen hundred. Of two thousand we attacked with.'

'Armed?'

'Seven hundred.' Scleros seemed unmoved by the information.

Von Klas looked between the pillars at the churning sky. He saw something, vague flitting black spots like flies. He had seen them before, untold millions of miles away, on an insignificant moon of Hydraphur. They were devastating eldar attack craft: Raiders.

'NO ALIEN MUST LIVE. Bring me the head of the man-scum who dared defy my will.' Kypselon gave his order in a stern, quiet voice, knowing it would be transmitted into the very consciousness of every eldar under his control.

His ornate strike craft touched down and all around him flowed a tide of his followers, a wave that crashed against the makeshift barricades and swept over them. The first were absorbed by the slaves, those that were armed keeping low against their barricades and pouring splinter fire into their foes. Warriors fell broken to the floor, a hundred at a stroke, but they could be replaced.

From within the depths of the front lines a horde of slaves armed with little save fear and anger poured out. They were led by a shaven-headed maniac with a splinter pistol in each hand, the fury in its eyes infecting the slaves formed up around it, who attacked with crude blades and clubs.

Yae's wyches went to meet them, dancing gleefully between the barbarians, lashing out with their silver blades, slicing through the pale skinny bodies of the slaves. But the slaves still would not fall back, still they charged forward, even as their leader died under Yae's twin blades. Countless slaves died, slashed to pieces or riddled with splinter rounds. Heavy fire from stolen dark lances and splinter cannons scythed through the eldar warriors, but then Yae broke through, and again the slaves' blood swirled ankle-deep on the temple floor.

Kypselon ordered his craft forward through the carnage. Before him lay only one target: the human filth who had started it all, he of the colder heart, standing defiant by the great skull altar, still bearing the weapons he had stolen from Verredaek.

Alerting Verredaek's miserable translator slave with a cuff to the head, Kypselon landed within earshot of the human, where they could talk above the cries of the dead. The eldar body-guard stood aside. Kypselon spoke.

'Who are you to defy my will?' he said via the translator.

'I am Commissar von Klas, of Hydraphur,' replied the alien, almost as if he wasn't afraid. 'You may remember. When you took my command prisoner, you picked out a handful of us to kill at your leisure. Ten per cent.'

Kypselon thought for a second. He was old, he had killed so many...

Then he remembered.

'Of course,' he said with a smile of pride. 'You're the one in ten.'

The human, von Klas, smiled coldly. 'No, the one in a million.'

Kypselon noticed the young one too late, the one in a dirty dark red uniform, with the web of metal across the side of his face, skulking at the foot of the altar. It pressed down a plunger on the control it was holding.

A dozen explosive charges stolen from the factory went off at once. They blasted the bases out from the pillars, sending great shards of bone shearing down from the ceiling. They crushed eldar and slave alike, and punched through the hulls of the eldar Raiders. Only Kypselon's craft managed to dodge out between the pillars.

Half the warriors were buried as a cloud of dust rose to obscure the imploding mass of bone which had once represented Kypselon's endless career of murder and savage glory. Broken skulls rained down from a sky the colour of dead flesh.

Kypselon felt that emotion he had not felt for a very long time. The feeling that he had lost control.

'Death to men!' he hissed to anyone who could hear. 'I want no slave sullying my city! Kill them all! Every one! This disgusting species shall never again face me and live!'

WHEN VON KLAS awoke he was manacled to the cold metal floor of a cell. The skin on his back was raw from the lash. He was unable to focus properly; the taste of blood was in his mouth.

In the minimal light he could see that his legs had been broken, and were lying out in front of him like useless twigs. He was probably dying. But had he won? He drifted into unconsciousness again.

Days or weeks later, he could no longer tell, the cell door was opened and another two prisoners were thrown in. One was human, a girl, with straggly hair that had once been blonde, who crawled like a beaten dog.

The other was an eldar, thin and feeble without his armour and his legions of elite guards, his eyes dull, his wrinkling skin bruised. He stared at von Klas and started with recognition. Then he spoke. The translator took up his dark sibilant language in Imperial Gothic automatically, working from an instinct that had been bored into her soul.

'I knew you had a cold heart, human,' Kypselon said, with something approaching admiration.

Von Klas laughed darkly, even though it hurt his raw throat. 'What was it in the end? What finished you?'

Kypselon shook his head gravely. 'Uergax. We had no slaves, we had no factories, no expendable troops. We were crippled. He had the mandrakes, the incubi. He carved the Broken Spine apart as if he had been born to it.' The archon slumped to the cell floor, and von Klas saw the old eldar's fires of ambition were out.

'Your Raiders turned up as blips on our scanners,' said the human who called himself a commissar. 'Seventy-two hours later, the only survivor of seventeen whole platoons was me, but I had my orders. I was to eliminate any threats and a commissar either fulfils his orders or dies. I fulfilled mine.'

He looked Kypselon deep in his unknowable alien eyes. 'We humans aren't as stupid as you eldar believe. Remember my words, when Uergax comes to execute us both. I know I'll get a blade through the neck, like any other animal.

'But I imagine that it will take far, far longer for *you* to die.'

BATTLE OF THE ARCHAEOSAURS
Barrington J. Bayley

WITHIN ITS OVAL frame of enamelled copper, the holo-plate displayed the nearly perfect sphere of a planet fringed with cloud and shining seas. Fleet Captain Karlache slapped a knob, causing the image of the world to rotate at a faster rate.

'The mapping is incomplete, having been carried out from orbit by the first surveyor ship to arrive,' Karlache explained. He struck the knob again, making the image halt and then move around in small jerks until a pear-shaped continent became visible. He positioned an arrow in the middle of it. 'This is where the first landing was made, on the sole inhabited continent. The initial survey had reported a sparse human population which, like many settlements dating from the Dark Age of Technology, had lost the technical arts and degenerated to the Stone Age. As you know, Imperial policy in such circumstances is to land amid the populated area and take control immediately. A single battalion, lightly armed, was deemed more than sufficient to subdue a primitive people, establish a military base, and secure the planet for the Imperium. As you also know by now, it was wiped out almost immediately, without a single survivor.'

The captain looked around at his guests. They were seated in his private cabin – with its darkly gleaming panelled walls embellished with icons of the Emperor, and its ribbed and curved ceiling – aboard the troopship he commanded, the *Mobilitatum*. With a thousand troopers aboard, the *Mobilitatum* was approaching Planet ABL 1034, the planet on the screen, as was its sister ship, the *Straterium*. Some distance to their rear came two immense travel pods containing Warlord Titans, the *Lex et Annihilato* and the *Principio non Tactica*, two prime examples of the mightiest land-war machines ever to exist.

Their commanders, Princeps Gaerius and Princeps Efferim, sat across the cabin, men of stern appearance in their diamond-shaped peaked caps, skulls stitched onto their epaulets. Also present were Imperial Guard Colonel Costos and Commissar Henderak, both of the Fifth Helvetian Regiment.

It was most unusual for sealed orders to be entrusted to a Fleet captain rather than to an Imperial Guard officer, but security was of the essence. Public morale dictated that as few as possible should know what had happened on Planet ABL l034. 'A stronger expedition equipped with Leman Russ battle tanks and Basilisk mobile artillery was then despatched to the same location. It met a similar fate. Messages despatched to the orbiting transports spoke of giant beasts which the natives were using as battle weapons. Only one brief visual transmission was received.'

Planet ABL l034 vanished from the holo-plate. A blurred, shaking picture replaced it, showing a huge shape looming over the camera. Colossus-like legs, a vast neck, jaws that could have swallowed the cabin in which the officers watched – then nothing. The screen went blank.

'Large animals have been trained for use in battle on many primitive planets, including on ancient Terra,' Captain Karlache continued. 'Such forms of warfare have never presented the least problem to the Imperial Guard. The difference here would appear to be one of size. The Imperium has simply not encountered beasts this huge before.'

Again the Fleet captain manipulated the knobs in front of the enamel-decorated holo-plate. A procession of lumbering creatures crossed the visual area, some with long necks and thick tails. The outline of a man in the corner of the screen gave some idea as to their size, which was much larger than any living Terran animal. 'Genetors of the Adeptus Mechanicus, by studying fossil records, have established that beasts such as these lived on Earth a hundred million years ago. Similar animals are common throughout the galaxy but are too unmanageable to be trained for war. In any case, they could be downed with a single shot. How even larger beasts are able to be utilised on the target planet is a mystery. However, Mechanicus Genitors have named them "archaeosaurs" because of their resemblance to the ancient Earth animals.'

Again the scene on the holo-plate changed to show clouds and filaments formed of stars. An arrow picked out the star that warmed Planet ABL 1034. 'The archaeosaur planet has a strategic value, as you can see for yourselves. It guards the crossing point between no less than three star systems, all of them of interest to the Imperium. It has been ordered that the planet will not be permitted to be lost by default. It must be occupied. That is why two Warlord Titans have been assigned to the next landing, so that there may be no question of further defeat.'

Colonel Costos coughed softly. 'While not wishing to criticise command decisions, is it not an overreaction to call on the Adeptus Titanicus in this case? Our Fifth Helvetian Regiment is battle-hardened, down to less than half its original strength.' He made this last statement with pride. Imperial Guard regiments generally dwindled in proportion to the number of engagements they had fought, their final remnants eventually being absorbed elsewhere. A regiment at full strength meant an inexperienced regiment. 'The second landing was made by elements of the First Ixist, a newly raised regiment that had never seen an engagement before. It is certain the whole affair was carelessly executed, the natives underestimated. It is sometimes a fatal error to suppose that primitive people need not be taken seriously in military terms. I have known men armed with nothing but stone axes to overrun a Guard outpost in a sneak attack.'

Commissar Henderak nodded in judicious agreement. 'Either that, or the First Ixist had not enough faith in the Emperor!'

On hearing this, Princeps Gaerius looked askance at the commissar, disdain flitting across his face. The Adeptus Titanicus was an ancient order, predating the Ministorum which promulgated the Cult of the Emperor, and it was unique among the Imperium's fighting forces in coming under the Adeptus Mechanicus. Its officers mostly followed the Martian religion, worshipping the Emperor as the Machine God and Totality of All Knowledge. The icons on the bridge of Gaerius's Titan were quite different from the 'holy' images he saw here. Tek sigils and arcane formulae overlaid the Emperor's stern visage. In his eyes, Imperial Guard commissars, with their emotional ranting about faith, were little short of lunatics.

The look on Gaerius's face did not go unnoticed by Captain Karlache. Surreptitiously he studied the princeps. He was hook-nosed, a feature common among Titanicus officers – a consequence, no doubt, of the hereditary strain in the Adeptus. Privately, Karlache agreed with Colonel Costos that the mission was a trivial misuse of such extraordinary machines. He wondered if Gaerius and Efferim thought so too. Not that they would ever voice such an opinion. The discipline of Titan officers was legendary.

For the first time, Princeps Gaerius spoke, his voice dry and sardonic. 'There is little to go on, it seems. But no matter. We of the Adeptus, at any rate, have little to fear. Let us get down on-planet and bring this business to a speedy finish.'

LANDING A TITAN was not a simple matter. This was the time when the monstrous machines were most at risk. On the bridge of the Lex et Annihilato, Princeps Gaerius took the command seat. Beside him were his bridge officers: Tactical Officer Viridens, Weapons Moderati Knifesmith, and Chief Engineer Moriens. Down below, sweating with fear, huddled the Titan's five dozen ordinary crewmen. Command had been temporarily handed to the four-man landing-and-ascent crew of the transport pod, who now were seated before the command podium which in turn was hooked through to the pod's controls.

The conning plate currently showed the view outside the pod. Feet first, the Titan was lowering itself through Planet ABL 1034's atmosphere. In the distance, the pod carrying the Principio non Tactica with Princeps Efferim and his crew could be seen. Heated air flamed around it, turning the pod white-hot.

The Titans were to be the first to land. The Imperial Guard would arrive under their protection. Using consummate skill to keep the tall pod stable as it fell, the crew steered the Lex et Annihilato towards its designated landing place. Deceleration over, they soared over a landscape of mountains, valleys, and plains interspersed with dense forests. It appeared to be a fertile world, Princeps Gaerius thought. No wonder it had been colonised, long ago in the Dark Age of Technology. Now it would become more than just a strategic outpost. He could see it someday becoming a productive agricultural world, perhaps later even a forge world or a hive world. He leaned close to the conning plate with this thought in mind, imagining how the landscape would look in the future.

'What in the All-Knowing's Name is that?' The exclamation was torn from his throat. 'Steersman, take us back over that ridge!'

The pod officer glanced back at him nervously. 'That will be tricky, princeps.'

'Take us back, I say!'

Although technically Gaerius was not in command of the Titan at this moment, the pod officer dared not defy him. Instead, he muttered to the men on either side of him. Carefully, consulting continually with one another, they eased the pod back over to the other side of the ridge and hovered. Oaths now came involuntarily from the mouths of all Gaerius's officers.

Five huge hulks lay toppled on their sides in a broad fern-clad valley. They must have lain there for centuries, for they were rusting away, dissolving with age, riddled with holes and covered in lichen.

Had they been standing they would not have been as tall as the Warlord Titans, but they were broader, monstrous rotund shapes. Tactical Officer Viridens gasped out shocked words.

'Ork Gargants!'

It was indeed astonishing to see these mighty machines, the crude ork version of Titans, felled and abandoned on a primitive world. Gaerius looked thoughtfully on the scene. 'It seems the orks have also tried to take this world at some time in the past.'

'And they were defeated?' Weapons Moderati Knifesmith ground out. 'It's hardly credible!'

'Hardly defeated by the natives,' Gaerius told him confidently. 'Orks usually end up fighting among themselves. In any case, we have nothing to fear. Whenever a Titan has met a Gargant, the Titan has prevailed.'

Gargants were best described as caricatures of Titans. In place of power bundles, they were worked by clumsy, clanking beams and cogwheels. And they were steam-driven! In place of fission reactors, banks of furnaces were fed by teams of stokers!

But then, no one could build such superb machines as those of the Adeptus Titanicus. They were all thousands of years old, and even though continually repaired and renewed, they still retained the special occult qualities of the Dark Age of Technology. The Adeptus Mechanicus had tried to build brand-new Titans themselves, but the fruits of their efforts never performed nearly as well.

'Enough!' Gaerius said shortly. 'On, pilot.'

The great pod eased itself back over the ridge. Far in the distance, Gaerius saw what looked like a herd of animals, but there was no time now to magnify the image. The slow thunder of the landing engine faded as the pod was lowered gently onto a plain scattered about with overturned artillery, smashed tanks, and flattened drop shuttles. This was where the second expedition had met its grisly fate, and this was where the Imperium would now, finally, exert its will.

Planet ABL 1034 was a low-gravity planet, perfect for the operation of Titans, which originally had been designed for use on Mars. The huge pod opened up and trundled away over the moss. The Lex et Annihilato was revealed in all its prodigious glory, roughly the shape of a man and the height of a 12-storey building, bristling with armament. Half a mile away stood its match, the Principio non Tactica.

Princeps Gaerius smiled. Whenever he saw two Titans standing on the same landscape, twinned colossi, he felt an urge to engage in a duel, to have the machines striding towards one another with shoulder cannon blazing. He was sure that his colleague Princeps Efferim, on the bridge situated within the cranium of the Principio non Tactica, felt the same. It had never been his luck to engage with a Chaos Titan, possibly the only worthy opponent of the Adeptus. But one day…

The landing crew left the bridge. Chief Engineer Moriens left too, descending into the body of the Warlord to rally the cowering crewmen. Now the drop shuttles were coming in, Imperial Guard detachments piling out and setting up a perimeter around the watchful Titans. More shuttles landed and disgorged Basilisk artillery, Leman Russ tanks and Rhino armoured carriers.

For the third time, Planet ABL 1034 was claimed for the Imperium. For a while, the landing force would merely hold its ground, scanning the terrain from within the craniums of the Warlords, waiting to see if an attack would come. If it did not, the Titans would stride out to seek the Emperor's revenge.

GUARDSMAN LECHE and Colour Sergeant Hangist were the last two left in the prisoner cage. In his tattered uniform, Osmin Leche – smeared with mud and pale of face – stared from between the rough-hewn timbers at the stone-age village which sprawled all round him.

He had always thought of stone-age humans as shambling and brutish, a picture reinforced by the pre-landing morale lectures. But the people he saw striding among the fern-thatched huts were nothing like that. They were tall, muscled men, proud of bearing. They were gracious, equally proud women. They were agile, healthy children. It was he, Osmin Leche, who felt like a frightened primitive. By contrast, the natives, who should have cowered in fear and awe at contact with the Imperium, had shown no fear at all.

And no wonder. Far off, the guardsman could see one of the natives' battle beasts ambling across the horizon. It was like watching a mountain move, a mountain with a long neck carrying a huge head like a rock outcrop, and an impossibly long and massive tail. From where Leche cowered, the human beings which he knew swarmed over the beast were too small to be visible. He shuddered, remembering the attack which had killed most of his comrades.

Colour Sergeant Hangist squatted in a corner of the cage, his head in his hands. One thing was true about the stone age primitives, and that was their cruelty. There had been fifty captives in the cage to begin with. The villagers had been killing one per day, always by some different method. Their ingenuity seemed inexhaustible.

While the commissar had been alive, Leche had been able to keep his own spirits up to some extent. The commissar had exhorted them constantly to keep faith in the Emperor, and he had encouraged them to believe that rescue was possible. The villagers had seemed to be amused by his hectoring, though of course they could not understand it. They had kept him till nearly last. He had been killed the day before.

True, it had been inspiring to witness the commissar's grim fortitude as he was torn apart, limb by limb. Only at the very end did his torturers succeed in wringing cries of agony from him. But the spectacle had finally broken Colour Sergeant Hangist. And it had broken Guardsman Leche too.

Leche shivered. He trembled. The Imperium was far away. The Emperor was but a word.

He glanced again at the distant archaeosaur, to use the name given the beasts in the morale lectures. It had turned and was approaching the village.

Then a creaking sound from behind made him turn. The cage's gate was opening. Bronze-skinned stone-age men entered. They dragged out the whimpering, sobbing Emperor's Guardsmen to face their doom.

THERE WAS A PECULIARITY to Planet ABL 1034. Cloud formations were all of the same type, a series of evenly spaced ribs or striations high in the sky, stretching from horizon to horizon. No one in the expeditionary force asked himself what produced this phenomenon. That was a task for an adept, and to the military mind, planetary peculiarities were too numerous to be worth thinking about. But as the striped cloud cover raced across the sky, it broke up the light of the hard, white sun and produced a rippling effect on the ground below.

Princeps Gaerius found the rapidly shifting light and shade eerie but also restful. The expedition had not so far been challenged, and the officers were enjoying a meal in the open air. Artillery and tracked vehicles grumbled and clanked around them.

It was a traditional courtesy for a princeps to eat with Imperial Guard officers during a combined operation, though both Gaerius and Efferim would much have preferred to be with the rest of their bridge crews, supervising a meticulous checking of their Warlords. Commissar Henderak was consulting the Imperial Tarot. Reverently he unfolded the purple velvet cloth in which the deck was wrapped, pushed aside the remains of the meal and laid out three cards to form a triangle, tapping each in turn.

The surfaces of the cards glittered and swirled, flashing with colour. The card at the apex of the triangle was the Significator. It was the first to clear and form an image. The Emperor appeared, seated on a throne carved from a single gigantic diamond, glaring out at the beholder.

The card on the left was the next to stabilise. It showed Universal Force, a snake with its tail in its mouth, whirling endlessly against a background of receding galaxies. The final card cleared almost immediately after it to show The Galactic Realm, producing one of several images by which that card manifested itself. A maiden in a flowing gown stood on a landscape, star formations in the sky at her back, pouring multicoloured liquid from two large pitchers she held, one in each hand. The liquid flooded the landscape, carrying away cities and forests.

The commissar banged his fist on the table. 'The meaning is clear!' he intoned. 'Might will prevail!'

'Of course,' Princeps Efferim drawled, glancing casually at the triangle of images. 'What else could the cards show if they tell the truth?'

'Yes, what else?' Commissar Henderak said feverishly. 'Though the message contains an ambiguity. One must judge carefully, when interpreting the Emperor's Tarot. True, the presence of The Emperor as Significator confirms that the message relates to our current operation. But Universal Force does not necessarily refer to the forces of the Divine Emperor. Forces opposed to His Terribilitas could be implied. Also, the Galactic Realm...'

The commissar's eyes widened as he redirected his gaze back to the final card. The image was changing, the landscape writhing and rising up around the feet of the maiden, threatening to topple her.

'Imperator Divinitas!' he gasped in horror. 'We are undone!'

Gaerius's patience had reached its limit. With a grunt of disgust, he swept the cards from the table. 'Enough of your superstition, faith cultist,' he snarled. 'True holiness is the holiness of the machine. Suggest defeat for our Titans on a planet of animals, and you are ripe for reprocessing as a servitor!'

Commissar Henderak leapt to his feet, fury on his face. It was not that he heard the princeps's words as an insult to himself personally. He heard them as an insult to the Emperor. He made a sudden movement, as if reaching for his laspistol.

Colonel Costos was about to intervene, but excited shouting from the perimeter interrupted the exchange. A veteran sergeant ran up and saluted hastily.

'Native war-beasts advancing on the camp, colonel!'

Princeps Gaerius laughed, sounding like a drain emptying. 'Now you will see!'

'BRING THE TWO SLAVES forward!' The order was barked out by the clan hetman. He stood in the middle of the village compound, wavy blond hair flowing down his hard-muscled back, a stone axe thrust into his belt of woven fern leaves. Colour Sergeant Hangist and Guardsman Leche were flung at his feet, where they cringed like dogs, peering left and right.

'These are not warriors!' the hetman roared at the villagers who were gathered round him. 'These are slaves of the Giant Shining Men, the real warriors who have come again from the sky to do battle with us. That is why the gods gave us the Defenders: to help us fight the Giant Shining Warriors!'

Leche and Hangist could not, of course, understand a syllable of what the hetman was saying. All they understood by this time was that every second they remained alive and untortured was a miracle. At the same time, the knowledge that pain and death were coming closer second by second struck stark fear into their souls. Leche gibbered as he was once more wrenched to his feet. Hangist groaned with despair.

And then they saw them again. There were two of them, coming closer, pacing the plain one after the other, looming against the sky: archaeosaurs. They were like mottled grey and brown mountains with massive, reptilian heads on the end of long, sinuous necks, the weight balanced by enormous rippling tails as long as the bodies themselves.

This was the second time they had seen such monsters. The first time was when the beasts had destroyed the Imperial Guard camp. Leman Russ tanks had been unable to stop them. Basilisk artillery had been unable to stop them. They had trampled everything, moving surprisingly quickly on their eight sturdy legs, four on a side, thicker than any tree trunk. Guardsman Leche found it incredible, almost unimaginable, that there could be animals as huge as these.

Either one of the beasts could have trampled the village to dust by merely strolling through it, but instead they halted far outside its bounds, heads swaying. Despite their size, they looked placid enough for the moment. Leche knew that really massive animals would have to be plant-eaters, and there was no grass on this planet, only ferns and moss – endless fern forests and fern-covered plains. He could imagine the wide swathes the beasts would cut through such forests as they fed.

With whoops and shouts, the villagers dragged Leche and Hangist out of the village. Being sacrificed to the monsters would at least be quicker than the deaths suffered by many of his comrades, Leche thought. They came nearer, and now men could be seen crawling over the vast bodies as if on hillsides. The guardsman could also see house-like structures erected on their backs, and – what seemed most weird – one such structure atop each massive head.

The steadily flickering daylight of Planet ABL 1034 gave the scene an unreal, disjointed appearance. Now Guardsman Leche could see how the tribesmen climbed onto the huge beasts. Rope ladders hung down from their sides and trailed over the ground. Leche found himself at the foot of one. A tribesman mounted a rung, seized hold of Leche by one arm, and jerked him upward. Haplessly the young man was hauled up the ladder, soon forced to assist in the climb or fall a lethal distance to the ground below.

Leche saw Colour Sergeant Hangist being dragged towards the second archaeosaur. Once the guardsman passed the point where the ropes fell away from the beast's hide, he saw how easy it was to move about on top of the archaeosaur. The immensely thick and tough hide was corrugated. On the lower slopes of the animal-mountain, one could walk in these corrugations as though in a trough or trench. Scrambling over these, he and his captors came close to the gigantic spine, where the corrugations smoothed out somewhat and it was like making one's way on the top of a heaving hill.

Leche now realised that the beast's hide was in fact armoured. Up here it was like stepping on steel or adamantium. Tribesmen dotted the vast back. The hetman had made his way here already. He bellowed and gestured. Leche was propelled forward, towards the beast's head. Even facing certain death, Leche found time for a touch of pure curiosity about what was to happen. Certainly this was an unusual way to die, an adventure he would have enjoyed telling to his comrades of the First Ixist – if there had been any way he could have survived it.

The archaeosaur's neck, though long, was not all that lengthy as compared with the huge body. It had, after all, only to reach ground level in order to feed, so it was little longer than the eight comparatively stubby legs. Traversing it was like walking up a mountain trail. And there, set on top of the giant reptilian head, was a square hut or covered platform. It was open at the front and back, and three tribesmen squatted in it. Leche got an odd feeling. It was like looking at a primitive version of the bridge of some fearsome war machine!

Leche was pushed through the hut and out the other side. In passing, he saw what at first he took to be a dozen bony spines projecting from the top of the archaeosaur's skull, but then he realised that they were rudely shaped stone spikes hammered into the animal's head! Before he could wonder what these were for his fate was revealed to him. Forward of the hut, also mounted on the beast's head, not far behind the eyes, stood a timber X-shape. Guardsman Leche's captors fastened him to this, limbs spread, and left him there.

Leche could hear the beast's stertorous breathing. It sounded like nothing so much as the engine of a Leman Russ tank. Turning his head, he was soon able to see Colour Sergeant Hangist spread-eagled on an identical X-beam above the eyes of the second war-beast.

So here Guardsman Leche was: a mascot, an emblem, a figurehead, and perhaps a taunt to the enemy. The archaeosaurs were going into battle. Against another tribe? Or a third Imperial Guard expedition?

From behind him came banging, clinking noises. The Imperial Guard officers who had faced these war-beasts had been at a loss to know how the primitive tribesmen control-led them. Here was the answer, though Leche could not look around far enough to see it. The stone-age people had lived on Planet ABL 1034 for a long time, and they had learned much. The stone spikes had been driven through the archaeosaur's skull to precise points within the tiny brain. By banging the spikes with his stone hammer and making them vibrate, the mahout could stimulate nerve centres at will. One spike and the creature would advance. Another spike and it would retreat.

Others, and it would turn left, turn right, fly into a rage, and attack. Another, and it would spew fire!

The hetman barked an order. The squatting mahout banged one spike, then another. The two archaeosaurs lumbered off, away from the village.

Towards the Giant Shining Warriors.

'HERE THEY COME,' said Princeps Gaerius. 'Ready to move out!' The bridge crewmen of the Lex et Annihilato took up their positions, pulling down the control sets to link with the metal sockets set into their skulls.

As commander, only Gaerius himself was free of such an interface. Chief Engineer Moriens was most encumbered. His head almost disappeared amid a nest of pipes, tubes and leads. It was his responsibility to keep contact with the whole internal machinery of the Warlord, to supervise its running crew, and to keep everything functioning whatever the damage. Tactical Officer Viridens would actually guide the giant battle machine, moving it like his own body at Gaerius's orders, with a direct neural connection to the power bundles.

The chief engineer was also effectively blind, seeing nothing outside. Gaerius, Moriens and Weapons Moderati Knifesmith had access to the conning holos. Gaerius looked to the right, where the companion Warlord Principio non Tactica stood, also gearing itself up to move.

The Lex et Annihilato roared. Warlord Titans had the imprinted mental nature of the grizzly bear, a powerful bad-tempered animal native to Terra, and this sometimes made them difficult to handle. The Principio non Tactica also roared. At a word from Gaerius, they each took a gigantic step forward, carefully treading in the spaces cleared for them. A few steps more, and they were outside the camp and striding towards the horizon.

'There are only two of them,' Gaerius murmured. 'I had expected more.'

At first it was difficult to estimate the size of the archaeosaurs as they loped onward. It was the speed of their approach, perhaps, that made them seem not as large as they really were. Moving with a shuffling motion on their eight sturdy legs, they appeared to Gaerius's eye scarcely larger than Terran dinosaurs. He relaxed. This should take no more than moments, after which the natives were unlikely to have any stomach for further action.

Gaerius, as Acting Group Commander, outranked Efferim for the duration of the engagement. He spoke briefly into his communicator, issuing orders to his fellow princeps. Fibre bundles humming like swarms of angry hornets, leg shanks clanging, the twin Titans strode out towards their primitive challengers.

And then Gaerius caught his breath in surprise. The brief blurred transmission from the destroyed second expedition had not prepared him for what he now saw. The archaeosaurs were enormous – bigger than he would have believed remotely possible for any land animal, even taking the low gravity into account. The monster's head, when raised, reared even higher than the Warlord's!

That was not the only comparison between the two. Behind the Titans, using them for protection like mice scurrying behind a man, came the Imperial Guard force: tanks, mobile artillery, and infantry. It was the same on the other side. A ragged column of at least a thousand nearly naked primitives, armed with spears and stone axes, trailed behind the archaeosaur, ready to take on whatever their battle-beasts left alive.

How did the creatures stand up? Their bones must be made of steel, he thought with incredulity– or adamantium. Still, they could not conceivably withstand the Titans' armament. He barked orders again. The Warlords angled out to approach the archaeosaurs from their flanks and get an easier target, then their huge legs pumped faster, propelling them almost at a run.

By now, Tactical Officer and Weapons Moderati had almost become a single personality, joined by the grizzly-bear-essence imprinted on the Lex et Annihilato. The shoulder cannon swivelled, aimed at the flank of one of the impossibly huge beasts, and opened up. A shattering noise echoed through the cranium of the Titan as a volley of shells went hurtling towards the defenceless target.

Disbelievingly, Princeps Gaerius watched as the entire volley bounced off the beast's armoured back. Some exploded in mid-air; others flew away and fell to the ground. The archaeosaur, however, seemed unhurt by the explosions. It lumbered around to face the Titan with its smouldering, yellow eyes. Now Gaerius saw that what he had taken to be a fringe or crest on the creature's skull was actually an artificial structure in the form of a covered platform, and within it squatted men. Did these men manage to control the animal? If so, how?

But there was something else. Set in front of the platform an X-beam had been erected. To this – uniform torn and ragged, face covered in dirt – was bound a guardsman.

Up to now, Gaerius's feelings for the enemy – whom he had scarcely considered an enemy, so inferior were they – had been neutral. Now his heart filled with hatred.

'Poor wretch,' he muttered to himself. There was no way he could help the prisoner, who was sure to die along with the archaeosaur. He put him from his mind.

He doubted that Weapon Moderati Knifesmith's aim was good enough to hit the swaying head. 'Aim lower!' he ordered. 'The belly will have less armour!'

Again the shoulder cannon roared their ferocious violence. This time, several shells struck home, creating a brief smoke screen. When it cleared, Gaerius expected to see the smashed carcass of the archaeosaur lying on its side, twitching. He gaped with renewed astonishment to see the monster still standing. True, some of the shells had penetrated the hide and left deep gaping wounds. Yet the archaeosaur was unshaken. It was as if it did not even feel the torn flesh and flowing blood.

And it was still on the move, turning to face the Titan. Gaerius was about to order another volley, but first he glanced towards the Principio non Tactica and momentarily froze. The second archaeosaur, also dripping blood from a cannon volley, was charging towards the Warlord at a run. Suddenly its jaws gaped open, and from between its rows of teeth came a white-hot gout of fire which enveloped the upper part of the Principio.

To the astounded princeps, it looked just like a plasma weapon – something with which he had not thought to equip the Warlords. Who would have thought to need it on a world like this? He did not know of the archaeosaurs' prodigious digestive system with its twenty-three stomachs, building up acetylene gas at high pressure, or of the unusual metabolism which mixed pure phosphorus into that acetylene. When the archaeosaur belched, which it did when angry or when made to do so by a bang on the appropriate stone spike, the acetylene was squirted out and ignited by the phosphorus on contact with the air. Evolution had devised the phenomenon as a defence against predators. It was even more effective as a weapon.

The Principio's bridge must have been completely blinded during the discharge, though the void shields would have protected the crew from the heat. But there was a second tactic to the archaeosaur's attack. It reared up on its four hind legs. It now towered over the Warlord. When Princeps Efferim's view cleared, he saw the vast beast come crashing down on his landwar machine in an attempt to topple it.

'Assist Principio!' Gaerius shouted. 'All weapons!'

The Lex et Annihilato swivelled. Moderati Knifesmith let loose with both shoulder cannon and the belly lasgun. The Principio staggered back, its own belly lasgun also opening up, trying desperately to keep its footing against the monstrous weight of the angry beast. It probably would have succeeded, but the archaeosaur had yet another trick. It turned aside. The vast tail came swinging round and crashed into the body of the Titan, where the power source and main engines were located. The carapace buckled.

Now a red steam obscured the view as Principio's two heavy lasguns bit into the beast and vaporised huge amounts of its blood. Through Gaerius's communicator came a faint voice – that of Efferim's chief engineer

'Void shields down.'

Then, with utter horror, Princeps Gaerius saw the Principio non Tactica fall, first losing its balance, unable to correct the momentum imparted by the archaeosaur's tail, then one foot lifting off the ground, then the huge structure descending with slow majesty in the low gravity, until it smashed into the hard earth.

Once a Titan was toppled, there was virtually no chance of it getting to its feet again. Princeps Gaerius shrieked orders, turning his attention back to the archaeosaur threatening the Annihilato.

'The head! Aim for the head!'

Alert to the fate that had overtaken the sister Titan, Viridens backed away, jinking aside to prevent the creature mounting a similar assault, even though it was clear by now that the archaeosaurs were more agile than their bulk gave them any right to be. Shoulder cannon barked, and both missed the waving head as it turned on its sinuous neck to follow the Warlord.

Gaerius was dimly aware of the other archaeosaur trampling the fallen Principio non Tactica, rending and splitting the defenceless carapace. Briefly the lasgun hissed out again, but it was unable to target the beast.

Then Gaerius glimpsed a final indignity. Men were spilling out of the cracks in the casing like maggots from a festering body. And he could see what they were fleeing from: a blinding-white, ravening glow in the interior. The Warlord's fission reactor was in meltdown, its fuel elements fused together by the force of the archaeosaur's trampling.

Now Gaerius knew what had happened to the Gargants. And now, its business finished, the second archaeosaur was coming to join its brother. It was frightening how the mountain of an animal was still able to move with great chunks torn out of it by four repeat shoulder cannon and two heavy lasguns. It seemed the monsters were unstoppable. The bones of the beast were even exposed, a lustrous grey in colour. Gaerius could well believe they were made of iron or even steel.

'Aim right, Moderati! Aim right! Look out for the tail!'

The warning came too late. The tail lashed out swifter than the eye could follow and struck the Titan on one knee. The Warlord juddered. A muffled battle report came from Chief Engineer Moriens.

'Left leg disabled.'

Despite himself terror struck into Princeps Gaerius's soul. His Titan had lost mobility. And two archaeosaurs were bent on toppling and trampling it.

'The brain!' he insisted. 'You must go for the brain!'

Weapons Moderati Knifesmith did not need urging. He was still trying to target the head on which Guardsman Leche was strapped like a sacrificial victim. It was easier as the beast came closer. With a feeling of desperation he watched shell after shell bounce off the giant skull. Was there any brain in it? Was it pure metal-laden bone through and through?

Tactical Officer Viridens shifted the Warlord's good leg, attempting as best he could to brace the Titan against the strain that was to come. Both archaeosaurs spewed streams of burning phosphorus-acetylene, temporarily blinding the bridge crew. When the white-hot fumes cleared they faced the dreadful sight of two battle-beasts rearing on their hind legs, blotting out the sky.

Moderati Knifesmith realised that everything now depended on him, and that it would all be over in the next few seconds. In an act of intense concentration, he divided his firepower. He aimed one shoulder cannon up at the lower jaw of the first archaeosaur. At the same time, he levelled the belly lasgun and the other shoulder cannon together at the same target: one of the deep wounds in the second, grievously injured animal.

The hiss and racket of the weapons was brief. A single shell passed through the archaeosaur's jaw and entered the skull to explode within it and blast it to pieces. Meantime both cannon shells and laser beam ate their way deep into the innards of the other beast, inflicting explosion after explosion at the centre of the massive body. The enormous spine shattered. Both beasts fell, one soundlessly, one with mangled roars, to lie writhing in its death throes.

Luckily neither had fallen against the Warlord. Princeps Gaerius breathed a sigh.

'Well done, Knifesmith!' He turned to the Chief Engineer. 'Moriens, effect repairs immediately.'

Muffled by the mask-like neural interface, Moriens replied. 'Yes, princeps.'

Imperial Guard units were already attacking the fleeing tribesmen, causing terrible carnage Guardsman Osmin Leche, having fainted with terror, had died without feeling anything. And no one had heard the death-scream of Colour Sergeant Hangist as he was carried falling to the ground.

THE FIRES IN the village burned low that night. Women keened for their lost men, children cried for their fathers and brothers. The new hetman spoke gravely.

'We have acted with honour,' he said. 'We sent only two Defenders to fight two Giant Shining Warriors. Now here is only one other course of action. We must use the whole herd.'

'But that is dishonour!' protested a young warrior, one of the few to survive.

'When we fight another tribe, then there is honour,' the hetman pronounced. 'Beast is pitted against beast. The vanquished grants the victor tribute of grazing, tools and women, and offers battle the following year. Here there is no honour. The Giant Shining Warriors from the sky have come to take our world. They must know they cannot.'

The men pondered his words, and could find no fault with them.

THE FLICKERING DAWN had come, and repairs to the Lex et Annihilato were complete, when the herd came loping over the horizon. Princeps Gaerius stared aghast. He had assumed from yesterday's battle that the archaeosaurs were rare. Yet here were a hundred animals at least. And they were running straight for the Imperial Guard camp.

He looked stony-faced at Knifesmith, Viridens and Moriens. Stricken, they glared back at him.

Using the conning magnifier, he saw that the onrushing animals were bare of artificial structures. They were not under anyone's direct control – except for four or five 'managed' beasts at the back, and these were driving the others on. The herd was being stampeded.

There was nothing for it but to go down fighting. No officer trained by the Collegio Titanicus would do anything else. Gaerius clenched his fists. 'Battle stations!'

His order went unquestioned. All three bridge officers pulled down their interfaces. Klaxons sounded in the body of the Titan. The ground was shaking. An enormous pounding, as though the planet was breaking up, could be heard even here in the bridge.

The Warlord strode out to its doom, lasgun zipping, shoulder cannon roaring until all magazines were empty. Not a single archaeosaur was downed, but the lasgun, powered by the fission reactor, kept firing until it was destroyed. When the Warlord was caught in the onrush, the press of the creature's steely flesh was so hard that it could not even fall but was instead ground between numerous immense bodies. By the time the herd had passed, the Lex et Annihilato was smashed to fragments. Only the cranium was still intact.

TWENTY LIGHT YEARS distant, the destruction of the third expedition to Planet ABL 1034 was evaluated almost immediately. A visual account of the initial battle, in which one Titan was destroyed, had been retrieved. In the final hour, Colonel Costos of the Fifth Helvetian, showing great bravery, had managed to send a shaky record of the final dreadful events.

The commission was broad-ranging. Imperial Guard Tactical

Staff officers accompanied by the obligatory commissar, Collegio Titanicus staff officers, and a priest of the Adeptus Terra, sat round a varnished teak table. They had watched the visual records, including the bridge logs from the Lex et Annihilato and the Principio non Tactica. All had been shocked to see what a people who did not even know how to smelt metal could do.

'The planet cannot be abandoned,' the Adeptus Terra dignitary pronounced. 'It must be occupied, even if only to deny it to others. What are the options?'

The Collegio Titanicus officer spoke sadly. 'We should not send more of our Titans against those monsters. We cannot afford such losses.'

The commissar, present as a representative of the Ministorum, stirred. 'The Cult of the Emperor has succeeded in worse places. We can take the long approach. Infiltrate trained missionaries into the local culture. Given time, they will create a religion favourable to the Imperium. We can then move in and take over a friendly population.'

'No! We cannot risk it!'

The cry had come from the Collegio Titanicus officer. His face was pained. 'Don't you see? The archaeosaurs are a direct danger to us! Our Dark Age Titans constantly decrease in number, even though slowly. None that are vanquished can be replaced. But these archaeosaurs are animals! They breed! If they get loose into the galaxy, they can be bred without limit! What if the orks get hold of them?'

It must have been hard for a senior officer of the Adeptus Titanicus to speak so. His voice was anguished. 'With respect, the commissar's plan will take too long to execute. Meantime, there is always the risk of an alien race – such as the orks – stepping in, learning from the natives, and eventually deploying these beasts against us!'

'We could do the same,' the commissar pointed out smoothly.

The suggestion that archaeosaurs might supplant the Adeptus Titanicus plainly horrified the Collegio officer. He shook his head vigorously. 'It is far too dangerous. There is only one real option. Exterminatus!'

'That will deny us the use of the planet, too, for centuries to come,' the commissar said. 'I advocate the gentler course.'

They pondered. And then a shivering stillness seemed to come upon them. It was as though a ghostly presence had passed through the assembly. Several of those present looked up, softly murmuring the same word.

'Exterminatus.'

TIGHTLY BOUND to an X-beam far above the ground, on the swaying head of a giant beast, Princeps Gaerius raged with shame and frustration. Colonel Costos had been right. Primitive peoples were not stupid. They were bright. How, by the Emperor, had they ever learned to bend the archaeosaurs to their will? Could the Adeptus Mechanicus have done any better? Could it have done as well?

Gaerius was forced to admit the natives' cleverness and courage. But they had destroyed his beloved Annihilato! They had humiliated the Adeptus Titanicus! For that, only hatred!

A quarter of a mile to his right, Weapons Moderati Knifesmith swayed atop a second battle beast. Tactical Officer Viridens was on a third beast to his left. Chief Engineer Moriens was luckier. He had not survived the final fall of the Lex et Annihilato's cranium.

Gaerius raised his face to the sky and cried out with all his soul, as though he could cast his cry through the warp.

'Exterminatus!' he pleaded. '*Exterminatus!*'

KNOW THINE ENEMY
Gav Thorpe

THE MASSIVE, slab-sided fuselage of the Thunderhawk gunship shook and rattled as it plunged through the upper atmosphere of the planet Slato. The roaring of its massive jets and the rumbling of the air against the armoured hull filled the interior with a deafening cacophony. The air glowed around the falling gunship as the armoured beak of its cockpit and the leading edge of its stubby wings glowed white-hot with the friction of its entry from orbit.

Brother Ramesis, chaplain of the 4th Company of the Salamanders Space Marine Chapter, felt the craft hit an area of low pressure and drop several hundred feet in a couple of seconds, pushing him up into the harness which secured him to the inner side of the gunship's fuselage. As the Thunderhawk plummeted deeper into the thick cloud of Slato's skies the passage became smoother, and half a minute later the pilot activated the standby lights. The padded restraints arched up into the wall above Ramesis's head with a hiss of hydraulics and he stretched his arms, the servos within his powered armour whirring quietly as they matched the movement. He felt pressure on his back as the Thunderhawk's machinery implanted his backpack into the socket along his armour's spine, then dropped the ablative shoulder pads down on either side of his head. Now fully armoured, Ramesis stood up and walked steadily along the decking of the Thunderhawk, passing his gaze over the twenty-six assembled Space Marines. Each was conducting their own pre-battle rituals: checking weapons, comms or armour one last time, wishing each other the Emperor's benevolence or just praying quietly.

Ramesis activated a rune set into a bulkhead and the door to the small chapel-room slid out of sight. Stepping inside, the chaplain lit an ornate brazier in the middle of the altar and then knelt on one knee before it, bringing his clenched fists to his forehead in a sign of worship. Standing, he took his rosarius, the Shield of the Emperor, from the reliquary to the left of the altar. Kneeling again, he cupped the great arcane device in both hands, running his fingers around its circular edge, seeing his face mirrored in the twelve gems set in concentric circles on its black enamelled surface.

'Beneficent Emperor, who rules the stars and guideth mankind,' Ramesis chanted as his thumbs gently pressed the jewels on the rosarius in the ritual pattern, 'Cast thy divine protection over me, your eternal servant. Though I gladly shed my blood in your honour, keep me from ignoble death so that I might continue to serve thy greatness. I live that I might serve thee. As I serve thee in life, may I serve thee in death.'

As he completed his ritual, the rosarius hummed into life. Ramesis could feel the Emperor's protective aura pulsing from its depths and it gladdened his soul. Hanging the rosarius's heavy chain around his neck, Ramesis stood and turned to the reliquary to the right. From within the intricately carved wooden box, fashioned by his own hand during his time as a Chaplain Novitiate, Ramesis took out his crozius arcanum, grasping its two-foot haft tightly in both gauntleted hands. Again Ramesis knelt before the altar clutching the crozius to his chest, its eagle-shaped head resting against the similar eagle blazon embossed on the armoured plastron across his chest.

'Beneficent Emperor, who ruleth the stars and guideth mankind. Guideth my hand that I might smite thine enemies. Invest this weapon with thine anger. Let mine arm be the instrument of thy divine wrath. As you keep me in life, let me bring death to thine enemies.'

With the invocation complete, Ramesis slid the firing stud in the haft of the crozius into its forward, active position. With a simple press of his finger, the eagle of the crozius would be surrounded by a shimmering disruption field, capable of smashing bone and shattering the thickest armour. Truly, the ways of the Machine God are miraculous, Ramesis thought.

As the final part of the Consecration to Battle, Ramesis hung his crozius from his belt and took his golden, skull-faced helm from its position in front of the flickering brazier.

'Beneficent Emperor, who rules the stars and guideth Mankind. Let mine eyes look upon your magnificence. Let mine eyes see truly all things fair and foul. Let mine eyes tell friend from foe that I might know thine enemy.' Ramesis placed the helm over his head, twisting it slightly so that the vacuum seals clamped into place. He turned a dial on his left wrist and the helmet pressurised with the rest of the power armoured suit.

'Tactical display,' the chaplain commanded his armour, and his vision was filled with an enhanced image of the outside: details of temperature, atmospheric pressure, light density and other factors were superimposed over his sight. As he rolled his head left and right to check the suit's calibration, Ramesis swiftly completed the other pre-battle procedures, double-checking the suit's power and exhaust assembly, the internal environment monitors, targeting crosshairs and myriad other systems that would keep him alive in the midst of battle, even in the depths of space.

The comm-speaker inside Ramesis's helmet chimed and the pilot informed him they were soon to land.

Ramesis strode out into the main chamber, where the other Space Marines of his force waited for him, their quietly sincere conversations showing they were eager for battle too. At his approach, though, they fell silent.

'Today we are joined by Brother Xavier, who has proved himself worthy enough to move on from his initiation.' The Space Marines raised their fists in praise of the newcomer, who bowed his head in thanks.

'Brother Xavier has served in Tenth Company for twenty-five years, and many are his battle honours,' Ramesis informed them. 'I am pleased to welcome him to our company and this, his first conflict as a full battle-brother, is indeed an hon-

ourable and auspicious one. We have come to this world to fulfil our duty as the protectors of mankind., There is no mission
more sacred or righteous in its cause.

'Several weeks ago an expedition from the newly founded
colony on this world discovered something ancient and terrible. Their explorers found an alien device, a thing of great evil
– for it has been placed here by the eldar.'

The Salamanders hissed and snarled in anger, for their
Chapter had a long history of fighting eldar pirates. Their home
planet of Nocturne had been plagued by the alien corsairs for
millennia before the Emperor had arrived to bring them salva-
tion. Ramesis himself had fought against the eldar on
numerous occasions and was unreserved in his loathing of the
capricious aliens.

'We have been told by the worshippers of the Machine God
that this device is a gateway, a portal to the Immaterium,' the
chaplain continued solemnly. 'Soldiers from the colony's garrison were despatched to guard this portal while it is
investigated, to ensure that the eldar did not attempt to use this
gateway to attack Slato. However, they are few and our divine
claim to this world, as well as the lives of two hundred thousand colonists, requires that we aid them. We have learned in
the last few hours that the eldar have indeed attacked Slato.
Even as we descend, their warriors are assaulting the Emperor's
servants at the portal. Our augurs and surveyors tell us that they
are relatively few in number at present, but if they gain access
to their gateway then they will be able to bring on untold numbers of reinforcements. If that happens, our fight to protect this
world will be all that much harder.'

Ramesis allowed a moment for his battle-brothers to digest
this news. He was glad to be facing the eldar again, for the
deaths of many of his ancestors stained their hands and he
looked forward to every opportunity to repay the blood-debt.

'Let us pray!' Ramesis commanded the assembled Space
Marines. They turned to face him and bowed their heads in
acquiescence. As Ramesis spoke he walked along the two lines
of warriors, touching each on the chest with the palm of his
hand, passing on the blessing of the Emperor and their
Primarch.

'May the Emperor look kindly on our endeavours today,' he
chanted. 'May his eternal spirit steer us ever on the path of

light. May revered Vulkan, Primarch of our Chapter, watch over us. May we have the strength and wisdom that we will not fail them in honour and duty. Praise the Emperor!'

'Praise the Emperor!' the Space Marines replied in a deep chorus. At that moment a siren sounded twice and the pilot's voice sounded over the comm-net.

'Alien interceptors on an attack approach,' the pilot said hastily. 'Assume battle positions.'

The Space Marines each stepped back into the small alcove which served as their resting place during transportation, grabbing hold of the brass grip rails to steady themselves. Hurriedly Ramesis ducked back into the chapel to extinguish the sacred brazier before taking his own position. The Thunderhawk banked sharply to starboard for a moment, the artificial muscles within Ramesis's armour easily compensating for the movement. The gunship continued to zigzag sluggishly to evade the eldar fighters, before a sudden screech rent the air and a bolt of energy smashed against the armoured fuselage. The blast was mirrored inside the hull in a spray of violet energy, and Brother Lysonis was hurled to the decking. Ramesis took a step forward to aid the veteran-sergeant, but his comrade held up a hand to indicate he was well, before slowly standing up. Sparks of energy crackled around a gash in his abdominal armour, but there was no blood. The blast had just inflicted a glancing hit on the Space Marine. As Lysonis reclaimed his place in one of the unoccupied alcoves, the gunship's reeling interior echoed with the sound of more energy bolts hitting the hull. Another fusillade was followed by the thump of a detonation, sending the gunship falling to one side.

'We've lost two engines,' the pilot informed them in a calm voice. 'Prepare for emergency landing!'

Ramesis felt his weight lightening as the Thunderhawk pushed forward into a steep dive, rushing down towards Slato's surface. For perhaps half a minute the rapid descent continued until the pilot fired the retro-jets, all but stopping the gunship dead in mid-air. The sudden increase in g-forces would have crushed a normal man, but Ramesis hardly even noticed, protected by the strength of his genetically modified physique and further enhanced by his ancient suit of power armour. With a skidding impact the Thunderhawk hit the ground a moment later, sliding to the right for several seconds before coming to a halt. Within a heartbeat the assault ramp had been lowered and Ramesis was charging out, the rest of his force pounding down the ramp behind him.

'THIS IS Brother-Captain Nubean. We have made landfall in the high ground, at position secundus-deca as intended. Ramesis, lead your force to point secundus-octus; I will converge on your position from the other side.' Even carried across several miles by the comm-net, Nubean's voice was as clear to Ramesis as if he were next to him. The chaplain signalled an affirmative and then switched frequencies to address the Space Marines under his own command.

'Advance by squads, pattern Enflamus. Squads Delphus and Lysonis will lead; squad Malesti will form rear guard,' Ramesis ordered in a clipped, precise tone. The three sergeants signalled confirmation and the two lead squads set off at a trot, the long strides of their power armoured legs covering the ground quickly. Ramesis fell in with Veteran Sergeant Malesti, whom he had known since he was first inducted into the Chapter. They had fought together as scouts in the Tenth Company and though Ramesis had advanced more rapidly in the Chapter's hierarchy, they still shared a special friendship. As they ran along, Ramesis modified the comm-net controller on his wrist so that he could talk with Malesti alone.

'eldar again, my brother. We will have to be vigilant.' Though Ramesis's words seemed grim, he was in a light mood. It had been several weeks since he had been in battle and had looked forward with anticipation to fighting once more against the Emperor's enemies.

'We have defeated the eldar before,' Malesti replied. 'We know their guile. Their arcane trickeries and sorceries will not avail them against us this time.'

'I share your confidence, brother,' Ramesis said. 'Captain Nubean is a strong commander. The honour of the Fourth Company prospers under his guidance.'

'And yours!' Malesti added with a chuckle. 'In the years you have been our chaplain, our battle-brothers' faith has been sure and steady. They conduct themselves with honour and respect, and do all that we ask of them and more. They do not fail in their duties as warriors of the Adeptus Astartes and they shall not fail us this day either.'

'They'll fight like steppe-lions, of that I'm sure!' Ramesis remarked.

They continued in silence for a while, jogging easily through the waist-high grasses of the plain, turned into a blaze of gold by Slato's setting star. A few miles to the north ahead of them, the plains rose quickly into the foothills that eventually became a sharp mountain range. In every other direction stretched leagues of cereal plants, heavy with grain. The majority of Slato's landmass was given over to farming. Food grown here would feed the workers on mining worlds and industrial hive planets. Without such agri-worlds, the Imperium's labour forces would starve and the eternal manufacturing of arms and armour would cease, spelling the end for mankind's presence in the sector. It was paramount that Slato did not fall into the hands of the eldar.

IN THE LAST rays of the alien sun, Ramesis's force was continuing its forced march, making their way swiftly along one of the mountain valleys. But for the last few minutes, the sound of cannonfire had been echoing off the valley's steep sides.

'It appears the eldar are engaged in another attack,' Malesti was speculating. 'Landing behind the accursed aliens' position may prove to be an advantage: we can catch them between our guns and those of the guardsmen at the portal. The Emperor has blessed us.'

'Beware of over-confidence, my brother,' Ramesis warned. 'The eldar are as slippery as a lava serpent and twice as venomous. They may have left a rearguard to protect them from such an attack.'

'True,' Malesti said. 'That is why we have come with two separate forces, so that if one were delayed the other may still fight through. With the Emperor's blessing…' Malesti's voice trailed away. His attention had become fixed on something ahead. Ramesis followed his gaze and saw that the two squads leading the march had halted. He was about to signal Sergeant Lysonis when the comm-net chimed in his ear.

'Chaplain Ramesis, this is Sergeant Lysonis. The valley ahead is filled with woodland, a possible ambush site. Request orders.'

'I'll be at your position shortly. Stay alert,' Ramesis commanded.

A minute had passed before Ramesis and Squad Malesti reached the other Space Marines where they were half-hidden in the long grass and rocks of the valley floor. The woodland ahead nestled firmly in the base of the valley which they had been following, stretching up the mountain slopes to either side. It was impossible to tell how far along the valley the woods continued, but Ramesis did not even consider the option of circumnavigating it. To do so would cost valuable time and still offered no surety that they would reach the site of the gateway unhindered. Ramesis peered at the small forest, trying to discern any activity in the shadowy depths between the thin, tightly clustered boles of the trees.

'Sergeant Lysonis, activate your auspex. See if you can detect anything within those woods.' Ramesis's order was quiet but authoritative.

'We risk the eldar detecting the signal, chaplain. They may not know we are here yet.' Lysonis cautioned.

'Rest assured, sergeant,' Ramesis informed him, 'The eldar are very aware of our presence. Even if their machines did not locate us, their mind-magic will undoubtedly have detected our presence by now.'

The sergeant's head was bowed as he unhooked the auspex from his utility belt and adjusted the dials. As he held it in one hand, passing it left and right in the direction of the woods, its screen threw a flickering green glow onto the black paint of his armour, harshly lighting the helmet from underneath, so that he almost looked like some daemon from the pits of Chaos. Lysonis adjusted one of the many brass dials set next to the display, then tapped a switch into a different position.

'There are definitely human-sized life signals within the woods, chaplain, possibly a dozen or more,' Lysonis reported, replacing the arcane device on his belt and pulling his power sword from its scabbard.

Ramesis looked at the trees once more, seeking any sign of movement or life. There were none. After glancing at the chronometer reading on his visual display, the chaplain made a decision.

'We do not have time to circumnavigate the woods. Prepare for attack. May the Emperor guide our weapons.' As he spoke, Ramesis strode to the front of the gathered Space Marines.

'For the Emperor and Vulkan!' Ramesis cried as he sprinted forward, the actuators of his armour turning every step into a bounding leap across the plain. Around him the Salamanders charged forward too, echoing his battle cry. The air was filled by a soft whistling noise and Ramesis noticed tiny slivers of crystal starting to patter off the armour of the Space Marines around him. Looking into the woods once again, half-seen shadows of movement caught Ramesis's attention as another volley of fire swept into the Space Marines. Behind him Ramesis heard a startled cry. He looked back over his shoulder to see what had happened. One of the Space Marines of Squad Delphus, Brother Lastus, was clutching at his helmet with one hand. Another member of the squad turned on his heel to grab Lastus's arm and haul him forwards. As the chaplain looked on, the toxins contained within the crystal sliver were already seeping into Lastus's bloodstream. The Space Marine gave a choked cry and his body began to shudder. The power armour amplified the shivering Space Marine's movements into flailing paroxysms as Lastus dropped his boltgun and fell to one knee.

'Sniper's needle hit Brother Lastus in the eye-plate,' Sergeant Delphus reported over the comm-link.

'Bring him with us!' Ramesis ordered as he turned his attention back to the woods. The first of the Space Marines were fifty paces from the trees now. Squad Lysonis stopped their advance and as one they raised their bolters and let loose a salvo of fire. Explosive bolts tore through the woodland, smashing swathes of shredded leaf and bark into the air, shattering branches and punching gaping holes into the boles of the trees. Ramesis heard a high-pitched cry and a figure staggered forward from the shadows, a hand raised to its shoulder where bright red blood was spilling down the ever-shifting camouflage colours of its cape. It was tall and swathed in a long coat that shifted colour to match the shades of the trees and grass. Ramesis aimed his pistol, the crosshair imposed over his vision fixing on the eldar's hooded face. He could see its thin, pointed nose, the delicate features of its high cheeks and brow, and a pair of large eyes glittering with alien intelligence. The chaplain squeezed softly on the trigger and a moment later the eldar's skull exploded, the headless body flung forward several yards by the bolt's detonation.

As he reached the treeline, Ramesis found three more alien bodies. The first had two massive holes blown in its chest, another's leg was ripped off at the hip while the third had been turned into an almost unidentifiable crimson mess by several simultaneous bolter hits. Looking back across the grasslands, Ramesis saw Lastus being carried between two of his battle-brothers who were firing their bolters with their free hands. The wounded Marine was still twitching as his system tried to clear away the alien poisons. The armour of another Space Marine lay close by, sprawled in the grass like a casually discarded doll. The chaplain could see a neat hole in the flexible armour of the warrior's left hip joint where the needle shot had entered. The shot must have hit a major artery for it to have killed the bio-enhanced Space Marine so quickly.

'May thy soul be forever in the light of the Emperor. By His grace he has taken you into his embrace. Serve Him as well in death as your sacrifice served Him in life,' intoned Ramesis, whilst inwardly cursing his force's lack of an apothecary. He could not afford for one of his warriors to carry the dead Space Marine's body and by the time the apothecary from Captain Nubean's formation could arrive, the fallen fighter's gene-seed would be useless. And every gene-seed not recovered was lost forever, weakening the Chapter.

Glancing around, Ramesis saw that all of the remaining men had reached the shelter of the trees. Of the eldar there was no sign. For the next few minutes the dim light was occasionally broken by the orange glow cast by the jets of fire from Squad Delphus's flamer as the Space Marines methodically swept through the trees for any surviving eldar. Ramesis sent Squad Malesti ahead to ascertain whether the route to the rendezvous with Captain Nubean was clear, then sought out Brother Lastus.

The chaplain found him crouched with his back against the trunk of a tree, thumbing bolts from a pouch at his belt into a boltgun magazine. Beside him was his helmet, with the left eyepiece cracked. Blood was dried across the left side of Lastus's face, a reddish stain against his dark skin, and his left eye had been stitched shut. The rest of his face was marked by the scars of the Salamanders' ritual branding. Three dragon-heads were scorched into his forehead, each representing a commendation from the company captain, whilst several lines were scarred along his nose and chin, each scar burnt forever as recognition for a particularly noteworthy kill. As Ramesis approached, Lastus looked up.

'I'd swear that devil-spawned eldar had been aiming for Brother Nitrus next to me. No accuracy, these aliens!' the Space Marine joked.

'How are you faring, brother?' Ramesis asked, crouching next to Lastus and removing his own helmet.

'I can fight on,' Lastus declared with a wide grin that curled the lines of his scars into ragged swirls. 'The toxin is still affecting my hearing and smell, but my vision is almost clear. Well, through this one, anyway.' He stuck a thumb towards his good eye.

'And how is your aim, Brother Lastus?' Ramesis asked. He needed to know how much he could rely upon his battle-brother in a firefight.

'Still true, lord,' Lastus assured him. The Space Marine gestured towards his helmet. 'That's an old Mark VI Regis pattern. It can compensate for the loss of one eye by boosting another signal through the remaining optical link. I won't even realise I'm handicapped. It fits a bit tightly – I almost asked for a different helmet when the armour was given to me – but praise the Emperor I persevered with it.'

Ramesis stood up and told Lastus to report back to Sergeant Delphus. With a salute the battle-brother fixed his helmet back on and strode off towards the other Space Marines.

Sergeant Malesti strode up to Ramesis and reported that the firesweep was complete; no other eldar had been discovered.

'Understood,' Ramesis replied, rubbing a hand through the short curls of his hair before donning his own helmet once more. 'Lead the force to the ridge. The eldar definitely know now from which direction we approach, and Captain Nubean will not want to tarry long waiting for us.'

RAMESIS AND his force arrived at the rendezvous point first. As the sun dipped below the horizon, Ramesis's vision was augmented by the aura-intensifier of his helmet, bathing his view of the landscape in a red sheen. From the crest of a ridge the chaplain could see the repeated glow of the Imperial Guard guns, further up into the mountains. It was another hour before Captain Nubean and his Space Marines marched into view. With the aid of the artificial eyes of his armour, the chaplain could see the shimmering heat surrounding the advancing force, plumes of pure white jetting from the exhaust vents cut into their armoured backpacks. Their guns glowed a dim red, which Ramesis knew could only mean they had been involved in a protracted battle. As they came closer, Ramesis did a quick head count: there were twenty-one of them, seven less than had set out. Several more appeared to be wounded and as Captain Nubean approached with his command squad, Ramesis could see that Apothecary Suda's reductor was covered in the dark red of Space Marine blood; he had been busy extracting the progenoid glands from the missing warriors. The gene-seed he had recovered would allow the Chapter to create more Space Marines to replace those that had fallen.

'We were ambushed shortly after insertion,' Nubean explained as he stopped in front of Ramesis. 'They came in fast, carried inside two fast, skimming transports, our weapons unable to penetrate the force shields protecting the vehicles. There was another anti-grav tank there too, gliding out around us, trying to pick us off with rapid volleys from a pulse laser. Brother Kolenn managed to take it down with his lascannon, but not after Squad Mauria lost three warriors. We were mostly facing regular line troops, which did not present much of a challenge. Their shuriken catapults were unable to penetrate our armour, while our bolters punched them off their feet with every shot! It was the specialists, the ones they call Striking Scorpions, that caused me the most consternation – we've fought them before, Ramesis…'

'I remember. It was on Corronis IV. Close combat experts, with those infernal laser dischargers in their helmets,' Ramesis said, gesturing with a finger either side of his jaw to imitate the aliens' strange mandible-like weaponry.

'That's them,' Nubean agreed. 'Their armour was as good as ours; our bolters were virtually useless. They had managed to slip behind us, elusive scum. It was Squad Goria that they attacked first. Their leader had some kind of power glove, punched through Sergeant Goria's chest with ease. We managed to stave off the others by getting a crossfire on the alien wretches, and once that distraction had been disposed of we could concentrate our fire on the close combat fighters. We left none of them alive,' Nubean finished with a grim smile.

The captain pointed to a Space Marine whose left arm ended at the elbow in a blackened stump; with his other arm the wounded warrior was gesturing expansively to Sergeant Lysonis, not at all disconcerted by his injury.

'Brother Kahli's plasma gun detonated, but he brought two of the enemy down first,' Nubean explained. 'That's the fourth time in the last seven missions I have had a plasma weapon failure, though this is the first time it has been so catastrophic. I will have words with the Master of the Forges when we return. It matters not that our plasma weapons are ancient artefacts, I need them to be better maintained.'

The captain turned his gaze towards the distant flashes of fire coming from the distant Imperial Guard encampment. 'We must press on. I want to reach the Imperial Guardsmen before dawn,' he said, turning his attention back to Ramesis. 'It was well we did not try to mount an airborne landing at the battle sector itself. We came across a pair of the enemy's anti-aircraft vehicles about four miles back. They have gigantic crystalline lasers; they would have shot the Thunderhawks out of the sky with ease.' With a thin smile, the captain directed Ramesis's attention to two thin columns of smoke to the south. 'Still, they won't be causing us any more worries.'

The captain's face grew serious again. 'I only wish we had more time for proper reconnaissance, but the Imperial Guard cannot be expected to hold their defence while scouts locate the main eldar positions.'

'I've never known the eldar to form a static camp, captain,' Ramesis commented.

'That is true,' the captain agreed, his helmet moving slightly as he nodded his head. 'If we had waited to find them we may have wasted what precious time we have. As you once taught us, Ramesis, we must always temper action with wisdom. Though we live for battle, a war is fought with wits as well as weapons.'

'I'm afraid I cannot take the credit for that, brother,' Ramesis confessed with a wry smile. 'I took it from the sermons of Chaplain Gorbiam, my tutor during my time as a Novitiate.'

The captain removed his helmet and took a deep breath. His forehead was pierced by eight service studs, each representing ten years of loyal duty to the Emperor. A pink scar cut from his right cheek to his chin, standing out against the supple sheen of his dark skin. Like the other Salamanders, his face and throat were covered with burns, each medal of honour intricately etched into his flesh. His dark eyes gazed solemnly out into the darkness, the weight of several hundred years of battle hung in that look. With a nod to himself, the captain replaced his helmet.

'Enough talk. Move our battle-brothers out.'

THE SPACE MARINES advanced more cautiously, sending out regular patrols to search for eldar ambush sites. Ramesis was with Brother-Captain Nubean and Brother-Epistolary Zambias of the Chapter's librarium. They had been marching for half an hour when Zambias held up a hand and Nubean signalled a halt. Without a word the librarian took off his helm and stared up into the sky where the stars of the galactic rim were scattered across the cloudless night like a fine dust. The librarian's face was gaunt, his bald head glistened with waxy sweat. His eyes were milky white with no pupils, as though he were blind, yet he gazed up into the heavens with a furrowed brow, as if searching for something. Ramesis saw a pale eldritch light playing around the psyker's eyes as he used his powers to scan the surroundings for other minds.

With a slow blink and a long exhalation, Zambias closed his mind once more. 'The eldar have broken off their attack. They are moving further north,' he told Nubean and Ramesis.

'Then we advance quickly while they regroup!' Nubean barked, waving a hand forward to signal the surrounding squads to start moving again.

'Have you no clues as to the eldar's intent?' Ramesis asked Zambias as they broke into a run.

'Their witchery is strong, as you know, brother-chaplain. I cannot penetrate their minds, I can only sense their presence. It leaves a foul stain upon the air, a corruption on the aura of this world. These lands belong to the Emperor, they abhor the presence of these vile aliens,' the librarian explained, his clenched fist showing his anger at the aliens' desecration of Slato.

'I have pondered upon this myself, brothers,' Nubean said. 'I have been in contact with the lieutenant in charge of the Imperial Garrison and there are a number of factors which puzzle me. I would welcome your guidance in these matters.'

'With our weapons we bring the Emperor's judgement; with our minds we bring his wisdom,' Zambias replied, putting his helmet back on.

'Three times the eldar have launched a full frontal assault on the Imperial positions,' Nubean said. 'That is unusual. The eldar are as fast as lightning on the plains, striking then disappearing as quickly. They know they are no match for massed guns, yet three times they have hurled themselves onto the tanks and squads of the Imperial Guardsmen.'

'I believe they are acting in haste,' Zambias answered after a moment's consideration. 'The force they left to waylay Ramesis was small, composed entirely of their so-called "Rangers", experts in infiltration, disruption and delaying tactics. Even the host they sent against us was not a large proportion of their warriors, if the auguries assessed their strength correctly. It seems they are concentrating everything they can spare on the portal and the humans defending it. Their usual strategy of hit and run would bleed us dry if we did not take the offensive, ensuring them a good chance of victory. Yet here they are, throwing their warriors into the teeth of the Imperial army. They are desperate to break through, that much I am certain.'

'What matter is it whether they are desperate or nonchalant? They will die under our bolters either way!' Ramesis spat, taking his bolt pistol from its holster and brandishing it fiercely at the horizon. 'If they choose to make themselves easier targets then we should be grateful. I have little stomach for fighting the eldar. They slink and crawl and slither like serpents, never standing and fighting like honourable warriors. Their witchcraft is potent, their machines of war fast and manoeuvrable; it will be better for us that they forego such tactics to stand and fight for once.'

'That is true,' Nubean agreed with a nod. 'We fight for a just cause, for the eldar cannot be allowed access to their infernal portal. If they reach their device they'll bring more of their kind to this world and slaughter the colonists, and it will be lost to the Emperor. We must ensure that does not happen.'

'Why do we not destroy the portal and end this matter immediately?' asked Ramesis.

'There is an agent of the Machine God in the Imperial Guard force,' replied Zambias. 'I believe he wishes it preserved for study.'

'Ach! The Machine God. Politics.' Ramesis's simple statement conveyed his contempt. 'I do not pretend to understand why we waste time with such matters. We fight, we kill, we are victorious. That is what it means to be a Salamander.'

'And what would we be without our armour and our weapons, Ramesis?' Nubean gently chided the chaplain. 'You above all others know that we exist only to protect the Emperor's domains and his servants. If the Mechanicus wish to examine this thing, as foolish as it seems to us, it is our duty to protect them whilst they do so.'

As he pondered this, Ramesis cast a look at the mountains around him. The light of Slato's twin moons had not reached into the valley yet and everything was swathed in shadow. They were jogging easily through the long wild grass, their passage only broken by the odd clump of withered mountain trees or cluster of tumbled boulders.

'That is another curious matter here, brothers,' Nubean said, picking up on Ramesis's earlier words. 'The eldar excel at the sneak attack, the hidden blow, but they forewarned the garrison of their approach. They sent them an ultimatum – allow access to their portal or be destroyed. Why would they give up the element of surprise, when perhaps they could have swept away the defences with a single conclusive assault?'

'Perhaps they wished to terrorise the guardsmen, in the hope that they would not have to fight at all?' Ramesis offered, not trying to hide his lack of faith in the courage of the Imperial Guard.

'Equally, an attack with total surprise might have swept aside all resistance and given them access to the reinforcements they desire,' Nubean countered, adjusting his right shoulder pad as he jogged along, so that it sat better on its actuators.

'Ramesis is correct,' Zambias said, pulling his force sword from its scabbard. Psychic energy flowed through the blade, causing faint blue flames to play along its length. 'It matters not what their devious scheme is. They will fall before the blade of the Emperor's anger all the same.'

THE SPACE MARINES reached the pickets of the Imperial Guard force without encountering any more eldar, though twice Zambias informed them that an enemy psyker had tried to break through the Epistolary's psychic shield. The Imperial Guard were in poor shape. The charred hulls of both of their tanks sat smoking in the darkness. The bodies of the dead were lined up, their faces covered by helmets, in a line that stretched for thirty paces. Ramesis could see the thirty yards of killing ground which the guardsmen had cleared in front of their line. It was scorched, pockmarked with craters and shell holes, yet there was no sign of any eldar dead. Ramesis presumed that the enemy had taken them back when they had been forced to withdraw from the sheer weight of the Guard's short-range volleys of las-fire.

The few surviving Imperial Guard squads sat around campfires, their long greatcoats and peaked helmets ragged and stained from battle. Their lieutenant hurried through the darkness to greet the newcomers. His eyes were ringed with fatigue and stress and his dark blue tunic was unbuttoned. A bandage was wrapped around the thigh of his left leg, blood seeping from beneath it in a red stain across his white breeches He saluted to Captain Nubean in the manner of his regiment, one finger to the peak of his cap.

'Lieutenant Raskil of the Fourth Levillian, seconded to the Adeptus Mechanicus on garrison duty,' he said. 'Praise the Immortal Emperor that you are here to save us.'

Nubean looked down at the officer, the tip of whose head only reached to the Space Marine's chest eagle.

'You are mistaken, lieutenant,' he told Raskil. 'We are not here to save you. We are here to protect the portal from the foul eldar. Your survival is only important with regard to that mission.'

The lieutenant stepped back as if slapped, mouth gaping wide. Before he could say anything more, the hulking form of Brother Zambias was towering over him.

'Where is this alien artefact, lieutenant? I wish to examine it,' the librarian asked. The Imperial Guardsman was still taken aback by Nubean's reprimand.

'I'll, er... I'll take you there myself. Do you wish to rest and eat a little before we see it?' Raskil offered.

Ramesis felt his anger rising. This impudent human was suggesting their physical needs took priority over their mission objectives. He stomped towards the lieutenant, but Nubean interposed himself, holding up a hand to halt Ramesis's approach.

'We do not require any sustenance yet, lieutenant,' the captain interjected swiftly. 'However, we must attend to the defence of this position before any other matters. Please detail your sergeants to work with my brothers. Your men can rest for the remainder of the night, my squads will stand watch until daybreak.'

'You realise that night here lasts for eighteen hours?' Raskil asked.

'We are aware of Slato's rotational cycle, lieutenant,' Nubean said, his voice betraying his confusion at the officer's inquiry.

'And your men are going to stand watch until daybreak, some ten hours away?' Raskil continued incredulously. 'I can detail some men for watch duty, it isn't a problem.'

That was too much for Ramesis. He stepped around Captain Nubean and stared down at Raskil.

'Your men require food and sleep. We do not!' Ramesis felt like he was stating the obvious. 'If your men do not receive these things, their combat performance is adversely affected. We have no such weakness. We can fight for a month on the proteins contained within our armour recycling systems alone. You also suffer from stress-related physical and mental disorders over protracted periods of conflict, which is why I will ignore these insults. Our brothers will stand watch. Please do not question the captain's wisdom again.'

Lieutenant Raskil gave a worried glance at the three giant Space Marines standing around him. Looking across the camp he saw the other Space Marines moving into positions from which they could keep watch to the north and south, along the valley. He wasn't surprised to notice his own men giving the massive warriors a wide berth, moving out of their way when they approached.

'Follow me then. Magos Simeniz has been analysing the... the objective for several days,' he said finally, setting off to the rear of the encampment.

RASKIL LED RAMESIS and the other Marines into an even, bowl-shaped depression which was surrounded on three sides by steep cliffs, just behind the eastern side of the ridge where the guardsmen had set up their defence. The artefact at its centre was instantly recognisable as eldar in design. The obelisk stood roughly twice the height of a man and was constructed from a deep purple stone. eldar runes were painted in gold leaf along its length. Delicate strands of silver wire hung from rods in the ground around the portal, tracing out a hexagram. The air was filled with a hissing sound, which was emitting from a square box, two foot across and covered in dials and valves, which was sat nearby and linked up to the wires by coils of cables. The whole area was lit by the flickering flames of three braziers placed in a triangle around the dell. As they strode towards the alien creation, a stooping robed figure shuffled into sight from behind the machinery.

'Ah, Raskil, there you–' the figure started, then halted as he noticed the Space Marines for the first time. As he turned to regard them, the flames illuminated the face beneath the heavy cowl of his robe. Parchment-like skin hung in fleshless folds from his cheeks and his back seemed permanently hunched. From his right eye socket protruded a strange optical device with several different sized lenses which slid back and forth as he adjusted his focus. His nose was also absent, an air hose coiling from the middle of his misshapen face to a small cylinder at his belt.

'Come, see this!' Simeniz offered, beckoning to them with his right hand, from which protruded a number of small antennas. He led them to the far side of the analysis machine and pointed to one of the numerous screens showing a succession of sine waves and curving graphs. The Adeptus Mechanicus agent pulled a small plug from a receptacle implanted into the side of his forehead and plugged it into a matching socket in the machine, the wire linking him to the plug glistening with a thin sheen of blood. The screen which he had indicated began to change as the tech-priest chanted a low, almost sub-vocal, invocation. The outline of the artefact appeared in solid green lines and as the adept chanted faster, swirling orange dots began to form into concentric ovals that span in a seemingly arhythmic pattern around the centre of the monolith.

'You see?' Simeniz demanded, stabbing a finger at the screen with obvious excitement.

'We do not understand the workings of this machine,' Nubean said, looking blankly at the ever-moving image.

The tech-priest gave a snort of derision and flicked a switch which locked the moving shapes in place, before pulling the mind-plug from its socket.

'That is a definite warp-coil energy wave,' the tech-priest said slowly, as a patient adult would address a child. 'Our suspicions were correct: this edifice is capable of opening a warp gate, enabling objects to pass through. Rather large objects if my calculations are correct. However, there have been some anomalies. The wave signature is not consistent with any point of warp-interface we are aware of. It is as if it led to somewhere that is part of the warp, yet is separate from it.

'Also, it has been increasing in magnitude since my arrival. I am certain that someone is trying to activate it remotely.'

'Can you prevent that happening?' Ramesis asked, looking up at the great obelisk. The construction seemed to absorb the light from the braziers rather than reflecting it, staying in constant shadow. Being near to such an alien thing, with the scent of otherworldly evil hanging in the air, made Ramesis's spine tingle with some preternatural sensation of foreboding.

'I could potentially destabilise the warp field, but that could prove catastrophic if I am incorrect,' the tech-priest suggested, with a shrug of his slight shoulders.

'Be prepared to do so if I give the order,' Nubean said. 'We will endeavour to preserve this portal intact for your study, but our orders are to prevent the eldar from fully activating it. We will destroy it if necessary, for the lives of two hundred thousand colonists could be in danger.'

'Colonists?' Simeniz asked with a sneer. 'There are always more colonists – but we might not find another specimen of this quality for another five centuries.'

'If the eldar reach this portal, then it will be lost to us anyway,' Zambias said. The librarian held out his hands to either side and walked slowly towards the portal stone, gradually bringing his hands together in front of him as he did so.

'I can feel evil in this place. Ancient, alien evil,' he said, turning back to the group.

'We will be ready for it,' Ramesis answered confidently.

IT WAS STILL several hours before daybreak when the eldar attacked again. Ramesis had been with Zambias and Nubean for the whole night, positioning their warriors and the Imperial Guard for the best defence. The bulk of the force was stationed watching the northern approaches, where the eldar had attacked from before. However, Nubean had ordered Ramesis and a small contingent to guard the south, in case the eldar used their swift skimmer vehicles to launch their attack from the other direction. There were forty-four other Space Marines, as well as some sixty Imperial Guardsmen, and Ramesis was feeling confident that they could hold out. He was with Squad Lysonis when the first firing erupted to the north, on the right flank of the defenders.

The Imperial Guardsmen sent a steady stream of volleys into the darkness, the harsh white flare of their lasguns burning brightly against the dark. Sleek beams of blue energy struck back from the shadows, followed by a succession of flickering plasma bolts which impacted into the ground with blinding explosions. Ramesis's suit had automatically imposed a filter over his visor to stop his vision being impaired by the glaring light of the attacks, but he knew that the guardsmen would have difficulty seeing anything in the darkness. As he watched, a fist-sized star of energy shot from the gloom and impacted into the chest of a guardsman, flinging his ragged corpse a dozen yards across the ground. Ramesis could hear the bellowed orders of the Imperial Guard sergeants, and in the occasional seconds of near-silence his ears picked up the shrill whine of eldar shuriken catapults tearing through the night air.

'We hold here. That may simply be a diversionary attack,' he told Lysonis, turning his attention away from the firefight that was raging a hundred paces to his right. Checking to his left, Ramesis saw the heat auras of several eldar craft skimming forward slowly, silently stalking towards the Imperial position.

'Magnify,' he told his suit, and his field of vision suddenly zoomed in on the faint shimmering lines of three eldar war machines. They flitted a couple of yards above the ground, dodging between the scattered rocks and trees. They were long and sleek, with a curved armoured canopy at the front and an exposed gun cradle to the back. Ramesis recognised them instantly as the craft he had been told the eldar called Serpents or Vypers, something like that; swift two-man attack vehicles armed with a lethal heavy weapon. As they came closer, the sleek, menacing lines of the craft could be seen more clearly, gliding steadily towards the Imperial defenders.

There was no need for him to warn his brothers; he could see they were tracking the eldar's progress as well. Taking a deep breath to steady himself he pulled his bolt pistol and crozius from his belt and waited patiently for the aliens to get within range. A sudden glow from the slender weapon of the closest craft indicated a heat build-up, and a moment later a blue bolt of energy sliced out of the night, punching cleanly through the armour of Brother Kammia where he stood on the hillside fifty yards to Ramesis's right. The Space Marine stood there for a second as if nothing had happened, faint wisps of vapour steaming from the gaping hole through his torso. Then the warrior's legs folded under him and he fell to the ground, his armour clattering noisily as if suddenly empty.

The Space Marines reacted immediately, a lion's roar tearing the sky apart as they opened fire with their bolters in a mass volley of fire. Each bolt traced into the shadows on a tiny tail of flame, to explode a second later with a distinctive cracking noise. Ramesis watched the tiny eruptions spatter across the hull of the lead craft, shrapnel sent flying in all directions. As Ramesis switched his optics to normal view again, the Space Marine beside him, Brother Arthetis, braced his legs and brought his missile launcher to his shoulders. The Vypers were swinging past, the gunners swivelling their elegant weapons to direct their fire against the Space Marines. Arthetis swung at the waist to point the tubular missile launcher at the closest, before pulling back heavily on the trigger. A blossom of orange fire erupted from the back of the missile launcher. For a second it appeared that the missile had not seen its targets; its course would take it straight past the last Vyper. Then the spirit within the missile became aware of the aliens swooping past and with a small flicker of a guidance jet it altered course. A moment later the krak warhead exploded, turning the rearmost of the three craft into a rapidly expanding ball of flame which tumbled into the ground with another explosion.

The Space Marines tracked the surviving Vypers, continuing to fire their bolters. Ramesis saw one bolt impact into a control plane before detonating, shearing the fin off completely. Its stability lost, the craft dived towards the ground and the chaplain saw the gunner lift his arms to shield his face a moment before the nose ploughed into the dirt. The skimmer's momentum sent the craft cartwheeling down the hillside, shards of curved armour flung in all directions. The last surviving Vyper flitted back into the shadows of the crags and disappeared from view.

THE BATTLE HAD raged for a couple of hours, the eldar preferring to dart in and inflict some casualties before withdrawing back into the darkness, rather than mounting a full-scale assault.

Such tactics made it almost impossible to judge the eldar's numbers, but the shattered wrecks of two of their grav-tanks littered the ridgeline now, and Lysonis had reported over fifty of their dead found in the surrounding area. During the last assault Ramesis had been caught in a hail of fire from a shuriken catapult, an alien creation that could send a storm of razor-sharp discs slicing through their target. The chaplain's ancient armour had held firm, though, and a row of the monomolecular-edged discs spread in a neat line from just below his left shoulder to his right hip. When the battle was won he would have Techmarine Orlinia carefully remove them so that Ramesis could keep them as a memento of the battle. He would repaint the armour himself, however, and thank it for the protection it had given him.

It had been over an hour since the last attack and Captain Nubean, convinced by the lapse of time that this was not some kind of feint, had led his command squad and Squad Delphus after them, determined to harass them and stop them regrouping. He had been gone for perhaps a quarter of an Imperial hour now, having left Ramesis in charge of the remaining Imperial forces.

Those forces were much depleted. The eldar attacks had been highly efficient; only twenty nine of the guardsmen and twenty-seven Space Marines were fit for fighting. Ramesis knew that many of his fallen battle-brothers would fight on if asked, but it was imperative that they allowed their enhanced bodies every opportunity to heal themselves so that they might fight at full effectiveness later when they were really needed. Most of the troopers who had fallen were dead, shredded by shuriken, blown apart by starcannon plasma bolts or torn in half by high-powered laser weapons. Ramesis was looking at one corpse in particular, that of a young corporal whose face looked so serene and at peace. Strange, Ramesis thought in a detached fashion, considering his legs and half his spine have been vaporised. Then Ramesis's comm-link chimed and the body was instantly forgotten.

'I'm returning with some of the eldar,' he heard Numean reporting.

The connection was cut before he had a chance to reply, but Ramesis was delighted that the captain had captured some of the filthy aliens so that they could be interrogated as to their plans and the strength of their army. It was not long before Ramesis caught sight of the returning Space Marines. Nubean was striding purposefully up the hill, accompanied by Zambias. His bodyguard was behind him, and between their massive torsos Ramesis caught occasional glimpses of the alien captives.

All three wore long flowing robes and tall, jewel-encrusted helms. Their slight forms seemed emaciated next to the immense physiques of the Space Marines, but the aliens were slightly taller. Intricately shaped eldar runes hung from their garments on fine threads, swaying gently as they walked forward. The one in the centre was the most ornamented and Ramesis realised with a start that this must be one of the legendary Farseers, the powerful psykers said to command the eldar. The other two were Warlocks; he had encountered them before, powerful battle-witches who were obviously serving as some kind of honour guard for the Farseer. All three moved with an effortless grace, easily keeping pace with the Space Marines despite the long strides of the captain and librarian. Nubean and Zambias were about ten yards away now, and Ramesis could clearly make out the three aliens following them. Something was nagging at the back of his mind, but before he could work out what was amiss Nubean was stood directly in front of him.

'Come, brother! We have matters to discuss, and urgently,' Nubean said without formality, already striding past Ramesis in the direction of the portal.

It was then that Ramesis realised that the eldar were not bound in any way at all, and with a shock he noticed they still carried their weapons: shuriken pistols in finely-crafted holsters and long swords carried in scabbards hung with many tassels and runes.

'What devilry is this?' the chaplain demanded, sighting his pistol at the Farseer. It was obvious that the Space Marines were under some kind of foul influence of the eldar's psychic powers.

'Calm yourself, Ramesis!' Nubean shouted back, putting himself between the chaplain and his target. 'The situation has changed. Put down your weapon.'

'Weak-minded fool!' Ramesis hissed, pointing his bolt pistol at the captain. 'This is some cursed eldar mind-trick!'

Zambias once more stepped between the chaplain and captain, laying his heavily-gauntleted hand on Ramesis's pistol.

'There is no trickery here, brother,' the librarian assured him calmly. 'We are both free from influence.' Zambias's helmet was hung from his belt and Ramesis could see his eyes were normal, betraying no sign of mental powers being used.

Ramesis hesitated for a moment and studied the librarian's face. Seeing nothing but the honourable and honest face he had come to know and respect over the last few years, he took a reluctant step back, lowering his pistol. The three eldar strode past without even glancing at the chaplain, acting as if nothing at all had happened. Their alien haughtiness infuriated Ramesis but he managed to keep his anger in check – for the meantime.

THE PORTAL WAS being guarded by Brothers Amadeus, Xavier and Joachim, and they eyed the group of eldar accompanying Nubean very suspiciously. Raskil's men and the other Space Marines were left watching the valley, in case this was a subtle ploy to lure the Emperor's servants into some false sense of confidence and security. As the group entered the natural bowl containing the eldar artefact, Magos Simeniz looked up from where he was adjusting the wire hexagram around the portal, his jaw dropping almost comically when he noticed the nature of his visitors.

'What are they doing here?' he demanded, stepping protectively in front of his analytical engine. The Farseer took a pace forward and raised his hand in some kind of alien gesture, his fingers splaying open and then closing into a half-fist. When he spoke, the eldar's voice was musical, every syllable and sound perfectly formed and intoned, spoken without hesitation.

'I am here to deactivate the opening-ward, the device of power you call a portal,' the Farseer waved an arm hung with several thick golden bracelets in a fluid gesture towards the obelisk.

'This is trickery! You will open the gateway to your fiendish home and bring more of your warriors,' Ramesis claimed, striding to stand next to Simeniz.

'Interference would not please us,' the Farseer said gently, with an inclination of his head. 'The voices of our home and forefathers have sent us here, the runes guiding my dancing path to your presence. There is one who comes here, born in nightmare and feeding on fear. He is Kha-rehk, leader of the Fanged Maw. He comes and slaughters you all, sating his thirst with your peoples' essence.'

Ramesis stared at the eldar leader, fixing his gaze on the two green, gem-like ovals he assumed served as eyepieces in the helmet. It was impossible to tell what the Farseer was feeling or thinking; the alien's bowed head could be a demand or acquiescence. Captain Nubean removed his helmet as he joined the chaplain, Magos Simeniz scurrying close behind. The captain's eyes were troubled and Ramesis could see that the responsibility he held was weighing heavily on his shoulders.

'Everything has been explained. Well, I think I understand,' Nubean told the others. 'A band of eldar renegades are trying to use this portal to attack the colonists. This Farseer has arrived to close the portal completely, so that it can never be used again. We must act quickly to sever this bridge between realms.'

'No!' Simeniz cried suddenly, a crazed look in his natural eye. 'They're trying to keep it a secret from us! They want to hide their wonderful technology from the Machine God!' With a hiss the tech-priest launched himself at the Farseer, his fingers spread like claws. Ramesis reached out to grab the deranged adept but the Farseer acted more swiftly. The eldar psyker made a short gesture with the fingers of his raised hand and Simeniz's head was surrounded by a faint rippling nimbus of yellow light, stopping him in his tracks. Zambias had taken a step forward, his hand on the hilt of his force sword, but no sooner had he moved then one of the Warlocks was barring his path, a glowing witchblade brandished in its hands.

'Release him!' Nubean demanded and the Farseer flicked its fingers again with an almost bored shrug. Simeniz fainted to the ground. As Ramesis stooped to one knee to check he was alive, the tech-priest opened his eye and groaned sleepily.

'It told me things,' Simeniz whispered. 'Showed me a glimpse of the portal. It was wonderful.' The tech-priest struggled to his feet and gazed wide-eyed at the Farseer, who had turned its attention to the portal itself.

'What do you care about our colonists?' Ramesis demanded of the eldar.

'Nothing,' the psyker admitted with a dismissive wave of a long-fingered hand. 'More of your warriors discover the butchery and seek answers. You stumble across our Craftworld as she drifts peacefully through the stars. You do not understand what has happened and the guilt for the spilling of blood is laid upon us. Your warships gather and attack us. We destroy all of them, but many of my kin die doing so. We wish to avoid this outcome. We did not wish to fight against you. If the Dark Kin break free from the webway we will need the strength of both our forces to turn them back.'

'How do you know this?' Ramesis asked, still convinced that the eldar were trying to trick them somehow.

'How do you know that you are awake? Or even alive?' the Farseer said.

'Speak plainly!' Ramesis demanded.

'We waste time!' the eldar leader snapped back. 'I will gladly leave you all to die in the most agonising manners, if you would kindly leave assurances that my kin are not responsible for your deaths or the eradication of your intrusive little dunghill of a town. I must close the webway arch and I must be doing it now!'

The Farseer raised its hand and pointed at the portal, chanting softly in its own strange, melodic language. As Ramesis watched, the analytical engine gave a shriek. Simeniz leapt to man the status displays, his fingers working furiously at a series of switches and dials.

'The… the portal's beginning to open,' he said in an awed whisper. All eyes turned towards the stone. A dark corona of energy was forming around the obelisk, tendrils of white power crawling along its surface. A dull hum filled the air and as they watched the silver wire of Simeniz's analysis matrix began to melt.

'Treachery!' Ramesis bellowed, bringing up his bolt pistol and firing at the Farseer. There was a flare of psychic energy and the bolt dropped to the ground, unexploded. Behind the Farseer, Ramesis saw Zambias exchanging sword blows with the Warlock in front of him. Amadeus, Xavier and Joachim fired their bolters at the other Warlock, but the eldar side-stepped neatly past the volley and struck out, its witchblade slicing across Amadeus's chest with sparks of psychic power.

Ramesis pressed his thumb to the power stud of his crozius and turned back to the Farseer. Suddenly, the chaplain's mind exploded. He felt quicksilver shards of mental energy piercing his soul. It seemed as if the universe itself was shrieking in his ears and light as bright as the sun blinded him. Gritting his teeth, Ramesis forced his eyes to focus on the Farseer, who was still standing calmly in the middle of the hollow, his attention fixed on the portal, one hand still outstretched towards it.

'Vulkan give me strength!' Ramesis cried, throwing off the Farseer's mental attack with a sudden surge of willpower. Ramesis was two strides from the eldar when it snapped its head towards him like a mantis spying its prey. The Farseer opened its right hand and its witchblade leapt from the sheath across its back and settled into his grip. Ramesis brought his crozius around in a vicious back-handed strike, smashing the power weapon into the alien's head. Gems scattered across the ground as the Farseer reeled. Ramesis brought his arm back for another attack, but the eldar reacted quickly, spinning on its heel to deliver a double-handed blow with its witchblade. Ramesis thought the eldar had missed for a moment until he brought his arm forward to strike again with the crozius. In a moment of disbelief, Ramesis noticed that his right arm stopped just above the wrist. Glancing down in a detached fashion, the chaplain saw his crozius lying on the ground, his gloved hand still gripping its haft.

The witchblade slashed out again and Ramesis dived to one side, the alien weapon smashing across his left shoulder pad. Sparks fountained into the air from the severed auto-actuators as Ramesis rolled and regained his feet. The Farseer seemed to glide towards the chaplain, advancing without walking, the Witchblade blazing with power. The eldar took a wide-stepped stance, its robes billowing in a psychic gale of power, and brought the blade in a slow circle around its head. Ramesis noticed that one of the eye-jewels had been shattered and he could see part of the Farseer's face. An almond shaped-eye stared back at him with contempt in its gaze. As the Farseer advanced, the eye's yellow iris began to glow, filling up with tiny sparks of energy until it was a small star of white light.

With a thunderous explosion of energy, the Farseer was knocked down onto one knee. Behind the sprawling eldar stood Xavier, Ramesis's crozius gripped in both hands. The Space Marine struck down again and again, battering the Farseer's head and back until the alien stopped moving, its blood seeping into the dirt. Looking around, Ramesis saw that both Warlocks were dead too. Brother Amadeus was on his back, Zambias helping him hold in the organs that were trying to spill from the massive slash through his chest bone. Simeniz was cowering on the ground, sobbing gently, covering his eyes. Nubean strode over and grabbed the back of the tech-priest's robes in one hand and lifted him off the ground.

'Stop the portal opening!' he demanded, hurling Simeniz towards the logic machine.

The portal-stone was glowing white-hot with energy. A cold wind seemed to emanate from its surface causing the braziers to flicker madly. The tech-priest set to work, while Ramesis strode to where Xavier was standing over the Farseer, alien blood dripping from the crozius arcanum in his hands.

'This is a good omen, brother!' Ramesis grinned, pointing towards the crozius. 'The Emperor has obviously marked you as special. When we return to Nocturne I will enter your name into the Novitiate of the Promethean Cult. You will make a fine chaplain one day.

'Thank you, brother. I pray to live up to your expectations,' Xavier replied, the honour shining in his eyes.

Ramesis clapped his left hand on the young Space Marine's shoulder pad and looked at the stump of his other arm. Already his genetically-modified blood had clotted and stopped the bleeding, his power armour releasing pain-numbing elixirs into the nerves around the injury. When they returned to the fortress-monastery, the Master of the Forges would fit him with an artificial hand. Such prosthetics were common amongst the Salamanders. There would be no shame in it.

'I think I'm too late,' Ramesis heard Simeniz mutter.

All eyes turned to the tech-priest where he stood hunched over the analyser.

'What did you say?' Nubean demanded, his dark eyes narrowed.

'I'm too late...' Simeniz repeated, pointing at the portal. The white energy had formed into a swirling ring of power many paces across, a purplish shadow staining its centre. The air was filled with a piercing whining noise, somehow loud but also just at the edge of hearing at the same time. Without any order being given, the Space Marines began to back away from the alien artefact, taking up a position on the crest of the rise.

Captain Nubean was shouting over the comm-net, demanding all squads to assemble on the hill.

With a crack louder than thunder the portal yawned open, creating a massive oval of pure blackness that stretched three dozen yards across the whole width of the depression. Within the blackness of the void there blinked cold, distant stars. Nothing happened for several heartbeats, then suddenly the renegades burst from the ellipse of energy. Gunfire flashed out of nowhere and more eldar leapt into view, each of their rifles spewing a hail of deadly crystal splinters. More eldar riding midnight-black jet bikes covered in scything blades flashed into existence, their screaming engines sending them racing past the startled humans. The Space Marines and Imperial Guardsmen opened fire as more and more evil creatures slid into existence. The skin of these eldar was pale to the point of being white, contrasting harshly with the black of their armour, which was made of flexible plates festooned with glittering blades. Hooks and barbs hung from chains around their wrists, loins and necks, and many of them wore extravagantly coloured crests on their high-fluted helmets.

Watching as the dark portal spat forth a sleek anti-grav vehicle packed full of howling warriors, Ramesis knew at the last that the alien Farseer had been right. Their force could not hold against the alien host on its own. The war engine glided slowly forward, menacing in its calmness. The creatures aboard it brandished cruel curved and serrated blades, and fired pistols indiscriminately into the mass of Imperial servants before them. The exotic cannon mounted on the prow of the renegades' craft spat a ball of dark energy at the Space Marines, slicing easily through the armour of Brother Lastus. More and more warriors leapt through into the world, accompanied by packs of alien beasts which had no skin, their flesh and muscles clearly visible in the light of the constant gun fire. With ear-splitting howls the hunting pack bounded up the slope, their fanged jaws and clawed feet tearing a bloody path through the Imperial Guardsmen. More skimmers were sliding into view, bearing a seemingly endless stream of depraved and vicious warriors.

Firing his bolt pistol at the charging aliens, Ramesis knew a fear like he had never experienced before. If their forces had been combined with the original eldar force, without being weakened by days of fighting each other, they would have been able to stem the tide of renegades pouring through the breach in reality. Now the servants of the Emperor stood alone. Ramesis knew that they were doomed; their only hope of victory had been shattered by his own hatred and inflexibility.

Determined that he would not die alone, Ramesis snatched the powersword clenched in the hand of Malesti, who lay dead in the dust. The hollow was full of the aliens' corpses, yet more and more seemed to spill forth into the battle. Screaming with rage, the chaplain charged into the centre of the throng. Ramesis was surrounded by their warriors as he hacked blindly left and right, felling an enemy with each blow. The whining of anti-grav engines was deafening and the chaplain was knocked to one knee by the downblast of something large sweeping overhead. The noise of guns and blade-on-blade swirled around him, accompanied by a cacophony of screams which were suddenly drowned out by a deafening bellow of inhuman rage. He was hemmed in on all sides by shadowy warriors, his armour rent and torn from the blows of his enemies, his real enemies. As the darkness closed in on him the last sight he had was of their thin faces laughing with cruel glee.

THE WRATH OF KHÂRN
William King

'BLOOD FOR THE Blood God!' bellowed Khârn the Betrayer, charging forward through the hail of bolter fire, towards the Temple of Superlative Indulgence. The bolter shells ricocheting off his breastplate did not even slow him down. The Chaos Space Marine smiled to himself. The ancient ceramite of his armour had protected him for over ten thousand years. He felt certain it would not let him down today. All around him warriors fell, clutching their wounds, crying in pain and fear.

More souls offered up on the altar of battle to the Supreme Lord of Carnage, Khârn thought and grinned maniacally. Surely the Blood God would be pleased this day.

Ahead of him, Khârn saw one of his fellow berzerkers fall, his body riddled with shells, his armour cracked and melted by plasma fire. The berzerker howled with rage and frustration, knowing that he was not going to be in at the kill, that he would give Khorne no more offerings on this or any other day. In frustration, the dying warrior set his chainsword to maximum power and took off his own head with one swift stroke. His blood rose in a red fountain to slake Khorne's thirst.

As he passed, Khârn kicked the fallen warrior's head, sending it flying over the defenders' parapet. At least this way his fallen comrade would witness Khârn slaughter the Slaanesh worshippers in the few delicious moments before he died. Under the circumstances, it was the least reward Khârn could grant such a devout warrior.

The Betrayer leapt over a pile of corpses, snapping off a shot with his plasma pistol. One of the Slaanesh cultists fell, clutching the ruins of his melted face. Gorechild, Khârn's daemonic axe, howled in his hands. Khârn brandished it above his head and bellowed his challenge to the sick, yellow sky of the Daemon World.

'Skulls for the skull throne!' Khârn howled. On every side, frothing Berzerkers echoed his cry. More shells whined all around him. He ignored them the way he would ignore the buzz of annoying insects. More of his fellows fell but Khârn stood untouched, secure in the blessing of the Blood God, knowing that it would not be his turn today.

All was going according to plan. A tide of Khorne's warriors flowed across the bomb-cratered plains towards the towering redoubt of the Slaanesh worshippers. Support fire from the Chaos Titan artillery had reduced most of the walls around the ancient temple complex to just so much rubble. The disgusting murals painted in fluorescent colours had been reduced to atoms. The obscene minarets that crowned the towers had been blasted into well-deserved oblivion. Lewd statues lay like colossal, limbless corpses, gazing at the sky with blank marble eyes. Even as Khârn watched, missiles blazed down from the sky and smashed another section of the defensive wall to blood-covered fragments. Huge clouds of dust billowed. The ground shook. The explosions rumbled like distant thunder. Sick joy bubbled through Khârn's veins at the prospect of imminent violence.

This was what he lived for, these moments of action where he could once again prove his superiority to all other warriors in the service of his exalted lord. In all his ten thousand year existence, Khârn had found no joy to touch the joy of battle, no lust greater than his lust for blood. Here on the field of mortal combat, he was more than in his element, he was at the site of his heart's desire. It was the thing that had caused him to betray his oath of allegiance to the Emperor of Mankind, his genetic destiny as a Space Marine and even his old comrades in the World Eaters Legion. He had never regretted those decisions even for an instant. The bliss of battle was reward enough to stay any doubts.

He jumped the ditch before the parapet, ignoring the poisoned spikes which lined the pit bottom and promised an ecstatic death to any that fell upon them. He scrambled up the loose scree of the rock face and vaulted over the low wall, planting his boot firmly into the face of a defender as he did so. The man screamed and fell back, trying to stem the flow of blood from his broken nose. Khârn swung Gorechild and ended his whining forever.

'Death is upon you!' Khârn roared as he dived into a mass of depraved cultists. Gorechild lashed out. Its teeth bit into hardened ceramite, spraying sparks in all directions. The blow passed through the target's armour, opening its victim from stomach to sternum. The wretch fell back, clutching at his ropy entrails. Khârn despatched him with a backhand swipe and fell upon his fellows, slaying right and left, killing with every blow. Frantically the cultists' leader bellowed orders, but it was too late. Khârn was among them, and no man had ever been able to boast of facing Khârn in close combat and living.

The numbers 2243, then 2244, blinked before his eyes. The ancient gothic lettering of the digital death-counter, superimposed on Khârn's field of vision, incremented quickly. Khârn was proud of this archaic device, presented by Warmaster Horus himself in ancient times. Its like could not be made in this degenerate age. Khârn grinned proudly as his tally of offerings for this campaign continued to rise. He still had a long way to go to match his personal best but that was not going to stop him trying.

Men screamed and howled as they died. Khârn roared with pleasure, killing everything within his reach, revelling in the crunch of bone and the spray of blood. The rest of the Khornate force took advantage of the destruction the Betrayer had caused. They swarmed over the walls in a howling mass and dismembered the Slaanesh worshippers. Already demoralised by the death of their leader, not even these fanatical worshippers of the Lord of Pleasure could stand their ground. Their morale broken, they panicked and fled.

Such pathetic oafs were barely worth the killing, Khârn decided, lashing out reflexively and killing those Slaanesh worshippers who passed too to close him as they fled. 2246, 2247,

2248 went the death counter. It was time to get on with his mission. It was time to find the thing he had come here to destroy – the ancient daemonic artefact known as the Heart of Desire.

'Attack!' Khârn bellowed and charged through the gaping mouth of the leering stone head that was the entrance to the main temple building.

INSIDE IT WAS quiet, as if the roar of battle could not penetrate the walls. The air stank of strange perfumes. The walls had a porous, fleshy look. The pink-tinged light was odd; it shimmered all around, coming from no discernible source. Khârn switched to the auto-sensor systems within his helm, just in case there was some trickery here.

Leather-clad priestesses, their faces domino-masked, emerged from padded doorways. They lashed at Khârn with whips that sent surges of pain and pleasure through his body. Another man, one less hardened than Khârn, might have been overwhelmed by the sensation but Khârn had spent millennia in the service of his god, and what passed through him now was but a pale shadow compared to the battle lust that mastered him. He chopped through the snake-like flesh of the living lash. Poison blood spurted forth. The woman screamed as if he had cut her. Looking closer he saw that she and the whip were one. A leering daemonic head tipped the weapon's handle and had buried its fangs into her wrist. Khârn's interest was sated. He killed the priestess with one back-handed swipe of Gorechild.

A strange, strangled cry of rage and hate warned him of a new threat. He turned and saw that one of the other Berzerkers, less spiritually pure than himself, had been overcome by the whip's evil. The man had torn off his helmet and his face was distorted by a sick and dreamy smile that had no place on the features of one chosen by Khorne. Like a sleepwalker he advanced on Khârn and lashed out with his chainsword. Khârn laughed as he parried the blow and killed the man with his return stroke.

A quick glance told him that all the priestesses were dead and that most of his followers had slain their drugged brethren. Good, thought Khârn, but part of him was disappointed. He had hoped that more of his fellows would be overcome by treachery. It was good to measure himself against true warriors, not these decadent worshippers of an effete god. Gorechild howled with frustrated bloodlust, writhing in his hand as if it would turn on him if he did not feed it more blood and sinew soon. Khârn knew how the axe felt. He turned, gestured for his companions to follow him and raced off down the corridor.

'Follow me,' he shouted. 'To the slaughter!'

Passing through a huge arch, the former Space Marines entered the inner sanctum of the temple and Khârn knew that they had found what they had come for. Light poured in through the stained glass ceiling. As he watched, Khârn realised that the light was not coming through the glass, but from the glass itself. The illustrations glowed with an eerie internal light and they moved. A riotous assembly of men and women, mutants and daemons enacted every foul deed that the depraved followers of a debauched god could imagine. And, Khârn noted, they could imagine quite a lot.

Khârn raised his pistol and opened fire, but the glass merely absorbed the weapon's energy. Something like a faint moan of pleasure filled the chamber and mocking laughter drew Khârn's attention to the throne which dominated the far end of the huge chamber. It was carved from a single gem that pulsed and changed colour, going from amber to lavender to pink to lime and then back through a flickering, random assortment of iridescent colours that made no sense and hurt the eye. Khârn knew without having to be told that this throne was the Heart of Desire. Senses honed by thousands of years of exposure to the stuff of Chaos told him that the thing fairly radiated power. Inside was the trapped essence of a daemon prince, held forever at the whim of Slaanesh as punishment for some ancient treachery. The man sitting so regally on the throne was merely a puppet and barely worth Khârn's notice, save as something to be squashed like a bug.

The man looked down on Khârn as if he had the temerity to feel the same way about Khorne's most devoted follower. His left hand stroked the hair of the leashed and naked woman who crouched like a pet at his feet. His right hand held an obscenely shaped runesword, which glowed with a blasphemous light.

Khârn strode forward to confront his new foe. The clatter of ceramite-encased feet on marble told him that his fellow berzerkers followed. In a matter of a hundred strides, Khârn found himself at the foot of the dais, and some odd, mystical force compelled him to stop and stare.

Khârn did not doubt that he was face-to-face with the cult leader. The man had the foul, debauched look of an ancient and immortal devotee of Slaanesh. His face was pale and gaunt; make-up concealed the dark shadows under his eyes. An obscene helmet covered the top of his head. As he stood, his pink and lime cloak billowed out behind him. Tight bands of studded leather armour girdled his naked chest, revealing lurid and disturbing tattoos.

'Welcome to the Heart of Desire,' the Slaanesh worshipper said in a soft, insinuating voice which somehow carried clearly across the chamber and compelled immediate, respectful attention. Khârn was instantly on his guard, sensing the magic within that voice, the persuasive power which could twist mortals to its owner's will. He struggled to keep the fury that burned eternally in his breast from subsiding under the influence of those slyly enthralling tones. 'What do you wish?'

'Your death!' the Betrayer roared, yet he felt his bloodlust being subdued by that oddly comforting voice.

The cult leader sighed. 'You worshippers of Khorne are so drearily predictable. Always the same tedious, unimaginative retort. I suppose it comes from following that mono-maniacal deity of yours. Still, you are hardly to be blamed for your god's dullness, I suppose.'

'When Khorne has devoured your soul, you will pay for such blasphemy!' Khârn shouted. His followers shouted their approval but with less enthusiasm than Khârn would have expected. For some reason, the man on the throne did not appear to be worried by the presence of so many armed men in his sanctum.

'Somehow I doubt it, old chap. You see, my soul has long been pledged to thrice-blessed Slaanesh, so unless Khorne wants to stick his talon down Slaanesh's throat or some other orifice, he'll have a hard time getting at it.'

'Enough of this prattle!' Khârn roared. 'Death is upon you!'

'Oh! Be sensible,' the cultist said, raising his hand. Khârn felt a tide of pleasure flow over him, like that he had felt from the whip earlier but a thousand times stronger. All around him he heard his men moan and gasp.

'Think! You can spend an eternity of pleasure being caressed by the power of Lord Slaanesh, while your soul slowly rots and sinks into his comforting embrace. Anything you want, anything you have ever desired, can be yours. All you have to do is swear allegiance to Slaanesh. Believe me, it's no trouble.'

As the cult leader spoke, images flickered through Khârn's mind. He saw visions of his youth and all the joys he had known, before the rebellion of Horus and the Battle for Terra. Somehow it all looked so clear and fresh and appealing, and it almost brought moisture to his tear ducts. He saw endless banquets of food and wine. For a moment, his palate was stimulated by all manner of strange and wonderful tastes, and his brain tingled with a myriad pleasures and stimulations. Visions of diaphanously clad maidens danced before his eyes, beckoning enticingly.

For a moment, despite of himself, Khârn felt an almost unthinkable temptation to betray his ancient oath to the Blood God. This was powerful sorcery indeed! He shook his head and bit his lip until the blood flowed. 'No true warrior of Khorne would fall for this pitiful trick!' he bellowed.

'All hail Slaanesh!' one of his followers cried.

'Praise to the great Lord of Pleasure!' shouted another.

'Let us grovel and adore him,' a third said, as the whole force cast themselves down onto their knees.

Khârn turned to look at his men, disbelief and outrage filling his mind. It seemed that they did not possess his iron-willed belief in Khorne's power, that they were prepared to betray him for a few tawdry promises of pleasure. In every face, in every posture, he saw slack-jawed worship of the posturing peacock on the throne. He knew that there was only one thing to be done under the circumstances.

The Slaanesh leader obviously felt the same. 'Kill him!' he cried. 'Offer up his soul to Slaanesh and unspeakable ecstasy shall be your reward!'

The first of Khârn's comrades raised his bolt pistol and squeezed the trigger. Khârn threw himself to one side and the shell whipped past his head. The Betrayer rewarded the traitor with a taste of Gorechild. The chain-axe screeched as it bit through armour in a mighty sweep that clove him clean in two.

The warrior gave a muted whine as his Slaanesh-corrupted soul went straight to the warp.

Suddenly the rest of the berzerkers were upon him. Khârn found himself fighting for his immortal life. These were no mere Slaanesh cultists. Newly tainted though they might be, they had once been worthy followers of Khorne, fierce, deadly and full of bloodlust. Mighty maces bludgeoned Khârn. Huge chainswords threatened to tear his rune-encrusted armour. Bolter shells tore chunks from his chest-plate. Khârn fought on, undismayed, filled with the joy of battle, taking fierce pleasure every time Gorechild took another life. At last, these were worthy foes! The body count swiftly ticked on to 2460 and continued to rise.

Instinctively Khârn side-stepped a blow that tore off one of the metal skulls which dangled from his belt. The Betrayer swore he would replace it with the attacker's own skull. His return stroke made good his vow. He whirled Gorechild in a great figure-of-eight and cleared a space all around him, sending two more traitors to make their excuses to the Blood God. Insane bloodlust surged through him, overcoming even the soporific influence of the Heart of Desire and for a moment Khârn fought with his full unfettered power. He became transformed into an unstoppable engine of destruction and nothing could stand against him.

Khârn's heart pounded. The blood sang through his veins and the desire to kill made him howl uncontrollably. Bones crunched beneath his axe. His pistol blew away the life of its targets. He stamped on the heads of the fallen, crushing them to jelly. Khârn ignored pain, ignored any idea of self-preservation, and fought for the pure love of fighting. He killed and he killed.

ALL TOO SOON it was over, and Khârn stood alone in a circle of corpses. His breathing rasped from his chest. Blood seeped through a dozen small punctures in his armour. He felt like a rib might have been broken by that last blow of the mace but he was triumphant. His counter read 2485. He sensed the presence of one more victim and turned to confront the figure on the dais.

The cultists' leader stood looking down at him with a faint expression of mingled disbelief and distaste on his face. The naked girl had fled. The throne pulsed enticingly.

'It's true what they say,' the man said with a delicious sigh. 'If you want anything done properly, you have to do it yourself.'

The insinuating voice drove Khârn's fury from him, and left him feeling tired and spent. The cultist strode down from the dais. Khârn felt almost too weary to parry his blow. He knew he must throw off this enchantment quickly. The runesword bit into his armour and a wave of mingled pain and pleasure passed through Khârn like poison. Summoning his last reserves of rage, he threw himself into the attack. He would show this effete fop who was the true warrior here.

Khârn hacked. Gorechild bit into the tattoos of the man's wrist. Gobbets of flesh and droplets of blood whirled away from the axe's teeth. The rank smell of hot bone filled the air as the hand separated from the arm – and began to crawl away with a life of its own. Khârn stamped on it and a rictus of pain appeared on its owner's face, as if the hand was still attached.

Khârn swung. The cultist's head separated from its shoulders. The body swung its blade, a puppet still controlled by the strings of its master's will. It bit into Khârn and the wave of sensation almost drove him to his knees.

'Nice trick!' roared Khârn, feeling the hand squirm beneath his boot. 'But I've seen it before.'

He brought his chain-axe down on the head and cleaved it in two. The body fell to the ground, a puppet with its strings cut. 2486, Khârn thought with some satisfaction.

The Betrayer advanced upon the throne. It pulsed enticingly before him. Within its multiple facets he thought he saw the face of a beautiful woman, the most beautiful he had ever seen – and the most evil. Her hair was long and golden, and her eyes were blue. Her lips were full and red, and the small, white fangs that protruded from her mouth in no way marred her perfection. She looked at Khârn beseechingly, and he knew at once he was face to face with the Daemon trapped within the Heart of Desire.

Welcome, Khârn, a seductive voice said within his head. *I knew you would triumph. I knew you would be the conqueror. I knew you would be my new master.*

The voice was thrilling. By comparison, the cult leader's voice had been but a pale echo. But the voice was also deceptive. Proud as he was, mighty as he knew himself to be, Khârn knew that no man could truly be the master of a daemon, not even a fallen Space Marine like himself. He knew that his soul was once more in peril, that he should do something. But yet again he found himself enthralled by the persuasiveness of a Slaanesh worshipper's voice.

Be seated! Become the new ruler of this world, then go forth and blast those meddlesome interlopers from the face of your planet.

Khârn fought to hold himself steady while the throne pulsed hypnotically before him, and the smell of heavy musk filled his nostrils. He knew that once he sat he would be trapped, just as the daemon was trapped. He would become a slave to the thing imprisoned within the throne. His will would be drained and he would become a decadent and effete shadow of the Khârn he had once been. Yet his limbs began to move almost of their own accord, his feet slowly but surely carrying him towards the throne.

Once more, visions of an eternity of corrupt pleasure danced in Khârn's mind. Once more he saw himself indulging in every excess. The daemon promised him every ecstasy imaginable and it was well within its power to grant such pleasures. He knew it would be a simple thing for him to triumph on its behalf. All he had to do was step outside and announce that he had destroyed the Heart of Desire. He was Khârn. He would be believed, and after that it would be a simple matter to lure the Khorne worshippers to ecstatic servitude or joyful destruction.

And would they not deserve it? Already he was known as the Betrayer, when all he had done was be more loyal to his god than the spineless weaklings he had slaughtered. And with that the daemon's voice fell silent and the visions stopped, as if the thing in the throne realised its mistake, but too late.

For Khârn was loyal to Khorne and there was only room for that one thing within his savage heart. He had betrayed and killed his comrades in the World Eaters because they had not remained true to Khorne's ideals and would have fled from the field of battle without either conquering or being destroyed.

The reminder gave him the strength. He turned and looked back at the room. The reek of blood and dismembered bodies filled his nostrils like perfume. He remembered the joy of the combat. The thrill of overcoming his former comrades. He looked out on a room filled with corpses and a floor carpeted with blood. He was the only living thing here and he had made it so. He realised that, compared to this pleasure, this sense of conquest and victory, what the daemon offered was only a pale shadow.

Khârn turned and brought Gorechild smashing down upon the foul throne. His axe howled thirstily as it drank deep of the ancient and corrupt soul imprisoned within. Once more he felt the thrill of victory, and knew no regrets for rejecting the daemon's offer.

2487. Life just doesn't get any better than this, Khârn thought.

ANCIENT HISTORY
Andy Chambers

Cross the Stars and fight for glory
But 'ware the heaven's wrath.
Take yer salt and hear a shipmen's story.
Listen to tales of the gulf,
Of stars that sing and worlds what lie
Beyond the ghosts of the rim.
But remember, lads, there ain't no words
For every void-born thing.

— Shipmen's labour-chant,
Gothic Sector, Segmentum Obscurus

NATHAN RAN DOWN the stinking alley, panting and sweating. He could hear shouts and a scuffle behind him as they pounced on Kendrikson. His mind raced faster than his feet across the cracked slabs. Poor old Kendrikson. Still – better him than me. He leapt over a prostrate body almost invisible in the darkness as the irony of the situation struck home. At least that's the last time he'll try to get me killed.

At the corner he risked a glance back. A lone streetlume cast a pool of yellow illumination over a scene which looked suspiciously like one from some Ministorum morality play. Four

burly, shaven headed men in dun-coloured coveralls were hauling Kendrikson to his feet. He seemed unduly surprised, nay
stunned, to be cast in the starring role of the eponymous incau-
tious reveller laid low by local ruffians, cultists or worse –
surely a punishment from the God-Emperor for his carelessness and self-indulgence.

The image was shattered when the officer stepped out from
the shadows to congratulate the men on their catch. Nathan
had never seen an Imperial Naval officer before but he had no
doubt that he was looking at one now. Tall, poised, immacu-
lately dressed in tailored uniform coat and a pair of glossy
black boots which had probably never trodden the dust of a
planet for more than a few hours. He would surely be a junior
officer to be in charge of a gang like that, trawling through the
back alleys of Juniptown to fill out some labour team aboard
his ship. Junior or not, he radiated the absolute assuredness
that only generations of breeding and a lifetime of training
engenders.

Nathan started to back away as his mind raced on. There
were rumours that Imperial ships would come from Port Maw
to Lethe, but everyone said that sort of thing when there was a
war among the stars. Half the people hoped the fleet would
come and save them from Sanctus-knows-what, while the
other half were afraid that the fleet would bring the war to their
doorstep. Nobody had ever thought that the Navy would come
to steal a tithe of men and take them away on ships. Men who,
if only half the stories were true, would never be seen again.

Kendrikson was off for a cruise and there was nothing
Nathan could do about it. He certainly didn't intend take on a
pressgang single-handed.

'Well, well,' said a finely cultured voice from behind him. 'It
looks like young Rae missed one – get him lads!'

A blow struck his head, bright stars flashed before his eyes
and he fell into waiting arms which bore him off even as his
consciousness slipped away.

NATHAN WOKE TO the sound of a voice speaking. It sounded
deep, resonant and faintly amused. He was amongst a crowd,
being propped up by a stranger. The voice rolled on through
his confused awakening like martial music: proud and insistent.

'...I could take this ship twice around the galaxy and wander the void for a hundred years if the Emperor wished it. One thing would bring me back to the hallowed worlds of humanity before we'd been out for more than a year! Crew! You lucky fellows have won the chance to serve aboard one of the sector's finest ships, the *Retribution*. Remember that name with pride and affection and all else should come naturally.'

Nathan must have looked confused because the stranger, a thin, dark man with tired eyes, whispered to him: 'It's the captain. 'Ere to welcome us aboard – sez it'll likely be the first and last time we see's 'im.'

Nathan blinked and gazed about him.

A vast, curving wall disappeared out of sight above them. It was pierced by arches showing a night sky speckled with stars. Halfway up it a buttressed gallery swelled outwards and it was from there that the captain spoke. His voice must have been amplified somehow, because a normal man's voice would have been drowned by a distant rumble which seemed to radiate from the worn stone floor they stood upon. A jolt of panic shot through Nathan as he realised they must be aboard some ship. No, an Imperial warship, he corrected himself. Even as he watched the stars in the windows were sliding across it almost imperceptibly. They were already underway.

NATHAN WAS INDUCTED into a gun crew: number six gun of the port deck, known to its crew as Balthasar. Him, Kendrikson, the tired-eyed man – who introduced himself as Fetchin – and five others were beaten, stripped, shaved, deloused, tattooed with their serial numbers and issued with dun-coloured coveralls, apparently tailored so that their one size would fit no one. The gun officer for Balthasar, a Lieutenant Gabriel, seemed decent enough and didn't revel in their humiliation. He and his enforcers, his armsmen, simply crushed their individuality and made it clear that they were to obey orders and cause no trouble. He was even good enough to explain to them that men were a commodity on a warship, like food or fuel or ammunition. When the ship ran out, it came to a world to resupply. Simple as that.

Even before the lieutenant had finished his little speech, Nathan had hardened his resolve to escape at the first opportunity.

They were set to work in a gunroom, a cavernous, hangar-like space which reeked of grease and ozone. It was part-filled by cranes and gantries but dominated by the breech of Balthasar, apparently some sort of gigantic cannon as big as a house and nested at the centre of an insane web of power coils, chains, coolant pipes, wiring, hydraulic rams and less easily identified attachments. By the unspoken rule which applies to all new recruits, the old hands set them to work on the most mundane, laborious and unwelcome tasks in the gunroom. In this case that meant long, hard work-shifts scraping off corrosion – which an old hand named Kron helpfully pointed out bloomed like a weed in the moist, oxygen-rich air inside the ship – or chipping away frozen coolant from the branches of piping. They ate on the gundeck too, with their food arriving on square metal trays through an aperture in the wall.

Food breaks were accompanied by the arrival of the crewmen the old hands referred to as armsmen. They came through one of the two heavy pressure doors which led into the gunroom, from the direction which Nathan had nominated as 'south'. The armsmen wore leather harnesses over their coveralls and carried long clubs and stubby pistols or shotguns. They kept a respectful distance while the guncrew ate, but their attitude spoke of a readiness to do harm if necessary. Once the food was consumed and the trays returned to their slot, the armsmen left through the north door, presumably to perform the same, apparently pointless function in the next gunroom.

Again, it was Kron who explained the purpose of the arms-men's vigil to the new recruits. 'They're here to make sure everyone gets their own share, lads.' Kron told them. 'An' that nobody takes what isn't theirs.'

Fetchin seemed shocked. 'So yer can't even keep a crumb for later? Or swap some wi' yer mate.'

Kron's answering grin was an ugly sight, particularly because he, like many of the old hands, had been patched with steel over old injuries. In Kron's case the tech-priests had left him with a half-skull of polished metal and set with a red-glowing eye. 'Not unless you want a few extra lumps to nurse, no,' he chortled.

Seeing disbelief still written on their faces he added more quietly: 'Was a time, years ago, when we had a… bad captain. He didn't keep a watch, boys. Was alright at first, the bully boys didn't take too much and no one starved. But then we were caught in a storm 'tween Esperance and the K-star for months, the ether was torn apart by cross-chasers and remnants so much that it was all the navigators could do to keep us from being lost. Pretty soon men's hunger made 'em desperate, an' desperate men'll do terrible things.'

Kron closed his real eye, blocking out bad memories.

Nathan had seen plenty of desperate men around Juniptown in Wet season, when work was scarce or non-existent.

'I've seen floors swimming with blood after fights over a husk of bread. The captain's right to keep a watch,' he said.

Kron looked at him curiously for a moment and then nodded. 'That's right, lad. Better to be harsh now than deadly later.'

Food was palmed and traded and fought over anyway, but in a quiet, cautious fashion which Nathan suspected the armsmen chose to overlook. Several times he tried to speak with Kendrikson but each time his old rival ignored him or, if Nathan pressed him harder, fled away from him. The old hands brooked no fighting so Nathan took it no further. He judged that the old hands were right: punishments for fighting were liable to be swift and brutal.

At the end of each workshift the crew slept in a low bunkroom beneath the gundeck. armsmen arrived to drive them below, although they needed little persuasion to drop their tools and find their way down into the gloomy, red-lit chamber. There were no exits from the bunkroom saving the hatch which led back up to the gunroom. cleansing and purging was undertaken in ridiculously small metal cubicles off the bunkroom. Nathan watched and waited but opportunities for escape never presented themselves. Soon work-shifts and sleep-shifts rolled relentlessly past until all sense of time was lost, until there was only toil and rest from toil, and then toil renewed.

IT WAS ONLY after the ship had left the Lethe system and passed into warp space that Nathan began to understand why men were a commodity. The warp made everything different somehow. Even the cavernous gundeck felt claustrophobic and oppressive, as if immense pressures existed just beyond the hull. Then the dreams had started, nightmares which left the mind dark and full of half-formed images upon waking. Some men screamed and wept in their sleep without knowing why, and others just grew more and more introverted and silent. Fetchin was one of these and Nathan had seen a weird light coming into his eyes long before it happened.

It was the end of the work-shift. The crew were straggling down the hatch to the bunkroom, more reluctant now that the dreams had come. Fetchin was last of all, listlessly scouring at a corrosion spot long after the others had moved away. The armsmen stepped forward with hard faces and Fetchin backed away with a stooped, almost scuttling gait. Almost at the top of the ladder, Nathan stopped and turned, his mind fumbling for some encouraging words which might persuade Fetchin to go below.

Before he could speak Fetchin backed into another of the guncrew. The man cursed and roughly thrust Fetchin away. From there it seemed as if Fetchin was possessed by devils. He pounced on the man with a snarl and bore him down. A horribly throttled gurgle escaped the thrashing pair and Fetchin rolled away, his lips and chin bloody with the ruin of the man's throat. Two men tried to pin the devil-Fetchin's arms but he slipped through their grasp like an eel, raking clawed fingers across their eyes with a hysterical, wordless scream.

The armsmen came pelting up and the first to reach the scene swung at Fetchin's shoulder with his long club, probably aiming to break his collarbone. The blow never connected. Fetchin grasped the downrushing arm with preternatural speed and swung the Armsman away with a horrible cracking, popping sound which spoke of dislocated joints and snapping bones. The madman turned suddenly and bounded towards the bunkroom hatch. Men scattered as his last manic leap sent him hurtling straight at Nathan.

Nathan saw the animal fire in Fetchin's eyes in the age-long instant as he leapt and felt his guts turn icy. There was not a scrap, not a hint of the mild, world-weary colleague he had come to know. All reason was lost in that glare, and Nathan was frozen in it.

Suddenly Kron was between them, so quick that Nathan didn't even see him step in the way. Kron swept the flailing arms aside and punched two stiffened fingers into Fetchin's windpipe before his feet had touched the ground. Fetchin was knocked sprawling by the impact and let out a low growl as he skidded across the deckplates. Nathan felt shocked; Kron's deadly accurate blow should have left Fetchin dead or unconscious, he felt sure.

Click-clack BOOM.

The sound of the shot echoed around the gunroom. A frozen tableau was left in its wake. An Armsman stood with shotgun levelled, smoke curling from the muzzle. Fetchin slid down the bulkhead leaving a bloody smear, a fist-sized wedge of raw flesh and entrails blasted from his midriff. Nathan, splattered with still-warm blood, not able to understand how Kron had moved so fast.

The armsmen drove them below with kicks and blows before another word was said. Kron was surprisingly kind and turfed out the old hand who bunked below him so that Nathan did not have to sleep beneath Fetchin's empty berth. When they were brought up for the next work-shift a scoured spot on the bulkhead was all that was left of Fetchin.

NATHAN WOKE to the sound of screaming. He lurched up with a half-strangled yelp, almost braining himself on the bottom of Kron's bunk. He stared wildly about him, gulping for breath. The oppressive red light of the bunkroom still surrounded him, the cloying odour of sour sweat and grease still fought the sharp tang of coolant in the air down here. The room was quiet save for the drip of the condensers and the assurance of night noises made by forty sleeping men.

Nathan wiped a shaky hand across his eyes and peered over towards Kendrikson. If anyone had screamed it would have been Kendrikson; he had nightmares nearly every sleep-shift. They all did, but Kendrikson just couldn't take it. Perhaps he had a guilty conscience, or perhaps he was just some dumb thief who was completely terrified by being shut up in one of the Emperor's warships. But Kendrikson's bunk was empty; he must have gone to relieve himself.

The scream came again, but it was tinny and distant, carried along by the conduits from another bunkroom. Pity the poor devils in there, thought Nathan, every one of them wide awake and praying the screamer didn't go berserk and start clawing and biting at them. That he didn't turn into a wild beast like Fetchin had.

Nathan lay back in the narrow bunk and tried to recapture sleep. He tried to imagine all the other shipmen doing the same. Start with this gundeck. Kron had told him there were forty guns with forty crews each, that's sixteen hundred, another gundeck on the other side for three thousand two hundred. Then there were the lance turrets, port and starboard, nobody seemed to know just how big the crews for those beasts were, call it another sixteen hundred a piece. This was working well, his eyelids were drooping. That was six and a half thousand souls (give or take). The torps probably had a crew much bigger than a single gun but less than a whole deck – maybe a thousand. That made seven and a half... engines must be at least two or three thousand more...

A rasping cough snapped him back to full wakefulness. A bittersweet cloud of smoke was drifting down from the bunk above. Nathan sighed. Kron, it was always Kron. 'Ain't sleeping too good?'

'Nah. Bad dreams,' Nathan replied. Kron was the oldest hand on the gundeck. Even Lieutenant Gabriel listened to him, sometimes, so it often paid to listen too.

'Really? Not like Fetchin, I hope,' Kron wheezed. It was a statement – or a cruel joke – not a question.

Nathan decided to take it as a joke and chuckled quietly. 'No, not like Fetchin,' he said. 'Just more dreams of the ship.'

Kron harrumphed quietly and another cloud of smoke wafted downwards, the feeble breath of the recyclers apparently insufficient to even pull it up and away. 'It's lucky to dream of the ship,' Kron said, his voice sounded a little wistful to Nathan, as though Kron were talking to himself. 'I used to dream of it a lot when I was young.'

Nathan wouldn't like to have to guess Kron's years. Apparent age varied so much from one world to another that it was a long shot at best. Take into account all the warp-time Kron must have had and Nathan would be naming a figure somewhere between sixty and three hundred. In the time it took him to think that, a slithering sound came from above and suddenly Kron was there, pipe in hand, right beside Nathan's bunk. The red light turned his polished skull, with its sharp nose and glowing eye into a gargoyle's head. His living eye twinkled.

'Come walk with me, young Nathan. Let's go up on deck.'

Nathan sat up and warily eased himself out of the bunk. 'What about the armsmen?' Nathan asked. Kron just snorted and started to pick his way, soft as a cat, to the hatch.

The gunroom was dark, its spars and columns rearing up with cathedral-like splendour into a gloom broken only by the jewel-like gleam of ready-lights and power indicators. They edged around to the far side of Balthasar over snaking cables, Kron sure-footed and Nathan trailing behind. As they rounded one of the pillars Nathan froze as he heard a squeak of oiled leather. Kron stepped on and virtually walked into an Armsman.

The Armsman brought up a torch and snapped it on, a little too quickly and awkwardly to have been lying in wait for them. Nathan slipped back round the pillar and out of sight so he didn't hear what was said, but after a few muttered words the armsmen swung away, whistling a little ditty and heading for the far end of the gunroom.

'Yeh can come out, lad,' Kron called. 'Ole Leopold won't bother us.'

Nathan came forward. 'I'd thought they would never stoop to fraternising with gunners, the armsmen I mean,' he said.

'Not while others're about, but come sleepshift they'll talk and trade like anyone else – they're crew just like us, just trusted enough to bear arms all th' time.' Kron seated himself on a stanchion and gestured expansively to another. Nathan took a last glance round before warily sitting also.

Kron gazed at him steadily while he got out his pipe again. 'So what's your story, young Nathan?' he asked.

'I don't have a story,' Nathan replied carefully. 'If this is about Kendrikson, my business is with him alone and I'll thank you not to intrude.' That earned an arched eyebrow and Nathan suddenly felt he was mistaken, Kron hadn't brought him up here to find out what was going on between him and Kendrikson.

'No,' Kron said, 'I mean, tell a story. That's how it's done among shipmen. When we want to really talk we tells a story, that way we can tell our secrets without saying them right out so others might hear.'

When Kron said that, he looked meaningfully at the outer hull plates, which Nathan could see from here were covered with writings, layered one over the other, marching lines of faded gothic script which continued up and out of sight towards the ceiling.

A sudden chill crept down Nathan's spine. He was sure he heard a vague creak of metal up at the north end of the gunroom. 'What do you mean? What "others"?' he hissed.

Kron raised a hand to stop him 'That's jest what I mean. Let me tell you a story about how mankind got among the stars: a tale of ancient times.'

Kron began to speak clearly and surely, without the customary drawls and breaks in his speech. It was almost as if he were reading from a book, or reciting a tale told many, many times before.

'ONCE, LONG AGO, Man lived on just one island. The broad oceans surrounded him and he believed himself alone. In time, Man's stature grew and he caught sight of other isles far off across the deep ocean. Since he had seen everything on his island, climbed every peak and looked under every stone, he became curious about the other islands and tried to reach them. He soon found the oceans too deep and cold for him to get far, not nearly a hundredth of the way to the next island. So Man returned and put his hand to other things for an age.

'But in time food and water and air ran short on Man's island and he looked to the far islands again. Because he could not bear the cold of the ocean deeps, he fashioned Men of Stone to go in his place, and the Stone Men fashioned Men of Steel to become their hands and eyes. And the Stone Men went forth with their servants and swam in the deep oceans. They found many strange things on the far islands, but none as strange or as wicked as the things that swam in the depths between them; ancient, hungry things older than Man himself.

'But these beasts of the deep hungered for the true life of Man, not the half-life of Stone, so the Stone Men swam unmolested. At first all was well and the Men of Stone planted Man's Seed on many islands, and in time Man learned to travel the oceans himself, hiding in Stone ships to keep out the cold and the hunger of the beasts. All was well and Men spread to many islands far across the ocean, such that some even forgot how they came to be there and that they ever came from just one island at all.'

Kron's tale wound on, telling of how the stone men became estranged from humanity by their journeys through the void. This led to a time of strife when the Men of Steel turned against their stone masters and mankind was riven asunder by wars. A thousand worlds were scoured by the ancient, terrible weapons of those days before the Men of Stone were overthrown, and a million more burned as flesh fought against steel. Worst of all, the beasts arose and were worshipped as gods by the survivors. Once proud and mighty, Man was reduced to a rabble of grovelling slaves. Finally one came who freed man from his shackles and showed him a new way to reach for the stars. This path was forged from neither stone nor steel but simple faith. Faith guarded Man from the beasts of the void as steel or stone could never do.

NATHAN CAME to himself with a start. Kron's sonorous voice had lulled him into a strange, half-dreaming state. He looked back at the wall and its inscrutable scripture. *Faith*. Faith kept the beasts at bay. Beasts that turned men into creatures like Fetchin. Each line of script covering the wall was a prayer to the God-Emperor for protection. Centuries of devotion layered like stratified rock to keep whatever was out there... out there. He could feel Kron's expectant gaze upon him, the red eye burning like a ruddy star in the gloom. Nathan uncomfortably tried to ignore the scratching noises he thought he heard coming from the gloom. Just nerves, he told himself, or rats, of course. Still, no harm in watching the shadows.

'I don't know many tales,' Nathan hedged, trying to recall one about the Emperor or the Great Crusade. He felt Kron's tale must be a parable of ancient times, set before the Crusades. They were spoken of only through the preachings of the Ecclesiarchy. In the Lethe system, a legendary time of right-eousness and purity recalled in the Ministorum's most reverential sermons, usually as a comparison to the immorality and irreverence of modern times.

'Tell us about you and yon Kendrikson then,' Kron prompted.

Inwardly Nathan cringed, but he sensed that Kron could be a big help to his chances of survival, let alone escape, and he had told a tale first. Warily, Nathan began.

'Me and Kendrikson don't go back far, but in the short time I've known him I've decided that I need to kill him. My youthful prospects were not exceptionally good, truthfully they were much given over to petty crime and associating with undesirables. However, thanks to Kendrikson I'm now an unwilling recruit in the Emperor's Navy. That appears to mean lifetime incarceration in a steel cube twenty paces across until death by insane shipmate, starvation, disease or enemy action intercedes. This wasn't my first choice in life.'

Nathan stood suddenly There was no doubt about it now, someone or something was creeping towards them as stealthily as it – or they – could manage. He gently lifted a steel hookbar from the deck and held it ready. Kron, seeing his look and actions, similarly armed himself with a long spanner. All the while Nathan kept talking, so as not to alert their stalkers. He told Kron about how he and Kendrikson had both served on the *Pandora*, an ageing lugger hauling ore and oxygen between the outer mines of Lethe. He even told him about how they had both actually been in the pay of a businessman dedicated to transporting goods of a rare, valuable and illegal nature with no questions asked.

Nathan had just got to their last voyage on the *Pandora*, and how Kendrikson had sold him out to the pirates when their skulking stalkers attacked. They came out of the shadows in a rush, three pale shapes and one dun coloured one. Nathan made a two-handed swing at the first to reach him. The steel hookbar caught it on the side of the head with a meaty crack and it dropped as if poleaxed.

It was a man. Pale, near naked, with a matted beard and bloodied shock of hair. A second leapt forward, jagged blade swinging, while Nathan was still recovering from his initial blow. He managed an awkward parry with the hookbar and the man pulled his blade back for another hack. Nathan followed through with his block and crashed the end of the hookbar into the wildman's elbow, making him yell and drop his blade. The third dove in between them and drove Nathan back with a flurry of blows.

He blocked a few strikes with the ungainly bar, but gave ground and almost stumbled on a trailing pipe. In desperation he ducked under a cable conduit as his assailant made an overhead cut. The blade sliced into the shoc-lines with a shower of fat sparks. The man convulsed and his face clamped into a rictus grin of agony as current flowed remorselessly between blade and deck through him. As Nathan dashed past him he was starting to smoulder, the blade glowing orange in his deathgrip.

The second man had retrieved his blade and made as if to strike as Nathan ran up, but the superior reach of the hookbar finally paid off. Nathan slammed it bodily into his ribs. The momentum of his charge skewered the man on its cruel head, splintering ribs and ripping open a gouting wound. Nathan abandoned the wedged bar and plucked the blade out of the man's fingers, giving thanks that his enemies seemed disorientated and slow, as if they were half-starved or dim-witted.

Nathan sprang forward towards the last foe, a figure in shipman's coveralls bending over the prone body of Kron. Nathan's nape hairs prickled as the figure lurched up. Blue wych-fires writhed about his limbs like angry snakes and sparks poured from its fingertips. By some reflex Nathan ducked away from a hissing bolt of energy which lashed out from an outstretched hand. It still caught him across the left shoulder and sent fiery needles of agony lancing into his very bones.

If he could have shouted in agony he would have, but his lips only parted in a soundless gasp as a wave of numbness washed through him. Nathan fell to his knees on the deck and fought his unresponsive body as it dragged him down, down. The figure stepped closer. Through blurring eyes Nathan could see the complex weaving of tattoos beneath his skin, glowing through it with lightning-brightness. Even the coveralls were rendered translucent by that glare, and bones stood out coal-black as he raised a spectral hand in a gesture full of menace.

With his final ounces of strength he struck back at his foe the only way he could, hurling the blade stiff-armed as he slid to the deck. Before he blacked out he felt a thunderclap of pressure and a wave of heat before blackness closed over him.

NATHAN'S EYES flickered open. He pulled himself up to a sitting position and retched. Only moments had passed. Smoke was still rising from the corpse beside him and the sweet stench of cooked flesh hung in the air. The thrown blade protruded from the corpse's larynx, and Nathan knew he should never gamble again after fluking that shot. But, despite the blade, the massive burns across the body looked like they had been just as fatal. Vagrant flickers of static still trailed along rigor-stretched limbs. Nathan mustered his courage and stared into the blackened face. It was Kendrikson, patently no mere smuggler after all. He stepped well clear of the corpse as he staggered groggily to where Kron lay.

Faint breath sighed from Kron's lips and the burns on his body didn't look fatal. Nathan paused at this, his head throbbing and mouth dry with fear, and considered how he might be able to judge such a thing given his lack of experience. Regardless, he could not simply leave Kron lying insensible so he decided to follow his instincts and attempt to revive him somehow. By shaking him and calling Kron's name, Nathan was soon rewarded with a moaning and stirring. Seconds later Kron's real eye flickered open; his redgem-eye remained dim.

'Wh-wh-what? Wh-where am I?' he whispered with trembling lips.

'On the gundeck,' Nathan replied. 'There was a fight...'

He broke off. Kron had raised his hands and was touching his metal half skull and dim jewel-eye. 'It's still on me!' he suddenly yelped. 'Get it off before it can crash-start!'

Nathan stood in shock. Kron's voice was different and he was starting to thrash around in a most un-Kron-like fashion. Nathan snatched for his wrists in fear that he might injure himself and the strange voice grew shrill with panic. 'No! Don't let it take me... don't let it...' Kron's new voice trailed away and his body slackened in Nathan's grip. As Nathan lowered him gently to the deck he noticed Kron's jewel-eye was flickering back to life.

'Ai, Nathan,' Kron said, his voice normal. 'Lost my way there for a sec. Ye were about to tell me how ye escaped from the pirates?'

Nathan stared at him. Kron seemed to have no recollection of the fight or his bizarre behaviour. Nathan squatted down, watching Kron carefully as he slowly looked about, taking in the carnage around him.

'There was a fight,' Nathan explained again. 'Kendrikson and some new friends tried to kill us, well, perhaps just kill me and capture you.'

Kron stood with no apparent signs of pain or weakness, and walked over to Kendrikson's corpse, where he bent down and retrieved a half-melted spanner. 'I struck him with this,' he told Nathan. 'I didn't realise he was a Luminen.' Kron fell silent, staring down at Nathan with that red, cyclopean eye for a long, long minute.

Nathan had a greasy feeling of fear in his stomach as he gazed back. Kron was obviously not entirely whole or sane. He had called Kendrikson a Luminen, a word which stirred disturbing memories in Nathan's mind. It might be best not to remind Kron of his equally disturbing words and actions. Better now to find out about the Luminen Kendrikson and his allies. Kron was holding Kendrikson's scorched head in his hands now.

'Why do ye think they were out to catch poor Kron?' the old man asked. Kron turned away to hide the act, but his hands still made an ugly cracking noise as they crushed Kendrikson's skull.

'I have absolutely no idea who they were,' Nathan snapped, 'let alone what they wanted with you! Kendrikson was… was… I don't know, possessed? What is a Luminen?'

Kron clicked his tongue a few times, a curiously mechanical sound like that of the *Pandora's* clattering old logic engine. Before he could reply there was a flicker of lights at the south end of the gunroom; echoing shouts followed. Kron turned and scurried towards the north end without a word. After a second's indecision, Nathan followed, struggling to keep sight of Kron's disappearing back while not tripping on a cable or cracking his head on a stanchion.

He caught up with Kron as he bent over a thick pipe in a shadowed corner beside the script-marked outer wall. The pipe was made of many rings of metal half the height of a man. Kron pulled apart two of the rings and slipped inside, turning to hold the rings apart and jerking his head for Nathan to follow. He ducked within, realising as the rings creaked back into place that he had heard the same noise before Kendrikson and his allies had attacked.

They belly-crawled along the pipe in silence, the way lit only by Kron's cyclopean eye. Bundles of wires ran along the bottom of the pipe, most filthy and blackened but some more recent, their bright colours encarmined by Kron's unflinching gaze. Dozens of dog-eared labels clung precariously to the different bundles. Many were torn off or unreadable, others bore legends such as *Lwr diff*, *aaz/3180* or *Ar.ctrl 126.13kw* in careful gothic script.

The pipe gave out in to a black crack, chasm-deep with cabling spilling off into its depths like a frozen waterfall. Kron led Nathan on to a short bridge of pipes that crossed to the other wall which was splotched with bright blobs of enormous silver like soldering marks. At the far side Nathan stopped, unnerved by Kron's continuing silence and the cold, lightless spaces he was being led into. Time for some answers.

'Kron,' he whispered, 'where are we? And where do you think you're taking me?'

Kron turned to face him before replying. 'She's an old ship, lad. She fought and sailed the void for nigh eighteen centuries in the Emperor's fleet, an' before that she slept in a hulk for another twenty. That's where I–' Kron clamped his mouth shut and his eye blazed. He gazed round warily before speaking again. 'We're between the hull plates here. Yon weld marks are from when she took a salvo in the flank during the assault on Tricentia.'

'And where are we going?'

'Somewhere that's safe, where we can hide 'til the armsmen finish their search; hide an' talk in peace.'

'Won't the armsmen follow us down here?'

'Nay lad, wi'out a fully armed servitor crew an' a tech-priest they couldn'a use their guns for fear of cracking somethin',' Kron said.

'And where is this sanctuary of yours?'

'Not ten strides yonder.' Kron pointed.

Nathan took a long, hard look at the narrow ledge of rotting cables that ran along the wall from the end of the pipe bridge. His burnt and aching body already throbbed from the efforts he had forced it through after the fight. Now, as the flush of adrenaline left him and the icy chill in the air replaced it, he doubted his arms and legs could carry him on such a precarious path. He hesitated and swayed involuntarily on the bridge, which suddenly seemed rather precarious in itself now he came to think about it.

'Kron, I don't think…'

Too late, the old man was swinging off along the ledge with the agility of a monkey. With him, the wan red light that served as the only illumination was vanishing fast.

Nathan hesitated only a moment before a hot flush of anger drove him forward onto the ledge. He'd be damned if he would let this walking enigma disguised as an old man abandon him to the dark and potentially more of Kendrikson's feral allies. He grasped a shoulder-high seam of wiring and pulled himself firmly over to get a foot on the cabling, trusting his weight to it as he pulled his other foot into place. Bloody-minded determination hauled him along three paces of the ledge. He made two more with his heart in his mouth and fingers fumbling blindly for purchase on the wires before his foot slipped off the cables.

His body swung out alarmingly, and only his recently gained handholds on the wiring-seam stopped him pitching off the treacherous ledge. He desperately scrabbled to get his foot back on it. His hands were as weak as water and his heart was thumping so hard his arms quivered. After a few seconds of naked terror he got his foot back on and hugged himself to the wall, teetering as his legs shook. He couldn't let go of the wiring now, his legs were too weak to trust and his hands couldn't hold his weight for much longer. He couldn't go forward, he couldn't go back. Every iota of his strength was necessary just to hold him where he was, with the blackness below sucking at his remaining scraps of vigour.

Nathan clutched closer still to the wall and plucked up his courage, carefully shuffling one foot along the cabling. He shifted some weight to it and shakily drew the other foot closer. With a supreme effort of will he unhooked one hand from the wires and reached out to grasp them further along. Then he rested and sweated before shuffling his foot forward again. So he went for the remaining five paces: slide, grip, shuffle, rest; slide, grip, shuffle, rest; slide, grip...

NATHAN ALMOST FELL into the opening when he came to it. The horrible sensation that he might fall off just as he pulled himself to safety was almost overwhelming. Once inside the opening he sat trembling for only a moment, before summoning the energy to crawl further away from the edge.

The interior of the narrow space looked like the choir stall of some Ministorum chapel. Narrow seats crammed along either wall beneath gothic arches of tubular metal. At the far end a porthole of stained glass was lit fitfully from behind by swirling colours. Kron stood silhouetted against the glass. He turned to face Nathan and pressure doors rolled shut behind him, shutting the dank breath of the crevasse outside. 'Well done, lad. I was thinking ye weren't goin' to make it.' His voice sounded as smooth and calming as the raspy little goblin could make it.

'What the hell did you leave me alone out there for?' Nathan demanded.

'To see if you're as tough as I'm thinking ye are.'

'Oh really, and do I pass muster?'

'I'll be needing to hear the end of your story to know that.'

'That's got nothing to do with this!'

'Come, lad, I can tell by the look in yer eyes that you don't think that's true. "Coincidence" is just a name that fools use for events they don't understand.'

Nathan blinked at Kron and gave a mental shrug. What harm could it do to finish the story if it gave Kron one less thing to be evasive about? 'All right, but then you better give me some answers or I'll crawl right back out of here and tell it to the armsmen.

'As I said, I opened the inner hatch to the cargo bay. Once it was open I overrode the outer hatch controls and hung on tight. I knew the drums in the bay were badly secured because me and Kendrikson had been too busy watching each other to make a decent job of it. The outer hatch blowing was enough to break them free and dump them into the void between the *Pandora* and the pirates. I was almost crushed by the stampede of metal cylinders but by the Emperor's grace and a strong grip I was able to keep a hold and stayed on the ship instead of being flung out among the cartwheeling drums outside.

'A few seconds later the first drum connected with the docking thrusters of the pirate ship. I'd been playing for time, just hoping to upset their approach, but the drums were filled with liquid oxygen. The touch of the thrusters was enough to make them explode like bombs. Dozens of the cylinders exploded in slow, slow motion, the tendrils of fire reaching back further into the cloud and detonating the rest. The escalation scared me badly and I hauled myself within the inner hatch and closed it an instant before the expanding bubble of flames washed across the *Pandora*. The deck bucked and the handful of drums which had not escaped with their fellows rolled around and clashed angrily.

'In a second the shock wave had passed and I looked out the hatch to see the pirate ship spiralling off, fires clinging to it and debris leaking from it like a blood-trail. I went forward and up to the bridge where that slob Captain Lage was defecating in his britches. Lage claimed that Kendrikson had held him at gunpoint and forced him to cut the engines and wait for the other ship. Minutes before the explosion Kendrikson had taken a raft and left the ship. Naturally he had taken all of the archaeotech we had been smuggling with him.

'I was surprised when I heard Kendrikson had been seen in Juniptown on Leath. I'd thought he was dead or long gone. I knew I could pick up a bounty for his head so I went hunting for him in the back alleys, which is home turf for me. But both me and Kendrikson were seized by men from the *Retribution*. And that is how I began my new career in the Imperial Navy...'

'Ye never actually knew Kendrikson?' Kron asked softly.

'No, I knew of him, worked with him, but he avoided me and most people from what I heard, he was a guy so weird he didn't even have a nickname. He was just "Kendrikson", and that said it all. Alright, I've told you my tale now it's time for you to give me some answers. No stories, just tell me the truth. 'Who were those men with Kendrikson?' Nathan glared at Kron, daring him not to answer, to push him over the edge into screaming fury.

'Them's muties, shipmen that's spent too long sailin' the void an' lost their faith. The beast song's in their heart now and they live like lice on the innards o' the ship; sometimes they'll even grab compartments and feast on the poor shipboys if they can. Once in a century the captain'll put the ship into port and flush her guts with poison to clear 'em out but 'tween times there's always muties in the crossways and trunks. Seein' as we're in a big war right now there's more than ever, and they'll be lookin' to call the beasts aboard all the time, invite 'em in as it were. Out there's whole squadrons who've succumbed to the beasts in men's hearts in past times, ones I reckon we'll be fightin' soon enough. Kendrikson probably pretended he were possessed to scare 'em into obeying him. The pirates' ship ye saw, did it have a mark on it? A rune or sigil?'

'Yes it did, most do. I don't see–'

'Did ye see it well enough to know it again?'

'Yes, but I'm asking the questions now.' Nathan had recovered enough energy to stand and hauled himself up to face Kron. 'What's a Luminen? I asked you before and you didn't answer but now you're going to tell me. What made Kendrikson a Luminen and how did that give him lightning in his veins and the power to melt steel like wax?' Nathan took a step closer, looming over Kron in the narrow space. 'Tell me!'

Kron grinned up at him before turning and pointing at the stained glass. 'I bet the pirates' symbol looked like that.'

Nathan gaped. The intricate, geometric designs of the window centred around a central icon. A halo of gold with rays so short and square that they looked like crenellations on a castle wall. In the centre was a grinning skull, picked out in loving detail with strands of platinum wire and swirls of crushed diamond. He snapped his gaze back to Kron. 'What does it mean?'

'It answers both your questions, lad. Kendrikson and yon pirates came from the same place. They made him a Luminen, took him an' made crystal stacks of his bones an' electro grafts of his brain, gave 'im skinplants and electros so's he could summon lightning an' channel it an' much more. He was a war-child of the Machine God, what the uninitiated call an electro-priest, though not one in a hundred can hide his power an' look like a normal man like he did.'

'The Machine God – you mean the tech-priests of Mars, don't you, the Adeptus Mechanicus?'

Kron nodded solemnly and Nathan suffered a painful insight into the awesome power that organisation wielded within the all-powerful Imperium. Tech-priests ministered to machines and engines on every civilised world, every interstellar ship. The Navy might man its ships but the tech-priests ran them. Their prayers and runes brought life to cold, dead metal and their Forge worlds produced weapons in their billions for the Emperor's eternal war against aliens, heretics and traitors. In theory at least killing Kendrikson made him one of the latter. A sobering thought indeed.

'All right then, what's this place. Those look like shuttle controls. Am I right in presuming that it's an escape pod of some sort?'

'Aye lad, a cutter. Good for a planetary hop if ye don't mind the waiting as she's a mite slow.'

'Given what I've just heard I'd jump ship now if we weren't in the warp.'

'Death by fulguration if they catch ye,' Kron muttered with an honest-looking shudder.

'Well, we can't go back. If they find out who Kendrikson was and who killed him I'd wager they'll come up with something even more unpleasant.'

'Nay, lad, if anyone knew who Kendrikson was he wouldnae have been in the gunrooms. Tech-priests only come to repair battle damage and such.'

'So Kendrikson was originally out to get back the archaeotech for the tech-priests and got pressganged accidentally, but why didn't he tell the Navy who he was? They would have let him go for sure.'

'Many times servants o' the Emperor bury their real selves behind false memgrams and such, makes 'em hard to ferret out even wi' soul-seers. Their real purposes run in the background, watching the puppet show through the eyes and ears until they're in position to accomplish their mission. Then they become a whole different person. The Luminen part was just standing by for orders, but it must have decided that you needed killin' to keep its past buried.' Kron let that sink in for a few seconds before passing judgement on the matter.

'No one'll know we did for 'im if we get back before roll call, 'cept Leopold mebbe and he ain't going to say for fear o' bein' called derelict.'

Nathan was safe as long as Kron didn't rat on him, but he had a feeling that Kron was happy to keep their secret for the time being. They were partners in crime. 'I'm willing to bet that there's another way back into the crew quarters without crossing the gunroom.'

Kron grinned.

'HAJJ. ·

  'Isiah.

  'Kendrikson.'

The sergeant-at-arms leant over and whispered something to Lieutenant Gabriel, who paused over the great ledger he had open before him. Nathan swallowed hard. This was where Kron's theory came to the crunch. Getting back from the cutter had been easier than he had hoped. A narrow culvert led back from the crevasse into the cubicles by the bunkroom. Nathan had carefully memorised every twist of the trunking and was determined to go back and familiarise himself further with it in the very next sleep shift. But for now he must see whether the Angel of Retribution was at Kendrikson's side or not.

Lieutenant Gabriel gazed at the assembled company, eyes blinking as if he were struggling to recall Kendrikson's face. He turned and murmured a question to the sergeant, who shook his head curtly in response. Gabriel made a small mark in the ledger and continued.

'Krait.

'Komoth.'

Roll call held an additional pleasant surprise: when Lieutenant Gabriel assigned the duty roster Nathan found himself placed on the Opticon crew. His momentary puzzlement was soon answered when it became clear that he was to be Kron's apprentice. He stole a look at the old man, who looked blandly innocent of course, and made a mental note of the apparent influence he could wield. Nathan wondered what the role of apprentice entailed, and for that matter what the Opticon was. A dim memory floated forward that the Opticon was involved in observation outside the ship. He certainly knew that the Opticon crew usually worked high up on the main gantries above Balthasar's breech on what amounted to an extra half-deck a good twelve metres up spiral steps of skeletal ironwork.

Whatever the duties, they could scarcely be as onerous and repetitive as the labours he was tasked with at present. As he ascended he could see other members of the guncrew moving to repair the damage he and Kron had caused in their desperate fight. The bodies were gone but charred cabling and slashed conduits were visible. Nathan wondered grimly how often they had repaired such damage without knowing its cause. The adage that 'ignorance is bliss' seemed to dominate shipboard life, but with good cause if what Kron had said about the muties was true. The grim pressures of warp travel became all the more nightmarish with the thought that there were malevolent entities clustered beyond the hull. Beasts that thirsted for human lives and souls, whose subconscious calls drove men mad. Nathan suddenly stopped climbing the steps as the thought struck him that he was going to help Kron observe those beasts and the Empyrean, the alternate dimension that they swam in.

The curses of the men behind made him move on, accompanied by a perverse desire to see the sinister beasts. He had mixed feelings when he reached the raised deck and saw a row of five shuttered arches lining the hull wall. There were ten in the Opticon crew and the burly rating named Isiah placed two men at each shutter. At first Nathan and Kron busied themselves greasing the shutter runners and cogs at its head and foot. After a quarter watch or so Isiah received a message from the comm-box he carried and relayed an order to raise the shutters. Kron smartly threw a lever and the shutter rose smoothly up to reveal an expanse of black glass which rose higher than his head and as wide as his outstretched arms. As Nathan glanced around at the other crews he noted a sense of nervous anticipation behind their actions, as if raising the shutters was an act of hidden significance.

Nathan was still gazing expectantly at the black glass when the scream of a siren shocked him rigid. The titanic blast of noise seemed to make the very deck plates tremble and was followed by a booming voice which rang like the word of the God-Emperor: 'ALERT STATUS ALL STATIONS!'

Kron turned and ran for a set of lockers at the side of the Opticon chamber, hotly pursued by the rest of the crew. The men started pulling on pressure suits which Kron dragged from the lockers. The significance of the situation was becoming readily apparent to Nathan by now. They were going into battle, very soon. Those ridiculously cumbersome-looking, heavy, rubberised pressure suits and thick-bowled helmets could be all that stood between them and the void.

To his surprise, Nathan managed to finish clamping himself into a suit before anyone else.

The helmet locked down onto a broad ring across the shoulders of the suit but had a visor made up of different layers, the last of which was little more than a slit in the armour plate. He slid back all the layers and saw Kron had done the same. Nathan felt relieved that he wouldn't have to breathe the stale, sweaty air inside the suit just yet. 'How long does this oxygen last?' he asked Kron, tapping the dented brass cylinder plumbed into the side of the suit's chest.

'A watch or so for somun' as big as ye.'

'Just eight hours? They don't want us to get any ideas about wandering off, do they?'

'Ye can always get more air on the ship and if ye... part company wi the ship an' ye're not picked up they wouldnae be able to find ye anyway. Ye'd be drifted too far into the void.'

'Alright, what do–'

The deck lurched beneath their feet and there was a sickening sensation of falling for a second. Isiah shouted at them to get to their stations. Nathan noted that the rating now bore a pistol and what looked suspiciously like a shock-maul and sprang to his post as best as the suit's heavy boots would allow.

The monolithic siren blasted twice. A commanding voice spoke: 'BATTLE STATIONS. BRACE FOR IMPACT!'

The deck shuddered and dropped again. This time the falling was longer. Nathan slid the visor down, grabbed a stanchion and braced his legs. He felt sick and hollow. The suit was stifling. He fought an urge to tear the helmet off and scream his lungs out. An insistent, intellectual part of his brain kept telling him to be calm and that the ship was simply preparing itself and surging majestically into battle. But the animal instincts of his body felt every jar and shake as an infernal choir of death screams.

The ship lurched and fell again. This time Nathan actually felt his feet leave the floor. He felt as though part of him was being torn away, all the roiling emotion in his body began coalescing into a tearing sense of dislocation. A tangible shock rang along the length of the ship and Nathan realised they had left warpspace.

The black glass of the Opticon flashed white and then cleared to show a scene of awesome beauty. A night-sky bisected by titanic thunderheads of cloud reared above a fiery sunset. Static lightning cobwebbed the depths and climbed up to blush the clouds with purple. Stars stood out sharp and clear, their own fires made to seem cold by their distance.

'The void never looked so beautiful or terrible before,' Nathan whispered, his fear drained away by the majesty of it all. Kron's voice crackled in his earpieces.

'That's right lad, 'cause through this glass ye see as the ship does; heat, light, magnetism, radiants and etherics are all clear to her.' Kron slid out a large circular lens which was attached to the window frame by a system of brass rods and runners. The thick frame of the lens held two number counters and two raised icons. Kron expertly tracked it across the surface of the window. The numbered wheels of the counters span in response, one horizontal, one vertical.

The ship shuddered again, and Nathan swayed against the window, his helmet ringing off the unyielding surface alarmingly. The sensation of almost being pitched out into the void was enough to make his palms sweat inside the cursedly thick gloves. As he straightened up, Isiah was barking orders to the crews to search different co-ordinates. Kron slid the lens across until the metriculators showed 238.00 by 141.00, their search area. At that spot the lens resolved a dark area which had shown occasional vagrant twinklings into an asteroid field, rolling mountains of stone lit by the star's fiery light.

'What are we looking for, Kron, just rocks?' Nathan asked with shaky levity. The old man was tracking the lens back and forth across the field with deft, economical movements. Each time he reached its periphery he depressed one of the runes, and the tumbling stones shown in the lens were outlined in red with strings of numbers showing speed and distance which remained in the glass after the lens slid away.

'Anythin' that might show us where the foe's a'lurkin; a glint here, or a bloom o' heat there.' Kron never took his eye from the lens as he spoke, Nathan slid back his topmost, armoured visor so that he could see better.

'You mean engine heat trails like those?' he stated, pointing to a set of needle-thin arcs which shimmered near the edge of the field.

'CONTACT! MARK-TWO-FOUR-ZERO BY ONE-THREE-SEVEN!' Kron roared, Isiah shouting it back, word for word, over the crackling comm.

The lens now showed broad, vaporous trails of red which curved back around the furthest asteroids. There looked to be four to Nathan, although they were already merging and dissipating.

'They're closing in, lad, I can smell it.'

Kron tracked the lens along the trails and cursed as they disappeared behind a glowing streamer of dust. Moments later an incandescent spearhead of heat blossomed out of the cloud, dust and lightning rolled off it in plumes as the lens starkly announced it as *Enemy vessel [class: Unknown]. 51,000l. Closing.*

A burst of activity on the deck below drew Nathan's attention. Through the grilled floor he could see Balthasar's breech had been swung open and the gunners were hauling flat plates covered in short spikes into the open maw. Even through his thick suit he could hear the gunners' cheers as they slammed the sub-munitions home. On the lens light and shadow now etched out the enemy, showed the silhouette of crenallated battlements and barbed buttresses as the spearhead rolled abeam on the white-hot stabs of myriad thrusters. *Grand cruiser*, the display read, *Repulsive* class.

A ripple of serried flames geysered from the *Repulsive's* flank as she completed the turn, and a storm of black specks arrowed towards them. Nathan gasped in horror as a heartbeat later the specks started to explode in gouts of flame. At first they looked distant, small puffs of colour against the void, but the projectiles kept coming, surging forward through the fiery chains to detonate in turn. In moments their view of the enemy was obscured by a firestorm which was rippling ever closer. The flames filled every window in the Opticon by the time Nathan slammed his visor fully shut.

The *Repulsive's* salvo crashed down on the ship itself with hurricane force. Nathan staggered as the deck rolled beneath him and a mighty, rushing wind roared beyond the hull. A lash of dazzling purple light blazed through the glass, cutting the incendiary cloud like elemental lightning. It was gone in an instant before it returned in a retina-burning sweep which slammed into the ship with a bone-jarring impact. Nathan's spine crawled with the sensation of unseen energies straining and crackling before a rush of scorching heat washed over him.

At last he was glad of the suit's cumbersome protection, though even with it he felt as though he had been suddenly cast into a great oven. The heat was a palpable thing, pushing down on him like a great hand and burning his throat as he tried to breathe. Nathan saw several of the Opticon crew collapse into pathetic heaps, one with flames licking about him. After what seemed like hours but could only have been seconds of heart-stopping fear the burning suddenly stopped, leaving a horrible tang of smouldering rubber inside his helmet. Sirens blasted and an almighty voice boomed over the chaos: 'PORT WEAPONS PREPARE TO LOCK-ON. TARGET MARK-TWO-SIX-NINE BY ONE-SIX-ZERO.'

Iron discipline drove the shipmen to their tasks, that and the grim instinct that to live they must fight and win. The ship had been wounded but it could still fight back. Fires were doused, the dead and injured dragged away. The firestorm was lessening and a moment later the decks ceased to rattle as the ship finally burst clear of the enemies' salvo pattern. Kron's breath rasped in Nathan's earpiece as they slid the lens back over the grand cruiser contact. The *Retribution* was coming across the enemies' bow, and the metriculator's count showed the enemy as closing.

'LOCK ON.'

Kron activated the second rune on the lens frame. A stylised cog superimposed by the Imperial eagle sprang into existence within the lens but the runners seemed to be jammed and Nathan had to help him drag the device over the target contact. The lens showed the ornate spearhead foreshortening into a shark-finned ziggurat of bronze as they pulled across the front of her. Where the icon rested the hull of the grand cruiser was illuminated as if by a ghostly radiance which played over shimmering walls of force.

'FIRE MAIN BATTERIES!'

The lights dimmed for a moment as capacitors charged and then the ship resounded with the clamour of the guns. Nathan felt the pressure of unseen forces hit him like a slap as forty guns hurled their payloads across the void. A moment later he saw the spreading cloud of projectiles cleaving towards the enemy. No spreading storms of fire this time, the munitions detonated right beneath the enemy's prow. Invisible walls fell beneath the onslaught and a rain of destruction crashed across the battlements of the ziggurat-fortress. Debris haloes puffed from it like smoke rings.

'FIRE MAIN LANCE ARRAYS.'

Ravening white spears of pure power stabbed at the foe, tearing red-glowing gouges across its hull, globs of molten metal spun away and flames leapt from the wounds. The grand cruiser lurched visibly under the impacts, and began to twist away from the salvo. Even as it did so, two heat trails appeared from behind the grand cruiser, coming up fast to slash at its rear with a spiralling net of laser bolts. Nathan felt a flush of relief. The other two ships must be allies, and now their mutual enemy was caught between two fires. Below, the gunners were rushing to reload Balthasar for another shot, while a small team struggled to pin a whipping power line which sparked furiously. He looked back at the lens in time to see a swarm of bright flares pulling away from the enemy cruiser's prow. Ominously the tiny heat trails curved to alter course towards them and it soon became apparent that although these new weapons were not as fast as the projectiles fired before, they were considerably bigger. Sirens blared.

'ALL STATIONS PREPARE TO REPEL BOARDERS.'

The relief Nathan had felt rapidly evaporated. The enemy must have launched boarding torpedoes, simple attack craft packed with the troops, bombs, incendiaries, corrosives, nerve agents and other hellish weapons necessary to wreak havoc if they got aboard. It was bad enough to be caught up in the titanic duel between warships but now the enemy was coming to strike at them face to face, all the time with the prospect of being crushed like an insect by the pulverising contest going on outside. Isiah rapidly passed out weapons from an arms-locker: blades, shock mauls, stubby autopistols and chunky shotguns. Nathan found himself equipped with a worn-looking pump gun and a clip of shells. He risked a glance at the windows as he was fumbling to slot the shot-filled cylinders into the breech of the gun. They now showed finger-long missiles with beaked prows powering, as it seemed, straight for him on harsh coronas of light. The sirens blared a repeating four-tone alarm.

'PORT TURRET STATIONS: OPEN FIRE!'

Nathan cursed as he dropped a shell onto the grating; his fingers felt like sausages in the thick suit gloves. Outside lasers sketched livid traceries across the void as the short-range turrets laid down their barrage, shells and missiles exploded in gouts of orange incandescence as the *Retribution's* barbettes joined in. The first rank of the beaked projectiles were consumed or broken open and tiny, struggling figures spilled into the void as they spiralled away. But still more torpedoes surged through the barrage and angled in, cutting their flaring drives on a final approach.

Nathan slammed the last shell into place and carefully pumped the action to chamber a round. At the last instant before impact the torpedoes appeared to swell enormously, becoming as big as shuttles before they disappeared from view. A ringing impact threw Nathan to the quivering deck and an endless cacophony of screaming, tearing metal followed. It was so loud it made him quail at the bone-crushing violence of it, of the sheer force that was ripping through the metres of armour plate to breach the hull.

Finally the tearing slowed and stopped until only the screams of injured gunners and the hiss of escaping air penetrated Nathan's helmet. The Opticon deck had twisted and now part of it sagged away towards the lower deck. Nathan crawled to the edge and saw there was terrible carnage below. A great crocodile-snout of steel and brass projected through the hull plates near Balthasar's breech. Deckplates were twisted back; stanchions and pipes had been bent into an insane ironwork jungle with flowers of steam and spraying fluids. The surviving gunners were taking up defensive positions, aiming their assortment of shotguns and pistols at the invader.

As they did so, cannons coughed into life around the crocodile's snout. Gunflashes strobed as the autoweapons hammered explosive rounds across the interior of the gunroom. Men were blasted asunder where the rounds struck and hot shrapnel whickered around the metal walls injuring others. The snout was grinding open now and a horde of nightmarish figures spilled out of it to add their fire to the fight. At first they appeared like men in the flickering light, but their insane glee marked them apart. They capered as the gunners' pitifully few weapons tore into them, filling that crocodile maw with twitching bodies. They roared with mad laughter as they blazed back with their own guns and threw devilish bombs which burst into pools of hungry, incandescent flame wherever they landed.

Nathan sighted on a twisted figure as it pulled back its arm to throw. The pump gun crashed and the figure fell into a burning pool of its own making. The flames spread, engulfed the crocodile snout and the next two who tried to rush through it were eaten alive by the incendiary. Even so a group of the attackers were out in the gunroom now, dashing through the wreckage to hurl themselves on the gunners. Vicious hand-to-hand combats broke out all across the deck, the foes' hooks and crooked blades clashing against the gunner's pry bars and line gaffes.

The pump gun was useless now the melee had reduced all ordered fighting to a shambles.

'We've got to help them!' Nathan shouted to Kron.

Kron's helm nodded ponderously back and they both slid themselves down the twisted Opticon deck to drop down onto the gundeck. Isiah and two other survivors of the opticon crew followed and they waded into the brawl in a loose knot. Nathan used his gun as a club, smashing the skull of a black-clad figure who was about to gut a fallen gunner. He winced as the gun crunched into its misshapen head, fearing the ageing weapon would fall apart in his hands.

He pumped the action to chamber a round to reassure himself it still could, just as two figures leapt at him out of the smoke. Their mad eyes glared from behind leather hoods, looking so like Fetchin's that Nathan almost hesitated before he blasted one in the midriff with the shotgun. He pumped the slide to chamber another round but it jammed halfway. Cursing, he swung the gun up to block a saw-bladed knife as the other foe slashed at him but he was borne back as his attacker leapt bodily onto him, pinning the useless gun between their bodies. Panic stole Nathan's strength as he struggled against its maniacal attack. Drool spilled across his face as the creature tore away his helmet with its free hand and pushed him to the deck.

Nathan dropped his gun and scrabbled to keep a grip on the knife-hand as his foe leaned his weight against it, pushing it inexorably towards his exposed neck. For a long second Nathan saw every detail of the thing astride him with horrible clarity. Flames billowed behind a head made jagged by the short horns thrusting out through its leather mask. Cartilage-textured tubes twisted in and out of its flesh like parasitic worms. It was either naked or covered in human hides marked with brands and stigmata. It stank like a week-old corpse and it muttered mad, excited prayers as it bent to the task of murdering him. If what he had been told was true this thing must have been human once. Every shred of its humanity was gone now, eaten up by insane gods that had reduced it to living offal that worshipped its own butcher.

Sickness lent Nathan an awful strength, a burning desire to wipe out these horrors that had been unleashed on them. With a supreme effort born of revulsion Nathan shoved the creature back. Suddenly it convulsed, then slumped and its dead weight bore him back down again.

Nathan rolled free to see Kron pulling an axe from the abomination's neck. Isiah and the others had disappeared into smoke. only corpses surrounded Nathan and Kron. Nathan's helmet visor had been smashed, rendering it useless. Without it he realised how thin the air was becoming. The flames all around were turning ghostly as they hungrily ate at what remained. Even the screams and sounds of combat were becoming subtly muffled.

'We have to stop more of them getting aboard!' Kron shouted to him through his own damnably intact helmet.

Nathan nodded his understanding and grabbed up some firebombs from the corpse and found a short halberd from among the fallen before heading for the heart of the inferno. He felt filled with a kind of righteous fury at the turn of events, like things couldn't get any worse and it was time for some payback. Somebody had to pay for him landing up in a situation as dire as this, and with Kendrikson already dead it was going to have to be their insane, murderous enemy.

The snout stood open as before. The flames were dying away in its maw and Nathan could see more twisted figures gathering to rush through. He fumbled to find an activation stud on the rune-etched bomb before giving up and simply lobbing it as the figures started to run forward. Then another, and a third from Kron, turning the entryway into a sea of corrosive fire as the bombs burst on impact. Nathan turned to shout to Kron an instant before an armoured giant burst through the conflagration with a brazen roar.

Before Nathan could react the heavy pistol in its fist barked twice and Kron was thrown back with a flash and shower of blood. Nathan felt an icy bolt of fear trying to force his feet to run but it was already too late. The figure charged forward with nightmarish speed, an ironclad monster of myth, skull-helmed and laden with death, a screeching chainsword in its other fist slashing down at him in an unstoppable arc.

Nathan hurled himself aside and brought up the halberd to block the slash. It was a mistake. The power of the blow threw him back, jolting his arms as the shrieking teeth of the saw tore chunks from the halberd's steel haft in a shower of sparks. The giant wielded its huge blade with ease, and in the blink of an eye its shrieking blade circled and swept down at him again. Nathan leapt back but the sweep of the chainsword tore the head from the halberd and slid along the arm of his suit, chewing through it and tearing at his flesh. A cold flush of painlessness told Nathan that the injury was severe; his body was already trying to shut out the agony.

In desperation Nathan thrust the jagged end of the halberd haft into the thing's barrel chest. It rang off an armoured plate and buried itself deep in a nest of cables beneath where its ribs should have been. The giant warrior didn't even flinch as it sent him sprawling with a blow from its heavy pistol.

Death was close. One of his eyes was blind and Nathan felt an abnormal calm as he accepted that these were his last seconds of life. The world seemed to slow to an insect crawl as the armoured warrior stepped towards him, raising its keening sword for a killing blow. Nathan felt only a pang of disappointment that he would never know more of Kron's strange wisdom; so much must have died with him. The pounding of Nathan's last heartbeats sounded like a distantly thumping drum.

Thump. One armoured boot crunched down. Flecks of blood span away from the motion-captured teeth of the chainsword as it soared upward. Nathan looked down at his right arm and saw it was crimson from shoulder to wrist. Everything wavered as he started to black out.

Thump. The other boot crashed down. The blade was raised almost to the top of its arc. Nathan was aware of movement where Kron had fallen, and a tiny spark of hope flared that he might still be alive, might save Nathan somehow if only he were quick and could defeat this unstoppable colossus. Logic sneered at his paltry hopes from the dark recesses of his brain.

Thump. The blade began to sweep down, gathering momentum. Nathan's world was shrinking, the vision from his remaining eye darkening till he could barely see. Paltry hopes and all conscious thought was corroded away by the sea of agony raging through his arm.

Thump. Nathan saw the blade had entered his dimmed world and part of him welcomed it, teeth flashing bright as a shark's hungry smile in the gloom. The pain would be over soon, that could only be good. A spectral hand seemed to reaching over him to touch the blade, as if the God-Emperor himself were placing a benediction on his slaughter. The hand was crawling with blue fires and sparks cascaded from its fingertips.

Thump. A flash of light leapt from hand to blade, and with it the chainsword exploded and was hurled away from the giant's fist. The hulking warrior staggered and started to raise his pistol. Kron stepped forward into Nathan's circle of vision and raised a hand.

Thump. A ravening bolt of brilliance crackled from Kron's hand onto the warrior's chest plate and rent it asunder in a thunderclap. The mighty figure was thrown off its feet, its pistol sending explosive rounds flashing off wildly from its owner's convulsing death-spasm.

Thump. The chainsword, molten and twisted rang down on the deckplates. Nathan clasped his left arm to his right shoulder and instantly felt warmth flood through his blood slick wounds. The armoured warrior crashed to the deck beside its smoking sword. Nathan tried to breathe more deeply to clear his head but found he couldn't. The orange flames all around were shrinking into bluish flickers. The air was nearly gone.

Kron squatted down beside him as the ship shook, as if from some internal explosion. Nathan could see the chest of Kron's suit was shredded and bloody, a death-shot surely. Wreckage dislodged by the shockwave crashed down nearby with horrible clangour. Kron didn't even flinch as he calmly removed his helmet. As the helmet came away, Kron's eye blazed as never before. It was glowing with the fierce light of furnace. Nathan tried to blot out the horrible intensity of that glare in his dimmed world but couldn't. It bored into him, so that it seemed like Kron the man was shrunk to nothing more than a wraith, that the crimson brilliance trailed behind it like smoke.

Kron's lips moved, but Nathan had to strain to hear their faint whisper through the rarefied air.

'Don't you worry, shipmate, Kron'll see to ye.'

'L-Luminen!' Nathan gasped.

'No,' Kron whispered.

Nathan's body was trembling uncontrollably as shock set in. His vision had almost dimmed completely, apart from a harsh, red light floating nearby.

'Not that at all.'

A helmet clamped down over Nathan's head, dimming the light and bringing a welcome darkness.

NATHAN AWOKE on the floor of the hidden cutter. His arm was in a sling and a bandage covered one of his eyes but he otherwise felt rested and healthy. Kron was sitting in one of the narrow pews, watching him.

'How de ye feel?' he inquired with genuine concern.

'Good,' Nathan grunted as he sat up. 'How long was I out?'

'Five hours. I took time to fix ye up, an' me too, and rest some 'fore we go back up to the gunroom.'

Nathan felt a sense of relief. He had feared Kron would ask him if he wanted to jump ship. The aftermath of a battle offered the best chance Nathan would likely get for an escape to go unnoticed. But somehow the prospect seemed a lot less appealing now he had seen what was out there waiting for mutineers and faithless men to fall into its clutches. In fact Nathan was feeling an unfamiliar amount of regard for the God-Emperor after his experiences, a craving for the protection the Ecclesiarchs promised could be gained from the blessings of the Holy Master of Mankind.

But that left him in here with Kron, not-a-Luminen Kron who could defeat a champion of the mad gods with his own lightning. No ordinary gunner, for sure. A servant of the Emperor? Somehow Nathan didn't think so. If anything he really did look like a gargoyle in this setting, a red-eyed piece of malevolence that had detached itself from the stonework and come down to blaspheme among it. Perhaps someone hiding out then, disguised among a faceless mass yet always moving from one world to another. It would be a superb cover. Unremarkable, beneath attention and yet guarded by the awesome might of an Imperial warship. Ultimately, whatever other misgivings Nathan might have, Kron had saved his life and that put him firmly in Kron's debt. He began to say so but Kron waved his thanks away.

'Don't be too thankful, lad. I had to fix your eye with what was to hand down here. I'm 'fraid I might have made a terrible job out of it. Take the bandage off. Tell me if ye can see.'

Nathan knew what was coming even before his fingers brushed cold steel around his eye. The lens of it was hard and slightly curved to the touch. He bore the metal-sealed scars of his first engagement as part of the Emperor's navy, but his vision was perfect. Nathan shuddered as he recalled Kron's unnerving personality shift after the fight with Kendrikson, when he had seemed like a slave desperate to escape his inactive bionic eye.

'Kron?' Nathan began tentatively. 'Who are you really?'

Kron chortled. 'A princeling who was stolen by gypsies.'

'Don't start that again.'

'Very well, I'll put it this way, lad... *Cross the stars and fight for glory...*'

SNARES & DELUSIONS
Matthew Farrer

THE TOWN SURROUNDS the obscenity, and the obscenity is eating the town. It has no name, this elegant pattern of buildings spread out beneath the wind on the dusty green hills. It is an oddity on this world, this town of dove-grey walls which seem to flow up out of the ground, their smooth lines and gentle angles forcing the eye to look in vain for any tool-marks or signs of shaping. Simplicity of shape and complexity of detail, like outcrops growing unworked from the soil, but natural rock could never grow in the delicate mandala of streets and paths, flowing across the hillside in a design so subtle that the eye can take it in for hours before it begins to understand how much the pattern delights.

Even the violence with which the obscenity has torn its way into the heart of the town has not eclipsed the art of its building, not yet. Despite the craters blasted into the buildings, the smoke in the streets, the dead scattered upon the ground, despite whatever invisible thing it is that is withering the grass and trees and silencing the song of the insects – the place still holds scraps of its beauty, for now.

The town has never needed a name. The Exodites speak of it as they ride their fierce dragons to and fro over the steppes and prairies, but they bring its uniqueness to mind without the coining of a label to go on a sign. For all that they are a warrior race of beast-riding and beast-hunting tribes, their language is the silky melody of all eldar and they are able to speak of the one little town on their world, its historians and artisans and seers, without its ever needing a name.

The obscenity is different. It drives its way out of the ground like the head of a murderous giant buried too shallow, buttresses bulging out from its walls like tendons pulled rigid on a neck as the head is thrown back to scream. Black iron gates gape and steel spines give an idiot glint from the parapets and niches. They are not there to defend. The thing leers and swaggers against the landscape in its power, sure that it is above attack. The spikes are there for cruelty, for execution and display. The obscenity is being built not for subjugating but for the pleasure of the subjugation.

It is growing. As small bands of figures grow from dots across the prairie, advance and join up and form into a procession through streets choked with the stink of death, they can see where buildings are being torn down and the earth beneath them ripped up to furnish more rock for the obscenity. There are rough patches, cavities along the side where new chambers and wings will be added, and the procession – the armoured figures gripping the chains, and the slim cloaked shapes staggering beneath the weight of them – passes the crowds of slaves, toiling in the dust, crying and groaning as the obscenity creeps outward and grows ever taller beneath their hands.

The town does not have a name, but the obscenity does. There is no eldar word for this red-black spear of rock, eating the town from within like a cancer, but it bears a name in the hacking, cawing language of the once-human creatures who drive the slaves ever harder to build it. It is called the Cathedral of the Fifth Blessing, and in its sick, buried heart its master is at prayers.

The air in the Deepmost Chapel was torn this way and that by the screams of the thralls, but Chaplain De Haan paid them no mind. The patterns on the warp-carved obelisk seemed to writhe, the lines and angles impossible by any sane geometry, and De Haan's eyes and brain shuddered as he tried to follow them. There had been times when he had relished or loathed the sensation in turn, even times when he had screamed when he looked at the pillar just as their mortal serfs were screaming now. That had been in the early days, when the Word Bearers had taken up the banner of Horus himself and Lorgar had still been crafting the great laws of faith in the Pentadict. Those laws had commanded contemplation of the work of Chaos as part of the Ritual of Turning, and now De Haan was calm as he felt the carvings send ripples though his sanity. *A lesson in self-disgust and abasement*, he had learned in his noviciate. *Realise that your mind is but a breath of mist in the face of the gale that is Chaos Undivided.* It was a useful lesson.

The time for contemplation was at an end, and he rose. The screams from the chapel floor, beneath the gallery where the Word Bearers themselves sat, went on. Although their mortal thralls were being herded out perhaps a dozen remained, those whose minds had not withstood the gaze at the column, who had begun to convulse on the floor and mutilate themselves. The slave-masters began to drag them toward the torturing pens; they would be adequate as sacrifices later. De Haan walked forward to the pulpit, turned to face the ranks of wine-dark armour and horned helms to begin his first sermon on this new world.

The cycle of worship laid down in the Pentadict decreed that sermon and prayers for that hour were to be about *hate*. There was a certain expectation in the air that plucked a little chord of pleasure at the base of the Chaplain's spine. Of all Lorgar's virtues hatred was the one De Haan prized most, the sea in which his soul swam, the light with which he saw the world. Some of his most beautiful blasphemies had been done in the name of hate. He knew he was revered as a scholar in the field.

The Sacristans moved to the dais below him and reached into the brocaded satchels they carried. They began to array objects on the dais: a banner of purple-and-gold silk tattered and scorched by gunfire in places; a slender eldar helmet and gauntlet in the same colours were set atop it. At the other end of the dais, a delicate crystal mask and a slender sword seemingly made from feather-light, smoky glass, a single pale gem set into the pommel. And beside them, carefully set exactly between the rest, a fist-sized stone, smooth and hard, that shone like a Phoenix egg even in the dimness of the Chapel. De Haan looked at them, heard the words in his mind: *All will be at an end.*

An exquisite shudder went through his body. He unclenched
his right hand from the pulpit rail, gripped his crozius in his
left and opened his mouth to preach. And something happened to the Revered Chaplain De Haan that had never
happened to him in his millennia as a Word Bearer: he found
himself mute.

HIGH CLOUDS HAD turned the sky dull and cool as De Haan
stood on the jutting rampart outside his war room. His eyes
narrowed behind his faceplate as if he were trying to stare
through the curve of the planet itself.

'This race has been allowed to *go on*, Meer. It has been
allowed to spread itself. They drink their wine on their craft-
worlds and stand under the sky on worlds like this. They crept
out across the galaxy like the glint of mildew.'

Meer, chief among his lieutenants, knew better than to
respond. He stood at the door which led out onto the rampart,
hands folded respectfully before him. He had heard De Haan
talk about the eldar many times.

'Not even the whining Emperor's puppies are like this. Nor
the mangy orks. Tyranids, feh, beneath our dignity. But these
things, these are an *affront*. To be assailed by them – ah! It
gnaws at my pride.' His hand squeezed the haft of his crozius
and the weapon's daemon-head hissed and cursed and spat its
displeasure. Only during the rituals would the thing keep
quiet. De Haan twisted it around and held it at a more digni-
fied angle. It was a symbol of his office, a chaplaincy in the only
Traitor Legion to remember and revere the importance of
Chaplains. It did not do to show it disrespect.

De Haan wondered why he had not been able to speak like
this in the chapel, why he had stood grasping for words, trying
to force thoughts to his lips. A sermon on hate, no less, and yet
he had stumbled over the words, choked on maddening dis-
tractions, images, snatches of voices, the swirl of memories he
was normally able to leave behind at prayer.

'The eyes of our Dark Master see far, Meer, and who am I to
set myself up beside them?' Meer remained silent, but De Haan
was speaking half to himself. 'The words fled me. My throat
was dry and empty. I am wondering, Meer, was it an omen? Do
they prey on my mind because they are so near? There was a...
a feel to this world, something in the words of our prisoners

and spies. Perhaps the Great Conspirator planned from the start that it would end here. To end here, Meer, to bring the sacrament into full flower! Imagine that.'

'I know you believe your enemy is here, revered,' came Meer's careful voice from behind him, 'but my counsel, and Traika's, is still that the time was not ripe for you to join us here.'

De Haan's fist tightened around the crozius again, and the head – now a fanged mouth and eye-stalk; it was always different each time he looked at it – yapped and spat again.

'The fortifications are still not complete, revered, and only threescore of our own brethren are in this citadel. The battle tanks and Dreadnoughts are still being readied, and the dissonance in this world's aura has made auguries hard. We still cannot scry far beyond what our own eyes could see. Our bridgehead is not secure, revered. Do you believe this is worth the risk? The reports we had of eldar here seem only to mean these savages, or perhaps mere pirates. We cannot be sure Varantha has passed near this system. We have seen no Craftworld eldar here, or–'

De Haan spun around. 'And I told you, Meer, that it is not suspicions and rumours which have drawn us here this time. I could feel the slippery eldar filth singing to me when I first heard the reports. I saw their faces dancing in the clouds when I looked from the bridge of our ship. What could this psychic 'dissonance' you complain of be, but the cowards trying to fog our minds and cover their tracks?'

'These eldar savages keep a thing called a World-Spirit, revered. They–'

'I *know* what is a World-Spirit – and what is the stink of a Farseer!' De Haan's voice did not quite go all the way to a roar, but it did not have to. There was a jitter in his vision and a rustle far off in his hearing as the systems in his armour, long since come to a Chaotic life of their own, tried to recoil from his anger. 'You were not given the sacrament, Meer! You do not carry the Fifth Blessing! I do, and I command you with it. I tell you that Varantha is here, and this is our doorway to it! I have known it in my soul since we broke from the warp!'

Meer bowed, accepting the rebuke, and De Haan slowly, deliberately turned his back. High in his vision he could see a point of light, visible even while the sun was up: their orbiting battle-barge. A space hulk full of Chaos Marines and their slaves and thralls, cultists doped with Frenzon with their explosive suicide collars clamped to their necks, mutants and beastfolk from the Eye of Terror and traitors of every stripe. Seeing it focused his thoughts again.

'We shall bring down our brethren soon enough. The engines and Dreadnoughts too. For now, fetch Nessun. And have the latest prisoner train brought before me.'

There was a scrape of ceramite on stone as Meer bowed again and turned to go, and by the time Meer had reached the bottom of the stairs De Haan was sinking back into reverie.

HE WAS THINKING of the cramped, fetid tunnels within the walls of the giant canal-cities of Sahch-V, where he and Meer and Alaema and barely a half-dozen Word Bearer squads had lived like rats in burrows for nearly two years, as around them their covert missionaries moved out through the cities and along the canals which brought life to the basalt plains, beginning their quiet preaching, their mission schools with their drugs and brainwashing rooms. He remembered the small chamber beneath the thermic pumps outside Vana City where the three of them had listened to their agents' reports and pored over their ever-spreading web of traitors and catspaws.

He remembered cries in the tunnels, in particular the voice of Belg, the scrawny cleft-chinned cult emissary loud in the coffin-like burrows as he shouted down the passages: 'We are lost! The missions are dying. Our rebellion is clipped before it begins!' Someone had shot Belg down in a fury before De Haan had had a chance to hear more, but he remembered the word that had gone flying through the base as the reports began to come in.

eldar!

And the second, the three syllables that had not yet – he could barely remember the feeling – become sweet poison in his brain, not yet become the black-burning obsession hanging in front of his eyes, the name they had not heard until the Warp Spiders had begun to hunt them through their chambers and drove them out to where the rest of the eldar lay waiting with shuriken and plasma-shot, fusion-beam and wraithcannon. Alaema had gone down with a lightning-wrapped witchblade through his gut, and De Haan had barely managed to drag himself and Meer away to the teleport point.

Varantha.

Oh, he remembered. Twenty-one centuries of remembering.

He remembered the sick anger that had seized him when he first spoke to the Imperial scholar they had captured as the wretch thrashed on the torture rack. Varantha meant 'Crown of our Steadfast Hopes'. Human traders spoke in awe of the gems it crafted, the rare flowers it bred, the beautiful metals its artisans worked. Varantha that passed through the western galactic margins, scraping the borders of the Halo where not even the Traitor Legions went, Varantha that was supposed to have passed through Hydraphur itself, the home of the Imperial Battlefleet Pacificus, coasting through the system's intricate double-ecliptic and away again before the whey-faced Imperials had even a suspicion it had been there.

Varantha that hated Chaos with a white heat. Varantha that had held off Karlsen of the Night Lords in his raids on the Clavian Belt until the Ultramarines had arrived, Varantha whose Farseers had tricked and feinted to lure the orks of Waaagh-Chobog into falling on the Iron Hands' fortresses on Taira-Shodan instead of the Imperial and Exodite worlds around them, Varantha whose warriors had driven Arhendros the Silken Whisper off the three worlds he had claimed for Slaanesh.

And Varantha that had balked the Word Bearers on Sahch-V, had unravelled their plans and made sure the great citadels and halls they would have built could never be. A Varantha witch blade had cut down De Haan's mentor, Varantha wraithships had driven their battle-barges and strikers out of the system. And when they had broken free of the warp outside the Cadian Gate, ready for their last final jump back to the Eye of Terror and sanctuary, it had been Varantha craft which had led the fleets of Ulthwe and Cadia, driving into the Chaos fleet like a bullet tearing into flesh.

Fighting Varantha, stalking the craftworld through a quarter of the galaxy, De Haan had discovered a capacity for hate he had never realised that even a Traitor Marine could possess. Every battle against the craftworld had been like a stroke of the bellows, fanning it ever hotter. The orbital refineries at Rhea, where the eldar had lured De Haan and his warband in – then disappeared, leaving the Word Bearers in the abandoned, genestealer-infested satellite compounds. The island chains of Herano's World where their Doomblaster had smashed the eldar psykers into the ocean at the campaign's opening, and De

Haan had led a joyous hunt through the jungles, mopping up the scattered and leaderless Guardians.

And at the last, the Farseer, staggering beneath the red-black clouds of Iante as artillery flashed and boomed across the distant horizon, watching De Haan as he circled it, stepping over its dead bodyguard. The calm resignation in its stance and the cold precision of its voice.

'So tell me then. What do you see for us, little insect?' De Haan had taunted.

'Why, you will set your eyes on the heart of Varantha, and all will come to an end,' it had replied, before a howling stroke of De Haan's crozius had torn it in half. He had felt the Spirit Stone shudder and pulse as he tore it free of the thing's breastplate with a sound like cracking bone, and he wondered every so often if the creature's soul was aware of who owned its stone now. He hoped it did.

It had not been long after that that he had been called to receive his sacrament, the Sacrament of the Fifth Blessing. The highest priests of his Chapter had recognised the depth of his spite and had praised him for it: the Fifth Blessing was hate, and the sacrament had appointed De Haan a holy vessel, freed him from his duties in order to lead a crusade that he might express that hate to the utmost, a great hymn to Lorgar carved across the galaxy in Varantha's wake. He could never think back on his sacrament without the hot red flames of pride flaring deep in what he thought was his soul.

He walked to the edge of his rampart and watched the slaves toiling at the walls far below. His arms convulsed, as though he could already feel eldar souls pulsing and struggling in his fingers, and the wave of malice which surged up his spine made him almost giddy.

'Revered?'

De Haan started at the voice and spun around. His crozius head, now some kind of grotesque insect, chittered something that sounded almost like words. He ignored it and found his concentration again.

'What have the threads of Fate brought us, Nessun?'

The other Marine hesitated. Nessun was no full-fledged sorcerer as the adepts of the Thousand Sons were, but by Lorgar's grace he had developed a spirit sight that could scry almost as well as the eldar warlocks they hunted. The mutation that had given him his warp eye had pushed it far out and up onto his brow, making an ungainly lump of his head. The ceramite of his armour had turned glass-clear over it, but De Haan and the others had long ago become used to the way the great milky eyeball pulsed and rolled between the horns of Nessun's helm.

'In the way of eldar, revered, there is little I can say for definite. I see shadows at the corners of my vision and echoes that I must interpret. You know that nothing is certain with these creatures.'

'Describe these shadows and echoes, Nessun. I am patient.'

'I have kept my gaze on the tribes here in the days since our first landing, revered, and watched as they fought our thralls and Brother Traika's vanguard force. There is a... texture to them that I have taught myself to recognise, by Lorgar's grace. But I have caught ripples, something dancing out of sight. I am not sure how I can explain it, revered. Imagine a figure standing just beyond the reach of light from a fire, so that sometimes its shape is touched by the firelight...'

'I think I understand.' De Haan wasn't aware that he had tensed until he felt his armour, alive like his helmet systems, shiver and creak as it tried to find a comfortable position.

'Revered, I am abased and humble before the foul glory of Chaos, but I must venture the guess that Craftworld eldar may be here. Here on this world. I have dimly seen the patterns that the minds of Farseers form when they assemble, and I have felt... *gaps* in my vision that I believe are warp gates, webway gates here and in orbit beyond the planet from our own ship, that have opened and closed and that they have not been able to hide...' He stopped short as De Haan drove gauntlet into fist, hissing with triumph, sending his armour shivering and flexing from the blow.

'An omen! My voice was bound in the chapel as an omen!' And he was about to speak again when Meer called from the war room.

'Most revered lord, the prisoners await you.'

There was something in Meer's voice that made De Haan almost run for the doorway.

TWO ELDAR STOOD in the great hall, heads bowed as De Haan strode to his throne and sat down, crozius across his knees. The arm of one hung brokenly; blood matted the other's hair. Both were dressed in rough cloth and hide tunics, and their lasers, the power chambers smashed, had been hung around their necks. Traika, the commander of their vanguard and Raptors, bowed to De Haan and made the sign of the Eightfold Arrow with the hand that had fused to his chainsword. Traika's legs had warped and lengthened too, now bending backward like an insect's, the armour over them lumpy and stretched. It had made him fleet of foot but gave him an odd, tilted way of standing.

'We found these in the south-west quarter where the hills steepen. We thought we had cleansed the area, revered, but these were part of an ambush on one of our scouring forces. The fight was fierce but we carried the day.'

'Praise Lorgar's dark light and the great will of Chaos,' De Haan intoned, and the two were led away into the cathedral's cells. Traika gestured and a third alien was dragged up the steps, limping and tripping. The thrall holding its chains tossed a dead power-lance and a tall bone helm onto the floor. The prisoner did not react, standing slumped with its hair in its face, its long cloak of golden-scaled hide hanging limply around it.

'The last survivor of a group of Dragon Knights we believe were scouting the northern border of our controlled zone. I will attend the tormenting of this one personally, revered. I had felt sure that our deep raids had gutted the last of the Exodite resistance on the prairies. We must find out how this new raid was organised so soon.' The thrall began to drag the knight out, and Meer walked over to stand beside the throne.

'Revered, this is the final prisoner. It was badly wounded, and did not survive the journey back to be brought before you, but we believed you would want to see it. The Raptors brought it down in the river-valley to the south and our bikers brought it here with all haste.'

With a scraping groan of wheels the thralls pushed forward an iron frame with a figure stretched in it, a figure whose rich purple and gold armour caught the sunlight coming through the still-unglazed windows and gave off a burnished glow. Behind it four more – strong beastfolk these, whose muscles rippled and corded with their burden – dragged something into view and dropped it crashing to the floor, stirring the rock-dust that still coated the hall from its building. A jet-bike, its canopy cracked open by bolt shells, the drive smashed and burnt from its crash, but the pennons hanging from its vanes perfectly clear: the stylised crown-and-starburst of Varantha.

For a long moment, De Haan was silent. Then he threw his arms wide as though he were about to embrace the corpse, and gave a bellow that echoed through the length of the hall.

'All will come to an end! Horus's eye, but the filthy little creature spoke the truth. The Craftworld's heart! It is here! The sacrament ends here, my brethren! *I will end it here!*'

'REVERED!' De Haan did not look back. His stride had lengthened as his pace had picked up, and he was practically jogging through the halls to the Deepmost Chapel, Meer and Nessun shouldering one another aside to keep up. The air in the fortress shivered as the great gongs they had hung over the barracks rang out again and again. Under the sound De Haan left a trail of angry murmurs in the air, curses and threats and dark prayers. Every so often he would slash his crozius viciously around him as if to knock the air itself out of his path.

He knew what Meer would be saying. More weak-spirited yapping, more about caution and rashness and the trickery of the eldar. But the warp gate was close. Varantha was close. The time when the heads of Varantha's Farseers were set on spikes atop his Land Raider was a breath away.

Why, you will set your eyes on the heart of Varantha, and all will come to an end.

The heart of the craftworld, the very heart of Varantha! He wondered how it would feel, walking from the webway gate into Varantha itself. The domes where the most ancient of their Farseers sat, their flesh crystallised and gleaming like diamond, waiting for the blow of an armoured fist that would send their souls screaming into the warp. The Grove of New Songs, that was what they called the forest-hall deep in Varantha where the few eldar children were born and weaned. De Haan had spent a hundred weeks agonising over whether he would kill the children or take them as slaves after he had poisoned and burned the trees. The Infinity Circuit, the wraithbone core which held the spirits of a billion dead eldar, had shone through his dreams like a galaxy aflame. Oh, to crack its lattice with his crozius and watch the warp tides pour in! It would need a special ceremony, the culmination of his crusade and sacrament, something he would have to plan.

And was Varantha possessed of engines, a world that could control its drift and sweep through space? He had never been able to discover that, but he began turning the idea over feverishly as he strode down the hallway to the chapel. To take command of Varantha, hollow out its core of eldar souls and fill them with sacrifices and the cries of daemons, to sail the fallen craftworld to the Eye of Terror itself! His head swam with the audacity: a world that would put their daemon-world fortresses and the asteroid seminaries at Milarro to shame. A corrupted world that would carry them through the galaxy, a great blight that would stand as a testament to their faith, their hate, their spite, their unholiness.

The rest of the Traitor Marines began to file in and take their places, and the slave-choir in their cells beneath the chapel floor raised a hymn of howls and cries as the choir-masters puffed drugs into their faces and yanked on the needles in their flesh. De Haan closed his eyes and could see the conquered Varantha still, a great twisted flower of black and crimson, sprawled against the stars. The shapes of the spires and walls, great plazas where the zealous would come to plead for the favour of Chaos, the cells and scriptoria where Lorgar's holy Pentadict would be copied and studied, the fighting pits where generations of new Word Bearers would be initiated. There would be pillars and statues greater than those they had raised after driving the White Scars from the island chains of Morag's World. There would be chamber after chamber of altars more richly decorated than those they had seized when they had sacked the treasury of Kintarre. There would be the slaughtering pens for the worship of Khorne, great libraries and chambers for meditating upon the lore of Tzeentch. There would be palaces of incense and music dedicated to Slaanesh, and cesspits for the rituals of self-defilement dedicated to Nurgle. And all just parts, even as the Chaos Gods were just facets, all parts of the great treacherous hymn, an obscene prayer in wraithbone and carved ceramite. The Sacred City of Chaos Undivided.

De Haan cradled his vision lovingly in his mind, and saw that it was good.

'LORGAR IS WITH US, Chaos is within us, damnation clothes us and none can stand against us.' Voices around the chapel echoed the blessing as De Haan held his rosarius aloft and made the sign of the Eightfold Arrow. For the second time that day he looked out over ranks of helms, leaned forward to look down at the bright eyes of the cultists and beastfolk crowded below him. But this time, his thoughts and his words were clear.

'Be it known to you, most devout of my comrades in Lorgar's footsteps, that we are gathered here once again in the observance of the Fifth Blessing of Lorgar, the blessing of hate. Bring your thoughts to the sacrament granted to me by the most high of our order, that I might light a dark beacon of spite for all the cosmos to see.' He paused, looked down again. The eldar artefacts had gone from the dais, locked away again by the Sacristans. It was not important – he did not need them now.

'Hatred earned me the great and honoured sacrament. Hatred has pleased the beautiful abomination of Chaos Undivided, and shone a light through the warp to Varantha. My beautiful hatred has brought us to their scent. After more than two millennia, the fulfilment of our sacred charter is near.' The memory of the Varantha Guardian, the knowledge of what they had found here, surged through him afresh: his head spun, his joints felt weak with exhilaration. His crozius head as he raised it was now a contorted nightmare-face, grimacing as if in ecstasy, mirroring his feelings.

'Soon we will be joined by our brothers, our fellow warriors and bearers of Lorgar's words. Even now the order goes out to land our machines of war, our bound Dreadnoughts. Within the week, my congregation, this world will have felt the full fury of our crusade and when the Exodites are scoured from it we shall march through the warp gate into the craftworld itself! Hone yourselves, my acolytes, hone your spite and fan your hate to the hottest, most bitter flame. None shall pass us in our devotion, none are as steeped in poisoned thoughts as we!' His voice hammered out and boomed against the walls of the chapel, intoxicating even with the power of its echoes. De Haan fought back an urge to laugh – this felt so right.

'In the beginning, even in the days before my pursuit earned me the sacrament, I had spoken to one of the degenerate Farseers the eldar claim to revere. At its death the maggot spoke a prophecy that the blessed oracles of our high temples have sworn to be true. Brethren, as I lead you to battle I will set my eyes on the heart of Varantha and then all will come to an end. I will cut down their last Farseer, I will break open the seals of their Infinity Circuit, I will shatter the heart and eye of their

home!' His voice had risen to a roar. 'All will come to an end!
Our crusade, our sacrament fulfilled! The eldar themselves
have sworn it will be so. What honours, what glories we will
build!'

Above him the gong rang again, and De Haan opened his
eyes and leaned forward.

'Look to your weapons, brothers. I will lead you now in the
Martio Imprimis. I tell you this: by the end of even this day we
will be at war!'

THE CHANT OF the *Martio Imprimis* was an old song and a good
one, crafted by Lorgar himself in the days before the Emperor
had turned on his Word Bearers and when even De Haan had
been only a youngblood initiate. The words were strange and
their meanings almost lost, but they filled him with a beautiful, electric energy. It rang in De Haan's blood even now. The
service in the Deepmost Chapel had been over for an hour but
the Word Bearers had caught something of their chaplain's
mood and as the teleport beam sent thundercracks and sickly
shimmers of light through the citadel's hangar, the Marines
chanted still as they selected weapons and directed the thralls
in moving the crates and engines away.

'Duxhai!' The crusade's chief artisan, still swaying a little
from his teleport, turned as De Haan called him. He stepped
back into a deep kneeling bow as De Haan strode across the
hangar floor and left the moving of the icon-encrusted
Razorback tanks to his seconds.

'Is it true, revered lord? I was told you have received omens
and that Varantha itself is in our grip. They are singing hymns in
all the halls and chambers of our fortress. Look!' The old Marine
pointed to the nearest tank's turret, where splashes of blood glistened. 'They have already made sacrifices over our wargear.'

'It is true, Duxhai, and it is fitting that our brethren in orbit
are making their thanks and obeisances. Lorgar has exalted us.
I have been shown the way.'

Duxhai had worked on his armour himself over the centuries, making it a glorious construction of red and gold. Chaos
had worked on it too: the studs and rivets on its carapace had
all turned to eyes, yellow slit-pupiled eyes, which stared at De
Haan now but rolled forward to watch Meer walk into the
hangar. De Haan pointed to the Razorbacks.

'Give praise, Meer! See how Brother Duxhai's skills have transformed these? Captured barely a year ago, and already adorned and consecrated for service! These will carry Traika's vanguard squads into the teeth of the Varantha lines!'

'Our revered chaplain's own Land Raider will be brought down next,' put in Duxhai, 'and the transports are being readied to bring down the Dreadnoughts and Rhinos. We will be ready to move soon.'

'A dark blessing on you, brother, and thanks to the great foulness of Chaos. Revered, I must make a report.'

'Well?' De Haan was becoming nettled by Meer's manner, his shifty-eyed caution. He could see in the corner of his eyes that Duxhai had registered the offhand greeting also.

'Revered, we have lost contact with our patrols at the furthest sweep of the contested zone. I had our adepts move the communicators onto the outer balconies but there is still no way to raise them. The Raptors who went out to counterstrike at the areas where our own forces were ambushed cannot be reached either, and the bike squadron was due two hours ago but cannot be seen. The psychic haze has thickened, and Nessun's warp eye is almost blind. He reports a presence like a light through fog, but he cannot pinpoint it.'

'I will come to the war room, Meer. Wait for me there.' His lieutenant backed away, bowed and departed. 'Something in the air on this world turns my warriors to water, Duxhai. They whimper to me of "caution" and "fortification". Meer is a good warrior, but I should have made you my lieutenant for this world. I need your ferocity by me here.'

Duxhai bowed. 'I am honoured, revered. Lieutenant or no, I will gladly fight by your side. Allow me to prepare my weapons and I will meet you in the war room.'

De Haan nodded and waited a moment more, allowing the chanting of the Traitor Marines to soothe his ruffled nerves, before he strode away.

NESSUN WAS STANDING quietly in the war room when De Haan entered, head bowed, warp eye clouded. Meer and Traika were pacing, almost circling each other, clearly at odds. De Haan ordered them to report.

'Something is coming, revered!' Meer began. 'The slaves are restless, there have been revolts on the building crews! The eldar know something! We must prepare for assault!'

'We *must* make the assault!' Traika's rasping voice. 'We are Word Bearers, not Iron Warriors! We do not skulk behind walls. We take Lorgar's blessing to our enemies, His blessings of hate and fire and blood and agony!' The obscenely long fingers of Traika's left hand flexed and clenched, as if to claw the tension out of the air.

Listening to them, De Haan hesitated. For the first time he felt a tug, a tilt at the back of his mind that he could not identify. He could not see with Nessun's precision, no seer he, but ten thousand years in the Eye of Terror had tuned him to the coarser ebbs and flows as it had them all. Something was near. He raised his crozius for silence – its crown a snarling hound's head now – and looked to Nessun.

'Speak, Nessun! Stare through these walls. Tell me what you see!'

'Revered, I… am not sure. There are patterns, something moving… a ring, a wall… closing or opening, I cannot say… a mind… shapes, silent… rushing air…' His voice was becoming ragged, and De Haan cut him off.

'It's clear enough. Meer, Traika: you are both right. The eldar know of us.' He fought back a chuckle. 'And they fear us. Catch us off-guard, would they? A quick strike at the head, was it? Drive me off their trail?' And now he did laugh, feeling the tension lifting from his back.

'Time for our sortie, my brothers! Have the Razorbacks lowered to the ramp. Traika, assemble your veteran squads! Meer, have our space command ready a bombardment for when we–'

That was when the first plasma blast hit the side of the cathedral with a sound like the sky being torn apart. The thunderous roar died away amid vast dust clouds, the groan of masonry, frenzied shouts from up and down the halls. De Haan stared straight ahead for one speechless moment, then hurled himself to the balcony, the others behind him. And then they could only stand and watch.

The world had filled with enemies. Sleek eldar jet-bikes arrowed down from the sky to whip past the walls of the cathedral, and high above De Haan could hear the rumble of sonic booms as squadrons of larger alien assault craft crisscrossed over their heads. With sickening speed each distant blur in the air would grow and resolve into a raptor-sleek grav-tank, arcing in silently to spill a knot of infantry into the town before they rose and banked away again. In what seemed like a matter of heartbeats the fortress was ringed by a sea of advancing Guardians, their ranks dotted with gliding gun-platforms and dancing war-walkers, and the air swarmed with the eldar craft.

The aliens' assault started to be answered. Thumps and cracks came from the walls as the Word Bearers brought heavy weapons to bear and threads of tracer fire began reaching out to the purple-and-gold shapes that danced past on the wind. De Haan pushed to the edge of the balcony, heedless of the shapes above him and greedy for the sight of fireballs and smoke-trails, but he had time for no more than a glance before Meer and Traika pulled him away from the edge.

'Revered! With us! You must lead us. We cannot stay!' He cursed and almost raised his crozius to Meer, but the first laser beams had begun sweeping the balcony, carving at the rock and sending molten dribbles down the walls behind them. He nodded grimly and led them inside.

In the debris-swathed halls all was din and confusion. The slave-masters bellowed and flailed with their barbed whips, but their charges would not be ordered. De Haan realised someone had set off the Frenzon too early. Their thralls ran to and fro, shrieking and swinging their clubs, pistols spitting and making the stone chambers a hell of sparks and ricochets. Bullets spanged off De Haan's armour as he shouldered his way through the crowd of naked, bleeding berserkers.

'To me! They are upon us, we will cut them down here! To me!' and De Haan began the chant of the Martio Secundus. All around him Word Bearers turned and began to fall in behind him, dark red helms bearing down on him above the sea of bobbing cultist heads. Roars and growls began to mix with the cries of the mortals; the beastfolk were following too. De Haan gave a snarling grin behind his faceplate. *In Lorgar's name, we will make a fight of this yet.*

Reaching the great stair, they found that a whole part of wall had gone, simply vanished leaving smooth stone edges where a piece had been erased. A distort-cannon crater – and the ceiling above it was already beginning to groan and send down streams of dust. He ignored the danger, sent his chant ringing out again and charged through the crater to the hall beyond; the hangar and teleport dais were close.

Then, swooping and darting though the breaches their cannon had made, came the eldar, Aspect Warriors all in blue, thrumming wings spreading from their shoulders. Lasers stabbed down into the throng underneath them and grenades fell from their hands like petals.

'Fight!' De Haan bellowed, and now that he was in battle he roared the *Martio Tertius* and sent a fan of bolt shells screaming through the squadron, smashing two Hawks backwards into the wall in clouds of smoke. His crozius, twisted into the head of a one-eyed bull, was belching streams of red plasma that hung in the air when he moved it; it had not boasted the blue power-field of the Imperial croziae for eight thousand years.

The remaining Hawks tumbled gracefully in the air and glided towards the ruined wall, now with other shots chasing them, but then the braying of the beastfolk changed note. De Haan whirled to see three of them, firing wildly, looking about them in panic, caught in a silvery mist. All three seemed to twitch and heave and fall oddly out of shape before they collapsed into piles of filth on the stone floor. Beyond them, the two Warp Spider warriors sucked the filament clouds back into the muzzles of their weapons. While shells from De Haan and Meer took one apart, the other stepped back. With a gesture, the air flowed around it like water and it was gone.

Down the hall and up the broad stairs, running hard, Duxhai came pounding out of the smoke, plasma gun clutched in his hands. The hangar was filled with smoke and flashes of light.

'The hangar is gone, lord, taken. We opened the gates to take the tanks down the ramp to the ground, but they drove us back with their strange weapons, and their heavy tanks are bombarding us. The teleport platform is destroyed. I have said the *Martio Quartus* for our fallen, and my brothers have dug in to hold them at bay. But we cannot stay here.'

De Haan almost groaned aloud. 'I will not be driven like an animal! This is my fortress, I will stand to defend it!' But his soldier's instincts had taken charge and were giving the lie to his words: he was already moving back down the stairs to meet the last of the Marines and a gaggle of thralls struggling up to meet him. He looked at them for a moment, and did not flinch

as a Fire Prism fired through the hangar doors, opened a dazzling sphere of yellow-white fire over their heads.

'The Deepmost Chapel, then, and the Great Hall. We will cut
them down as they enter, until our brothers can land. When
the transports land the rest of our crusade the battle will turn
soon enough.'

They hammered down the stairs. Beside them a glare came
through the window-slits and then the rock wall flashed red-
hot and crumbled as the Marines next to it hurled themselves
away. The sleek alien tank which had opened the breach rose
out of sight and the jet-bikes behind it – no Guardian craft
these but the smoky grey-green and bright silver of the Shining
Spears – threw a delicate cat's cradle of lasers through the opening. Thralls yowled and fell, while the beastfolk sent bullets
and shot blasting out of the opening as the jet-bikes peeled off
and rose out of sight.

Then the Word Bearers were in the chapel, the shadowy space
and echoes calming De Haan, the familiar shape of the warp
obelisk giving him strength. They fanned out into the chamber,
around the upper gallery and the floor itself, needing no
orders: within seconds the doors were covered. The pack of
thralls and beastfolk huddled and muttered in the centre of the
chamber, clutching weapons.

'Revered, we… we are beset on every side.' Nessun's voice was
flat and hoarse with anger. 'I feel them at the gates, fighting our
brothers and slaves. But they are above us too, they are breach-
ing the upper walls and stepping onto the balconies from their
grav-sleds. And, and… most revered lord…'

Suddenly Nessun's voice was drenched with misery, and even
the heads of the warriors around him were turning. 'Our battle-barge. Our fortress. I see it reeling in space, revered… it is
ringed by the enemy… their ships dance away from our guns…
our brothers were preparing their landing, the shields had been
lowered for the teleport to work. The eldar are tearing at it…
my vision is dimming…'

There was silence in the chapel for a moment after Nessun's
voice died away. De Haan thought of trying to reach the senso-
ria array in the spires above them, then pushed the useless
thought away. The upper levels would be full of the eldar scum
by now, and by the time they could fight their way there his
ship would indeed have been blasted from the sky.

He looked around. 'Alone, then. Alone with our hatred. I will hear no talk of flight. They will break against us as a wave against a cliff.'

'Lorgar is with us, Chaos is within us, damnation clothes us and none can stand against us.'

As they all said the blessing De Haan's eyes moved from one to the next. Meer cradling his bolter, seemingly deep in thought, Duxhai standing haughtily with plasma-gun held at arms, Traika glaring about him for any sign of weakness in the others, chainsword starting to flex and rev. De Haan raised his crozius and strode from the chapel, the others following, and as if on a signal they heard the bombardment outside begin again.

IT WAS ONLY fitting that De Haan and his retinue marched into the north end of the ruined Great Hall at the same time that the eldar filled its south. They had blown in the walls and shot the bronze doors apart and were fanning out through the ruins. De Haan leapt down the steps into the hall, letting the dust and smoke blur his outline as shots clipped the columns around him and his men returned fire from the archway. A plasma grenade exploded nearby, an instant of scorching whiteness that betrayed the eldar: in the instant that it blinded them the Word Bearers had launched their own advance, scrambling and vaulting over the rubble. There were insect-quick movements ahead and De Haan fired by reflex, plucking the Guardians out of their positions before he had consciously registered their location. The soft thrum of shuriken guns was drowned out by the hammer-and-yowl of the Word Bearers' bolt shells.

A stream of white energy flashed by De Haan's shoulder as Duxhai felled two more eldar, but there were Dire Avengers in the eldar positions now, with quicker reflexes and a hawk-eye aim to catch Duxhai before he could move again. The shuriken were monomolecular, too fast and thin to properly see, but the air around Duxhai seemed to shimmer and flesh. Blood and ceramite gouted from his back as his torso flew apart, the eyes on his armour glazing over. He staggered back and De Haan jinked around him, launched himself into battle.

A grenade went off somewhere to his left and shrapnel clipped his armour. The Word Bearer felt the moist embrace of the plates around his body jump and twitch with the pain. He brought his crozius up and over, its wolf's head yowling with both joy and pain and belching thick red plasma. It caught the Avenger square on its jutting helmet and the creature twitched for a moment only before the glowing crimson mist ate it down to the bone. His bolt pistol hammered in his hand and two more eldar crashed backward, twitching and tumbling. Just beyond them, Traika cleared a fallen column in a great leap and landed among yellow-armoured Striking Scorpions whose chainswords sang and sparked against his own. In the rubble, Meer led the others in laying down a crossfire that strewed alien corpses across a third of the hall.

De Haan sang the *Martio Tertius* in a clear, strong voice and shot the nearest Scorpion in the back. Traika screamed laughter and swung at another, but as it back-pedalled another Scorpion, in the heavy intricate armour of an Exarch, glided forward and whirled a many-chained crystalline flail in an intricate figure that smashed both Traika's shoulders and left him standing, astonished and motionless, for a blow that stove in his helm and sent ceramite splinters flying. De Haan bellowed a battle-curse and his crozius head became a snake that lashed and hissed. Two short steps forward and he lunged, feinted and struck the flail out of the creature's hand. It reeled back into Meer's sights, the plasma eating at it even as shells riddled it, but in the time it took for De Haan to strike down the last Scorpion the hall was alive with eldar again, and Meer and Nessun were forced back and away from him by a shower of grenades and sighing filament webs as the blast from a distort-cannon scraped the roof off the hall and let in the raging sky.

Even as De Haan charged, fired and struck again and again, some distant part of him groaned. Faint, maddening alien thoughts brushed his own like spider-silk in the dark, and shadows danced at the upper edge of his vision as jet-bikes and Vypers circled. The air around him was alive with shuriken fire and energy bolts. The eldar melted away as he struck this way and that. Ancient stone burst into hot shards as he swung his crozius, but rage had taken his discipline and, like a man trying to snatch smoke in his fingers, he found himself standing and roaring wordlessly as the hall emptied once more and the shots died away.

THERE WERE NO voices, no cries from his companions. De Haan did not have to turn to look to know that this last assault had taken them all. Meer and Nessun were dead, and behind him he could hear the boom of masonry as his citadel began to crumble. The Prayer of Sacrifice and the *Martio Quartus* would not come to his numb lips, and he nodded to himself. Why should not his rites unravel along with everything else? The Chaos Star set in his rosarius was dead, lacklustre. He looked at it dully, and that was when he began to feel something tugging at his mind.

It was like an electrical tingle, or the distant sound of crickets; the way the air feels before a storm, or the thrum of distant war-machines. De Haan's warp-tuned mind rang with the nearby song of power. He remembered Nessun speaking of the pattern that Farseers' minds made when they assembled.

You will set your eyes…

Suddenly he was running again. No screams now, just a low moan in his throat, a tangle of savage emotions he could not have put a name to if he had tried. Blood trickled from his lips and his crozius thrummed and crackled. The gates of the cathedral hung like broken wings. He ducked between them to stand on the broad black steps of his dying fortress.

…on the heart of Varantha…

His crozius's head had fallen silent, and he looked at it in puzzlement. It had formed itself into a human face, mouth gaping, eyes wide. A face that De Haan recognised as his own, from back in the days before his helm had sealed itself to him.

Turn, De Haan. Turn And Face Me.

The voice did not come through his ears, but seemed to resonate out of the air and throughout his bones and brain. It was measured, almost sombre, but its simple force almost shook him to his knees. Slowly, he raised his head.

…and all will come to an end.

More than twice De Haan's height, the immense figure stood with its spear at rest. It took a step forward out of the smoke that had wreathed it, to the centre of the plaza. De Haan watched the blood drip from its hand and stain the grey stones on the ground. It stood and regarded him, and there was none of the expected madness or fury in the white-hot pits of its baleful eyes, only a brooding patience that was far more terrifying.

He took a step forward. All the fury had gone like the snuffing of a candle: now there was just wrenching despair which drove everything else from his mind. He wondered how long ago Varantha's Farseers had realised he was hunting them, how long ago they had begun cultivating his hate, how long ago they had begun to set this trap for him. He wondered if the Farseer whose prophecy he had thought to fulfil was laughing at him from within its Spirit Stone.

He stood alone on the steps, and the air was silent but for the hiss of heat from incandescent iron skin and the faint keening from the weapon in one giant hand.

Then the lines from the Pentadict danced through his mind, the lines with which Lorgar had closed his testament as his own death came upon him.

Pride and defiant hate, spite and harsh oblivion. Let the great jewelled knot of the Cosmos unravel in the dust.

He looked up again, his mind suddenly clear and calm. He raised his crozius, but the salute was not returned. No matter. He took a pace forward and down the steps, that volcanic gaze on him all the time. He walked faster, now jogging. He worked the action on his pistol with the heel of his hand. Running, its eyes on him.

Charging now, feet hammering, voice found at last in a wail of defiance, Chaplain De Haan ran like a daemon across his last battlefield to where the Avatar of Kaela-Mensha-Khaine stood, its smoking, shrieking spear in its vast hands, waiting for him.

HIVE FLEET HORROR
Barrington J. Bayley

'Will the pain go, apothecary?'

'It is nothing but a skin rash, young man,' Jako Jaxabarm said. 'This balm will speed its healing. But I wonder as to its cause. What is your occupation?'

'I work in the chemics factory outside the town.'

Jaxabarm nodded. He knew the factory. It produced industrial acids and materials used in the manufacture of high explosives. Having dealt with his patient's right arm, he began applying a thin layer of the soothing blue unguent to his left arm, murmuring a prayer as he did so. The rash was indeed angry, and if left untreated might have rotted away the flesh and left the sufferer in a parlous state. He looked sternly into the young man's pale face.

'What did you say your name is?'

'Drenthan Drews.'

'Well, Drenthan, you must tell your employer to supply you with protective sleeves, or else find work elsewhere.'

Drenthan Drews looked alarmed. 'I can't go demanding safety gear from the factory managers, apothecary. I would be dismissed instantly. Work is hard to find, and I have an ageing mother to support.'

Jako Jaxabarm's mind went hazy as he listened to the all-too-familiar litany, looking out of the window to the increasingly busy street. He plied his apothecary's trade at a corner table in a cheap cafe, where the owner tolerated him because he brought in extra customers. The planet, a semi-industrial world in the Ultima Segmentum, lay somewhere near the Kreel Nebula. The factory workers here were poor and downtrodden, though not as downtrodden and poverty-stricken as on some of the more fully industrialised worlds he had visited. Jaxabarm had wandered much in recent years, never staying in one place very long, always fearing the clap of an arbitrator's – or worse, an inquisitor's hand on his shoulder.

'Your work has caused this painful rash, young man,' he said pitilessly. 'It will heal now, but if you continue to work unprotected it will return, and eventually you will lose your arms.'

Drenthan Drews's shoulders slumped but Jaxabarm was not looking at him. He could not take his eyes off the street. Adeptus Arbites patrols had increased dramatically, and the city – indeed the whole planet – was filling up more and more with the Imperial Guard. There were naval ships in orbit, and it was even rumoured that Space Marines were on their way. The legendary Adeptus Astartes!

An attack was coming. But where from? And by whom? The populace had not been told.

His young patient noticed his interest and seemed to cheer up. His eyes brightened. 'Don't worry, apothecary! The Emperor's forces are here. They'll soon see the enemy off, whoever they are!'

'Yes, no doubt.'

Few had come to see him today. People had left the city in droves, feeling they would be safer in the countryside and many who remained stayed indoors. He snapped shut his apothecary's bag, rose from the table and left the cafe with a casual wave to the proprietor.

Drenthan Drews followed only a few steps behind him. He had gone but a short distance along the pavement when a hulking arbitrator stopped them both.

'Your papers,' he said gruffly.

Jaxabarm avoiding looking at the dark visor which all but covered the face of the arbitrator, or judge to use the popular term. He and Drews both fumbled for their shiny pass books.

The judge carefully examined them both, then applied his scanner to the electrostatic text. He studied the results for a long moment, then returned his hidden gaze to the apothecary.

'You are Jako Jaxabarm?'

Jaxabarm nodded, clutching his bag. 'Yes, arbitrator.'

'I believe you to be Genetor van Leedrix, of the Adeptus Mechanicus, wanted for escape from lawful custody. You are under arrest.'

'There is surely some mistake…'

Jaxabarm's words trailed off, as he realised that the dreaded hour had come. The arbitrator muttered into his throat mic. A grinding, bulky, black holding vehicle emerged from a nearby corner and drew up.

'This is a wanted criminal,' the Arbites said to his colleagues who piled out. He gestured to Drenthan Drews. 'Take his accomplice too.'

'He is nothing to do with it,' Jaxabarm protested. 'I am an apothecary. He is only a patient.'

'That's right!' Drews cried out in panic. 'I don't even know him! Please let me go!'

The officer ignored his words. He and Jaxabarm were thrown together into the holding vehicle's dark interior.

THEY EMERGED into daylight outside the florid frontage of Adeptus Arbites city headquarters. Armoured tracked shapes were roaring by, their clanking treads tearing up the road surface, vast turrets reversed to leave stubby cannon barrels trailing as they raced towards the city limits. Jaxabarm recognised them as Baneblade battle tanks.

Evidently Arbitrator headquarters now doubled as Imperial Guard headquarters too. The building bustled with unfamiliar uniforms. But Jaxabarm and his young patient glimpsed these only briefly as they were hustled through the throng, quickly searched, and Jaxabarm's apothecary's bag taken from him. Then they were pushed hastily down cast iron stairs and flung into a prisoner cage.

A barred door clanged shut behind them. The faint pleasant aroma of blue balm on Drenthan Drews's arms slowly filled the dim cell. There was already one occupant. To Jaxabarm's surprise it was an Imperial Guard soldier, uniform rumpled, headgear missing, hair tousled, who huddled in the corner, head down.

Drenthan Drews rounded on the man who had unwittingly caused his imprisonment 'What's happening? You aren't an apothecary at all! What are you? An engineer?'

'Better you shouldn't know,' Jaxabarm told him.

Drews looked blank. Jaxabarm took a step towards the guardsman.

'With what crime are you charged?'

The soldier peered up at him. His face was slack and despairing.

'Cowardice,' he muttered sullenly.

Arbitrators and the Imperial Guard were also using the same holding cells, it seemed. The guardsman appeared to be in state of shock. Was it possible he did not realise that the smartly dressed Jaxabarm was a prisoner too?

'This planet is being readied for an attack,' he said in commanding tones. 'Who is the enemy?'

'Not allowed to say.'

Jaxabarm drew himself up. 'I am Genetor Leedrix of the Adeptus Mechanicus. You may tell me. You must tell me. That is an order.'

The guardsman rolled on his side and turned his face away as he replied. Jaxabarm had to lean close to catch the words.

'Hive Fleet Kraken.'

Jaxabarm went stiff. Now it was he who was in shock.

HE HAD NEVER heard of Hive Fleet Kraken. But he knew of Hive Fleet Behemoth!

Two hundred and fifty years previously, the tyranids had come, from out of the darkness between the galaxies, in their huge fleet of organically engineered snail-ships. They had demolished world after inhabited world, leaving nothing but bare rock. If unopposed it would have done the same to the whole galaxy. It was the greatest threat the Imperium had ever faced, and it had taken so much of the Imperium's resources to defeat it.

As a young genetor, or adept of the Arcanum Genetica, van Leedrix had once been part of a team that was still studying preserved tyranid cadavers a hundred and fifty years after Hive Fleet Behemoth had been defeated. A tyranid warrior was a fearsome thing to behold. It was perhaps best described as resembling the warrior caste of a social insect such as a termite or an ant, except that it was by far more vicious-looking and about twice the size of a horse. Despite being highly intelligent, its behaviour was controlled in a way similar to that of social insects, by means of chemical pheromones released by the hive mind. All tyranid engineering was biological in character. It was known that the hive fleet had come to the galaxy looking for genetic material, but it was not really understood why.

That had been a hundred years ago. 'Jaxabarm' was older than he looked. He was one hundred and twenty-eight, in an Imperium where average life expectancy was perhaps about forty. His longevity was solely due to his membership of the Arcanum Genetica, for genetors were the great experts in extending human life. It was a privilege ostensibly granted only to the high priests of the Adeptus, the technomagi. But those who bestowed this gift quietly availed themselves of it too, a fact which the magi wisely ignored.

No wonder the Planetary Governor had made no announcement concerning the emergency. Few in the Imperium's million worlds knew that the tyranid invasion had even taken place two and a half centuries ago. The Imperium worked on the principle of secrecy – no one was told anything he did not absolutely need to know. Just to learn one of these secrets by accident could mean speedy death at the hands of one of the countless arms of the Administratum.

Thus, had Jaxabarm told Drenthan Drews why he was a renegade from the Arcanum Genetica, why he was on the run from the Adeptus Mechanicus, he would likely have sealed the young factory worker's fate. The existence of the tyranids was a secret he was entitled to know. But there was another secret, to which he had no entitlement.

Years ago his colleagues in the Arcanum had begun to wonder why his prayers and incantations were so much more efficacious than theirs, when it came to assembling DNA into useful biological inventions. Under examination, it was found that he was a latent psyker whose powers were only now beginning to develop. It was deemed that he was at risk of daemonic possession, and he was sentenced to speedy execution. Up until then he had had no inkling of the daemonic realm. To hear of it came as a huge surprise to him, and he had a feeling of resentment against his accusers – which they, of course, interpreted as yet more evidence of daemonic intervention.

Scant hours before his sentence was due to be carried out, he had contrived to escape. With luck, and with cunning born of desperation, he had survived until now.

For long it had been thought that the Imperium had seen the last of the tyranids. Now they were back, it seemed – a terrifying prospect! – in the form of a second hive fleet, given another name. This explained something else to Jaxabarm. His psychic talent was still developing. Occasionally he could hear people's thoughts. If he relaxed and opened his mind, he heard a background of whispering. But lately the whispering had turned into a deathly silence, as if an advancing wall had obliterated psychic space.

The wall of Hive Fleet Kraken? Jaxabarm turned his attention back to the huddling guardsman. 'Describe this enemy, this Hive Fleet Kraken,' he ordered, in the same peremptory tone as before. 'What are their warriors like?'

'They are monsters!' the guardsman replied in a strangled voice. 'Nothing can withstand them! Their claws can tear a tank apart!'

His voice fell. 'They don't just conquer planets, they dismantle them! I am one of the few survivors from the defence of Moloch. Moloch is gone! Every man, woman, child and animal was taken up into the hive fleet. It was the same with Devlan – Devlan is gone! And Salem, and Sotha – homeworld of the Emperor's Scythes! I tell you there is nothing you can do here.'

Jaxabarm sensed fear and despair from the man. But inside that, he sensed also a guardsman's discipline and courage. He suspected the prisoner had been incarcerated not so much for cowardice but to stop him from telling others yet to encounter the tyranids how bad the situation was.

He and Drew tilted their faces as a loudspeaker voice came echoing down the stairwell from the ground floor. He just managed to make out the words.

'Hormagaunt horde advancing from the south. Break out all arms and distribute to city population. Release and arm prisoners.'

Hormagaunts... Quite likely whoever had sent the message from the front knew only this one term to describe the terrors that were coming. But there would also be carnifexes, lictors and termagants, not to speak of the tyranid warriors themselves, and all the rest of the multiformed nightmare war biology that had so amazed the magi biologis of the Adeptus Mechanicus. The city was about to be overrun. And when that happened…

They heard footsteps and the clang of cell doors opening. An arbitrator appeared and flung open the gridiron gate.

'You are free. Leave the building. Join the defences.'

He tossed three lasguns into the cell and passed on.

This truly was a measure of desperation: a general levy to try to hold off the tyranid swarm. Jaxabarm picked up the lasguns, passed one to Drews and another to the Imperial Guardsman, who also had been listening intently to the booming voice. The guardsman gave Jaxabarm a stricken look, but accepted the weapon with apparent gratitude.

Then he turned the emitter muzzle to his own head and immediately pressed the firing stud. His body jerked, then went limp and slumped, a neat hole burned through his skull.

A wise choice, Jaxabarm thought, if all he had been told about Hive Fleet Behemoth was true. He nudged the shocked Drenthan.

'Come on.'

The building was emptying rapidly. Outside, a great deal had changed in a very short time. It had gone gloomy; the sky seemed overcast but glimmered with faint flashes, while stronger shafts of light speared up from somewhere nearby. They were laser beams from the land silos and from warships in orbit.

Jaxabarm peered, slitting his eyes, and began to see why the sky had darkened. The air was filled with spots or specks as the hive fleet disgorged its rain of death upon the planet, each spot a pod bearing some monstrous invader.

Clumsily Drew waved his lasgun. 'I don't know how to use this thing!'

'You point it and press that stud there,' Jaxabarm informed him. A screaming noise, inhuman and terrifying, like an insane siren, caught his attention. Beyond the Arbites building was a broad prospect. Up this, half a dozen Baneblade tanks were reversing at full speed, firing as they retreated. Pursuing them were carnifexes, a hundred at least, living engines of destruction running on pairs of jointed legs, four huge scythe-blades of limbs carried by each massive, rounded, chitinous body. It was from these monsters that the eerie screams came. The

Baneblades' shells blew a few apart, but most came inexorably
on. The very sight of them caused an almost uncontrollable
fear in Jaxabarm, and even more so in Drews. Then, from one
of the monstrosities, a crackling fireball issued and surged forward to engulf a Baneblade in a glowing nimbus. The tank
juddered and came to a sudden halt. In seconds carnifexes were
all around it. The two men watched appalled as scythe-limbs
carved through the Baneblade's armour, taking it apart. Briefly
they glimpsed the doomed crew within, in the moments before
there was nothing but splashes of blood.

Drenthan Drews whimpered. 'I've got to go to my mother! I
must help her!"

Jaxabarm said nothing to stop him, useless though the young
man's sentiment was. There was no help for anyone now. He
fondled the unfamiliar lasgun, wondering if it would be possible to take one of the tyranid scum with him.

Drews did not get any distance. It was as if the air above the
city gave birth to an evil harvest. Husky pods by the thousand
were tumbling down and cracking open as they hit streets or
buildings. From them billowed white floss which expanded
until, within seconds, it had covered the city in foam to a
height of fifty feet.

Jaxabarm and Drews, together with anyone else still within the
conurbation – everyone in the countryside too, perhaps – were
now trapped inside a mesh of sticky threads which made movement impossible. Jaxabarm could see little: all around him was
nothing but a suffuse white glow. He heard Drenthan calling out
to him in a muffled voice. 'Apothecary! Where are you?'

He heard other muffled voices, too, seemingly far away.
Finding he could still move his fingers, he pressed the lasgun
stud. The beam shot through the enveloping floss, frizzling it
but achieving nothing else. When he lifted his finger the floss
instantly closed in again to fill the narrow pipe he had drilled.

After a while he became dimly aware that, immobilised
though he might be, other things were able to move through
the mesh. Tiny spider-like creatures crawled and skittered along
the threads which made it up. Hulking shadow-shapes, visible
as vague blots, were blundering through it.

Tyranids.

Then he could feel the whole mass moving, piling up, rolling
along. At the same time his psyker sense started to open up

again. He could sense human beings all around him, all stuck in the gloop – tough, cynical judges, battle-eager Imperial Guard, men, women and children, all overwhelmed with dismay, bewilderment and terror.

He felt something near him. A large wet tongue licked his face. It belonged to a small animal of the sort commonly kept as a pet on this planet. Somehow it had ended up next to him. He turned his face away.

More time passed. Then eerie ululations sounded, penetrating the mesh. Jaxabarm felt a tugging or a pushing, he could not tell which. He heard a dragging noise. Then it went dark. He heard a loud hissing, and felt a savage force pressing him down towards the ground.

Except that it was not the ground. It was a floor of some kind. He knew what that pressing down meant: acceleration, G-force.

They had been transferred to the innards of another type of tyranid beast. One that served as a shuttlecraft. He wondered if he would get a chance to turn the lasgun on himself, as the guardsman had.

They were being taken aboard the hive fleet.

WHEN THE ACCELERATION ceased a peculiar cloying smell invaded Jaxabarm's nostrils and he lost consciousness. When he came to, the floss was melting into thin air all around him. The lasgun was gone from his hand. He flailed desperately to find it, but to no avail.

The worst of all nightmares was about to begin.

WHEN HIS HEAD cleared he went nearly mad with horror. He was but one of a tangle of people who lay on the floor of a round, crimson-walled tunnel which pulsed like a living thing – as, indeed, it was. The light, too, was reddish and murky, issuing from nodules dotted randomly about the walls, made hazy by a drifting mist. A distant but steady thudding or booming, as of a giant heartbeat, accompanied the tunnel's writhing pulse. An acid stench filled the air. Jaxabarm guessed it was the smell of the pheromones by which the hive mind controlled its creatures.

Drenthan Drews tugged at his sleeve.

'Where are we?' he hissed fearfully.

Jaxabarm did not answer. His heart was in his throat. Approaching down the tunnel from both ends came tyranid creatures. The dreadful sight caused a wailing and a sobbing and a screeching with terror of children among the humans. Uniformed arbitrators and guardsmen came to all fours, defenceless now and stripped of all the certainty of the human Imperium, staring paralysed at the pure bestial alienness into which they were now plunged.

The creatures were lictors, a mutation of the standard tyranid warrior which, though a vicious killing machine like all tyranid progeny, was highly intelligent and had feeder tentacles for consuming a victim's brain, thereby absorbing and analysing his memories and genetic data. Cold, expressionless eyes, as blank as a spider's, were set above chitinous mandibles filled with huge curved teeth. The lictors moved in, seized the nearest soft-bodied humans in barbed flesh hooks and inserted tentacles through eyes, temples or beneath the jaw. Those seized went limp almost instantly as the transfer of brain tissue began.

Drenthan Drews and Jaxabarm had both come to their feet, but Drews seemed about to faint. Holding him up, his heart pounding with terror, he glanced behind him to see that the lictors were not alone. Picking their way among them were four monstrosities unlike any he had seen or heard described during his days in the Arcanum Genetica. They were large, but moved delicately as if physically puny, and sported huge bloated heads decorated with chitinous patterns and surrounded by bony antler-like structures. Behind them moved an even larger monstrosity, so huge that it barely found room for itself in the tunnel. Twice the size of a normal tyranid warrior, this was a type of monster which Jaxabarm did recognise. It was a hive tyrant, believed by some magi biologis to be individual embodiments of the hive mind.

There was no place to run. Delicately, but with more than human strength, the unnamed creatures bent their moiré-patterned heads and used their forelimbs to select and pick up squirming humans, among them Jaxabarm and Drews. Helpless in the pincer-like grip, the screeching of the captured and soon-to-be-decorticated men, women and children ringing in their ears, they were carried down the tunnel and emerged into a more bulbous chamber.

The pheromonic smell here was different from in the tunnel, less acid, but nonetheless just as revolting. The hive tyrant stood in the entrance, swaying slightly. A grotesque scene was then enacted. Under the bloody light, a middle-aged man was laid down and stripped of his clothing. Two large-headed tyranids bent over him, pinning him down as he tried to crawl away, looking desperately towards his fellow humans as though appealing for help.

Then the dissection began. The tyranid creatures, white slime dripping from glands in their underbellies, seemed oblivious of the screams of utmost agony from their experimental subject as he was laid open without anaesthetic and his intestines were torn out and tossed here and there. Drews gagged and even Jaxabarm staggered.

And then he became aware of the psychic presence of the tyranids. It was weird, like nothing else he had ever experienced: an implacable, ferocious sentience which was ancient beyond imagining. It stood alone; no one would ever be able to speak to it.

Suddenly he felt as though his psyche had been torn apart like the human body on the floor of the chamber. The scene before his eyes vanished.

He was somewhere else. Somewhere dark, but filled with a seething and a rustling. He had entered the hive mind.

And now he understood what the tyranids were.

THE TYRANIDS WERE what ants and termites would be if they could evolve further and become intelligent. What made such intelligence incomprehensible was that the tyranids had never evolved emotions. They were aware that concepts such as sympathy and honour existed in the species they harvested, but they viewed them only in the abstract and dismissed them as evolutionary mistakes. Gene coding for emotion was never made use of by the hive fleets.

Yes, the tyranids were intelligent, but intelligence was not a quality particularly prized by the hive mind. A tyranid creature could reason, but it never did so out of self-interest. Intelligence, like everything else, served only tyranid hive instincts – or rather, it served the single great tyranid instinct, the one overwhelming, compulsive urge.

SURVIVE! AND SURVIVE FOREVER!

When the tyranids invaded a galaxy they took aboard vast amounts of foodstuffs and raw materials, but those were not what they came looking for. They knew that every system, whether mechanical or biological, eventually runs down. Most species lasted only a few million years. A few – like some Earth ants – managed to survive for up to a hundred million years. But sooner or later they perished as their DNA either failed to adapt or simply deteriorated through natural wear.

The tyranids had found the only possible remedy for this. They moved from galaxy to galaxy, harvesting fresh, newly evolved DNA with which to renew and reinvigorate their own. They were the universe's ultimate life form. Quite possibly they had existed forever, and would continue to exist forever. Quite possibly the universe contained an infinite number of hive fleets.

The Imperium of Man had beaten off one hive fleet. Perhaps it could beat off others. It would be a rare reversal for the tyranids, but that did not matter at all. In a few million years the Imperium would be gone, the human race would be gone, and some other hive fleet would arrive, meeting weaker resistance, and would leave the galaxy lifeless and desolate.

Then, a few billion years later, life would evolve all over again, on millions of planets.

And again a hive fleet would move in....

Jaxabarm did not think the hive tyrant was at all aware that he was eavesdropping on the hive mind. He was not worthy of notice. The tyranid did not respect human intelligence – they did not respect any intelligence, not even their own. All they saw in the human race was a species possessing young, vigorous DNA.

A VIOLENT BARKING noise snatched him abruptly out of the unholy contact. He saw three of the large-headed tyranids blown apart, then the fourth. A ragged hole had been blown in the wall of the chamber, too. Shreds of rubbery flesh, the substance of the snail-ship, flapped and trailed, oozing pink ichor. Crowding through the hole came armoured man-shapes with pointed visors, seemingly grotesquely hunchbacked, the all-enclosing armour itself hulking over the back of the helmet. Their red and purple colouring seemed to merge into the blood-hued innards of the snail-ship.

Space Marines! The rumour was true! And they were using their favourite hand weapon – the bolter! Explosive bolts rained against the chitinous hide of the hive tyrant, which being weaponless itself, backed away up the tunnel. The lictors, however, launched themselves immediately at the Marines, shooting off flesh hooks which scraped and scored the Marines' armour, trying to get to grips with them with their claws and teeth. Against these creatures, the explosive bolts were more effective. The Marines had a strategy: they aimed for the lictors' gaping mouths, exploding the bolts within the tyranid skull.

Jaxabarm knew what the response would be to an intrusion into the organic tyranid ship, itself but a genetically modified tyranid. Tyranid monsters in all their forms would be rushing to the spot from all over the snail-ship. A single squad of Spaces Marines would stand no chance.

As it was there were too many lictors for them. Two had already been overcome, borne down by the weight of the creatures, their armour ripped open. The others, making no attempt to help their comrades, prepared to retreat. Jaxabarm's hope that this was a rescue mission was quickly dashed. One of the Marines carried a chest or box which he placed on the floor of the chamber. Bolters still barking, the Marines backed through the hole they had made, ignoring the human captives and leaving them to their grisly fate.

A lictor now turned its attention to Jaxabarm, its acidic stench almost overpowering him. Shivering, he tried to evade its reaching claws.

Again came a bolter bark, so close it nearly deafened him. The lictor took the bolt in the jaw, shuddered and slumped. Looking round, Jaxabarm was startled to see Drews awkwardly holding a bolter he had taken from a dead Space Marine.

'This way, apothecary!'

Drews grabbed him by the arm and dragged him towards the hole through which the Marines had already disappeared, firing off the bolt gun in all directions. Jaxabarm's last glimpse of the murky chamber was of a lictor picking up the discarded chest in its forelimbs and inspecting it.

The path of the Marines was easy to follow. Rather than try to find their way through the maze of tunnels and passages, where they would be prey to ambush, they had chosen to blast their way through the tunnel walls. There was very little light in these tunnels. They met no tyranid warriors of any kind, only small, spider-like creatures which scuttled everywhere, taking no notice of them. In minutes they had come in sight of the departing Marines, who were about to embark – again through a hole blasted in the skin of the ship-creature – in a spacecraft of some kind.

'Help us! Help us!' Jaxabarm cried out.

For a moment he thought they would be abandoned. Then the last Marine to embark gestured to them hastily. They went through a circular metal port and found themselves in a cramped hold among the hulking Astartes adepts. The Marines began removing their headgear as the craft shot away from the tyranid ships. They were watching a small screen set like a port-hole in the side of the hold.

There, the snail-ship suddenly exploded, reddened chunks of it flying into space. Yet, in the distance, other glints could be seen, many of them. The hive fleet consisted of thousands of such ships.

What now? Jaxabarm began to think of the future. He was no longer the condemned Genetor van Dreelix. He was Jako Jaxabarm, apothecary, once again. The discovery of his alias had been made on a planet shortly to be reduced to rubble.

He would try to persuade Drenthan Drews to join the Imperial Guard and help defend the Imperium. Hive Fleet Kraken had to be repelled or humanity was doomed.

Not that the outcome was of any importance to the tyranids. To them, species evolved and perished like blades of grass. Galaxies condensed, blazed, then guttered out. The supposedly immortal Chaos gods would not even last that long. They would perish when the psyches which sustained them died out.

Only the tyranids lasted forever.

More Warhammer 40,000 from the Black Library

INTO THE MAELSTROM

An anthology of Warhammer 40,000 stories, edited by Marc Gascoigne & Andy Jones

'THE CHAOS ARMY had travelled from every continent, every shattered city, every ruined sector of Illium to gather on this patch of desert that had once been the control centre of the Imperial garrison. The sand beneath their feet had been scorched, melted and fused by a final, futile act of suicidal defiance: the detonation of the garrison's remaining nuclear stockpile.' – **Hell in a Bottle** by Simon Jowett

'HOARSE SCREAMS and the screech of tortured hot metal filled the air. Massive laser blasts were punching into the spaceship. They superheated the air that men breathed, set fire to everything that could burn and sent fireballs exploding through the crowded passageways.' – **Children of the Emperor** by Barrington J. Bayley

IN THE GRIM and gothic nightmare future of Warhammer 40,000, mankind teeters on the brink of extinction. INTO THE MAELSTROM is a storming collection of a dozen action-packed science fiction short stories set in this dark and brooding universe.

More Warhammer 40,000 from the Black Library

STATUS: DEADZONE

An anthology of Necromunda stories, edited by Marc Gascoigne & Andy Jones

'KNIFE-EDGE LIZ closed on Terrak Ran'Lo. The old man was moving for cover, crouching behind a side-table. She fell upon him, dragging him to the ground. His breath was wine-rancid, his eyes glazed with age. He looked at the woman, her face sprayed with the blood of the inquisitor, and his eyes span.

'"A message from the Underhive," Liz spat and pulled the trigger.' – **Rat in the Walls** *by Alex Hammond*

'OUTSIDE THE Last Gasp Saloon, Nathan Creed examined the scrap of parchment. If the map was genuine, Toxic Sump's dome was built directly on top of another, much older settlement. Who knew what ancient treasures lay buried beneath the ash? Creed took the cheroot from his mouth and spat into the dust. The prospector had known. Now he was dead.' – **Bad Spirits** *by Jonathan Green*

ON THE SAVAGE factory world of Necromunda, renegade gangs struggle for survival in the shattered tunnels and domes beneath the teeming hive-cities. STATUS: DEADZONE is an awesome anthology of dark science fiction short stories from the devastated urban hell of Necromunda.

More Warhammer 40,000 from the Black Library

13th LEGION
A Kage's Last Chancers novel
by Gav Thorpe

GLANCING OVER my shoulder I see that we're at the steps to the command tower now. You can follow the trail of our retreat, five dead Last Chancers lie among more than two dozen alien bodies and a swathe of shotgun cases and bolt pistol cartridges litters the floor. A few eldar manage to dart through our fusillade, almost naked except for a few pieces of bladed red armour strapped across vital body parts. Almost skipping with light steps, they duck left and right with unnatural speed. In their hands they hold vicious-looking whips and two-bladed daggers that drip with some kind of venom that smokes as it drops to the metal decking. Their fierce grins show exquisitely white teeth as they close for the kill, their bright oval eyes burning with unholy passion.

ACROSS A HUNDRED blasted war-zones, upon a dozen bloody worlds, the convict soldiers of the 13th Penal Legion fight a desperate battle for redemption in the eyes of the immortal Emperor. In this endless war against savage orks, merciless eldar and the insidious threat of Chaos, Lieutenant Kage and the Last Chancers must fight, not to win, but merely to survive!

More Warhammer 40,000 from the Black Library

FIRST & ONLY
A Gaunt's Ghosts novel
by Dan Abnett

'THE TANITH ARE strong fighters, general, so I have heard.' The
scar tissue of his cheek pinched and twitched slightly, as it
often did when he was tense. 'Gaunt is said to be a resourceful
leader.'

'You know him?' The general looked up, questioningly.

'I know *of* him, sir. In the main by reputation.'

GAUNT GOT TO his feet, wet with blood and Chaos pus. His
Ghosts were moving up the ramp to secure the position. Above
them, at the top of the elevator shaft, were over a million
Shriven, secure in their bunker batteries. Gaunt's expeditionary
force was inside, right at the heart of the enemy stronghold.
Commissar Ibram Gaunt smiled.

*IT IS THE nightmare future of Warhammer 40,000, and mankind
teeters on the brink of extinction. The galaxy-spanning Imperium is
riven with dangers, and in the Chaos-infested Sabbat system,
Imperial Commissar Gaunt must lead his men through as much in-
fighting amongst rival regiments as against the forces of Chaos.
FIRST AND ONLY is an epic saga of planetary conquest, grand
ambition, treachery and honour.*

More Warhammer 40,000 from the Black Library

GHOSTMAKER
A Gaunt's Ghosts novel
by Dan Abnett

THEY WERE A good two hours into the dark, black-trunked forests, tracks churning the filthy ooze and the roar of their engines resonating from the sickly canopy of leaves above, when Colonel Ortiz saw death.

It wore red, and stood in the trees to the right of the track, in plain sight, unmoving, watching his column of Basilisks as they passed along the trackway. It was the lack of movement that chilled Ortiz.

Almost twice a man's height, frighteningly broad, armour the colour of rusty blood, crested by recurve brass antlers. The face was a graven death's head. Daemon. Chaos Warrior. *World Eater!*

IN THE NIGHTMARE future of Warhammer 40,000, mankind teeters on the brink of extinction. The Imperial Guard are humanity's first line of defence against the remorseless assaults of the enemy. For the men of the Tanith First-and-Only and their fearless commander, Commissar Ibram Gaunt, it is a war in which they must be prepared to lay down, not just their bodies, but their very souls.

More Warhammer 40,000 from the Black Library

NECROPOLIS
A Gaunt's Ghosts novel
by Dan Abnett

GAUNT WAS SHAKING, and breathing hard. He'd lost his cap
somewhere, his jacket was torn and he was splattered with
blood. Something flickered behind him and he wheeled, his
blade flashing as it made contact. A tall, black figure lurched
backwards. It was thin but powerful, and much taller than him,
dressed in glossy black armour and a hooded cape. The visage
under the hood was feral and non-human, like the snarling
skull of a great wolfhound with the skin scraped off. It clutched
a sabre-bladed power sword in its gloved hands. The cold blue
energies of his own powersword clashed against the sparking,
blood red fires of the Darkwatcher's weapon.

*On THE SHATTERED world of Verghast, Gaunt and his Ghosts find
themselves embroiled within an ancient and deadly civil war as a
mighty hive-city is besieged by an unrelenting foe. When treachery
from within brings the city's defences crashing down, rivalry and
corruption threaten to bring the Tanith Ghosts to the brink of
defeat. Imperial Commissar Ibram Gaunt must find new allies and
new Ghosts if he is to save Vervunhive from the deadliest threat of
all – the dread legions of Chaos.*

More Warhammer 40,000 from the Black Library

SPACE WOLF
A Space Wolf novel
by William King

RAGNAR LEAPT UP from his hiding place, bolt pistol spitting death. The nightgangers could not help but notice where he was, and with a mighty roar of frenzied rage they raced towards him. Ragnar answered their war cry with a wolfish howl of his own, and was reassured to hear it echoed back from the throats of the surrounding Blood Claws. He pulled the trigger again and again as the frenzied mass of mutants approached, sending bolter shell after bolter shell rocketing into his targets. Ragnar laughed aloud, feeling the full battle rage come upon him. The beast roared within his soul, demanding to be unleashed.

IN THE GRIM future of Warhammer 40,000, the Space Marines of the Adeptus Astartes are humanity's last hope. On the planet Fenris, young Ragnar is chosen to be inducted into the noble yet savage Space Wolves Chapter. But with his ancient primal instincts unleashed by the implanting of the sacred Canis Helix, Ragnar must learn to control the beast within and fight for the greater good of the wolf pack.

More Warhammer 40,000 from the Black Library

RAGNAR'S CLAW
A Space Wolf novel
by William King

ONE OF THE enemy officers, wearing the peaked cap and greatcoat of a lieutenant, dared to stick his head above the parapet. Without breaking stride, Ragnar raised his bolt pistol and put a shell through the man's head. It exploded like a melon hit with a sledgehammer. Shouts of confusion echoed from behind the wall of sandbags, then a few heretics, braver and more experienced than the rest, stuck their heads up in order to take a shot at their attackers. Another mistake: a wave of withering fire from the Space Marines behind Ragnar scythed through them, sending their corpses tumbling back amongst their comrades.

FROM THE DEATHWORLD of Fenris come the Space Wolves, the most savage of the Emperor's Space Marines. RAGNAR'S CLAW explores the bloody beginnings of Space Wolf Ragnar's first mission as a young Blood Claw warrior. From the jungle hell of Galt to the polluted cities of Hive World Venam, Ragnar's mission takes him on an epic trek across the galaxy to face the very heart of evil itself.

Also from the Black Library

HAMMERS OF ULRIC

A Warhammer novel by Dan Abnett, Nik Vincent and James Wallis

ARIC RODE FORWARD across the corpse-strewn ground and helped Gruber to his feet. The older warrior was speckled with blood, but alive.

'See to von Glick and watch the standard. Give me your horse,' Gruber said to Aric.

Aric dismounted and returned to the banner of Vess as Gruber galloped back into the brutal fray.

Von Glick lay next to the standard, which was still stuck upright in the bloody earth. The lifeless bodies of almost a dozen beastmen lay around him.

'L-let me see…' von Glick breathed. Aric knelt beside him and raised his head. 'So, Anspach's bold plan worked…' breathed the veteran warrior. 'He's pleased… I'll wager.'

Aric started to laugh, then stopped. The old man was dead.

IN THE SAVAGE world of Warhammer, dark powers gather around the ancient mountain-top city of Middenheim, the City of the White Wolf. Only the noble Templar Knights of Ulric and a few unlikely allies stand to defend her against the insidious servants of Death.

Also from the Black Library

THE WINE OF DREAMS
A Warhammer novel by Brian Craig

THE SWORD FLEW from Reinmar's hand and he just had
time to think, as he was taken off his feet, that when he
landed – flat on his back – he would be wide open to
attack by a plunging dagger or flashing teeth. As the beastman leapt, Sigurd's arm lashed out in a great horizontal
arc, the palm of his hand held flat. As it impacted with
the beastman's neck Reinmar heard the snap that broke
the creature's spine.

As soon as that, it was over. But it was not a victory.
Now there was no possible room for doubt that there
were monsters abroad in the hills.

*DEEP WITHIN the shadowy foothills of the Grey Mountains, a
dark and deadly plot is uncovered by an innocent young mer-
chant. A mysterious stranger leads young Reinmar Weiland
to stumble upon the secrets of a sinister underworld hidden
beneath the very feet of the unsuspecting Empire – and learn
of a legendary elixir, the mysterious and forbidden Wine of
Dreams.*

Also from the Black Library

REALM OF CHAOS

An anthology of Warhammer stories edited by Marc Gascoigne & Andy Jones

'Markus was confused; the stranger's words were baffling his pain-numbed mind. "Just who are you, foul spawned deviant?"

'The warrior laughed again, slapping his hands on his knees. "I am called Estebar. My followers know me as the Master of Slaughter. And I have come for your soul."'
– **The Faithful Servant,** *by Gav Thorpe*

'The wolves are running again. I can haear them panting in the darkness. I race through the forest, trying to outpace them. Behind the wolves I sense another presence, something evil. I am in the place of blood again.' – **Dark Heart,** *by Jonathan Green*

IN THE DARK and gothic world of Warhammer, the ravaging armies of the Ruinous Powers sweep down from the savage north to assail the lands of men. REALM OF CHAOS is a searing collection of a dozen all-action fantasy short stories set in these desperate times.

IN THE GRIM DARKNESS OF THE FAR FUTURE, THERE IS ONLY WAR...

You can recreate the ferocious battles of the Imperial Guard and the Space Marines with WARHAMMER 40,000, Games Workshop's world famous game of a dark and gothic war-torn future. The galaxy-spanning Imperium of Man is riven with dangers: aliens such as the ravaging orks and the enigmatic eldar gather their forces to crush humanity – and in the warp, malevolent powers arm for war!

To find out more about Warhammer 40,000, as well as Games Workshop's whole range of exciting fantasy and science fiction games and miniatures, just call our specialist Trolls on the following numbers:

In the UK: 0115-91 40 000

In the US: 1-800-GAME

or look us up online at:

www.games-workshop.com